Émile Zola, George Moore

Piping Hot!

(Pot-bouille.)

Émile Zola, George Moore

Piping Hot!
(Pot-bouille.)

ISBN/EAN: 9783743454613

Printed in Europe, USA, Canada, Australia, Japan

Cover: Foto ©Andreas Hilbeck / pixelio.de

More available books at **www.hansebooks.com**

PIPING HOT!

(*POT-BOUILLE.*)

A REALISTIC NOVEL.

BY

ÉMILE ZOLA.

TRANSLATED FROM THE 63RD FRENCH EDITION.

Illustrated with Sixteen Page Engravings,

FROM DESIGNS BY GEORGES BELLENGER.

NEW EDITION.

LONDON:

VIZETELLY & CO., 42 CATHERINE STREET, STRAND.

1887.

PREFACE.

One day, in the middle of a long literary conversation, Théodore Duret said to me : "I have known in my life two men of supreme intelligence. I knew of both before the world knew of either. Never did I doubt, nor was it possible to doubt, but that they would one day or other gain the highest distinctions—those men were Léon Gambetta and Émile Zola."

Of Zola I am able to speak, and I can thoroughly realise how interesting it must have been to have watched him, at that time, when he was poor and unknown, obtaining acceptance of his articles with difficulty, and surrounded by the feeble and trivial in spirit, who, out of inborn ignorance and acquired idiocy, look with ridicule on those who believe that there is still a new word to say, still a new cry to cry.

I did not know Émile Zola in those days, but he must have been then as he is now, and I should find it difficult to understand how any man of average discrimination could speak with him for half-an-hour without recognising that he was one of those mighty monumental intelligences, the statues of a century, that remain and are gazed upon through the long pages of the world's history. This, at least, is the impression Émile Zola has always produced upon me. I have seen him in company, and company of no mean order, and when pitted against his compeers, the contrast has only made him appear grander, greater, nobler. The witty, the clever Alphonse Daudet, ever as ready for a supper party as a literary discussion, with all his splendid gifts, can do no more when Zola speaks than shelter himself behind an epigram ; Edmond De Goncourt, aristocratic, dignified, seated amid his Japanese water-colours, bronzes, and Louis XV. furniture, bitterly admits, if not that there is a greater naturalistic god than he, at least that there is a colossus whose strength he is unable to oppose.

This is the position Émile Zola takes amid his contemporaries. By some strange power of assimilation, he appropriates and makes his own of all things; ideas that before were scattered, dislocated, are suddenly united, fitted into their places. In speaking, as in writing, he always appears greater than his subject, and, Titan-like, grasps it as a whole; in speaking, as in writing, the strength and beauty of his style is an unfailing use of the right word; each phrase is a solid piece of masonry, and as he talks an edifice of thought rises architecturally perfect and complete in design.

And it is of this side of Émile Zola's genius that I wish particularly to speak—a side that has never been taken sufficiently into consideration, but which, nevertheless, is its ever-guiding and determinating quality. Émile Zola is to me a great epic poet, and he may be, I think, not inappropriately termed the Homer of modern life. For he, more than any other writer, it seems, possesses the power of seeing a subject as a whole, can divest it at will of all side issues, can seize with a firm, logical comprehension on the main lines of its construction, and that without losing sight of the remotest causes or the furthest consequences of its existence. It is here that his strength lies, and his is the strength which has conquered the world. Of his realism a great deal, of course, has been said, but only because it is the most obvious, not the most dominant quality of his work. The mistletoe invariably hides the oak from the eyes of the vulgar.

That Émile Zola has done well to characterise his creations with the vivid sentiment of modern life rather than the pale dream which reveals to us the past, that he was able to bend, to model, to make serviceable to his purpose the ephemeral habits and customs of our day, few will now deny. But this was only the off-shoot of his genius. That the colour of the nineteenth century with which he clothes the bodies of his heroes and heroines is not always exact, that none other has attempted to spin these garments before, I do not dispute. They will grow threadbare and fall to dust, even as the hide of the megatharium, of which only the colossal bones now remain to us wherewith to construct the fabric of the primeval world. And, in like manner, when the dream of the socialist is realized, when the burden of pleasure and work is proportioned out equally to all, and men live on a more strictly regulated plan than do either the ant or the bee, I believe that the gigantic skeleton of the Rougon-Macquart family will still continue to resist the ravages of time, and that western scientists will refer to it when disputing about the idiosyncrasies of a past civilization.

In the preceeding paragraph, I have said neither more nor less than my meaning, for I am convinced that the living history of no age has been as well written as the last half of the nineteenth century is in the Rougon-Macquart series. I pass over the question whether, in describing Renée's dress, a mistake was made in the price of lace, also whether the author was wrong in permitting himself the anachronism of describing a fête in the opera-house a couple of years before the building was completed. Errors of this kind do not appear to me to be worth considering. What I maintain is, that what Émile Zola has done, and what he alone has done—and I do not make an exception even in the case of the mighty Balzac—is to have conceived and constructed the frame-work of a complex civilization like ours, in all its worse ramifications. Never, it seems to me, was the existence of the epic faculty more amply demonstrated than by the genealogical tree of this now celebrated family.

The grandeur, the amplitude of this scheme will be seen at once. Adélaïde Fouque, a mad woman confined in a lunatic asylum at Plassans, is the first ancestor ; she is the transmitter of the original neurosis, which, regulated by his or her physical constitution, assumes various forms in each individual member of the family, and is developed according to the surroundings in which he or she lives. By Rougon this woman had two children ; by Macquart, with whom she cohabited on the death of her husband, she had three. Ursule Macquart married a man named Mouret, and their children are therefore cousins of the Rougon-Macquarts. This family has some forty or fifty members, who are distributed through the different grades of our social system. Some have attained the highest positions, as, Son Excellence Eugène Rougon, others have sunk to the lowest depths, as Gervaise in " L'Assommoir," but all are tainted with the hereditary malady. By it Nana is invincibly driven to prostitution; by it Étienne Lantier, in "Germinal," will be driven to crime; by it his brother, Claude, will be made a great painter. Protean-like is this disease. Sometimes it skips over a generation, sometimes lies almost latent, and the balance of the intelligence is but slightly disturbed, as in the instance of Octave in " Pot-Bouille," and Lazare in " La Joie de Vivre." But the mind of the latter is more distorted than is Octave's. Lazare lives in a perpetual fear of death, and is prevented from realizing any of his magnificent projects by his vacillating temperament; in him we have an example how a splendid intelligence may be drained away like water through an imperceptible crack in the vase, and how what might have been the fruit of a life withers like the flowers from which the nourishing liquid has been withdrawn.

And so in the Rougon-Macquart series we have instances of all kinds of psychical development and decay; and with an overt and an intuitive reading of character truly wonderful, Émile Zola makes us feel that as the north and south poles and torrid zones are hemmed about with a girdle of air, so an ever varying but ever recognisable kinship unites, sometimes, indeed, by an almost imperceptible thread, the ends the most opposed of this remarkable race, and is diffused through the different variation each individual member successively presents. Can we not trace a mysterious physical resemblance between Octave Mouret in " Le Bonheur des Dames " and Maxime in " La Curée ? " Is not the moral something by which Claude Lantier in " Le Ventre de Paris " escapes the fate of Lazare made apparent ? Then, again, does not the inherited neurosis that makes of Octave a millionaire, of

Lazare a wretched hypochondriac, of Claude Lantier a genius, of Maxime a symbol of ephemeral vice, reappear in a new and more deadly form in Jeanne, the hysterical child, in that most beautiful of beautiful books, " Une Page d'Amour ? "

As beasts at a fair are urged on by the goads of their drivers, so certain fate pushes this wretched family forward into irrevocable death that is awaiting it. At each generation they grow more nervous, more worn out, more ready to succumb beneath the ravages of the horrible disease that in a hundred different ways is sweeping them into the night of the grave.

Even from this imperfect outline, what majesty, what grandeur there is in this dark design ! Does not the great idea of fate receive a new and more terrible signification ? Is not the horror and gloom of the tragedy increased by the fact that the thought was born in the study of the scientist, and not in the cloud-palace of the dreamer ? What poet ever conceived an idea more vast ! and if further proof of the epic faculty with which I have credited Émile Zola be wanting, I have only to refer to Pascal Rougon. Noah survived the deluge. Pascal Rougon, by some miracle, escapes the inherited stain—he, and he alone, is completely free from it. He is a doctor, an advanced scientist, and he, in the twentieth volume, will analyse the terrible neurosis that has devastated his family.

In the upbuilding of this enormous edifice, Émile Zola shows the same constructive talent as he did in its conception. The energy he displays is marvellous. Every year a wing, courtyard, cupola, or tower is added, and each is as varied as the most imaginative could desire. Without looking further back than " L'Assommoir," let us consider what has been done. In this work, we have a study of the life of the working people in Paris, written, for the sake of preserving the " milieu," for the most part in their own language. It shows how the workers of our great social machine live, and must live, in ignorance and misery; it shows, as never was shown before, what the accident of birth means; it shows in a new way, and, to my mind, in as grand a way as did the laments of the chorus in the Greek play, the irrevocability of fate. "L'Assommoir" was followed by "Une Page d'Amour," a beautiful Parisian idyl. Here we see the "bourgeois" at their best. We have seven descriptions of Paris seen from a distance of which Turner might be proud; we have a picture of a children's costume ball which Meissonier might fall down and worship; we have the portrait of a beautiful and virtuous woman with her love story told, as it were, over the dying head of Jeanne (her little girl), the child whose nervous sensibilities are so delicate that she trembles with jealousy when she suspects that behind her back her mother is looking at the doctor. After "Une Page d'Amour" comes "Nana," and with her we are transported to a world of pleasure-seekers; vicious men and women who have no thought but the killing of time and the gratification of their lusts. Nana is the Messaline of modern days, and, obeying the epic tendency of his genius, Émile Zola has instituted a comparison between the death of the "gilded fly," conceived in drunkenness and debauchery, and the harlot city of the third Emperor, which, rotten with vice, falls before the victorious arms of the Germans.

"Nana" and "Une Page d'Amour" are psychological and philological studies of two radically different types of women; in both works, and likewise in "L'Assommoir," there is much descriptive writing, and, doubtless, Émile Zola had this fact present in his mind when he set himself to write "Pot-Bouille," that terrible satire on the "bourgeoisie." He must have said, as his plan formulated itself in his mind, "this is a novel dealing with the home-life of the middle-classes : if I wish to avoid repeating myself, this book must contain a vast number of characters, and the descriptions must be reduced to a bare sufficiency, no more than will allow my readers to form an exact impression of the surroundings through which the action passes." "Pot-Bouille," or "Piping Hot!" as the present translation is called, is, therefore, an inquiry into the private lives of a number of individuals, who, while they follow different occupations, belong to the same class and live under the same roof. The house in the Rue de Choiseul is one of those immense "maisons bourgeoises," in which, apparently, an infinite number of people live. On the first floor, we find Monsieur Duveyrier, an "avocat de la cour," with his musical wife, Clotilde, and her father, Monsieur Vabre, a retired notary and proprietor of the house, who is absorbed in the preparation of an important statistical work; on the fourth floor are Madame Josserand, her two daughters, whom she is always trying to marry, her crazy son Saturnin, and her husband who spends his nights addressing advertising circulars at three francs a thousand, in order to eke out an additional something to help his family to ape an appearance of easy circumstances. On the third floor is an arcnitect, Monsieur Campardon, with his ailing, yet blooming, wife Rose, and her cousin, "l'autre Madame Campardon." There is also one of Monsieur Vabre's sons, and "a distinguished gentleman who comes one night a week to work."

These are the principal "locataires ;" but, in various odd corners, "des petits appartements qui donnent sur la cour," we find all sorts and conditions of people. First on the list is the government clerk Jules and his wife Marie. She is a weak-minded little thing who commits adultery without affection, without desire, and the frequency of her confinements excites the ire of her mother and father. Then come two young men, Octave and Trublot. The former plays a part similar to that of a tenor in an opera ; he is the accepted lover of the ladies. The latter is equally beloved by the maids. From the frequency of his visits, he may almost be said to live in the house ; he is constantly asked to dine by one or other of the inmates, and in the morning he is generally found hiding behind the door of one of the servants' rooms, waiting for an opportunity of descending the staircase unperceived by the terrible "concierge," the moral guardian of the house.

Other visitors who figure prominently in the story are Madame Josserand's brother, Uncle Bachelard, a dissipated widower, and his nephew Gueulin; the Abbé Mouret, ever ready to throw the mantle of religion over the back-slidings of his flock, and Madame Hédouin, the frigid directress of "The Ladies' Paradise," where Octave is originally engaged. The remaining "locataires" are Madame Juzeur, a lady who only reads poetry, and who was deserted by her husband after a single week of matrimonial bliss; a workwoman who has a garret under the slates; and last, but not least, an author who lives on the second floor. He is rarely ever seen, he makes no one's acquaintance, and thereby excites the enmity of everyone.

All these, the author of course excepted, pass and re-pass before the reader, and each is at once individual and representative; even the maid-servants—who only answer "yes" and "no" to their masters and mistresses—are adroitly characterised. We see them in their kitchens engaged in their daily occupations: while peeling onions and gutting rabbits and fish they call to and abuse each other from window to window. There is Julie, the belle of the attics, of whose perfume and pomatum Trublot makes liberal use when he honours her with a visit; there is fat Adèle whose dirty habits and slovenly ways make of her a butt whereat is levelled the ridicule and scorn of her fellow-servants; there are the lovers, Hippolyte and Clémence, whose carnal intercourse affords to Madame Duveyrier much ground for uneasiness, and in the end necessitates the intervention of the Abbé. Never were the manners and morals of servants so thoroughly sifted before, never was the relationship which their lives bear to those of their masters and mistresses so cunningly contrasted. The courtyard of the house echoes with their quarrelling voices, and it is there, in a scene of which Swift might be proud, that is spoken the last and terrible word of scorn which Émile Zola flings against the "bourgeoisie." From her kitchen window a fellow-servant of Julie's is congratulating her on being about to leave, and wishing that she may find a better place. To which Julie replies, "Toutes les baraques se ressemblent. Au jour d'aujourd'hui, qui a fait l'une a fait l'autre. C'est cochon et compagnie."

I do not know to what other work to go to find so much successful sketching of character. I had better, I think, explain the meaning I attach to this phrase, "sketching of character," for it is too common an error to associate the idea of superficiality with the word "sketch." The true artist never allows anything to leave his studio that he deems superficial, or even unfinished. The word unfinished is not found in his vocabulary; to him a sketch is as complete as a finished picture. In the former he has painted broadly and freely, wishing to render the vividness, the vitality of a first impression; in the latter he is anxious to render the subtlety of a more intellectual and consequently a less sensual emotion. The portrait of Madame Josserand is a case in point, it is certainly less minute than that of Hélène Mouret, but is not for that less finished. In both, the artist has achieved, and perfectly, the task he set himself. "Piping Hot!" cannot be better defined than as a portrait album in which many of our French neighbours may be readily recognized.

This merit will not fail to strike any intelligent reader; but the marvellous way the almost insurmountable difficulties of binding together the stories of the lives of the different inhabitants of the house in the Rue de Choiseul are overcome, none but a fellow-worker will be able to appreciate at their full value. Up and down the famous staircase we go, from one household to another, interested equally in each, disgusted equally with all. And this sentence leads us right up to the enemies' guns, brings us face to face with the two batteries from which the critics have directed their fire. The first is the truthfulness of the picture, the second is the coarseness with which it is painted. I will attempt to reply to both.

M. Albert Wolff in the "Figaro" declared that in a "maison bourgeoise" so far were "locataires" from being all on visiting terms, that it was of constant occurrence that the people on one floor not only did not know by sight but were ignorant of the names of those living above and below them; that the spectacle of a "maison bourgeoise," with the lodgers running up and down stairs

in and out of each other's apartments at all hours of the
night and day, was absolutely false; had never existed in
Paris, and was an invention of the writer. Without a
word of parley I admit the truth of this indictment. I
will admit that no house could be found in Paris where
from basement to attic the inhabitants are on such terms
of intimacy as they are in the house in the Rue de
Choiseul; but at the same time I deny that the extreme
isolation described by M. Wolff could be found or is even
possible in any house inhabited over a term of years by
the same people. Émile Zola has then done no more than
to exaggerate, to draw the strings that attach the different
parts a little tighter than they would be in nature. Art,
let there be no mistake on this point, be it romantic or
naturalistic, is a perpetual concession; and the character of the artist is determined by the selection he makes
amid the mass of conflicting issues that, all clamouring
equally to be chosen, present themselves to his mind.
In the case of Émile Zola, the epic faculty which has
been already mentioned as the dominant trait of his
genius naturally impelled him to make too perfect a
whole of the heterogeneous mass of material that he had
determined to construct from. The flaw is more obvious
than in his other works, but in "Piping Hot!" he has
only done what he has done since he first put pen to
paper, what he will continue to do till he ceases to write.
We will admit that to make all the people living in the
house in the Rue de Choiseul on visiting terms was a trick
of composition—*et puis?*

This was the point from which the critics who pretended to be guided by artistic considerations attacked
the book; the others entrenched themselves behind the
good old earthworks of morality, and primed their rusty
popguns. Now there was a time, and a very good time
it must have been, when a book was judged on its literary
merits; but of late years a new school of criticism has
come into fashion. Its manners are very summary indeed.
"Would you or would you not give that book to your
sister of sixteen to read?" If you hesitate you are lost;
for then the question is dismissed with a smile and you

are voted out of court. It would be vain to suggest that there are other people in the world besides your sister of sixteen summers.

I do not intend putting forward any well known paradox, that art is morals, and morals are art. That there are great and eternal moral laws which must be acted up to in art as in life I am more than ready to admit; but these are very different from the wretched conventionalities which have been arbitrarily imposed upon us in England. To begin with, it must be clear to the meanest intelligence that it would never do to judge the dead by the same standard as the living. If that were done, all the dramatists of the sixteenth century would have to go; those of the Restoration would follow. To burn Swift somebody lower in the social scale than Mr. Binns would have to be found, although he might do to commit Sterne to the flames. Byron, Shelley, yes, even Landor would have to go the same way. What would happen then, it is hard to-say; but it is not unfair to hint that if the burning were argued to its logical conclusion, some of the extra good people would find it difficult to show reason, if the intention of the author were not taken into account, why their most favourite reading should be saved from the general destruction.

Many writers have lately been trying to put their readers in the possession of infallible recipes for the production of good fiction; they would, to my mind, have employed their time and talents to far more purpose had they come boldly to the point and stated that the overflow of bad fiction with which we are inundated is owing to the influence of the circulating library, which, on one side, sustains a quantity of worthless writers who on their own merits would not sell a dozen copies of their books; and, on the other, deprives those who have something to say and are eager to say it of the liberty of doing so. It may be a sad fact, but it is nevertheless a fact, that literature and young girls are irreconcilable elements, and the sooner we leave off trying to reconcile them the better. At this vain endeavour the circulating library has been at work for the last twenty years, and what has been the result? A literature of bandboxes. Were Pope, Addison, Johnson, Fielding, Smollet, suddenly raised from their graves and started on reviewing "three vols.," think you that they would not all cry together, "This is a literature of bandboxes?"

We judge a pudding by the eating, and I judge Messrs. Mudie and Smith by what they have produced; for they, not the ladies and gentlemen who place their names on the title pages, are the authors of our fiction. And what a terrible brood to admit the parentage of! Let those who doubt put aside pre-conceived opinions, and forgetting the bolstered up reputation of the authors, read the volumes by the light of a little common sense. Cast a glance at those that lie in Miss Rhoda Broughton's lap. What a wheezing, drivelling lot of bairns they are! They have not a virtue amongst them, and their pinafore pages are sticky with childish sensualities.

And here we touch the keynote of the whole system. For mark you, you can say what you like provided you speak according to rule. Everything is agreed according to precedent. I could give a hundred instances, but one will suffice. On the publication of "Adam Bede" a howl was raised, but the book was alive; it finished by being accepted, and the libraries were obliged to give way. The employment of seduction in the fabulation of a story was therefore established. This would have been a great point gained, if Mr. Mudie had not succeeded in forcing on all succeeding writers George Eliot's manner of conducting her story. In "Adam Bede" we have Hetty described as an extremely fascinating dairymaid and Arthur as a noble-minded young man. After a good deal of flirtation they are shown to us walking through a wood together, and three months after we hear that Hetty is *enceinte.* Now, ever since the success of this book was assured, we have had numberless novels dealing with seductions, but invariably an interval of three months is allowed wherein the reader's fancy may disport until the truth be told.

Not being a select librarian I will not undertake to

say that the cause of morality is advanced by leaving the occurrence of the offence unmarked by a no more precise date than that of three months, but being a writer who loves and believes in his art, I fearlessly declare that such quibblery is not worthy of the consideration of serious men; and it was to break through this puerile conventionality that I was daring enough in my "Mummer's Wife" to write that Dick dragged Kate into the room and that the door was slammed behind her. And it is on this passage that the select circulating libraries base a refusal to take the book. And it is such illiterate censorship that has thrown English fiction into the abyss of nonsense in which it lies; it is for this reason and no other that the writers of the present day have ceased even to try to produce good work, and have resigned themselves to the task of turning out their humdrum stories of sentimental misunderstanding. Yet, strange to say, in every other department of art, an unceasing intellectual activity prevails. Our poetry, our histories, our biographies, our newspapers are strong and vigorous, pregnant with thought, trenchant in style; it is not until we turn to the novel that we find a wearisome absence of everything but drivel.

Though much that I would like to have said is still unsaid, the exigencies of space compel me to bring this notice to a close. However, this one thing I hope I have made clear: that it is my firm opinion that if fiction is to exist at all, the right to speak as he pleases on politics, morals, and religion must be granted to the writer, and that he on his side must take cognizance of other readers than sentimental young girls, who require to be provided with harmless occupation until something fresh turns up in the matrimonial market. Therefore the great literary battle of our day is not to be fought for either realism or romanticism, but for freedom of speech; and until that battle be gained I, for one, will continue fearlessly to hold out a hand of welcome to all comers who dare to attack the sovereignty of the circulating library.

The first of these is "Piping Hot!" and, I think, the pungent odour of life it exhales, as well as its scorching

satire on the middle-classes, will be relished by all who
prefer the fortifying brutalities of truth to the soft plati-
tudes of lies.   As a satire "Piping Hot!" must be read;
and as a satire it will rank with Juvenal, Voltaire, Pope,
and Swift.

GEORGE MOORE.

PIPING HOT!

(*POT-BOUILLE.*)

CHAPTER I.

In the Rue Neuve-Saint-Augustin, a block of vehicles arrested
the cab which was bringing Octave Mouret and his three trunks
from the Lyons railway station. The young man lowered one
of the windows, in spite of the already intense cold of that dull
November afternoon. He was surprised at the abrupt approach
of twilight in this neighbourhood of narrow streets, all swarming with a busy crowd. The oaths of the drivers as they
lashed their snorting horses, the endless jostlings on the foot-
pavements, the serried line of shops swarming with attendants
and customers, bewildered him ; for, though he had dreamed
of a cleaner Paris than the one he beheld, he had never hoped
to find it so eager for trade, and he felt that it was publicly open
to the appetites of energetic young fellows.

The driver leant towards him.

" It's the Passage Choiseul you want, isn't it ? "

" No, the Rue de Choiseul. A new house, I think."

And the cab only had to turn the corner. The house was the
second one in the street : a big house four storeys high, the
stonework of which was scarcely discoloured, in the midst of
the dirty stucco of the adjoining old frontages. Octave, who
had alighted on to the pavement, measured it and studied it
with a mechanical glance, from the silk warehouse on the
ground floor to the projecting windows on the fourth floor
opening on to a narrow terrace. On the first floor, carved female
heads supported a highly elaborate cast-iron balcony. The
windows were surrounded with complicated frames, roughly
chiselled in the soft stone ; and, lower down, above the tall

doorway, two cupids were unrolling a scroll bearing the number, which at night-time was lighted up by a jet of gas from the inside.

A stout fair gentleman, who was coming out of the vestibule, stopped short on catching sight of Octave.

"What! you here!" exclaimed he. "Why, I was not expecting you till to-morrow!"

"The truth is," replied the young man, "I left Plassans a day earlier than I originally intended. Isn't the room ready?"

"Oh, yes. I took it a fortnight ago, and I furnished it at once in the way you desired. Wait a bit, I will take you to it."

He re-entered the house, though Octave begged he would not give himself the trouble. The driver had got the three trunks off the cab. Inside the doorkeeper's room, a dignified-looking man with a long face, clean-shaven like a diplomatist, was standing up gravely reading the "Monitcur." He deigned, however, to interest himself about these trunks which were being deposited in his doorway; and, taking a few steps forward, he asked his tenant, the architect of the third floor as he called him:

"Is this the person, Monsieur Campardon?"

"Yes, Monsieur Gourd, this is Monsieur Octave Mouret, for whom I have taken the room on the fourth floor. He will sleep there and take his meals with us. Monsieur Mouret is a friend of my wife's relations, and I beg you will show him every attention."

Octave was examining the entrance with its panels of imitation marble and its vaulted ceiling decorated with rosettes. The courtyard at the end was paved and cemented, and had a grand air of cold cleanliness; the only occupant was a coachman engaged in polishing a bit with a chamois leather at the entrance to the stables. There were no signs of the sun ever shining there.

Meanwhile, Monsieur Gourd was inspecting the trunks. He pushed them with his foot, and, their weight filling him with respect, he talked of fetching a porter to carry them up the servants' staircase.

"Madame Gourd, I'm going out," cried he, just putting his head inside his room.

It was like a drawing-room, with bright looking-glasses, a red flowered Wilton carpet and violet ebony furniture; and, through a partly opened door, one caught a glimpse of the bed-chamber with a bedstead hung with garnet rep. Madame Gourd, a very fat woman with yellow ribbons in her hair, was stretched out in an easy-chair with her hands clasped, and doing nothing.

"Well! let's go up," said the architect.

And seeing how impressed the young man seemed to be by Monsieur Gourd's black velvet cap and sky blue slippers, he added, as he pushed open the mahogany door of the vestibule:

"You know he was formerly the Duke de Vaugelade's valet."

"Ah!" simply ejaculated Octave.

"It's as I tell you, and he married the widow of a little bailiff of Mort-la-Ville. They even own a house there. But they are waiting until they have three thousand francs a year before going there to live. Oh! they are most respectable doorkeepers!"

The decorations of the vestibule and the staircase were gaudily luxurious. At the foot of the stairs was the figure of a woman, a kind of gilded Neapolitan, supporting on her head an amphora from which issued three gas-jets protected by ground glass globes. The panels of imitation white marble with pink borders succeeded each other at regular intervals up the wall of the staircase, whilst the cast-iron balustrade with its mahogany hand-rail was in imitation of old silver with clusters of golden leaves. A red carpet, secured with brass rods, covered the stairs. But what especially struck Octave on entering was a green-house temperature, a warm breath which seemed to be puffed from some mouth into his face.

"Hallo!" said he, "the staircase is warmed."

"Of course," replied Campardon. "All landlords who have the least self-respect go to that expense now. The house is a very fine one, very fine."

He looked about him as though he were sounding the walls with his architect's eyes.

"My dear fellow, you will see, it is a most comfortable place, and inhabited solely by highly respectable people!"

Then, slowly ascending, he mentioned the names of the different tenants. On each floor were two separate suites of apartments, one looking on to the street, the other on to the courtyard, and the polished mahogany doors of which faced each other. He began by saying a few words respecting Monsieur Auguste Vabre; he was the landlord's eldest son; since the spring he had rented the silk warehouse on the ground floor, and he also occupied the whole of the "entresol" above. Then, on the first floor the landlord's other son, Monsieur Théophile Vabre and his wife, resided in the apartment overlooking the courtyard ; and in the one overlooking the street lived the landlord himself, formerly a notary at Versailles, but who was now lodging with his son-in-law, Monsieur Duveyrier, a judge at the Court of Appeal.

"A fellow who is not yet forty-five," said Campardon, stopping short. "That's something remarkable, is it not ?"

He ascended two steps, and then suddenly turning round, he added :

"Water and gas on every floor."

Beneath the tall window on each landing, the panes of which, bordered with fretwork, lit up the staircase with a white light, was placed a narrow velvet covered bench. The architect observed that elderly persons could sit down and rest. Then, as he passed the second floor without naming the tenants :

"And there ?" asked Octave, pointing to the door of the principal suite.

"Oh ! there," said he, "persons whom one never sees, whom no one knows. The house could well do without them. Blemishes, you know, are to be found everywhere."

He gave a little snort of contempt.

"The gentleman writes books, I believe."

But on the third floor his smile of satisfaction reappeared. The apartments looking on to the courtyard were divided into two suites; they were occupied by Madame Juzeur, a little woman who was most unhappy, and a very distinguished gentleman who had taken a room to which he came once a week on business matters. Whilst giving these particulars, Campardon opened the door on the other side of the landing.

"And this is where I live," resumed he. "Wait a moment, I must get your key. We will first go up to your room ; you can see my wife afterwards."

During the two minutes he was left alone, Octave felt penetrated by the grave silence of the staircase. He leant over the balustrade, in the warm air which ascended from the vestibule ; he raised his head, listening if any noise came from above. It was the death-like peacefulness of a middle-class drawing-room, carefully shut in and not admitting a breath from outside. Behind the beautiful shining mahogany doors there seemed to be unfathomable depths of respectability.

"You will have some excellent neighbours," said Campardon, reappearing with the key ; "on the street side there are the Josserands, quite a family, the father who is cashier at the Saint-Joseph glass works, and also two marriageable daughters ;

and next to you the Pichons, the husband is a clerk ; they are
not rolling in wealth, but they are educated people. Everything has to be let, has it not ? even in a house like this."

From the third landing, the red carpet ceased and was replaced by a simple grey holland. Octave's vanity was slightly
ruffled. The staircase had, little by little, filled him with
respect ; he was deeply moved at inhabiting such a fine house
as the architect termed it. As, following the latter, he turned
into the passage leading to his room, he caught sight through
a partly open door of a young woman standing up before a
cradle. She raised her head at the noise. She was fair, with
clear and vacant eyes ; and all he carried away was this very
distinct look, for the young woman, suddenly blushing, pushed
the door to in the shame-faced way of a person taken by
surprise.

Campardon turned round to repeat :

" Water and gas on every floor, my dear fellow."

Then he pointed out a door which opened on to the servants'
staircase. Their rooms were up above. And stopping at the
end of the passage, he added :

" Here we are at last."

The room, which was square, pretty large, and hung with a
grey wall-paper with blue flowers, was furnished very simply.
Close to the alcove was a little dressing-closet with just room
enough to wash one's hands. Octave went straight to the
window, which admitted a greenish light. Below was the courtyard looking sad and clean, with its regular pavement, and the
shining brass tap of its cistern. And still not a human being,
nor even a noise ; nothing but the uniform windows, without a
bird-cage, without a flower-pot, displaying the monotony of their
white curtains. To hide the big bare wall of the house on the
left hand side, which shut in the square of the courtyard, the
windows had been repeated, imitation windows in paint, with
shutters eternally closed, behind which the walled-in life of the
neighbouring apartments appeared to continue.

" But I shall be very comfortable here ! " cried Octave delighted.

" I thought so," said Campardon. " Well ! I did everything
as though it had been for myself ; and, moreover, I carried out
the instructions contained in your letters. So the furniture
pleases you ? It is all that is necessary for a young man.
Later on, you can make any changes you like."

And, as Octave shook his hand, thanking him, and apologising for having given him so much trouble, he resumed in a serious tone of voice :

"Only, my boy, no rows here, and above all no women ! On my word of honour, if you were to bring a woman here it would revolutionize the whole house !"

"Be easy !" murmured the young man, feeling rather anxious.

"No, let me tell you, for it is I who would be compromised. You have seen the house. All middle-class people, and of extreme morality ! between ourselves, they affect it rather too much. Never a word, never more noise than you have heard just now. Ah, well ! Monsieur Gourd would at once fetch Monsieur Vabre, and we should both be in a nice pickle ! My dear fellow, I ask it of you for my own peace of mind : respect the house."

Octave, overpowered by so much virtue and respectability, swore to do so. Then, Campardon, casting a mistrustful glance around, and lowering his voice as though some one might have heard him, added with sparkling eyes :

"Outside it concerns nobody. Paris is big enough, is it not ? there is plenty of room. As for myself, I am at heart an artist, therefore I think nothing of it !"

A porter carried up the trunks. When everything was straight, the architect assisted paternally at Octave's toilet. Then, rising to his feet he said :

"Now we will go and see my wife."

Down on the third floor the maid, a slim, dark, and coquettish looking girl, said that madame was busy. Campardon, with a view of putting his young friend at ease, showed him over the rooms : first of all, there was the huge white and gold drawing-room, highly decorated with artificial mouldings, and situated between a green parlour which the architect had turned into a workroom and the bedroom, into which they could not enter, but the narrow shape of which, and the mauve wall-paper, he described. As he next ushered him into the dining-room, all in imitation wood, with an extraordinary complication of baguettes and coffers, Octave, enchanted, exclaimed :

"It is very handsome !"

On the ceiling, two big cracks cut right through the coffers, and, in a corner, the paint had peeled off and displayed the plaster.

"Yes, it creates an effect," slowly observed the architect, his eyes fixed on the ceiling. "You see, these kind of houses are built to create effect. Only, the walls will not bear much looking into. It is not twelve years old yet, and it is already cracking. One builds the frontage of handsome stone, with a lot of sculpture about it ; one gives three **coats** of varnish to the walls of the staircase ; one paints and gilds the rooms ; and all that flatters people, and inspires respect. Oh ! it is still solid, it will certainly last as long as we shall ! "

He led him again across the ante-room, which was lighted by a window of ground glass. To the left, looking on to the court-yard, there was a second bed-chamber where his daughter Angèle slept, and which, all in white, looked on this November afternoon as sad as a tomb. Then at the end of the passage, came the kitchen, into which he insisted on conducting Octave, saying that it was necessary to see everything.

" Walk in," repeated he, pushing open the door.

A terrible uproar issued from. it. In spite of the cold, the window was wide open. With their elbows on the rail, the dark maid and a fat cook, a dissolute looking old party, were leaning out into the narrow well of an inner courtyard, which lighted the kitchens of each floor, placed opposite to each other. They were both yelling with their backs bent, whilst, from the depths of this hole, arose the sounds of vulgar voices, mingled with oaths and bursts of laughter. It was like the overflow of some sewer : all the domestics of the house were there, easing their minds. Octave's thoughts reverted to the peaceful majesty of the grand staircase.

Just then the two women, warned by some instinct, turned round. They remained thunderstruck on beholding their master with a gentleman. There was a gentle whistle, windows were shut, and all was once more as silent as death.

" What is the matter, Lisa ? " asked Campardon.

" Sir," replied the maid, greatly excited, " it's that filthy Adèle again. She has thrown a rabbit's guts out of the window. You should speak to Monsieur Josserand, sir."

Campardon became very grave, anxious not to make any promise. He returned to his workroom, saying to Octave :

" You have seen all. On each floor, the rooms are arranged the same. I pay a rent of two thousand five hundred francs, and on a third floor, too ! Rents are rising every day. Monsieur Vabre must make about twenty-two thousand francs a year from his house. And it will increase still more, for there is a question of opening a wide thoroughfare from the Place de la Bourse to the new Opera-house. And he had the ground this is built upon almost for nothing, twelve years ago, after that great fire caused by a druggist's servant ! "

As they entered, Octave observed, hanging above a drawing-table, and in the full light from the window, a richly framed picture of a Virgin, displaying in her opened breast an enormous flaming heart. He could not repress a movement of surprise ; he looked at Campardon, whom he had known to be a rather wild fellow at Plassans.

"Ah ! I forgot to tell you," resumed the latter slightly colouring, "I have been appointed diocesan architect, yes, at Evreux. Oh ! a mere bagatelle as regards money, in all barely two thousand francs a year. But there is scarcely anything to do, a journey now and again ; for the rest I have an inspector there. And, you see, it is a great deal, when one can print on one's cards : 'government architect.' You can have no idea what an amount of work that procures me in the highest society."

Whilst speaking, he looked at the Virgin with the flaming heart.

"After all," continued he in a sudden fit of frankness, "I do not care a button for their paraphernalia ! "

But, on Octave bursting out laughing, the architect was seized with fear. Why confide in that young man ? He gave a side glance, and, putting on an air of compunction, he tried to smooth over what he had said.

"I do not care and yet I do care. Well ! yes, I am becoming like that. You will see, you will see, my friend : when you have lived a little longer, you will do as every one else."

And he spoke of his forty-two years, of the emptiness of life, posing for being very melancholy, which his robust health belied. In the artist's head which he had fashioned for himself, with flowing hair and beard trimmed in the Henri IV. style, one found the flat skull and square jaw of a middle-class man of limited intelligence and voracious appetites. When younger, he had a fatiguing gaiety.

Octave's eyes became fixed on a number of the "Gazette de France," which was lying amongst some plans. Then, Campardon, more and more ill at ease, rang for the maid to know if madame was at length disengaged. Yes, the doctor was just leaving, madame would be there directly.

"Is Madame Campardon unwell ? " asked the young man.

"No, she is the same as usual," said the architect in a bored tone of voice.

"Ah! and what is the matter with her?"

Again embarrassed, he did not give a straightforward answer.

"You know, there is always something going wrong with women. She has been in this state for the last thirteen years, ever since her confinement. Otherwise, she is as well as can be. You will even find her stouter."

Octave asked no further questions. Just then, Lisa returned, bringing a card; and the architect, begging to be excused, hastened to the drawing-room, telling the young man as he disappeared to talk to his wife and have patience. Octave had caught sight, on the door being quickly opened and closed, of the black mass of a cassock in the centre of the large white and gold apartment.

At the same moment, Madame Campardon entered from the ante-room. He scarcely knew her again. In other days, when a youngster, he had known her at Plassans, at her father's, Monsieur Domergue, government clerk of the works, she was thin and ugly, as puny-looking as a young girl suffering from the crisis of her puberty; and now he beheld her plump, with the clear and placid complexion of a nun, soft eyes, dimples, and a general appearance of an overfed she-cat. If she had not been able to grow pretty, she had ripened towards thirty, gaining a sweet savour and a nice fresh odour of autumn fruit. He remarked, however, that she walked with difficulty, her whole body wrapped, in a mignonette coloured silk dressing-gown, moving; which gave her a languid air.

"But you are a man, now!" said she gaily, holding out her hands. "How you have grown, since our last journey to the country!"

And she gazed at him: tall, dark, handsome, with his well kept moustache and beard. When he told her his age, twenty-two, she scarcely believed it: he looked twenty-five at least. He, whom the presence of a woman, even though she were the lowest of servants, filled with rapture, laughed melodiously, enveloping her with his eyes of the colour of old gold, and of the softness of velvet.

"Ah! yes," repeated he gently, "I have grown, I have grown. Do you recollect, when your cousin Gasparine used to buy me marbles?"

Then, he gave her news of her parents. Monsieur and Madame Domergue were living happily, in the house to which they had retired; they merely complained of being very lonely, bearing Campardon a grudge for having taken their little Rose from them, during a stay he had made at Plassans ou business. Then, the young mau tried to bring the conversation round to cousin Gasparine, having a precocious youngster's old curiosity to satisfy, in the matter of an hitherto unexplained adventure: the architect's mad passion for Gasparine, a tall lovely girl, but poor, and his sudden marriage with skinny Rose who had a dowry of thirty thousaud francs, and quite a tearful sceue, aud a quarrel, and the flight of the abandoned one to Paris, to an aunt who was a dressmaker. But Madame Campardou, whose placid complexiou preserved a rosy paleness, did not appear to understand. He was unable to draw a single particular from her.

"And your parents?" iuquired she in her turn. "How are Monsieur and Madame Mouret?"

"Very well, thank you," replied he. "My mother scarcely leaves her garden. You would find the house in the Rue de la Banne, just as you left it."

Madame Campardon, who seemed unable to remain standiug for long without feeling tired, had seated herself on a high drawing-chair, her legs stretched out in her dressing-gown ; and he, taking a low chair beside her, raised his head when speaking, with his air of habitual adoration. With his large shoulders, he was like a woman, he had a woman's feeling which at ouce admitted him to their hearts. So that, at the eud of ten minutes, they were both talking like two lady friends of long stauding.

"Now I am your boarder," said he, passing a handsome hand with neatly trimmed nails over his beard. "We shall get on well together, you will see. How charming it was of you to remember the Plassans youngster and to busy yourself about everything, at the first word!"

But she protested.

"No, do not thank me. I am a great deal too lazy, I never move. It was Achille who arranged everything. And, besides, was it not sufficient that my mother meutioned to us your desire to board in some family, for us to think at once of opeuiug our doors to you? You will not be with strangers, and will be compauy for us."

Then, he told her of his own affairs. After having obtaiued a bachelor's diploma, to please his family, he had just passed three years at Marseilles, in a big calico print warehouse, which had a factory in the neighbourhood of Plassans. He had a passion for trade, the trade in women's luxuries, into which enters a seduction, a slow possession by gilded words and adulatory glances. And he related, laughing victoriously, how he had made the five thousand francs, without which he would never have ventured on coming to Paris, for he had the prudence of a Jew beneath the exterior of an amiable giddy-headed fellow.

"Just fancy, they had a Pompadour calico, an old design, something marvellous. No one would bite at it; it had been stowed away in the cellars for two years past. Then, as I was about to travel through the departments of the Var and the Basses-Alpes, it occurred to me to purchase the whole of the stock and to sell it on my own account. Oh! such a success! an amazing success! The women quarrelled for the remnants; and to-day, there is not one there who is not wearing some of my calico. I must say that I talked them over so nicely! They were all with me, I might have done as I pleased with them."

And he laughed, whilst Madame Campardon, charmed, and troubled by thought of that Pompadour calico, questioned him: "Little bouquets on an unbleached ground, was it not?" She had been trying to obtain the same thing everywhere for a summer dressing-gown.

"I have travelled for two years, which is enough," resumed he. "Besides, there is Paris to conquer. I must immediately look out for something."

"What!" exclaimed she, "has not Achille told you? But he has a berth for you, and close by, too!"

He uttered his thanks, as surprised as though he were in fairy land, asking, by way of a joke, whether he would not find a wife and a hundred thousand francs a-year in his room that evening, when a young girl of fourteen, tall and ugly, with fair insipid-looking hair, pushed open the door, and gave a slight cry of fright.

"Come in and don't be afraid," said Madame Campardon. "It is Monsieur Octave Mouret, whom you have heard us speak of."

Then, turning towards the latter, she added:

"My daughter, Angèle. We did not bring her with us at our last journey. She was so delicate! But she is getting stouter now."

Angèle, with the awkwardness of girls in the ungrateful age, went and placed herself behind her mother, and cast glances at the smiling young man. Almost immediately, Campardon re-appeared, looking excited; and he could not contain himself, but told his wife in a few words of his good fortune: the Abbé

Mauduit, Vicar of Saint-Roch, had called about some work,
merely some repairs, but which might lead to many other things.
Then, annoyed at having spoken before Octave, and still quivering, he rapped one hand in the other, saying :

"Well ! well ! what are we going to do ? "

"Why, you were going out," said Octave. "Do not let me
disturb you."

"Achille," murmured Madame Campardon, "that berth, at
the Hédouins'—"

"Why, of course ! I was forgetting," exclaimed the architect. "My dear fellow, a place of first clerk at a large linendraper's. I know some one there who has said a word for you.
You are expected. It is not yet four o'clock ; shall I introduce
you now ? "

Octave hesitated, anxious about the bow of his necktie,
flurried by his mania for being neatly dressed. However, he
decided to go, when Madame Campardon assured him that he
looked very well. With a languid movement, she offered her
forehead to her husband, who kissed her with a great show of
tenderness, repeating :

"Good-bye, my darling—good-bye, my pet." ·

"Do not forget that we dine at seven," said she, accompanying them across the drawing-room, where they had left their hats.

Angèle followed them without the slightest grace. But her
music-master was waiting for her, and she at once commenced
to strum on the instrument with her bony fingers. Octave, who
was lingering in the ante-room, repeating his thanks, was unable
to make himself heard. And, as he went downstairs, the sound
of the piano seemed to follow him : in the midst of the warm
silence other pianos—from Madame Juzeur's, the Vabres', and
Duveyriers'—were answering, playing on each floor other airs,
which issued, distantly and religiously, from the calm solemnity
of the doors.

On reaching the street, Campardon turned into the Rue
Neuve-Saint-Augustin. He remained silent, with the absorbed
air of a man seeking for an opportunity to broach a subject. ·

"Do you remember Mademoiselle Gasparine ? " asked he, at
length. "She is first lady assistant at the Hédouins'. You
will see her."

Octave thought this a good time for satisfying his curiosity.

"Ah ! " said he. "Does she live with you ? "

"No ! no ! " exclaimed the architect, hastily, and as though
feeling hurt at the bare idea.

Then, as the young man appeared surprised at his vehemence, he gently continued, speaking in an embarrassed way:

"No; she and my wife no longer see each other. You know, in families— Well, I met her, and I could not refuse to shake hands, could I? more especially as she is not very well off, poor girl. So that, now, they have news of each other through me. In these old quarrels, one must leave the task of healing the wounds to time."

Octave was about to question him plainly on the subject of his marriage, when the architect suddenly put an end to the conversation by saying:

"Here we are!"

It was a large linendrapers, opening on to the narrow triangle of the Place Gaillon, at the corner of the Rue Neuve-Saint-Augustin and the Rue de la Michodière. Across two windows immediately above the shop was a signboard, with the words, "The Ladies' Paradise, founded in 1822," in faded gilt letters, whilst on the shop windows was inscribed, in red, the name of the firm, "Deleuze, Hédouin, & Co."

"It has not the modern style, but it is honest and solid," rapidly explained Campardon. "Monsieur Hédouin, formerly a clerk, married the daughter of the elder Deleuze, who died a couple of years ago; so that the business is now managed by the young couple—the old Deleuze and another partner, I think, both keep out of it. You will see Madame Hédouin. Oh! a woman with brains! Let us go in."

It so happened that Monsieur Hédouin was at Lille buying some linen; therefore Madame Hédouin received them. She was standing up, a penholder behind her ear, giving orders to two shopmen who were putting away some pieces of stuff on the shelves; and she appeared to him so tall, so admirably lovely, with her regular features and her tidy hair, so gravely smiling, in her black dress, with a turn-down collar and a man's tie, that Octave, not usually timid, could only stammer out a few observations. Everything was settled without any waste of words.

"Well!" said she, in her quiet way, and with her trades-woman's accustomed gracefulness, "you may as well look over the place, as you are not engaged."

She called one of her clerks, and put Octave under his guidance; then, after having politely replied to a question of Campardon's that Mademoiselle Gasparine was out on an errand, she turned her back and resumed her work, continuing to give her orders in her gentle and concise voice.

"Not there, Alexandre. Put the silks up at the top. Be careful, those are not the same make!"

Campardon, after hesitating, at length said to Octave that he would call again for him to take him back to dinner. Then, during two hours, the young man went over the warehouse. He found it badly lighted, small, encumbered with stock, which, overflowing from the basement, became heaped up in the corners, leaving only narrow passages between high walls of bales. On several different occasions he ran against Madame Hédouin, busy, and scuttling along the narrowest passages without ever catching her dress in anything. She seemed the very life and soul of the establishment, all the assistants belonging to which obeyed the slightest sign of her white hands. Octave felt hurt that she did not take more notice of him. Towards a quarter to seven, as he was coming up a last time from the basement, he was told that Campardon was on the first floor with Mademoiselle Gasparine. Up there was the hosiery department, which that young lady looked after. But, at the top of the winding staircase, the young man stopped abruptly behind a pyramid of pieces of calico systematically arranged, on hearing the architect talking most familiarly to Gasparine.

"I swear to you it is not so!" cried he, forgetting himself so far as to raise his voice.

A slight pause ensued.

"How is she now?" at length inquired the young woman.

"Well! always the same. It comes and goes. She feels that it is all over now. She will never get right again."

Gasparine resumed, in compassionate tones :

"My poor friend, it is you who are to be pitied. However, as you have been able to manage in another way, tell her how sorry I am to hear that she is still unwell—"

Campardon, without letting her finish, seized hold of her by the shoulders and kissed her roughly on the lips, in the gas-heated air already becoming heavy beneath the low ceiling. She returned his kiss, murmuring :

"To-morrow morning, if you can, at six o'clock I will remain in bed. Knock three times."

Octave, bewildered, and beginning to understand, coughed, and showed himself. Another surprise awaited him. Cousin Gasparine had become dried up, thin and angular, with her jaw projecting, and her hair coarse ; and all she had preserved of her former self were her large superb eyes, in a face that had now become cadaverous. With her jealous forehead, her ardent and obstinate mouth, she troubled him as much as Rose had charmed him by her tardy expansion of an indolent blonde.

Gasparine was polite, without effusiveness. She remembered Plassans—she talked to the young man of the old times. When they went off, Campardon and he, she shook their hands. Downstairs, Madame Hédouin simply said to Octave :

"To-morrow, then, sir."

Out in the street the young man, deafened by the cabs, jostled by the passers-by, could not help remarking that this lady was very beautiful, but that she did not seem particularly amiable. On the black and muddy pavement, the bright windows of freshly-painted shops, flaring with gas, cast broad rays of vivid light ; whilst the old shops, with their sombre displays, lit up in the interior only by smoking lamps, which burnt like distant stars, saddened the streets with masses of shadow. In the Rue Neuve-Saint-Augustin, just before turning into the Rue de Choiseul, the architect bowed on passing before one of these establishments.

A young woman, slim and elegant, dressed in a silk mantlet, was standing in the doorway, drawing a little boy of three towards her, so that he might not get run over. She was talking to an old bareheaded lady, the shopkeeper, no doubt, whom she addressed in a familiar manner. Octave could not distinguish her features in that dim light, beneath the dancing reflections of the neighbouring gas-jets ; she seemed to him to be pretty, he only saw two bright eyes, which were fixed a moment upon him like two flames. Behind her yawned the shop, damp like a cellar, and emitting an odour of saltpetre.

"That is Madame Vabre, the wife of Monsieur Théophile Vabre, the landlord's younger son. You know the people who live on the first floor," resumed Campardon, when he had gone a few steps. "Oh ! a most charming lady ! She was born in that shop, one of the best paying haberdashers of the neighbourhood, which her parents, Monsieur and Madame Louhette, still manage, for the sake of having something to occupy them. They have made some money there, I will warrant ! "

But Octave did not understand trade of that sort, in those holes of old Paris, where at one time a piece of stuff was sufficient sign. He swore that nothing in the world would ever make him consent to live in such a den. One surely caught some rare aches and pains there !

Whilst talking, they had reached the top of the stairs. They were being waited for. Madame Campardon had put on a grey

silk dress, had arranged her hair coquettishly, and looked very
neat and prim. Campardon kissed her on the neck, with the
emotion of a good husband.

"Good evening, my darling ; good evening, my pet."

And they passed into the dining-room. The dinner was
delightful. Madame Campardon at first talked of the Deleuzes
and the Hédouins—families respected throughout the neighbourhood, and whose members were well known ; a cousin who
was a stationer in the Rue Gaillon, an uncle who had an
umbrella shop in the Passage Choiseul, and nephews and nieces
in business all round about. Then the conversation turned,
and they talked of Angèle, who was sitting stiffly on her chair,
and eating with inert gestures. Her mother was bringing her
up at home, it was preferable ; and, not wishing to say more,
she blinked her eyes, to convey that young girls learnt very
naughty things at boarding-schools. The child had slyly
balanced her plate on her knife. Lisa, who was clearing the
cloth, missed breaking it, and exclaimed :

"It was your fault, mademoiselle ! "

A mad laugh, violently restrained, passed over Angèle's face.
Madame Campardon contented herself with shaking her head ;
and, when Lisa had left the room to fetch the dessert, she sang
her praises—very intelligent, very active, a regular Paris girl,
always knowing which way to turn. They might very well do
without Victoire, the cook, who was no longer very clean, on
account of her great age ; but she had seen her master born at
his father's—she was a family ruin which they respected. Then
as the maid returned with some baked apples :

"Conduct irreproachable," continued Madame Campardon in
Octave's ear. "I have discovered nothing against her as yet.
One holiday a month to go and embrace her old aunt, who lives
some distance off."

Octave observed Lisa. Seeing her nervous, flat-chested,
blear-eyed, the thought came to him that she must go in for a
precious fling, when at her old aunt's. However, he greatly
approved what the mother said, as she continued to give him
her views on education—a young girl is such a heavy responsibility, it is necessary to keep her clear even of the breaths of
the street. And, during this, Angèle, each time Lisa leant over
near her chair to remove a plate, pinched her in a friendly way,
whilst they both maintained their composure, without even
moving an eyelid.

"One should be virtuous for one's own sake," said the

architect learnedly, as though by way of conclusion to thoughts he had not expressed. "I do not care a button for public opinion ; I am an artist !"

After dinner, they remained in the drawing-room until midnight. It was a little jollification to celebrate Octave's arrival. Madame Campardon appeared to be very tired ; little by little she abandoned herself, leaning back on the sofa.

"Are you suffering, my darling ?" asked her husband.

"No," replied she in a low voice. "It is always the same thing."

She looked at him, and then gently asked :

"Did you see her at the Hédouins' ?"

"Yes. She asked after you."

Tears came to Rose's eyes.

"She is in good health, she is !"

"Come, come," said the architect, showering little kisses on her hair, forgetting they were not alone. "You will make yourself worse again. You know very well that I love you all the same, my poor pet !"

Octave, who had discreetly retired to the window, under the pretence of looking into the street, returned to study Madame Campardon's countenance, his curiosity again awakened, and wondering if she knew. But she had resumed her amiable and doleful expression, and was curled up in the depths of the sofa, like a woman who has to find her pleasure in herself, and who is forcibly resigned to receiving the caresses that fall to her share.

At length Octave wished them good-night. With his candlestick in his hand, he was still on the landing, when he heard the sound of silk dresses rustling over the stairs. He politely stood on one side. It was evidently the ladies of the fourth floor, Madame Josserand and her two daughters, returning from some party. As they passed, the mother, a superb and corpulent woman, stared in his face ; whilst the elder of the young ladies kept at a distance with a sour air, and the younger, giddily looked at him and laughed, in the full light of the candle. She was charming, this one, with her irregular but agreeable features, her clear complexion, and her auburn hair gilded with light reflections ; and she had a bold grace, the free gait of a young bride returning from a ball in a complicated costume of ribbons and lace, like unmarried girls do not wear. The trains disappeared along the balustrade : a door closed. Octave lingered a moment, greatly amused by the gaiety of her eyes.

He slowly ascended in his turn. A single gas-jet was burning, the staircase was slumbering in a heavy warmth. It seemed to him more wrapped up in itself than ever, with its chaste doors, its doors of rich mahogany, closing the entrances to virtuous alcoves. Not a sigh passed along, it was the silence of well-mannered people who hold their breath. Presently a slight noise was heard; Octave leant over and beheld Monsieur Gourd, in his cap and slippers, turning out the last gas-jet. Then all subsided, the house became enveloped by the solemnity of darkness, as though annihilated in the distinction and decency of its slumbers.

Octave, nevertheless, had great difficulty in getting to sleep. He kept feverishly turning over, his brain occupied with the new faces he had seen. Why the devil were the Campardons so amiable? Were they dreaming of marrying their daughter to him later on? Perhaps, too, the husband took him to board with them so that he might amuse and enliven the wife? And that poor lady, what peculiar complaint could she be suffering from? Then his ideas got more mixed; he saw shadows pass— little Madame Pichon, his neighbour, with her clear empty glances; beautiful Madame Hédouin, correct and grave in her black dress; and Madame Vabre's ardent eyes, and Mademoiselle Josserand's gay laugh. How they swarmed in a few hours in the streets of Paris! It had always been his dream, ladies who would take him by the hand and help him in his affairs. But these kept returning and mingling with fatiguing obstinacy. He knew not which to choose; he tried to keep his voice soft, his gestures cajoling. And suddenly, worn-out, exasperated, he yielded to his brutal inner nature, to the ferocious disdain in which he held woman, beneath his air of amorous adoration.

"Are they going to let me sleep at all?" said he out loud, turning violently on to his back. "The first who likes, it is the same to me, and all together if it pleases them! To sleep now, it will be daylight to-morrow."

CHAPTER II.

When Madame Josserand, preceded by her young ladies, left the evening party given by Madame Dambreville, who resided on a fourth floor in the Rue de Rivoli, at the corner of the Rue de l'Oratoire, she roughly slammed the street door, in the sudden outburst of a passion she had been keeping under for the past two hours. Berthe, her younger daughter, had again just gone and missed a husband.

"Well! what are you doing there?" said she angrily to the young girls, who were standing under the arcade and watching the cabs pass by. "Walk on! don't have any idea we are going to ride! To waste another two francs, eh?"

And as Hortense, the elder, murmured:

"It will be pleasant, with this mud. My shoes will never recover it."

"Walk on!" resumed the mother, all beside herself. "When you have no more shoes, you can stop in bed, that's all. A deal of good it is, taking you out!"

Berthe and Hortense bowed their heads and turned into the Rue de l'Oratoire. They held their long skirts up as high as they could over their crinolines, squeezing their shoulders together and shivering under their thin opera-cloaks. Madame Josserand followed behind, wrapped in an old fur cloak made of Calabar skins, looking as shabby as cats'. All three, without bonnets, had their hair enveloped in lace wraps, head-dresses which caused the last passers-by to look back, surprised at seeing them glide along the houses, one by one, with bent backs, and their eyes fixed on the puddles. And the mother's exasperation increased still more at the recollection of many similar returns home, for three winters past, hampered by their gay dresses, amidst the black mud of the streets and the jeers of belated blackguards. No, decidedly, she had had enough of dragging her young ladies about to the four corners of Paris, without daring to venture on the luxury of a cab, for fear of having to omit a dish from the morrow's dinner !

"And she makes marriages !" said she out loud, returning to Madame Dambreville, and talking alone to ease herself, without even addressing her daughters, who had turned down the Rue Saint-Honoré. "They are pretty, her marriages ! A lot of impertinent minxes, who come from no one knows where ! Ah ! if one was not obliged ! It's like her last success, that bride whom she brought out, to show us that it did not always fail ; a fine specimen ! a wretched child who had to be sent back to her convent for six months, after a little mistake, to be re-whitewashed !"

The young girls were crossing the Place du Palais-Royal, when a shower came on. It was a regular rout. They stopped, slipping, splashing, looking again at the vehicles passing empty along.

"Walk on !" cried the mother, pitilessly. "We are too near now ; it is not worth two francs. And your brother Léon, who refused to leave with us for fear of having to pay for the cab ! So much the better for him if he gets what he wants at that lady's , but we can say that it is not at all decent. A woman who is over fifty and who only receives young men ! An old nothing-much whom a high personage married to that fool Dambreville, appointing him head clerk !"

Hortense and Berthe trotted along in the rain, one before the other, without seeming to hear. When their mother thus eased herself, letting everything out, and forgetting the wholesome strictness with which she kept them, it was agreed that they should be deaf. Berthe, however, revolted on entering the gloomy and deserted Rue de l'Echelle.

"Oh, dear !" said she, "the heel of my shoe is coming off. I cannot go a step further !"

Madame Josserand's wrath became terrible.

"Just walk on ! Do I complain ? Is it my place to be out in the street at such a time and in such weather ? It would be different if you had a father like others ! But no, the fine gentleman stays at home taking his ease. It is always my turn to drag you about ; he would never accept the burden. Well ! I declare to you that I have had enough of it. Your father may take you out in future if he likes ; may the devil have me if ever again I accompany you to houses where I am plagued like that ! A man who deceived me as to his capacities, and who has never yet procured me the least pleasure ! Ah ! good heavens ! there is one I would not marry now, if it were to come over again !"

The young ladies no longer protested. They were already acquainted with this inexhaustible chapter of their mother's blighted hopes. With their lace wraps drawn over their faces, their shoes sopping wet, they rapidly followed the Rue Sainte-Anne. But, in the Rue de Choiseul, at the very door of her house, a last humiliation awaited Madame Josserand : the Duveyriers' carriage splashed her as it passed in.

On the stairs, the mother and the young ladies, worn out and enraged, recovered their gracefulness when they had to pass before Octave. Only, as soon as ever their door was closed behind them, they rushed through the dark apartment, knocking up against the furniture, and tumbled into the dining-room, where Monsieur Josserand was writing by the feeble light of a little lamp.

"Failed !" cried Madame Josserand, letting herself fall on to a chair.

And, with a rough gesture, she tore the lace wrap from her head, threw her fur cloak on to the back of her chair, and appeared in a flaring dress trimmed with black satin and cut very low in the neck, looking enormous, her shoulders still beautiful, and resembling a mare's shining flanks. Her square face, with its drooping cheeks and too big nose, expressed the tragic fury of a queen restraining herself from descending to the use of coarse, vulgar expressions.

"Ah !" said Monsieur Josserand simply, bewildered by this violent entrance.

He kept blinking his eyes and was seized with uneasiness. His wife positively crushed him when she displayed that giant throat, the full weight of which he seemed to feel on the nape of his neck. Dressed in an old thread-bare frock-coat which he was finishing to wear out at home, his face looking as though tempered and expunged by thirty-five years spent at an office desk, he watched her for a moment with his big lifeless blue eyes. Then, after thrusting his grey locks behind his ears, feeling very embarrassed and unable to find a word to say, he attempted to resume his work.

"But you do not seem to understand !" resumed Madame Josserand in a shrill voice. "I tell you that there is another marriage knocked on the head, and it is the fourth !"

"Yes, yes, I know, the fourth," murmured he. "It is annoying, very annoying."

And, to escape from his wife's terrifying nudity, he turned towards his. daughters with a good-natured smile. They also were removing their lace wraps and their opera-cloaks; the elder one was in blue and the younger in pink; their dresses, too, free in cut and over-trimmed, were like a provocation. Hortense, with her sallow complexion, and her face spoilt by a nose like her mother's, which gave her an air of disdainful obstinacy, had just turned twenty-three and looked twenty-eight; whilst Berthe, two years younger, retained all a child's gracefulness, having, however, the same features, but more delicate and dazzlingly white, and only menaced with the coarse family mask after she entered the fifties.

"It will do no good if you go on looking at us for ever!" cried Madame Josserand. "And, for God's sake, put your writing away; it worries my nerves!"

"But, my dear," said he peacefully, "I am addressing wrappers."

"Ah! yes, your wrappers at three francs a thousand! Is it with those three francs that you hope to marry your daughters?"

Beneath the feeble light of the little lamp, the table was indeed covered with large sheets of coarse paper, printed wrappers, the blanks of which Monsieur Josserand filled in for a large publisher who had several periodicals. As his salary as cashier did not suffice, he passed whole nights at this unprofitable labour, working in secret, and seized with shame at the idea that any one might discover their penury.

"Three francs are three francs," replied he in his slow, tired voice. "Those three francs will enable you to add ribbons to your dresses, and to offer some pastry to your guests on your Tuesdays at home."

He regretted his words as soon as he had uttered them; for he felt that they struck Madame Josserand full in the heart, in the most sensitive part of her wounded pride. A rush of blood purpled her shoulders; she seemed on the point of breaking out into revengeful utterances; then, by an effort of dignity, she merely stammered,

"Ah! good heavens! ah! good heavens!"

And she looked at her daughters; she magisterially crushed her husband beneath a shrug of her terrible shoulders, as much as to say, "Eh! you hear him? what an idiot!" The daughters nodded their heads. Then, seeing himself beaten, and laying down his pen with regret, the father opened the "Temps" newspaper, which he brought home every evening from his office.

"Is Saturnin asleep?" sharply inquired Madame Josserand, speaking of her younger son.

"Yes, long ago," replied he. "I also sent Adèle to bed. And Léon, did you see him at the Dambrevilles'?"

"Of course! he sleeps there!" she let out in a cry of rancour which she was unable to restrain.

The father, surprised, naively added,

"Ah! you think so?"

Hortense and Berthe had become deaf again. They faintly smiled, however, affecting to be busy with their shoes, which were in a pitiful state. To create a diversion, Madame Josserand tried to pick another quarrel with Monsieur Josserand; she begged him to take his newspaper away every morning, not to leave it lying about in the room all day, as he had done with the previous number, for instance, a number containing the report of an abominable trial, which his daughters might have read. She well recognised there his want of morality.

"Well, are we going to bed?" asked Hortense. "I am hungry."

"Oh! and I too!" said Berthe. "I am famishing."

"What! you are hungry!" cried Madame Josserand beside herself. "Did you not eat any cake there, then? What a couple of geese! You should have eaten some! I did."

The young ladies resisted. They were hungry, they were feeling quite ill. So the mother accompanied them to the kitchen, to see if they could discover anything. The father at once returned stealthily to his wrappers. He well knew that, without them, every little luxury in the home would have disappeared; and that was why, in spite of the scorn and unjust quarrels, he obstinately remained till daybreak engaged in this secret work, happy like the worthy man he was whenever he fancied that an extra piece of lace would hook a rich husband. As they were already stinting the food, without managing to save sufficient for the dresses and the Tuesday receptions, he resigned himself to his martyr-like labour, dressed in rags, whilst the mother and daughters wandered from drawing-room to drawing-room with flowers in their hair.

"What a stench there is here!" cried Madame Josserand on entering the kitchen. "To think that I can never get that slut Adèle to leave the window slightly open! She pretends that the room is so very cold in the morning."

She went and opened the window, and from the narrow court-yard separating the kitchens there rose an icy dampness, the unsavoury odour of a musty cellar. The candle which Berthe had lighted caused colossal shadows of naked shoulders to dance upon the wall.

"And what a state the place is in!" continued Madame Josserand, sniffing about, and poking her nose into all the dirty corners. "She has not scrubbed her table for a fortnight. Here are plates which have been waiting to be washed since the day before yesterday. On my word, it is disgusting! And her sink, just look! smell it now, smell her sink!"

Her rage was lashing itself. She tumbled the crockery about with her arms white with rice powder and bedecked with gold bangles; she trailed her flaring dress amidst the grease stains, catching it in cooking utensils thrown under the tables, risking her hardly earned luxury amongst the vegetable parings. At last, the discovery of a notched knife made her anger break all bounds.

"I will turn her into the street to-morrow morning!"

"You will be no better off," quietly remarked Hortense. "We are never able to keep anyone. This is the first who has stayed three months. The moment they begin to get a little decent and know how to make melted butter, off they go."

Madame Josserand bit her lips. As a matter of fact, Adèle alone, stupid and lousy, and only lately arrived from her native Brittany, could put up with the ridiculously vain penury of these middle-class people, who took advantage of her ignorance and her slovenliness to half starve her. Twenty times already, on account of a comb found on the bread or of some abominable stew which gave them all the colic, they had talked of sending her about her business; then, they had resigned themselves to putting up with her, in the presence of the difficulty of replacing her, for the pilferers themselves declined to be engaged, to enter that hole, where even the lumps of sugar were counted.

"I can't discover anything!" murmured Berthe, who was rummaging a cupboard.

The shelves had the melancholy emptiness and the false luxury of families where inferior meat is purchased, so as to be able to put flowers on the table. All that was lying about were some white and gold porcelain plates, perfectly empty, a crumb-brush, the silver-plated handle of which was all tarnished, and some cruets without a drain of oil or vinegar in them; there was not a forgotten crust, not a morsel of dessert, not a fruit, nor a sweet, nor a remnant of cheese. One could feel that Adèle's hunger never satisfied, lapped up the rare dribblets of sauce which her betters left at the bottoms of the dishes, to the extent of rubbing the gilt off.

"But she has gone and eaten all the rabbit!" cried Madame Josserand.

"True," said Hortense, "there was the tail piece. Ah! no, here it is. It would have surprised me if she had dared. I shall stick to it, you know. It is cold, but it is better than nothing!"

Berthe, on her side, was rummaging about, but without result. At length her hand encountered a bottle, in which her mother had diluted the contents of an old pot of jam, so as to manufacture some red currant syrup for her evening parties. She poured herself out half a glass, saying:

"Ah! an idea! I will soak some bread in this, as it is all there is!"

But Madame Josserand, all anxiety, looked at her sternly.

"Pray, don't restrain yourself, fill your glass whilst you are about it! It will be quite sufficient if I offer water to the ladies and gentlemen to-morrow, will it not?"

Fortunately, the discovery of another of Adèle's evil doings interrupted her reprimand. She was still turning about, searching for crimes, when she caught sight of a volume on the table; and then occurred a supreme explosion.

"Oh! the beast! she has again brought my Lamartine into the kitchen!"

It was a copy of "Jocelyn." She took it up and rubbed it hard, as though dusting it; and she kept repeating that she had twenty times forbidden her to leave it lying about in that way, to write her accounts upon. Berthe and Hortense, meanwhile, had shared the little piece of bread which remained; then carrying their suppers away with them, they said that they would undress first. The mother gave the icy cold stove a last glance, and returned to the dining-room, tightly holding her Lamartine beneath the massive flesh of her arm.

Monsieur Josserand continued writing. He trusted that his wife would be satisfied with crushing him with a glance of contempt as she crossed the room to go to bed. But she again dropped on to a chair, facing him, and looked at him fixedly without speaking. He felt this look, and was seized with such uneasiness, that his pen kept sputtering on the flimsy wrapper paper.

"So it was you who prevented Adèle making a cream for to-morrow evening?" said she at length.

He raised his head in amazement.

"I, my dear!"

"Oh! you will again deny it, as you always do. Then, why has she not made the cream I ordered? You know very well that before our party to-morrow uncle Bachelard is coming to dinner, it is his saint's-day, which is very awkward, happening as it does on my reception day. If there is no cream, we must have an ice, and that will be another five francs squandered!"

He did not attempt to exculpate himself. Not daring to resume his work, he began to play with his penholder. There was a brief pause.

"To-morrow morning," resumed Madame Josserand, "you will oblige me by calling on the Campardons and reminding them very politely, if you can, that we are expecting to see them in the evening. Their young man arrived this afternoon. Ask them to bring him with them. Do you understand? I wish him to come."

"What young man?"

"A young man; it would take too long to explain everything to you. I have obtained all necessary information about him. I am obliged to try everything, as you leave your daughters entirely to me, like a bundle of rubbish, without occupying yourself about marrying them any more than about marrying the Grand Turk."

The thought revived her anger.

"You see, I contain myself, but it is more, oh! it is more than I can stand! Say nothing, sir, say nothing, or really my anger will get the better of me."

He said nothing, but she vented her wrath upon him all the same.

"It has become unbearable! I warn you, that one of these mornings I shall go off, and leave you here with your two idiotic daughters. Was I born to live such a skinflint life as this? Always cutting farthings into four, never even having a decent pair of boots, and not being able to receive my friends decently! And all that through your fault! Ah! do not shake your head, do not exasperate me more than I am already! Yes, your fault! You deceived me, sir, basely deceived me. One should not marry a woman, when one is decided to let her want for everything. You played the boaster, you pretended you had a fine future before you, you were the friend of your employer's sons, of those brothers Bernheim, who, since, have merely made a fool of you. What ! You dare to pretend that they have not made a fool of you ! But you ought to be their partner by now ! It is you who made their business what it is, one of the first glass-houses in Paris, and you have remained their cashier, a subordinate, a hireling. Really ! you have no spirit ; hold your tongue."

"I got eight thousand francs a year," murmured the cashier. "It is a very good berth."

"A good berth, after more than thirty years' labour !" resumed Madame Josserand. "They grind you down, and you are delighted. Do you know what I would have done, had I been in your place ? well ! I would have put the business into my pocket twenty times over. It was so easy. I saw it when I married you, and since then I have never ceased advising you to do so. But it required some initiative and intelligence ; it was a question of not going to sleep on your leather-covered stool, like a blockhead."

"Come," interrupted Monsieur Josserand, " are you going to reproach me now with being honest ?"

She jumped up, and advanced towards him, flourishing her Lamartine.

"Honest ! in what way do you mean ? Begin by being honest towards me. Others do not count till afterwards, I hope ! And I repeat, sir, it is not honest to take a young girl in, pretending to be ambitious to become rich some day, and then to end by losing what little wits you had in looking after somebody else's cashbox. On my word, I was nicely swindled ! Ah ! if it were to happen over again, and if I had only known your family !"

She was walking violently about. He could not restrain a slight sign of impatience, in spite of his great desire for peace.

"You would do better to go to bed, Eléonore," said he. "It is past one o'clock, and I assure you this work is pressing. My family has done you no harm, so do not speak of it."

"Ah ! and why, pray ? Your family is no more sacred than another, I suppose. Every one at Clermont knows that your father, after selling his business of solicitor, let himself be ruined by a servant. You might have seen your daughters married long ago, had he not taken up with a strumpet when over seventy. There is another who has swindled me !"

Monsieur Josserand turned pale. He replied in a trembling voice, which rose higher as he went on :

"Listen, do not let us throw our relations at each other's

heads. Your father never paid me your dowry, the thirty
thousand francs he promised."

"Eh? what? thirty thousand francs!"

"Exactly; don't pretend to be surprised. And if my father
met with misfortunes, yours behaved in a most disgraceful way
towards us. I was never able to find out clearly what he left.
There were all sorts of underhand dealings, so that the school
in the Rue des Fossés-Saint-Victor should remain with your
sister's husband, that shabby usher who no longer recognises us
now. We were robbed as though in a wood."

Madame Josserand, now ghastly white, was choking with
rage before her husband's inconceivable revolt.

"Do not say a word against papa! For forty years he was
a credit to instruction. Go and talk of the Bachelard Academy
in the neighbourhood of the Panthéon! And as for my sister
and my brother-in-law, they are what they are. They have
robbed me, I know; but it is not for you to say so. I will not
permit it, understand that! Do I speak to you of your sister,
who eloped with an officer? Oh! you have indeed some nice
relations!"

"An officer who married her, madame. There is uncle
Bachelard, too, your brother, a man totally destitute of all
morality—"

"But you are becoming cracked, sir! He is rich, he earns
what he pleases as a commission merchant, and he has promised
to provide Berthe's dowry. Do you then respect nothing?"

"Ah! yes, provide Berthe's dowry! Will you bet that he
will give a sou, and that we shall not have had to put up with
his nasty habits for nothing? He makes me feel ashamed of
him every time he comes here. A liar, a rake, a person who
takes advantage of the situation, who for fifteen years past,
seeing us all on our knees before his fortune, has been taking
me every Saturday to spend two hours in his office, to go over
his books! It saves him five francs. We have never yet been
favoured with a single present from him."

Madame Josserand, catching her breath, was wrapped for a
moment in thought. Then she uttered this last cry :

"And you have a nephew in the police, sir!"

A fresh pause ensued. The light from the little lamp was
becoming dimmer, wrappers were flying about beneath Monsieur
Josserand's feverish gestures; and he looked his wife full in
the face—his wife in her low neck dress—determined to say
everything, and quivering with courage.

" With eight thousand francs a year one can do many things," resumed he. "You are always complaining. But you should not have arranged your housekeeping on a footing superior to our means. It is your mania for receiving and for paying visits, of having your at homes, of giving tea and pastry—"

She did not let him finish.

"Now we have come to it ! Shut me up in a box at once. Reproach me for not walking out as naked as my hand. And your daughters, sir, who will marry them if we never see any one ? We don't see many people as it is. It does well to sacrifice oneself, to be judged afterwards with such meanness of heart !"

" We have all of us, madame, sacrificed ourselves. Léon had to make way for his sisters ; and he left the house to earn his own living without any assistance from us. As for Saturnin, poor child, he does not even know how to read. And I deny myself everything ; I pass my nights—"

" Why did you have daughters then, sir ? You are surely not going to reproach them with their education, I hope ? Any other man in your place would be proud of Hortense's diploma and of Berthe's talents. The dear child again delighted every one this evening with her waltz, the 'Banks of the Oise,' and her last painting will certainly enchant our guests to-morrow. But you, sir, you are not even a father ; you would have sent your children to take cows to grass, instead of sending them to school."

" Well ! I took out an assurance for Berthe's benefit. Was it not you, madame, who, when the fourth payment became due, made use of the money to cover the drawing-room furniture ? And, since then, you have even negotiated the premiums that had been paid."

" Of course ! as you leave us to die of hunger. Ah ! you may indeed bite your fingers, if your daughters become old maids."

" Bite my fingers ! But, Jove's thunder ! it is you who frighten the likely men away, with your dresses and your ridiculous parties ! "

Never before had Monsieur Josserand gone so far. Madame Josserand, suffocating, stammered forth the words : "I—I ridiculous !" when the door opened. Hortense and Berthe were returning, in their petticoats and little calico jackets, their hair let down, and their feet in old slippers.

"Ah, well! it is too cold in our room!" said Berthe shivering. "The food freezes in your mouth. Here, at least, there has been a fire this evening."

And both dragging their chairs along the floor, seated themselves close to the stove, which still retained a little warmth. Hortense held her rabbit bone in the tips of her fingers, and was skilfully picking it. Berthe dipped pieces of bread in her glass of syrup. The parents, however, were so excited that they did not even appear to notice their arrival. They continued:

"Ridiculous—ridiculous, sir! I shall not be ridiculous again! Let my head be cut off if I wear out another pair of gloves in trying to get them husbands. It is your turn now! And try not to be more ridiculous than I have been!"

"I daresay, madame, now that you have exhibited them and compromised them everywhere! Whether you marry them or whether you don't, I don't care a button!"

"And I care less, Monsieur Josserand! I care so little that I will bundle them out into the street if you aggravate me much more. And if you have a mind to, you can follow them, the door is open. Ah, heavens! what a good riddance!"

The young ladies quietly listened, used to these lively recriminations. They were still eating, their little jackets dropping from their shoulders, and their bare skin gently rubbing against the lukewarm earthenware of the stove; and they looked charming in this undress, with their youth and their hearty appetites and their eyes heavy with sleep.

"You are very foolish to quarrel," at length observed Hortense, with her mouth full. "Mamma only spoils her temper, and papa will be ill again to-morrow at his office. It seems to me that we are old enough to be able to find husbands for ourselves."

This created a diversion. The father, thoroughly exhausted, made a feint of returning to his wrappers; and he sat with his nose over the paper, unable to write, his hands trembling violently. The mother, who had been moving about the room like an escaped lioness, went and planted herself in front of Hortense.

"If you are speaking for yourself," cried she, "you are a great ninny! Your Verdier will never marry you."

"That is my business," boldly replied the young girl.

After having contemptuously refused five or six suitors, a little clerk, the son of a tailor, and other young fellows whose prospects she did not consider good enough, she had ended by setting her cap at a barrister, whom she had met at the Dambrevilles', and who was already turned forty. She considered him very clever, and destined to make a name in the world. But the misfortune was that for fifteen years past Verdier had been living with a mistress, who in the neighbourhood even passed for his wife. She knew of this, though, and by no means let it trouble her.

"My child," said the father, raising his head once more, "I begged you not to think of this marriage. You know the situation."

She stopped sucking her bone, and said with an air of impatience :

"What of it ? Verdier has promised me he will leave her. She is a fool."

"You are wrong, Hortense, to speak in that way. And if he should also leave you one day to return to her whom you would have caused him to abandon ? "

"That is my business," sharply retorted the young woman.

Berthe listened, fully acquainted with this matter, the contingencies of which she discussed daily with her sister. She was, besides, like her father, all in favour of the poor woman, whom it was proposed to turn out into the street, after having performed a wife's duties for fifteen years. But Madame Josserand intervened.

"Leave off, do ! those wretched women always end by returning to the gutter. Only, it is Verdier who will never bring himself to leave her. He is fooling you, my dear. In your place, I would not wait a second for him ; I would try and find some one else."

Hortense's voice became sourer still, whilst two livid spots appeared on her cheeks.

"Mamma, you know how I am. I want him, and I will have him. I will never marry any one else, even though he kept me waiting a hundred years."

The mother shrugged her shoulders.

"And you call others fools ! "

But the young girl rose up, quivering with rage.

"Here ! don't go pitching into me ! " cried she. "I have finished my rabbit. I prefer to go to bed. As you are unable to find us husbands, you must let us find them in our own way."

And she withdrew, violently slamming the door behind her.

Madame Josserand turned majestically towards her husband, and uttered this profound remark :

"That, sir, is the result of your bringing up !"

Monsieur Josserand did not protest ; he was occupied in dotting his thumb nail with ink, whilst waiting till they allowed him to resume his writing. Berthe, who had eaten her bread, dipped a finger in the glass to finish up her syrup. She felt comfortable, with her back nice and warm, and did not hurry herself, being undesirous of encountering her sister's quarrelsome temper in their bedroom.

"Ah ! and that is the reward !" continued Madame Josserand, resuming her walk to and fro across the dining-room. "For twenty years one wears oneself out for these young ladies, one goes in want of everything in order to make them accomplished women, and they will not even let one have the satisfaction of seeing them married according to one's own fancy. It would be different. if they had ever been refused a single thing ! But I have never kept. a sou for myself, and have even gone without clothes to dress them as though we had an income of fifty thousand francs. No, really, it is too absurd ! When those hussies have had a careful education, have got just as much religion as is necessary, and the airs of rich girls, they leave you in the lurch, they talk of marrying barristers, adventurers, who lead lives of debauchery !"

She stopped before Berthe, and, menacing her with her finger, said :

"As for you, if you follow your sister's example, you will have me to deal with."

Then she recommenced stamping round the room, speaking to herself, jumping from one idea to another, contradicting herself with the brazenness of a woman who will always be in the right.

"I did what I ought to do, and were it to be done over again I should do the same. In life, it is only the most shamefaced who lose. Money is money ; when one has none, one may as well retire. Whenever I had twenty sous, I always said I had forty ; for that is real wisdom, it is better to be envied than pitied. It is no use having a good education if one has not good clothes to wear, for then people despise you. It is not just, but it is so. I would sooner wear dirty petticoats than a cotton dress. Feed on potatoes, but have a chicken when you have any one to dinner. And only fools would say the contrary !"

She looked fixedly at her husband, to whom these last re-flections were addressed. The latter, worn out, and declining another battle, had the cowardice to declare :

"It is true ; money is everything in our days."

"You hear," resumed Madame · Josserand, returning towards her daughter. "Go straight ahead and try to give us satis-faction. How is it you let this marriage fall through ?"

Berthe understood that her turn had come.

"I don't know, mamma," murmured she

"A second head-clerk in a government office," continued the mother ; "not yet thirty, with a splendid future before him. Every month he would be bringing you his money ; it is some-thing substantial that, there is nothing like it. You have been up to some tomfoolery again, just the same as with the others."

"I have not, mamma, I assure you. He must have obtained some information—have heard that I had no money."

But Madame Josserand cried out at this.

"And the dowry that your uncle is going to give you ! Every one knows about that dowry. No, there is something else ; he withdrew too abruptly. When dancing you passed into the parlour."

Berthe became confused.

"Yes, mamma. And, as we were alone, he even tried to do some naughty things ; he kissed me, seizing hold of me like that. Then I was frightened ; I pushed him up against the furniture—"

Her mother, again overcome with rage, interrupted her.

"Pushed him up against the furniture, ah I the wretched girl pushed him up against the furniture !"

"But, mamma, he held me—"

"What of it ? He held you, that was nothing ! A fat lot of good it is sending such fools to school I Whatever did they teach you, eh ? "

A rush of colour rose to the young girl's cheeks and shoulders. Tears filled her eyes, whilst she looked as confused as a violated virgin.

"It was not my fault ; he looked so wicked. I did not know what to do."

"Did not know what to do ! she did not know what to do ! Have I not told you a hundred times that your fears are ri-diculous ? It is your lot to live in society. When a man is rough, it is because he loves you, and there is always a way of keeping him in his place in a nice manner. For a kiss behind a door ! in truth now, ought you to mention such a thing to us, your parents ? And you push people against the furniture, and you drive away your suitors ! ”

She assumed a doctoral air as she continued :

“ It is ended ; I despair of doing anything with you, you are too stupid, my girl. One would have to coach you in everything, and that would be awkward. As you have no fortune, understand at least that you must hook the men by some other means. One should be amiable, have loving eyes, abandon one’s hand occasionally, allow a little playfulness, without seeming to do so ; in short, one should angle for a husband. You make a great mistake, if you think it improves your eyes to cry like a fool ! ”

Berthe was sobbing.

“ You aggravate me—leave off crying. Monsieur Josserand, just tell your daughter not to spoil her face by crying in that way. It will be too much if she becomes ugly ! ”

“ My child,” said the father, “ be reasonable ; listen to your mother’s good advice. You must not spoil your good looks, my darling.”

“ And what irritates me is that she is not so bad when she likes,” resumed Madame Josserand. “ Come, wipe your eyes, look at me as if I was a gentleman courting you. You smile, you drop your fan, so that the gentleman, in picking it up, slightly touches your fingers. That is not the way. You are holding you head up too stifly, you look like a sick hen. Lean back more, show your neck ; it is too young to be hidden.”

“ Then, like this, mamma ? ”

“ Yes, that is better. And never be stiff, be supple. Men do not care for planks. And, above all, if they go too far do not play the simpleton. A man who goes too far is done for, my dear.”

The drawing-room clock struck two ; and, in the excitement of that prolonged vigil, in her desire now become furious for an immediate marriage, the mother forgot herself in thinking out loud, making her daughter turn about like a papier-mache doll. The latter, without spirit or will, abandoned herself ; but she felt very heavy at heart, fear and shame brought a lump to her throat. Suddenly, in the midst of a silvery laugh which her mother was forcing her to attempt, she burst into sobs, her face all upset :

“ No ! no ! it pains me ! ” stammered she.

For a second, Madame Josserand remained incensed and amazed. Ever since she left the Dambrevilles', her hand had been itching, there were slaps in the air. Then, she landed Berthe a clout with all her might.

"Take that! you are too aggravating! What a fool! On my word, the men are right!"

In the shock, her Lamartine, which she had kept under her arm, fell to the floor. She picked it up, wiped it, and without adding another word, she retired into the bedroom, royally drawing her ball-dress around her.

"It was bound to end thus," murmured Monsieur Josserand, not daring to detain his daughter, who went off also, holding her cheek and crying louder than ever.

But, as Berthe felt her way across the ante-room, she found her brother Saturnin up, barefooted and listening. Saturnin was a big, ill-formed fellow of twenty-five, with wild-looking eyes, and who had remained childish after an attack of brain-fever. Without being mad, he terrified the household by attacks of blind violence, whenever he was thwarted. Berthe, alone, was able to subdue him with a look. He had nursed her when she was still quite a child, through a long illness, obedient as a dog to her little invalid girl's caprices; and, ever since he had saved her, he was seized with an adoration for her, into which entered every kind of love.

"Has she been beating you again?" asked he in a low and ardent voice.

Berthe, uneasy at finding him there, tried to send him away.

"Go to bed, it is nothing to do with you."

"Yes, it is. I will not have her beat you! She woke me up, she was shouting so. She had better not try it on again, or I will strike her!"

Then, she seized him by the wrists, and spoke to him as to a disobedient animal. He submitted at once, and stuttered, crying like a little boy:

"It hurts you very much, does it not? Where is the sore place. that I may kiss it?"

And, having found her cheek in the dark, he kissed it, wetting it with his tears, as he repeated:

"It is well, now, it is well, now."

Meanwhile, Monsieur Josserand, left alone, had laid down his pen, his heart was so full of grief. At the end of a few minutes, he got up gently to go and listen at the doors. Madame Josserand was snoring. No sounds of crying issued from his daughters' room. All was dark and peaceful. Then he returned, feeling slightly relieved. He saw to the lamp which was smoking, and mechanically resumed his writing. Two big tears, unfelt by him, dropped on to the wrappers, in the solemn silence of the slumbering house.

CHAPTER III.

So soon as the fish was served, skate of doubtful freshness with
black butter, which that bungler Adèle had drowned in a flood
of vinegar, Hortense and Berthe, seated on the right and left of
uncle Bachelard, incited him to drink, filling his glass one after
the other, and repeating :

"It's your saint's-day, drink now, drink!   Here's your health,
uncle !"

They had plotted together to make him give them twenty
francs. ˙ Every year, their providant mother placed them thus
on˙either side of her brother, abandoning him to them.   But it
was a difficult task, and required all the greediness of two girls
prompted by dreams of Louis XV. shoes and five button gloves.
To get him to give the twenty francs, it was necessary to make
the uncle completely drunk.   He was ferociously miserly whenever he found himself amongst his relations, though out of
doors he squandered in crapulous boozes the eighty thousand
francs he made each year out of his commission business.   Fortunately, that evening, he was already half fuddled when he
arrived, having passed the afternoon with the wife of a dyer of
the Faubourg Montmartre, who kept a stock of Marseilles vermouth expressly for him.

"Your health, my little ducks !" replied he each time, with
his thick husky voice, as he emptied his glass.

Covered with jewellery, a rose in his button-hole, enormous
in build, he filled the middle of the table, with his broad
shoulders of a boozing and brawling tradesman, who has wallowed in every vice.   His false teeth lit up with too harsh a
whiteness his ravaged face, the big red nose of which blazed beneath the snowy crest of his short cropped hair ; and, now and
again, his eyelids dropped of themselves over his pale and misty
eyes.   Gueulin, the son of one of his wife's sisters, affirmed that
his uncle had not been sober during the ten years he had been
a widower.

"Narcisse, a little skate, I can recommend it," said Madame Josserand, smiling at her brother's tipsy condition, though at heart it made her feel rather disgusted.

She was sitting opposite to him, having little Gueulin on her left, and another young man on her right, Hector Trublot, to whom she was desirous of showing some politeness. She usually took advantage of family gatherings like the present to get rid of certain invitations she had to return; and it was thus that a lady living in the house, Madame Juzeur, was also present, seated next to Monsieur Josserand. As the uncle behaved very badly at table, and it was the expectation of his fortune alone which enabled them to put up with him without absolute disgust, she only had intimate acquaintances to meet him or else persons whom she thought it was no longer worth while trying to dazzle. For instance, she had at one time thought of finding a son-in-law in young Trublot, who was employed at a stockbroker's, whilst waiting till his father, a wealthy man, purchased him a share in the business; but, Trublot having professed a determined objection to matrimony, she no longer stood upon ceremony with him, even placing him next to Saturnin, who had never known how to eat decently. Berthe, who always had a seat beside her brother, was commissioned to subdue him with a look, whenever he put his fingers too much into the gravy.

After the fish came a meat pie, and the young ladies thought the moment arrived to commence their attack.

"Take another glass, uncle!" said Hortense. "It is your saint's day. Don't you give anything when it's your saint's-day ?"

"Dear me ! why of course," added Berthe naïvely. "People always give something on their saint's-day. You must give us twenty francs."

On hearing them speak of money, Bachelard at once exaggerated his tipsy condition. It was his usual dodge; his eyelids dropped, and he became quite idiotic.

"Eh ? what ?" stuttered he.

"Twenty francs. You know very well what twenty francs are, it is no use your pretending you don't," resumed Berthe. "Give us twenty francs, and we will love you, oh ! we will love you so much !"

They threw their arms round his neck, called him the most endearing names, and kissed his inflamed face without the least repugnance for the horrid odour of debauchery which he exhaled. Monsieur Josserand, whom these continual fumes of absinthe, tobacco and musk upset, had a feeling of disgust on seeing his daughters' virgin charms rubbing up against those infamies gathered in the vilest places.

"Leave him alone!" cried he.

"Why?" asked Madame Josserand, giving her husband a terrible look. "They are amusing themselves. If Narcisse wishes to give them twenty francs, he is quite at liberty to do so."

"Monsieur Bachelard is so good to them!" complacently murmured little Madame Juzeur.

But the uncle struggled, becoming more idiotic than ever, and repeating, with his mouth full of saliva:

"It's funny. I don't know, word of honour! I don't know."

Then, Hortense and Berthe, exchanging a glance, released him. No doubt he had not had enough to drink. And they again resorted to filling his glass, laughing like courtesans who intend robbing a man. Their bare arms, of an adorable youthful plumpness, kept passing every minute under the uncle's big flaming nose.

Meanwhile, Trublot, like a quiet fellow who takes his pleasures alone, was watching Adèle as she turned heavily round the table. Being very short-sighted he thought her pretty, with her pronounced Breton features and her hair the colour of dirty hemp. When she brought in the roast, a piece of veal, she leant right over his shoulder, to reach the centre of the table; and he, pretending to pick up his napkin, gave her a good pinch on the calf of her leg. The servant, not understanding, looked at him, as though he had asked her for some bread.

"What is it?" said Madame Josserand. "Did she knock against you, sir? Oh! that girl! she is so awkward! But, you know, she is quite new to the work; she will be better when she has had a little training."

"No doubt, there is no harm done," replied Trublot, stroking his bushy black beard with the serenity of a young Indian god.

The conversation was becoming more animated in the dining-room, at first icy cold, and now gradually warming with the fumes of the dishes. Madame Juzeur was once more confiding to Monsieur Josserand the dreariness of her thirty years of solitary existence. She raised her eyes to heaven, and contented herself with this discreet allusion to the drama of her life: her husband had left her after ten days of married bliss, and no one knew why; she said nothing more. Now, she lived by herself in a lodging that was as soft as down and always closed, and which was frequented by priests.

"It is so sad, at my age!" murmured she languishingly, cutting up her veal with delicate gestures.

"A very unfortunate little woman," whispered Madame Josserand in Trublot's ear, with an air of profound sympathy.

But Trublot glanced indifferently at this clear-eyed devotee, so full of reserve and hidden meanings. She was not his style.

Then there was a regular panic. Saturnin, whom Berthe was not watching so closely, being too busy with her uncle, had amused himself by cutting up his meat into various designs on his plate. This poor creature exasperated his mother, who was both afraid and ashamed of him; she did not know how to get rid of him, not daring through pride to make a workman of him, after having sacrificed him to his sisters by having removed him from the school where his slumbering intelligence was too long awakening; and, during the years he had been hanging about the house, useless and stinted, she was in a constant state of fright whenever she had to let him appear before company. Her pride suffered cruelly.

"Saturnin!" cried she.

But Saturnin began to chuckle, delighted with the mess he had made in his plate. He did not respect his mother, but called her roundly a great liar and a horrid nuisance, with the perspicacity of madmen who think out loud. Things certainly seemed to be going wrong. He would have thrown his plate at her head, if Berthe, reminded of her duties, had not looked him straight in the face. He tried to resist; then the fire in his eyes died out; he remained gloomy and depressed on his chair, as though in a dream, until the end of the meal.

"I hope, Gueulin, that you have brought your flute?" asked Madame Josserand, trying to dispel her guests' uneasiness.

Gueulin was an amateur flute-player, but solely in the houses where he was treated without ceremony.

"My flute! Of course I have," replied he.

He was absent-minded, his carroty hair and whiskers were more bristly than usual, as he watched with deep interest the young ladies' manœuvres around their uncle. Employed at an assurance office, he would go straight to Bachelard on leaving off work, and stick to him, visiting the same cafés and the same disreputable places. Behind the big, ill-shaped body of the one, the little pale face of the other was sure always to be seen.

"Cheerily, there! stick to him!" said he, suddenly, like a true sportsman.

The uncle was indeed losing ground. When, after the vegetables, French beans swimming in water, Adèle placed a vanilla and currant ice on the table, it caused unexpected delight amongst the guests; and the young ladies took advantage of the situation to make the uncle drink half of the bottle of champagne, which Madame Josserand had bought for three francs of a neighbouring grocer. He was becoming quite affec-tionate, and forgetting his pretended idiocy.

"Eh, twenty francs! Why twenty francs? Ah! you want twenty francs! But I have not got them, really now. Ask Gueulin. Is it not true, Gueulin, that I forgot my purse, and that you had to pay at the café? If I had them, my little ducks, I would give them to you, you are so nice."

Gueulin was laughing in his cool way, making a noise like a pulley that required greasing. And he murmured:

"The old swindler!"

Then, suddenly, unable to restrain himself, he cried:

"Search him!"

So Hortense and Berthe again threw themselves on the uncle, this time without the least restraint. The desire for the twenty francs, which their good education had hitherto kept within bounds, bereft them of their senses in the end, and they forgot everything else. The one, with both hands, examined his waist-coat pockets, whilst the other buried her fingers inside the pockets of his frock-coat. The uncle, however, pressed back on his chair, still struggled; but he gradually burst out into a laugh—a laugh broken by drunken hiccoughs.

"On my word of honour, I haven't a sou! Leave off, do; you're tickling me."

"In the trousers!" energetically exclaimed Gueulin, excited by the spectacle.

And Berthe resolutely searched one of the trouser pockets. Their hands trembled; they were both becoming exceedingly rough, and could have smacked the uncle. But Berthe uttered a cry of victory: from the depths of the pocket she brought forth a handful of money, which she spread out in a plate; and there, amongst a heap of coppers and pieces of silver, was a twenty-franc piece.

"I have it!" said she, her face all red, her hair undone, as she tossed the coin in the air and caught it again.

There was a general clapping of hands, every one thought it

very funny.   It created quite a hubbub, and was the success of
the dinner.   Madame Josserand looked at her daughters with a
mother's tender smile.   The uncle, who was gathering up his
money, sententiously observed that, when one wanted twenty
francs, one should earn them.   And the young ladies, worn out
and satisfied, were panting on his right and left, their lips still
trembling in the enervation of their desire.

A bell was heard to ring.   They had been eating slowly, and
the other guests were already arriving.   Monsieur Josserand,
who had decided to laugh like his wife, enjoyed singing some of
Béranger's songs at table ; but as this outraged his better half's
poetic tastes, she compelled him to keep quiet.   She got the
dessert over as quickly as possible, more especially as, since the
forced present of the twenty francs, the uncle had been trying
to pick a quarrel, complaining that his nephew, Léon, had not
deigned to put himself out to come and wish him many
happy returns of the day.   Léon was only coming to the evening party.   At length, as they were rising from table, Adèle
said that the architect from the floor below and a young man
were in the drawing-room.

"Ah ! yes, that young man," murmured Madame Juzeur,
accepting Monsieur Josserand's arm.   "So you have invited
him ? I saw him to-day talking to the doorkeeper.   He is very
good-looking."

Madame Josserand was taking Trublot's arm, when Saturnin,
who had been left by himself at the table, and who had not been
roused from slumbering with his eyes open by all the uproar
about the twenty francs, kicked back his chair, in a sudden
outburst of fury, shouting :

: "I won't have it, damnation !   I won't have it ! "

It was the very thing his mother always dreaded.   She sig-
nalled to Monsieur Josserand to take Madame Juzeur away.
Then she freed herself from Trublot, who understood, and disappeared ; but he probably made a mistake, for he went off in
the direction of the kitchen, close upon Adèle's heels.   Bachelard and Gueulin, without troubling themselves about the
maniac, as they called him, chuckled in a corner, whilst play-
fully slapping one another.

"He was so peculiar, I felt there would be something this
evening," murmured Madame Josserand, uneasily.   "Berthe,
come quick ! "

But Berthe was showing the twenty-franc piece to Hortense.
Saturnin had caught up a knife.   He repeated :

HORTENSE AND BERTHE SEARCHING UNCLE BACHELARD'S POCKETS.

p. 50.

"Damnation! I won't have it! I'll rip their stomachs open!"

"Berthe!" called her mother in despair.

And, when the young girl hastened to the spot, she only just had time to seize him by the hand and prevent him from entering the drawing-room. She shook him angrily, whilst he tried to explain, with his madman's logic.

"Let me be, I must settle them. I tell you it's best. I've had enough of their dirty ways. They'll sell the whole lot of us."

"Oh! this is too much!" cried Berthe. "What is the matter with you? what are you talking about?"

He looked at her in a bewildered way, trembling with a gloomy rage, and stuttered:

"They're going to marry you again. Never, you hear! I won't have you hurt."

The young girl could not help laughing. Where had he got the idea from that they were going to marry her? But he nodded his head: he knew it, he felt it. And as his mother intervened to try and calm him, he grasped his knife so tightly that she drew back. However, she trembled for fear he should be overheard, and hastily told Berthe to take him away and lock him in his room; whilst he, becoming crazier than ever, raised his voice:

"1 won't have you married, I won't have you hurt. If they marry you, I'll rip their stomachs open."

Then Berthe put her hands on his shoulders, and looked him straight in the face.

"Listen," said she, "keep quiet, or I will not love you any more."

He staggered, despair softened the expression of his face, his eyes filled with tears.

"You won't love me any more, you won't love me any more. Don't say that. Oh! I implore you, say that you will love me still, say that you will love me always, and that you will never love any one else."

She had seized him by the wrist, and she led him away as gentle as a child.

In the drawing-room Madame Josserand, exaggerating her intimacy, called Campardon her dear neighbour. Why had Madame Campardon not done her the great pleasure of coming also? and on the architect replying that his wife still continued poorly, she exclaimed that they would have been delighted to have received her in her dressing-gown and her slippers. But her smile never left Octave, who was conversing with Mon-

LIBRARY
UNIVERSITY OF ILLINOIS

sieur Josserand; all her amiability was directed towards him, over Campardon's shoulder. When her husband introduced the young man to her, her cordiality was so great that the latter felt quite uncomfortable.

Other guests were arriving; stout mothers with skinny daughters, fathers and uncles scarcely roused from their office drowsiness, pushing before them flocks of marriageable young ladies. Two lamps, with pink paper shades, lit up the drawing-room with a pale light, which only faintly displayed the old, worn, yellow velvet covered furniture, the scratched piano, and the three smoky Swiss views, which looked like black stains on the cold, bare, white and gold panels. And, in this miserly light, the guests—poor, and, so to say, worn-out figures, without resignation, and whose attire was the cause of much pinching and saving—seemed to become obliterated. Madame Josserand wore her fiery costume of the day before; only, with a view of throwing dust in people's eyes, she had passed the day in sewing sleeves on to the body, and in making herself a lace tippet to cover her shoulders; whilst her two daughters, seated beside her in their dirty cotton jackets, vigorously plied their needles, rearranging with new trimmings their only presentable dresses, which they had been thus altering bit by bit ever since the previous winter.

After each ring at the bell, the sound of whispering issued from the ante-chamber. They conversed in low tones in the gloomy drawing-room, where the forced laugh of some young lady jarred at times like a false note. Behind little Madame Juzeur, Bachelard and Gueulin were nudging each other, and making smutty remarks; and Madame Josserand watched them with an alarmed look, for she dreaded her brother's vulgar behaviour. But Madame Juzeur might hear anything; her lips quivered, and she smiled with angelic sweetness as she listened to the naughty stories. Uncle Bachelard had the reputation of being a dangerous man. His nephew, on the contrary, was chaste. No matter how splendid the opportunities were, Gueulin declined to have anything to do with women upon principle, not that he disdained them, but because he dreaded the morrows of bliss: always very unpleasant, he said.

Berthe at length appeared, and went hurriedly up to her mother.

"Ah, well! I have had a deal of trouble!" whispered she in her ear. "He would not go to bed, so I double-locked the door. But I am afraid he will break everything in the room."

Madame Josserand violently tugged at her dress. Octave, who was close to them, had turned his head.

"My daughter, Berthe, Monsieur Mouret," said she, in her most gracious manner, as she introduced them. "Monsieur Octave Mouret, my darling."

And she looked at her daughter. The latter was well acquainted with this look, which was like an order to clear for action, and which recalled to her the lessons of the night before. She at once obeyed, with the complaisance and the indifference of a girl who no longer stops to examine the person she is to marry. She prettily recited her little part with the easy grace of a Parisian already weary of the world, and acquainted with every subject, and she talked enthusiastically of the South, where she had never been. Octave, used to the stiffness of provincial virgins, was delighted with this little woman's cackle and her sociable manner.

Presently, Trublot, who had not been seen since dinner was over, entered stealthily from the dining-room ; and Berthe, catching sight of him, asked thoughtlessly where he had been. He remained silent, at which she felt very confused ; then, to put an end to the awkward pause which ensued, she introduced the two young men to each other. Her mother had not taken her eyes off her ; she had assumed the attitude of a commander-in-chief, and directed the campaign from the easy-chair in which she had settled herself. When she judged that the first engagement had given all the result that could have been expected from it, she recalled her daughter with a sign, and said to her, in a low voice :

"Wait till the Vabre's are here before commencing your music. And play loud."

Octave, left alone with Trublot, began to engage him in conversation.

"A charming person."

"Yes, not bad."

"The young lady in blue is her elder sister, is she not ? She is not so good-looking."

"Of course not ; she is thinner !"

Trublot, who looked without seeing with his near-sighted eyes, had the broad shoulders of a solid male, obstinate in his tastes. He had come back from the kitchen perfectly satisfied, crunching little black things which Octave recognised with surprise to be coffee berries.

"I say," asked he abruptly, "the women are plump in the South, are they not ?"

Octave smiled, and at once became on an excellent footing with Trublot. They had many ideas in common which brought them closer together. They exchanged confidences on an out-of-the-way sofa ; the one talked of his employer at " The Ladies' Paradise," Madame Hédouin, a confoundedly fine woman, but too cold ; the other said that he had been put on to the correspondence, from nine to five, at his stockbroker's, Monsieur Desmarquay, where there was a stunning maid servant. Just then the drawing-room door opened, and three persons entered.

" They are the Vabres," murmured Trublot, bending over towards his new friend. " Auguste, the tall one, he who has a face like a sick sheep, is the landlord's eldest son—thirty-three years old, ever suffering from headaches which make his eyes start from his head, and which, some years ago, prevented him from continuing to learn Latin ; a sullen fellow who has gone in for trade. The other, Théophile, that abortion with carroty hair and thin beard, that little old-looking man of twenty-eight, ever shaking with fits of coughing and of rage, tried a dozen different trades, and then married the young woman who leads the way, Madame Valérie—"

" I have already seen her," interrupted Octave. " She is the daughter of a haberdasher of the neighbourhood, is she not? But how those veils deceive one ! I thought her pretty. She is only peculiar, with her shrivelled face and her leaden complexion."

" She is another who is not my ideal," sententiously resumed Trublot. " She has superb eyes, and that is enough for some men. But she's a thin piece of goods."

Madame Josserand had risen to shake Valérie's hand.

" How is it," cried she, " that Monsieur Vabre is not with you ? and that neither Monsieur nor Madame Duveyrier have done us the honour of coming ? They promised us though. Ah ! it is very wrong of them ! "

The young woman made excuses for her father-in-law, whose age kept him at home, and who, moreover, preferred to work of an evening. As for her brother and sister-in-law, they had asked her to apologise for them, they having received an invitation to an official party, which they were obliged to attend. Madame Josserand bit her lips. She never missed one of the Saturdays at home of those stuck-up people on the first floor, who would have thought themselves dishonoured had they ascended, one Tuesday, to the fourth. No doubt her modest tea was not equal to their grand orchestral concerts. But,

patience ! when her two daughters were married, and she had
two sons-in-law and their relations to fill her drawing-room, she
also would go in for choruses.

"Get yourself ready," whispered she in Berthe's ear.

They were about thirty, and rather tightly packed, for the
parlour, having been turned into a bedroom for the young
ladies, was not thrown open. The new arrivals distributed
handshakes round. Valérie seated herself beside Madame
Juzeur, whilst Bachelard and Gueulin made unpleasant remarks
out loud about Théophile Vabre, whom they thought it funny to
call "good for nothing." Monsieur Josserand—who in his own
home kept himself so much in the background that one would
have taken him for a guest, and whom one would fail to find
when wanted, even though he were standing close by—was in a
corner listening in a bewildered way to a story related by one
of his old friends, Bonnaud. He knew Bonnaud, who was formerly the general accountant of the Northern railway, and
whose daughter had married in the previous spring? Well!
Bonnaud had just discovered that his son-in-law, a very respectable-looking man, was an ex-clown, who had lived for ten years
at the expense of a female circus-rider.

"Silence ! silence !" murmured some good-natured voices.

Berthe had opened the piano.

"Really !" explained Madame Josserand, "it is merely an
unpretentious piece, a simple reverie. Monsieur Mouret, you
like music, I think. Come nearer then. My daughter plays
pretty fairly—oh ! purely as an amateur, but with expression ;
yes, with a great deal of expression."

"Caught !" said Trublot in a low voice. "The sonata stroke."

Octave was obliged to leave his seat and stand up beside the
piano. To see the caressing attentions which Madame
Josserand showered upon him, it seemed as though she were
making Berthe play solely for him.

"'The Banks of the Oise,'" resumed she. "It is really very
pretty. Come begin, my love, and do not be confused.
Monsieur Mouret will be indulgent."

The young girl commenced the piece without being in the
least confused. Besides, her mother kept her eyes upon her
like a sergeant ready to punish with a blow the least theoretical
mistake. Her great regret was that the instrument, worn-out
by fifteen years of daily scales, did not possess the sonorous
tones of the Duveyriers' grand piano ; and her daughter never
played loud enough in her opinion.

After the sixth bar, Octave, looking thoughtful and nodding his head at each spirited passage, no longer listened. He looked at the audience, the politely absent-minded attention of the men, and the affected delight of the women, all that relaxation of persons for a moment at rest, but soon again to be harassed by the cares of every hour, the shadows of which, before long, would be once more reflected on their weary faces. Mothers were visibly dreaming that they were marrying their daughters, whilst a smile hovered about their mouths, revealing their fierce-loooking teeth in their unconscious abandonment; it was the mania of this drawing-room, a furious appetite for sons-in-law, which consumed these worthy middle-class mothers to the asthmatic sounds of the piano.

The daughters, who were very weary, were falling asleep, with their heads dropping on to their shoulders, forgetting to sit up erect. Octave, who had a certain contempt for young ladies, was more interested in Valérie—she looked decidedly ugly in her peculiar yellow silk dress, trimmed with black satin—and feeling ill at ease, yet attracted all the same, his gaze kept returning to her; whilst she, with a vague look in her eyes, and unnerved by the discordant music, was smiling like a crazy person.

At this moment quite a catastrophe occurred. A ring at the bell was heard, and a gentleman entered the room without the least regard for what was taking place.

"Oh! doctor!" said Madame Josserand angrily.

Doctor Juillerat made a gesture of apology, and stood stock-still. Berthe, at this moment, was executing a little passage with a slow and dreamy fingering, which the guests greeted with flattering murmurs. Ah! delightful! delicious! Madame Juzeur was almost swooning away, as though being tickled. Hortense, who was standing beside her sister, turning the pages, was sulkily listening for a ring at the bell amidst the avalanche of notes; and, when the doctor entered, she made such a gesture of disappointment that she tore one of the pages on the stand. But, suddenly, the piano trembled beneath Berthe's weak fingers, thrumming away like hammers; it was the end of the reverie, amidst a deafening uproar of clangorous chords.

There was a moment of hesitation. The audience was waking up again. Was it finished? Then the compliments burst out on all sides. Adorable! a superior talent!

"Mademoiselle is really a first-rate musician," said Octave, interrupted in his observations. "No one has ever given me such pleasure."

"Do you really mean it, sir ?" exclaimed Madame Josserand delighted. "She does not play badly, I must admit. Well ! we have never refused the child anything ; she is our treasure ! She possesses every talent she wished for. Ah ! sir, if you only knew her."

A confused murmur of voices again filled the drawing-room. Berthe very calmly received the praise showered upon her, and did not leave the piano, but sat waiting till her mother relieved her from fatigue-duty. The latter was already speaking to Octave of the surprising manner in which her daughter dashed off "The Harvesters," a brilliant gallop, when some dull and distant thuds created a stir amongst the guests. For several moments past there had been violent shocks, as though some one was trying to burst a door open. Everybody left off talking, and looked about inquiringly.

"What is it ?" Valérie ventured to ask. "I heard it before, during the finish of the piece."

Madame Josserand had turned quite pale. She had recognised Saturnin's blows. Ah ! the wretched lunatic ! and in her mind's eye she beheld him tumbling in amongst the guests. If he continued hammering like that, it would be another marriage done for !

"It is the kitchen door slamming," said she with a constrained smile. "Adèle never will shut it. Go and see, Berthe."

The young girl had also understood. She rose and disappeared. The noise ceased at once, but she did not return immediately. Uncle Bachelard, who had scandalously disturbed "The Banks of the Oise" with reflections uttered out loud, finished putting his sister out of countenance by calling to Gueulin that he felt awfully bored and was going to have a grog. They both returned to the dining-room, banging the door behind them.

"That dear old Narcisse, he is always original !" said Madame Josserand to Madame Juzeur and Valérie, between whom she had gone and seated herself. "His business occupies him so much ! You know, he has made almost a hundred thousand francs this year !"

Octave, at length free, had hastened to rejoin Trublot, who was half asleep on the sofa. Near them, a group surrounded Doctor Juillerat, the old medical man of the neighbourhood, not over brilliant, but who had become in course of time a good practitioner, and who had delivered all the mothers in their confinements and had attended all the daughters. He made a

speciality of women's ailments, which caused him to be in great
demand of an evening, the husbands all trying to obtain a
gratuitous consultation in some corner of the drawing-room.
Just then, Théophile was telling him that Valérie had had
another attack the day before; she was for ever having a
choking fit and complaining of a lump rising in her throat; and
he, too, was not very well, but his complaint was not the same.
Then he did nothing but speak of himself, and relate his vexations: he had commenced to read for the law, had engaged in
manufactures at a foundry, and had tried office management at
the Mont-de-Piété; then he had busied himself with photo-
graphy, and thought he had found a means of making vehicles
supply their own motive power; meanwhile, out of kindness, he
was travelling some piano-flutes, an invention of one of his
friends. And he complained of his wife: it was her fault if
nothing went right at home; she was killing him with her perpetual nervous attacks.

"Do pray give her something, doctor!" implored he, coughing and moaning, his eyes lit up with hatred, in the querulous
rage of his impotency.

Trublot watched him, full of contempt; and he laughed
silently as he glanced at Octave. Doctor Juillerat uttered
vague and calming words: no doubt, they would relieve her,
the dear lady. At fourteen, she was already stifling, in the
shop of the Rue Neuve-Saint-Augustin; he had attended her
for vertigo which always ended by bleeding at the nose; and,
as Théophile recalled with despair her languid gentleness when
a young girl, whilst now, fantastic and her temper changing
twenty times in a day, she absolutely tortured him, the doctor
merely shook his head. Marriage did not succeed with all
women.

"Of course!" murmured Trublot, "a father who has gone
off his chump by passing thirty years of his life in selling
needles and thread, a mother who has always had her face
covered with pimples, and that in an airless hole of old Paris,
no one can expect such people to have daughters like other
folks!"

Octave was surprised. He was losing some of his respect for
that drawing-room which he had entered with a provincial's
emotion. Curiosity was awakened within him, when he observed Campardon consulting the doctor in his turn, but in
whispers, like a sedate person desirous of letting no one become acquainted with his family mishaps.

"By the way, as you appear to know everything," said Octave to Trublot, "tell me what it is that Madame Campardon is suffering from. Every one puts on a very sad face whenever it is mentioned."

"Why, my dear fellow," replied the young man, "she has—"

And he whispered in Octave's ear. Whilst he listened, the latter's face first assumed a smile, and then became very long with a look of profound astonishment.

"It is not possible!" said he.

Then, Trublot gave his word of honour. He knew another lady in the same state.

"Besides," resumed he, "it sometimes happens after a confinement that—"

And he began to whisper again. Octave, convinced, became quite sad. He who had fancied all sorts of things, who had imagined quite a romance, the architect occupied elsewhere and drawing him towards his wife to amuse her! In any case he now knew that she was well guarded. The young men pressed up against each other, in the excitement caused by these feminine secrets which they were stirring up, forgetting that they might be overheard.

Madame Juzeur was just then confiding to Madame Josserand her impressions of Octave. She thought him very becoming, no doubt, but she preferred Monsieur Auguste Vabre. The latter, standing up in a corner of the drawing-room, remained silent, in his insignificance and with his usual evening headache.

"What surprises me, dear madame, is that you have not thought of him for your Berthe. A young man set up in business, who is prudence itself. And he is in want of a wife, I know that he is desirous of getting married."

Madame Josserand listened, surprised. She would never herself have thought of the linendraper. Madame Juzeur, however, insisted, for in her misfortune, she had the mania of working for the happiness of other women, which caused her to busy herself with everything relating to the tender passions of the house. She affirmed that Auguste never took his eyes off Berthe. In short, she invoked her experience of men : Monsieur Mouret would never let himself be caught, whilst that good Monsieur Vabre would be very easy and very advantageous. But Madame Josserand, weighing the latter with a glance, came decidedly to the conclusion that such a son-in-law would not be of much use in filling her drawing-room.

"My daughter detests him," said she, "and I would never oppose the dictates of her heart."

A tall thin young lady had just played a fantasia on the "Dame Blanche." As uncle Bachelard had fallen asleep in the dining-room, Gueulin reappeared and imitated the nightingale on his flute. No one listened, however, for the story about Bonnaud had spread. Monsieur Josserand was quite upset, the fathers held up their arms, the mothers were stifling. What! Bonnaud's son-in-law was a clown! Then who could one believe in now? and the parents, in their appetites for marriages, suffered regular nightmares, like so many distinguished convicts in evening dress. The fact was, that Bonnaud had been so delighted at the opportunity of getting rid of his daughter that he had not troubled much about references, in spite of his rigid prudence of an over-scrupulous general accountant.

"Mamma, the tea is served," said Berthe, as she and Adèle opened the folding doors.

And, whilst the company passed slowly into the dining-room, she went up to her mother and murmured :

"I have had enough of it! He wants me to stay and tell him stories, or he threatens to smash everything!"

On a grey cloth which was too narrow, was served one of those teas laboriously got together, a cake bought at a neighbouring baker's, with some mixed sweet biscuits, and some sandwiches on either side. At either end of the table quite a luxury of flowers, superb and costly roses, withdrew attention from the ancient dust on the biscuits, and the poor quality of the butter. The sight caused a commotion, and jealousies were kindled : really those Josserands were ruining themselves in trying to marry off their daughters. And the guests, having but poorly dined, and only thinking of going to bed with their bellies full, casting side glances at the bouquets, gorged themselves with weak tea and imprudently devoured the hard stale biscuits and the heavy cake. For those persons who did not like tea, Adèle handed round some glasses of red currant syrup. It was pronounced excellent.

Meanwhile, the uncle was asleep in a corner. They did not wake him, they even politely pretended not to see him. A lady talked of the fatigues of business. Berthe went from one to another, offering sandwiches, handing cups of tea, and asking the men if they would like any more sugar. But she was unable to attend to every one, and Madame Josserand was looking

TRUBLOT PINCHING ADÈLE AT THE JOSSERANDS' PARTY.

for her daughter Hortense, when she caught sight of her standing in the middle of the deserted drawing-room, talking to a gentleman, of whom one could only see the back.

"Ah! yes! he has come at last," she permitted, in her anger, to escape her.

There was some whispering. It was that Verdier, who had been living with a woman for fifteen years past, whilst waiting to marry Hortense. Every one knew the story, the young ladies exchanged glances; but they bit their lips, and avoided speaking of it, out of propriety. Octave, being made acquainted with it, examined the gentleman's back with interest. Trublot knew the mistress, a good girl, a reformed street-walker, who was better now, said he, than the best of wives, taking care of her man, and looking after his clothes; and he was full of a fraternal sympathy for her. Whilst they were being watched from the dining-room, Hortense was scolding Verdier with all the sulkiness of a badly brought up virgin for having come so late.

"Hallo! red currant syrup!" said Trublot, seeing Adèle standing before him, a tray in her hand.

He sniffed it and declined. But, as the servant turned round, a stout lady's elbow pushed her against him, and he pinched her back. She smiled, and returned to him with the tray.

"No, thanks," said he. "By-and-by."

Women were seated round the table, whilst the men were eating, standing up behind them. Exclamations were heard, an enthusiasm, which died away as the mouths were filled with food. The gentlemen were appealed to. Madame Josserand cried:

"Ah! yes, I was forgetting. Come and look, Monsieur Mouret, you who love the arts."

"Take care, the water-colour stroke!" murmured Trublot, who knew the house.

It was better than a water-colour. As though by chance, a porcelain bowl was standing on the table; right at the very bottom of it, surrounded by the brand new varnished bronze mounting, Greuze's "Young girl with the broken Pitcher" was painted in light colours, passing from pale lilac to faint blue. Berthe smiled in the midst of the praise.

"Mademoiselle possesses every talent," said Octave with his good-natured grace. "Oh! the colours are so well blended, and it is very accurate, very accurate!"

"I can guarantee that the design is!" resumed Madame Josserand, triumphantly. "There is not a hair too many or few.   Berthe copied it here, from an engraving.   There are really such a number of nude subjects at the Louvre, and the people there are at times so mixed ! "

She had lowered her voice when giving this last piece of information, desirous of letting the young man know that, though her daughter was an artist, she did not let that carry her beyond the limits of propriety.   She probably, however, thought Octave rather cold, she felt that the bowl had not met with the success she had anticipated, and she watched him with an anxious look, whilst Valérie and Madame Juzeur, who were drinking their fourth cup of tea, examined the painting and gave vent to little cries of admiration.

"You are looking at her again," said Trublot to Octave, on seeing him with his eyes fixed on Valérie.

"Why, yes," replied he, slightly confused.   "It is funny, she looks pretty just at this moment.   A warm woman, evidently.   I say, do you think one might venture ? "

"Warm, one never knows.   It is a peculiar fancy !   Anyhow, it would be better than marrying the girl."

"What girl ? " exclaimed Octave, forgetting himself. "What ! you think I am going to let myself be hooked ! Never !   My dear fellow, we don't marry at Marseilles ! "

Madame Josserand had drawn near.   The words came upon her like a stab in the heart.   Another fruitless campaign, another evening party wasted !   The blow was such, that she was obliged to lean against a chair, as she looked with despair at the now despoiled table, where all that remained was a burnt piece of the cake.   She had given up counting her defeats, but this one should be the last ; she took a frightful oath, swearing that she would no longer feed persons who came to see her solely to gorge.   And, upset and exasperated, she glanced round the dining-room, seeking into what man's arms she could throw her daughter, when she caught sight of Auguste resignedly standing against the wall and not having partaken of anything.

Just then, Berthe, with a smile on her face, was moving towards Octave, with a cup of tea in her hand.   She was continuing the campaign, obedient to her mother's wishes.   But the latter caught her by the arm and called her a silly fool under her breath.

"Take that cup to Monsieur Vabre, who has been waiting for an hour past," said she, graciously and very loud.

Then, whispering again in her daughter's ear, and giving her another of her warlike looks, she added :

"Be amiable, or you will have me to deal with !"

Berthe, for a moment put out of countenance, soon recovered herself. It often changed thus three times in an evening. She carried the cup to Auguste, with the smile which she had commenced for Octave ; she was amiable, talked of Lyons silks, and did the engaging young person who would look very well behind a counter. Auguste's hands trembled a little, and he was very red, as he was suffering a good deal from his head that evening.

Out of politeness, a few persons returned and sat down for some moments in the drawing-room. Having fed, they were all going off. When they looked for Verdier, he had already taken his departure ; and some young ladies, greatly put out, only carried away an indistinct view of his back. Campardon, without waiting for Octave, retired with the doctor, whom he detained on the landing, to ask him if there was really no more hope. During the tea, one of the lamps had gone out, emitting a stench of rancid oil, and the other lamp, the wick of which was all charred, lit up the room with so poor a light, . that the Vabres themselves rose to leave in spite of the attentions with which Madame Josserand overwhelmed them. Octave had preceded them into the ante-room, where he had a surprise : Trublot, who was looking for his hat, suddenly disappeared. He could only have gone off by the passage leading to the kitchen.

"Well ! wherever has he got to ? does he leave by the servants' staircase ?" murmured the young man.

But he did not seek to clear up the mystery. Valérie was there, looking for a lace neckerchief. The two brothers, Théophile and Auguste, were going downstairs, without troubling themselves about her. Octave, having found the neckerchief, handed it to her, with the air of admiration he put on when serving the pretty lady customers of "The Ladies' Paradise." She looked at him, and he felt certain that her eyes, on fixing themselves on his, had flashed forth flames.

"You are too kind, sir," said she, simply.

Madame Juzeur, who was the last to leave, enveloped them both in a tender and discreet smile. And when Octave, highly excited, had reached his cold chamber, he looked at himself for an instant in the glass, and he thought it worth while to make the attempt !

Meanwhile, Madame Josserand was wandering about the deserted room, without saying a word, and as though carried away by some gale of wind.   She had violently closed the piano and turned out the last lamp; then, passing into the dining-room, she began to blow out the candles so vigorously that the chandelier quite shook.   The sight of the despoiled table covered with dirty plates and empty cups, increased her rage; and she turned round it, casting terrible glances at her daughter Hortense, who, quietly sitting down, was devouring the piece of burnt cake.

"You are putting yourself in a fine state again, mamma," said the latter.   "Is it not going on all right, then?   For myself, I am satisfied.   He is purchasing some chemises for her to enable her to leave."

The mother shrugged her shoulders.

"Eh? you say that this proves nothing.   Very good, only steer your ship as well as I steer mine.   Here now is a cake which may flatter itself it is a precious bad one!   They must be a wretched lot to swallow such stuff."

Monsieur Josserand, who was always worn out by his wife's parties, was reposing on a chair; but he was in dread of an encounter, he feared that Madame Josserand might drive him before her in her furious promenade; and he drew close to Bachelard and Gueulin, who were seated at the table in front of Hortense.   The uncle, on awaking, had discovered a decanter of rum.   He was emptying it, and bitterly alluding to the twenty francs.

"It is not for the money," he kept repeating to his nephew, "it is the way the thing was done.   You know how I behave to women: I would give them the shirt off my back, but I do not like them to ask me for anything.   The moment they begin to ask, it annoys me, and I don't even chuck them a radish."

And, as his sister was about to remind him of his promises:

"Be quiet, Eléonore!   I know what I have to do for the child.   But, you see, when a woman asks, it is more than I can stand.   I have never been able to keep friends with one, have I now, Gueulin?   And besides, there is really such little respect shown me!   Léon has not even deigned to wish me many happy returns of the day."

Madame Josserand resumed her walk, clinching her fists.   It was true, there was Léon too, who promised and then disap-pointed her like the others.   There was one who would not sacrifice an evening to help to marry off his sisters!   She had just discovered a sweet biscuit, fallen behind one of the flower

vases, and was locking it up in a drawer when Berthe, who had
gone to release Saturnin, brought him back with her. She was
quieting him, whilst he, haggard and with a mistrustful look
in his eyes, was searching the corners, with the feverish excitement of a dog that has been long shut up.

"How stupid he is !" said Berthe, "he thinks that I have
just been married. And he is seeking for the husband ! Ah !
my poor Saturnin, you may seek. I tell you that it has come
to nothing ! You know very well that it never comes to anything."

Then, Madame Josserand's rage burst all bounds.

"Ah ! I swear to you that it sha'n't come to nothing next
time, even if I have to tie him to you myself! There is one
who shall pay for all the others. Yes, yes, Monsieur Josserand,
you may stare at me, as though you did not understand : the
wedding shall take place, and without you, if it does not please
you. You hear, Berthe? you have only to pick that one up !"

Saturnin appeared not to hear. He was looking under the
table. The young girl pointed to him ; but Madame Josserand
made a gesture which seemed to imply that he would be got
out of the way. And Berthe murmured :

"So then it is decidedly to be Monsieur Vabre? Oh ! it is
all the same to me. To think though that not a single sand-
wich has been saved for me !"

CHAPTER IV.

As early as the morrow, Octave commenced to occupy himself about Valérie. He studied her habits, and ascertained the hour when he would have a chance of meeting her on the stairs; and he arranged matters so that he could frequently go up to his room, taking advantage of his coming home to lunch at the Campardons', and leaving "The Ladies' Paradise" for a few minutes under some pretext or other. He soon noticed that, every day towards two o'clock, the young woman, who took her child to the Tuileries gardens, passed along the Rue Gaillon. Then he would stand at the door, wait till she came, and greet her with one of his handsome shopman's smiles. At each of their meetings, Valérie politely inclined her head and passed on; but he perceived her dark glance to be full of passionate fire; he found encouragement in her ravaged complexion and in the supple swing of her gait.

His plan was already formed, the bold plan of a seducer used to cavalierly overcoming the virtue of shop-girls. It was simply a question of luring Valérie inside his room on the fourth floor; the staircase was always silent and deserted, no one would discover them up there; and he laughed at the thought of the architect's moral admonitions; for taking a woman belonging to the house was not the same as bringing one into it.

One thing, however, made Octave uneasy. The passage separated the Pichons' kitchen from their dining-room, and this obliged them to constantly have their door open. At nine o'clock in the morning, the husband started off for his office, and did not return home until about five in the evening; and, on alternate days of the week, he went out again after his dinner to do some bookkeeping, from eight to midnight. Besides this, though, the young woman, who was very reserved— almost wildly timid—would push her door to, directly she heard Octave's footsteps. He never caught sight of more than her back, which always seemed to be flying away, with her light hair done up into a scanty chignon. Through that door kept discreetly ajar, he had, up till then, only beheld a small portion of the room : sad and clean looking furniture, linen of a dull whiteness in the grey light admitted through a window which he could not see, and the corner of a child's crib inside an inner room ; all the monotonous solitude of a wife occupied from morning to night with the recurring cares of a clerk's home. Moreover, there was never a sound ; the child seemed dumb and worn-out like the mother; one scarcely distinguished at times the soft murmur of some ballad which the latter would hum for hours together in an expiring voice. But Octave was none the less furious with the disdainful creature as he called her. She was playing the spy upon him perhaps. In any case, Valérie could never come up to him if the Pichons' door was thus being continually opened.

He was just beginning to think that things were taking the right course. One Sunday when the husband was absent, he had manœuvred in such a way as to be on the first-floor landing at the moment the young woman, wrapped in her dressing-gown, was leaving her sister-in-law's to return to her own apartments ; and she being obliged to speak to him, they had stood some minutes exchanging polite remarks. So he was hoping that next time she would ask him in. With a woman with such a temperament the rest would follow as a matter of course. That evening during dinner, there was some talk about Valérie at the Campardons'. Octave tried to draw the others out. But as Angèle was listening and casting sly glances at Lisa, who was handing round some leg of mutton and looking very serious, the parents at first did nothing but sing the young woman's praises. Moreover, the architect always stood up for the respectability of the house, with the vain conviction of a tenant who seemed to obtain from it a regular certificate of his own gentility.

"Oh ! my dear fellow, most respectable people. You saw them at the Josserands'. The husband is no fool ; he is full of ideas, he will end by discovering something very grand. As for the wife, she has some style about her, as we artists say."

Madame Campardon, who had been rather worse since the day before, and who was half reclining, though her illness did not prevent her eating thick underdone slices of meat, languidly murmured in her turn :

"That poor Monsieur Théophile, he is like me, he drags along. Ah ! great praise is due to Valérie, for it is not lively always having by one a man trembling with fever, and whose infirmity usually makes him quarrelsome and unjust."

During dessert, Octave, seated between the architect and his wife, learnt more than he asked. They forgot Angèle, they spoke in hints, with glances which underlined the double meanings of the words ; and, when they were at a loss for an expression, they bent towards him one after the other, and coarsely whispered the rest of the disclosure in his ear. In short, that Théophile was a stupid and impotent person, who deserved to be what his wife made him. As for Valérie, she was not worth much, she would have behaved just as badly even if her husband had been different, for with her, nature had so much the mastery. Moreover, no one was ignorant of the fact that, two months after her marriage, in despair at re- cognising that she would never have a child by her husband, and fearing she would lose her share of old Vabre's fortune if Théophile happened to die, she had her little Camille got for her by a butcher's man of the Rue Sainte-Anne.

Campardon bent down and whispered a last time in Octave's ear :

"Well ! you know, my dear fellow, a hysterical woman !"

And he put into the word all the middle-class wantonness of an indelicacy combined with the blobber-lipped smile of a father of a family whose imagination, abruptly let loose, revels in licentiousness. The conversation then took a different turn, they were speaking of the Pichons, and words of praise were not stinted.

"Oh ! they are indeed worthy people !" repeated Madame Campardon. "Sometimes, when Marie takes her little Lilitte out, I also let her take Angèle. And I assure you, Monsieur Mouret, I do not trust my daughter to everyone ; I must be absolutely certain of the person's morality. You love Marie very much, do you not, Angèle ? "

"Yes, mamma," answered the child.

The details continued. It was impossible to find a woman better brought up, or according to severer principles. And it was a pleasure to see how happy the husband was ! Such a nice little home, and so clean, and a couple that adored each other, who never said one word louder than another !

"Besides, they would not be allowed to remain in the house, if they did not behave themselves properly," said the architect gravely, forgetting his disclosures about Valérie. "We will only have respectable people here. On my word of honour ! I would give notice, the day that my daughter ran the risk of meeting disreputable women on the stairs."

That evening, he had secretly arranged to take cousin Gasparine to the Opéra-Comique.   He therefore went and fetched his hat at once, talking of a business matter which would keep him out till very late.   Rose though probably knew of the arrangement, for Octave heard her murmur, in her resigned and maternal voice, when her husband came to kiss her with his habitual effusive tenderness :

"Amuse yourself well, and do not catch cold on coming out."

On the morrow, Octave had an idea : it was to become acquainted with Madame Pichon, by rendering her a few neighbourly services ; in this way, if she ever caught Valérie, she would keep her eyes shut.   And an opportunity occurred that very day.   Madame Pichon was in the habit of taking Lilitte, then eighteen months old, out in a little basket-work perambulator, which raised Monsieur Gourd's ire ; the door-keeper would never permit it to be carried up the principal staircase, so that she had to take it up the servants' ; and as the door of her apartment was too narrow, she had to remove the wheels every time, which was quite a job.   It so happened that that day Octave was returning home, just as his neigh-bour, incommoded by her gloves, was giving herself a great deal of trouble to get the nuts off.   When she felt him standing up behind her, waiting till the passage was clear, she quite lost her head, and her hands trembled.

"But, madame, why do you take all that trouble?" asked he at length.   "It would be far simpler to put the perambul-ator at the end of the passage, behind my door."

She did not reply, her excessive timidity kept her squatting there, without strength to rise ; and, beneath the curtain of her bonnet, he beheld a hot blush invade the nape of her neck and her ears.   Then he insisted :

"I assure you, madame, it will not inconvenience me in the least."

Without waiting, he lifted up the perambulator and carried it in his easy way.   She was obliged to follow him ; but she remained so confused, so frightened by this important adventure in her uneventful every-day life, that she looked on, only able to stutter fragments of sentences.

"Dear me ! sir, it is too much trouble—I feel quite ashamed —you will find it very awkward.   My husband will be very pleased—"

And she entered her room and locked herself in, this time hermetically, with a sort of shame. Octave thought that she was stupid. The perambulator was a great deal in his way for it prevented him opening his door wide, and he had to slip into his room sideways. But his neighbour seemed to be won over, more especially as Monsieur Gourd consented to authorize the obstruction at that end of the passage, thanks to Campardon's influence.

Every Sunday, Marie's parents, Monsieur and Madame Vuillaume, came to spend the day. On the Sunday following, as Octave was going out, he beheld all the family seated taking their coffee, and he was discreetly hastening by, when the young woman, whispering quickly in her husband's ear, the latter jumped up, saying:

"Excuse me, sir, I am always out, I have not yet had an opportunity of thanking you. But I wish to tell you how pleased I was—"

Octave protested. At length he was obliged to give in. Though he had already had his coffee, they made him accept another cup. They gave him the place of honour, between Monsieur and Madame Vuillaume. Opposite to him, on the other side of the round table, Marie was again thrown into one of those confused conditions which at any minute, without apparent cause, brought all the blood from her heart to her face. He watched her, never having seen her at his ease. But, as Trublot said, she was not his fancy : she seemed to him wretched and washed out, with her flat face and her thin hair, though her features were refined and pretty. When she recovered herself a little, she laughed lightly as she again talked of the perambulator, about which she found a great deal to say.

"Jules, if you had only seen Monsieur Mouret carry it in his arms. Ah well ! it did not take long !"

Pichon again uttered his thanks. He was tall and thin, with a doleful look about him, already subdued to the routine of office life, his dull eyes full of the apathetic resignation displayed by circus horses.

"Pray say no more about it !" Octave ended by observing, " it is really not worth while. Madame, your coffee is exquisite. I have never drunk any like it."

She blushed again, and so much that her hands even became quite rosy.

"Do not spoil her, sir," said Monsieur Vuillaume gravely

"Her coffee is good, but there is better. And you see how proud she has become at once!"

"Pride is worth nothing," declared Madame Vuillaume. "We have always taught her to be modest."

They were both of them little and dried up, very old, and with dark-looking countenances; the wife wore a tight black dress, and the husband a thin frock-coat, on which only the mark of a big red ribbon was to be seen.

"Sir," resumed the latter, "I was decorated at the age of sixty, on the day I was pensioned off, after having been for thirty-nine years employed at the Ministry of Public Instruction. Well! sir, on that day I dined the same as on other days, and did not let pride interfere with any of my habits. The Cross was due to me, I know it. I was simply filled with gratitude."

His life was perfectly clear, he wished every one to know it. After twenty-five years' service, he had been promoted to four thousand francs. His pension, therefore, was two thousand. But he had had to re-engage himself in a subordinate position at fifteen hundred francs, as they had had their little Marie late in life when Madame Vuillaume was no longer expecting either son or daughter. Now that the child was established in life, they were living on the pension, by pinching themselves, in the Rue Durantin at Montmartre, where things were cheaper.

"I am sixty-three," said he, in conclusion, "and that is all about it, and that is all about it, son-in-law!"

Pichon looked at him in a silent and weary way, his eyes fixed on his red ribbon. Yes, it would be his own story if luck favoured him. He was the last born of a greengrocer who had spent the entire worth of her shop in her anxiety to make her son take a degree, just because all the neighbourhood said he was very intelligent; and she had died bankrupt eight days before his triumph at the Sorbonne. After three years of hardships at his uncle's, he had had the unexpected luck of getting a berth at the Ministry, which was to lead him to everything, and on the strength of which he had already married.

"When one does one's duty, the government does the same," murmured he, mechanically reckoning that he still had thirty-six years to wait before obtaining the right to wear a piece of red ribbon and to enjoy a pension of two thousand francs.

Then he turned towards Octave.

"You see, sir, it is the children who are such a heavy weight."

"No doubt," said Madame Vuillaume. "If we had had another we should never have made both ends meet. Therefore, remember, Jules, what I insisted upon when I gave you Marie : one child and no more, or else we shall quarrel ! It is only workpeople who have children like fowls lay eggs, without troubling themselves as to what it will cost them. It is true that they turn the youngsters out on to the streets, like flocks of animals, which make me feel sick when I pass by."

Octave had looked at Marie, thinking that this delicate subject would make her cheeks crimson; but she remained pale, approving her mother's words with ingenuous serenity. He was feeling awfully bored, and did not know how to retire. In the little cold dining-room these people thus spent their afternoon, slowly muttering a few words every five minutes, and always about their own affairs. Even dominoes disturbed them too much.

Madame Vuillaume now explained her notions. At the end of a long silence, which left all four of them in no way embarrassed as though they had felt the necessity of rearranging their ideas, she resumed :

"You have no child, sir ? It will come in time. Ah ! it is a responsibility, especially for a mother ! When my little one was born I was forty-nine, sir, an age when luckily one knows how to behave. A boy will get on anyhow, but a girl ! And I have the consolation of knowing that I have done my duty, oh, yes ! "

Then, she explained her plan of education, in short sentences. Honesty first. No playing on the stairs, the little one always kept at home and watched closely, for children think of nothing but evil. The doors and windows shut, never any draughts, which bring the wicked things of the street with them. Out of doors, never leave go of the child's hand, teach it to keep its eyes lowered to avoid seeing anything wrong. With regard to religion, it should not be overdone, just sufficient as a moral restraint. Then, when she has grown up, engage teachers instead of sending her to school, where the innocent ones are corrupted ; and assist also at the lessons, see that she does not learn what she should not know, hide all newspapers of course, and keep the bookcase locked.

"A young person always knows too much," declared the old lady coming to an end.

Whilst her mother spoke, Marie kept her eyes vaguely fixed on space. She once more beheld the little convent-like lodging, those narrow rooms in the Rue Durantin, where she was not even allowed to lean out of a window. It was one prolonged

childhood, all sorts of prohibitions which she did not understand, lines which her mother inked out on their fashion paper,
the black marks of which made her blush, lessons purified to
such an extent that even her teachers were embarrassed when
she questioned them. A very gentle childhood, however, the
soft warm growth of a greenhouse, a waking dream in which the
words uttered by the tongue, and the facts of every day life
acquired ridiculous meanings. And, even at that hour as she
gazed vacantly, and was filled with these recollections, a childish
smile hovered about her lips, as though she had remained in
ignorance spite even of her marriage.

"You will believe me if you like, sir," said Monsieur Vuillaume,
"but my daughter had not read a single novel when she was
past eighteen. Is it not true, Marie?"

"Yes, papa."

"I have George Sand's works very handsomely bound," he
continued, "and in spite of her mother's fears I decided, a few
months before her marriage, to permit her to read 'André,' a
perfectly innocent work, full of imagination, and which elevates
the soul. I am for a liberal education. Literature has certainly
its rights. The book produced an extraordinary effect upon
her, sir. She cried all night in her sleep: which proves that
there is nothing like a pure imagination to understand genius."

"It is so beautiful!" murmured the young woman, her eyes
sparkling.

But Pichon having enunciated this theory: no novels before
marriage, and as many as one likes afterwards—Madame
Vuillaume shook her head. She never read, and was none the
worse for it. Then, Marie gently spoke of her loneliness.

"Well! I sometimes take up a book. Jules chooses them
for me at the library in the Passage Choiseul. If I only played
the piano!"

For some time past, Octave had felt the necessity of saying
something.

"What! madame," exclaimed he, "you do not play!"

A slight awkwardness ensued. The parents talked of a succession of unfortunate circumstances, not wishing to admit that
they had not been willing to incur the expense. Madame
Vuillaume, moreover, affirmed that Marie sang in tune from
her birth; when she was a child she knew all sorts of very
pretty ballads, she had only to hear the tunes once to remember
them; and the mother spoke of a song about Spain, the story
of a captive weeping for her lover, which the child gave out

with an expression that would draw tears from the hardest hearts. But Marie remained disconsolate. She let this cry escape her, as she extended her hand in the direction of the inner room, where her little one was sleeping :

"Ah ! I swear that Lilitte shall learn to play the piano, even though I have to make the greatest sacrifices ! "

"Think first of bringing her up as we brought you up," said Madame Vuillaume, severely. "I certainly do not condemn music, it develops one's feelings. But, above all, watch over your daughter, keep every foul breath from her, strive that she may preserve her innocence."

She started off again, giving even more weight to religion, settling the number of times to go to confess each month, naming the masses that it was absolutely necessary to attend, all from the point of view of propriety. Then Octave, unable to bear any more of it, talked of an appointment which obliged him to go out. He had a singing in his ears, he felt that this conversation would continue in a like manner until the evening. And he hastened away, leaving the Vuillaumes and the Pichons telling one another, around the same cups of coffee slowly emptied, what they told each other every Sunday. As he was bowing a last time, Marie, suddenly and without any reason, became scarlet.

Ever since that afternoon, Octave hastened past the Pichons' door whenever he heard the slow tones of Monsieur and Madame Vuillaume on a Sunday. Moreover, he was entirely absorbed in his conquest of Valérie. In spite of the fiery glances of which he thought himself the object, she maintained an inexplicable reserve ; and in that he fancied he saw the play of a coquette. He even met her one day, as though by chance, in the Tuileries gardens, when she quietly began to talk of a storm of the day before ; which finally convinced him that she was devilish smart. And he was constantly on the staircase, watching for an opportunity of entering her apartments, decided if necessary upon being positively rude.

Now, every time that he passed her, Marie smiled and blushed. They exchanged the greetings of good neighbours. One morning, at lunch-time, as he brought her up a letter, which Monsieur Gourd had given him, to avoid having to go up the four flights of stairs himself, he found her in a sad way : she had seated Lilitte in her chemise on the round- table, and was trying to dress her again.

"What is the matter ?" asked the young man.

"Why, this child!" replied she. "I foolishly took her things off, because she was complaining. And now I don't know what to do, I don't know what to do!"

He looked at her in surprise. She was turning a skirt over and over, looking for the hooks. Then, she added :

"You see, her father always helps me to dress her in the morning before he goes out. I can never manage it by myself. It bothers me, it annoys me."

The child, meanwhile, tired of being in her chemise and frightened by the sight of Octave, was struggling and tumbling about on the table.

"Take care!" cried he, "she will fall."

It was quite a catastrophe. Marie looked as though she dare not touch her child's naked limbs. She continued contemplating her, with the surprise of a virgin, amazed at having been able to produce such a thing. However, assisted by Octave, who quieted the little one, she succeeded in dressing her again.

"How will you manage when you have a dozen?" asked he, 'aughing.

"But we shall never have any more!" answered she in a fright.

Then, he joked : she was wrong to be so sure, a child comes so easily !

"No! no!" repeated she obstinately. "You heard what mamma said, the other day. She forbade Jules to have any more. You do not know her ; it would lead to endless quarrels, if another came."

Octave was amused by the quiet way in which she discussed this question. He drew her out, without, however, succeeding in embarrassing her. She, moreover, did as her husband wished. No doubt, she loved children ; had she been allowed to desire others, she would not have said no. And, beneath this complacency, which was restricted to her mother's commands, the indifference of a woman whose maternity was still slumbering could be recognized. Lilitte occupied her like her home, which she looked after through duty. When she had washed up the breakfast things and taken the child for her walk, she continued her former young girl's existence, of a somnolent emptiness, lulled by the vague expectation of a joy which never came. Octave having remarked that she must feel very dull, being always alone, she seemed surprised : no, she was never dull, the days passed somehow or other, without her knowing, when she went to bed, how she had employed her time. Then, on Sun-

days, she sometimes went out with her husband; or her parents
called, or else she read.   If reading did not give her headaches,
she would have read from morning till night, now that she was
allowed to read everything.

"What is really annoying," resumed she, "is that they have
scarcely anything at the library in the Passage Choiseul.   For
instance, I wanted ' André,' to read it again, because it made me
cry so much the other time.   Well ! their copy has been stolen.
Besides that, my father refuses to lend me his, because Lilitte
might tear the pictures."

"But," said Octave, "my friend Campardon has all George
Saud's works.   I will ask him to lend me ' André ' for you."

She blushed, and her eyes sparkled.   He was really too kind !
And, when he left her, she stood before Lilitte, her arms hanging down by her sides, without an idea in her head, in the attitude which she maintained for whole afternoons together.   She
detested sewing, she did crochet work, always the same piece,
which she left lying about the room.

Octave brought her the book on the morrow, a Sunday.
Pichou had had to go out, to leave his card on one of his super-
iors.   And, as the young man found her dressed for walking,
she having just been on some errand in the neighbourhood, he
asked her out of curiosity whether she had been to church,
having the idea that she was religious.   She answered no.
Before marrying her off, her mother used to take her regularly
to mass.   During the six first months of her married life, she
continued going through force of habit, with the constant fear
of being too late.   Then, she scarcely knew why, after missing
a few times, she left off going altogether.   Her husband detested priests, and her mother never even mentioned them now.
Octave's question, however, disturbed her, as though it had
awakened within her things that had been long buried beneath
the idleness of her existence.

"I must go to Saint-Roch one of these mornings," said she.
"An occupation gone always leaves a void behind it."

And, on the pale face of this late child, born of parents too
old, there appeared the unhealthy regret of another existence,
dreamed of once upon a time, in the land of chimeras.   She could
conceal nothing, everything was reflected in her face, beneath
her skin, which had the softness and the transparency accompanying an attack of chlorosis.   Then, she gave way to her feelings, and caught hold of Octave's hands with a familiar gesture.

"Ah ! let me thank you for having brought me this book !

Come to-morrow after lunch. I will return it to you and tell you the effect that it produced on me. It will be amusing, will it not ? "

On leaving her, Octave thought that she was funny all the same. She was beginning to interest him, he contemplated speaking to Pichon so as to make him rouse her up a bit ; for the little woman, most decidedly, only wanted a shaking. It so happened that on the morrow he came across the clerk just as he was going off, and he accompanied him part of the way, at the risk of being late himself at " The Ladies' Paradise." But Pichon seemed to him to be even more benumbed than his wife, full of manias in their early stage, and entirely occupied with the dread of getting mud on his shoes in wet weather. He walked on his toes, and continually talked of the second head-clerk of his office. Octave, who was only animated by fraternal intentions in the matter, ended by leaving him in the Rue Saint-Honoré, after advising him to take Marie to the theatre frequently.

" Whatever for ? " asked Pichon in amazement.

" Because it is good for women. It makes them nicer."

" Ah ! you really think so ? "

He promised to give the matter his attention, and crossed the street, eyeing the cabs with terror, the only thing in life which worried him being the fear of getting splashed.

At lunch-time, Octave knocked at the Pichons' door for the book. Marie was reading, her elbows on the table, her hands buried in her dishevelled hair. She had just eaten an egg cooked in a tin pan which was lying in the centre of the hastily laid table without any cloth. Lilitte, forgotten on the floor, was sleeping with her nose on the pieces of a plate which she had no doubt broken.

" Well ? "

Marie did not answer at once. She was still wrapped in her morning dressing-gown, which, from the buttons being torn off, displayed her throat, in all the disorder of a woman just risen from her bed.

" I have scarcely read a hundred pages," she ended by saying. " My parents came yesterday."

And she spoke in a painful tone of voice, with a sourness about her mouth. When she was younger, she longed to live in the midst of the woods. She was for ever dreaming that she met a huntsman who was sounding his horn. He approached her and knelt down. This took place in a copse, very far away, where roses were blooming like in a park. Then, suddenly, they had been married, and afterwards lived there, wandering about till eternity. She, very happy, wished for nothing more; he, as tender and submissive as a slave, was continually at her feet.

" I had a talk with your husband this morning," said Octave. " You do not go out enough, and I have persuaded him to take you to the theatre."

But she shook her head, turning pale and shivering. A silence ensued. She again beheld the narrow dining-room with its cold light. Jules's image, sullen and correct, had suddenly cast a shadow over the huntsman of the romance whom she had been imagining, and the sound of whose horn in the distance again rang in her ears. Every now and then she listened: perhaps he was coming. Her husband had never taken her feet in his hands to kiss them; he had never either knelt beside her to tell her he adored her. Yet, she loved him well; but she was surprised that love did not contain more sweetness.

" What stifles me, you know," resumed she, returning to the book, " is when there are passages in novels about the characters telling one another of their love."

Octave then sat down. He wished to laugh, not caring for such sentimental trifling.

" I detest a lot of phrases," said he. " When two persons adore each other, the best thing is to prove it at once."

But she did not seem to understand, her eyes remained un-dimmed. He stretched out his hand, slightly touching hers, and leant over so close to her to observe a passage in the book that his breath warmed her shoulder through the open dressing-gown; yet she remained insensible. Then, he rose up, full of a contempt mingled with pity. As he was leaving, she said :

"I read very slowly, I shall not have finished it before to-morrow. It will be amusing to-morrow ! Look in during the evening."

He certainly had no designs upon her, and yet he felt indignant. He conceived a singular friendship for this young couple who exasperated him, they seemed to take life so stupidly. And the idea came to him of rendering them a service in spite of them ; he would take them out to dinner, make them tipsy, and then amuse himself by pushing them into each other's arms. When such fits of kindness got hold of him, he, who would not have lent ten francs, delighted in flinging his money out of the window, to bring two lovers together and give them joy.

Little Madame Pichon's coldness, however, brought Octave back to the ardent Valérie. This one, certainly, would not require to be breathed upon twice on the back of her neck. He was advancing in her favour : one day that she was going up-stairs before him, he had ventured to compliment her on her ankle, without her appearing displeased.

At length the opportunity so long watched for presented itself. It was the evening that Marie had made him promise to look in ; they would be alone to talk about the novel, as her husband was not to be home till very late. But the young man had preferred to go out, seized wi.h fright at the thought of this literary treat. However, he had decided to venture upon it, towards ten o'clock, when he met Valérie's maid on the first-floor landing with a scared look on her face, and who said to him :

"Madame has gone iuto hysterics, my master is out, and every one opposite has gone to the theatre. Pray come in. I am all alone, I don't know what to do."

Valérie was stretched out in an easy-chair in her bedroom, her limbs rigid. The maid had unlaced her stays, and her bosom was heaving. The attack subsided almost immediately. She opened her eyes, was surprised to see Octave there, and acted moreover as she might have done in the presence of a doctor.

" I must ask you to excuse me, sir," murmured she, her voice still choking. " I have only had this girl since yesterday, and she lost her head."

Her perfect coolness in adjusting her stays and fastening up her dress again, embarrassed the young man. He remained standing, swearing not to depart thus, yet not daring to sit down. She had sent away the maid, the sight of whom seemed to irritate her ; then she went to the window to breathe the cool outdoor air in long nervous inspirations, her mouth wide open. After a short silence, they commenced talking. She had first suffered from these attacks when fourteen years old ; Doctor Juillerat was tired of prescribing for her ; sometimes they seized her in the arms, sometimes in the loins. However, she was getting used to them ; she might as well have them as anything else, as no one was really perfectly well. And, whilst she talked, with scarcely any life in her limbs, he excited him-self with looking at her, he thought her provoking in the midst of her disorder, with her leaden complexion, her face upset by the attack as though by a whole night of love. Behind the black mass of her loose hair, which hung over her shoulders, he

fancied he beheld the husband's poor and beardless head. Then,
stretching out his hands, with the unrestrained gesture with
which he would have seized some harlot, he tried to take hold
of her.

"Well! what now?" asked she, in a voice full of surprise.

In her turn she looked at him, whilst her eyes were so cold,
her flesh so calm, that he felt frozen and let his hands fall with
an awkward slowness, fully aware of the ridiculousness of his
gesture. Then, in a last nervous gape which she stifled, she
slowly added :

"Ah ! my dear sir, if you only knew !"

And she shrugged her shoulders, without getting angry, as
though crushed beneath her contempt for man and her weariness
of him. Octave thought she was about to have him turned out
when he saw her move towards a bell-pull, dragging her loosely
fastened skirts along with her. But she merely required some
tea ; and she ordered it to be very weak and very hot. Altogether nonplussed, he muttered some excuses and made for the
door, whilst she again reclined in the depths of her easy-chair,
with the air of a chilly woman greatly in want of sleep.

On the stairs, Octave stopped at each landing. She did not
like that then ? He had just seen how indifferent she was,
without desire as without indignation, as difficult to deal with
as his employer, Madame Hédouin. Why did Campardon say
she was hysterical ? it was absurd to take him in by telling him
such humbug ; for had it not been for the architect's lie, he
would never have risked such an adventure. And he remained
quite bewildered by the result, his ideas of hysteria altogether
upset, and thinking of the different stories that were going
about. He recalled Trublot's words : one never knows what to
expect, with those crazy sort of people whose eyes shine like
balls of fire.

Up on his landing Octave, annoyed with all women, walked
as softly as he could. But the Pichons' door opened, and he
had to resign himself. Marie awaited him, standing in the
narrow room, which the charred wick of the lamp but imperfectly lighted. She had drawn the crib close to the table, and
Lilitte was sleeping there in the circle of the yellow light. The
lunch things had probably also served for the dinner, for the
closed book was lying beside a dirty plate full of radish ends.

"Have you finished it ?" asked Octave, surprised at the
young woman's silence

She seemed intoxicated, her face was swollen as though she had just awakened from a too heavy sleep.

"Yes, yes," said she, with an effort. . "Oh ! I have passed the day, my head in my hands, buried in it. When the fit takes one, one no longer knows where one is. I have such a stiff neck."

And, feeling pains all over her, she did not speak any more of the book, but was so full of her emotion and of confused dreams engendered by her reading, that she was choking. Her ears rang with the distant calls of the horn, blown by the huntsman of her romances, in the blue background of ideal loves. Then, without the least reason, she said that she had been to Saint-Roch that morning to hear the nine o'clock mass. She had wept a great deal, religion replaced everything.

"Ah ! I feel better," resumed she, heaving a deep sigh and standing still in front of Octave.

A pause ensued. She smiled at him with her candid eyes. He had never thought her so useless, with her scanty hair and her washed-out features. But as she continued looking at him, she became very pale and almost stumbled ; and he was obliged to put out his hands to support her.

"Good heavens ! good heavens !" stuttered she, sobbing.

He continued to hold her, feeling considerably embarrassed.

"You should take a little infusion. You have been reading too much."

"Yes, it upset me, when on closing the book I found myself alone. How kind you are, Monsieur Mouret ! I might have hurt myself, had it not been for you."

He looked for a chair on which to seat her.

"Shall I light a fire ? "

"No, thank you, it would dirty your hands. I have noticed that you always wear gloves."

And choking again at the idea, and suddenly feeling faint, she launched an awkward kiss into space as though in a dream, a kiss which slightly touched the young man's ear.

Octave received this kiss with amazement. The young woman's lips were as cold as ice. Then, when she had sank upon his breast in an abandonment of her whole frame, he was seized with a sudden desire, and sought to bear her into the inner room. But this brusque wooing roused Marie ; her womanly instinct revolted ; she struggled and called upon her mother, forgetting her husband, who was shortly to return; and her daughter who was sleeping near her.

“No, oh! no, no.　It is wrong.”

But he kept ardently repeating :

“No one will ever know—I shall never tell.”

“No, Monsieur Octave.　Do not spoil the happiness I have in knowing you.　It will do no good I assure you, and I had dreamed things—”

Then he left off speaking, having a revenge to take on woman-kind, and saying coarsely to himself: “You, at any rate, shall succumb!”　The door had not even been shut, the solemnity of the staircase seemed to ascend in the midst of the silence.　Lilitte was peacefully sleeping on the pillow of her crib.

When Marie and Octave rose up, they could find nothing to say to each other.　She, mechanically, went and looked at her daughter, took up the plate, and then laid it down again.　He remained silent, a prey to similar uneasiness, the adventure had been so unexpected ; and he recalled to mind how he had fraternally planned to restore the young woman to her husband’s arms.　Feeling the necessity of breaking that intolerable silence he ended by murmuring :

“You did not shut the door, then ?”

She glanced out on to the landing, and stammered :

“That is true, it was open.”

Her face wore an expression of disgust.　The young man too was now thinking that after all there was nothing the least funny in this adventure with a helpless woman, in the midst of that solitude.

“Dear me ! the book has fallen on the floor ! ” she continued, picking the volume up.

A corner of the cover was broken.　That drew them together, and afforded some relief.　Speech returned to them.　Marie appeared quite distressed.

“It was not my fault.　You see, I had covered it with paper for fear of soiling it.　We must have knocked it over, without doing so on purpose.”

“Was it there then ? ” asked Octave.　“I did not notice it. Oh ! for myself, I don’t care a bit !　But Campardon thinks so much of his books ! ”

They kept passing it from one to the other, trying to put the corner straight again.　Their fingers touched without a quiver. As they reflected on the consequences, they were quite dismayed at the accident which had happened to that handsome volume of George Sand.

"It was bound to end badly," concluded Marie, with tears in her eyes.

Octave was obliged to console her. He would invent some story, Campardon would not eat him. And their uneasiness returned, at the moment of separation. They would have liked at least to have said something amiable to each other; but the words choked them. Fortunately, a step was heard, it was the husband coming upstairs. Octave silently took her in his arms again and kissed her in his turn on the mouth. She once more complaisantly submitted, her lips icy cold as before. When he had noiselessly regained his room, he asked himself, as he took off his overcoat, whatever was it that she wanted? Women, he said, were decidedly very peculiar.

On the morrow, at the Campardons', just as lunch was finished, Octave was once more explaining that he had clumsily knocked the book over, when Marie entered the room. She was going to take Lilitte to the Tuileries gardens, and she had called to ask if they would allow Angèle to accompany her. And she smiled at Octave, without the least confusion, and glanced in her innocent way at the book lying on a chair.

"Why, I shall be only too pleased!" said Madame Campardon. "Angèle, go and put your hat on. I have no fear in trusting her with you."

Marie, looking very modest, in a simple dress of dark woollen stuff, talked of her husband, who had caught a cold the 'night before, and of the price of meat, which would soon prevent people buying it at all. Then, when she had left with Angèle, they all leant out of the windows to see them depart. Marie gently pushed Lilitte's perambulator along the pavement with her gloved hands; whilst Angèle, knowing that they were looking at her, walked beside her friend, with her eyes fixed on the ground.

"How respectable she looks!" exclaimed Madame Campardon. "And so gentle! so decorous!"

Then, slapping Octave on the shoulder, the architect said:

"Education is everything in a family, my dear fellow; there is nothing like it!"

CHAPTER V.

That evening, there was a reception and concert at the Duvey-riers'. Towards nine o'clock, Octave, who had been invited for the first time, was just finishing dressing. He was grave, and felt irritated with himself. Why had he missed fire with Valérie, a woman so well connected? And Berthe Josserand, ought he not to have reflected before refusing her? At the moment he was tying his white tie, the thought of Marie Pichon had become unbearable to him: five months in Paris, and nothing but that wretched adventure! It was as painful to him as a disgrace; for he well saw the emptiness and the uselessness of such a connection. And he vowed to himself, as he took up his gloves, that he would no longer waste his time in such a manner. He was decided to act, as he had at length got into society, where opportunities were certainly not wanting.

But, at the end of the passage, Marie was watching for him. Pichon not being there, he was obliged to go in for a moment.

"How smart you are!" murmured she.

They had never been invited to the Duveyriers', and that filled her with respect for the first floor drawing-room. Besides, she was jealous of no one, she had neither the strength nor the will to be so.

"I shall wait for you," resumed she holding up her forehead. "Do not come up too late; you can tell me how you amused yourself."

Octave had to deposit a kiss on her hair. Though relations were established between them, according to his fancy, when- ever a desire or want of something to do drew him to her, they did not as yet address each other very familiarly. He at length went downstairs; and she, leaning over the balustrade, followed him with her eyes.

At the same minute, quite a drama was enacting at the Josserands'. In the mind of the mother, the Duveyriers' party to which they were going, was to decide the question of a marriage between Berthe and Auguste Vabre. The latter, who had been vigorously attacked for a fortnight past, still hesitated, evidently entertaining doubts with respect to the dowry. So Madame Josserand, for the purpose of striking a decisive blow, had written to her brother, informing him of the contemplated marriage and reminding him of his promises, with the hope that, in his answer, he might say something that she could turn to account. And all the family were awaiting nine o'clock before the dining-room stove, dressed ready to go down, when Monsieur Gourd brought up a letter from uncle Bachelard which had been forgotten under Madame Gourd's snuff-box since the last delivery.

"Ah! at last!" said Madame Josserand, tearing open the envelope.

The father and the two daughters watched her anxiously as she read. Adèle, who had had to dress the ladies, was moving heavily about, clearing the table still covered with the dirty crockery from the dinner. But Madame Josserand turned ghastly pale.

"Nothing! nothing!" stuttered she, "not a clear sentence! He will see later on, at the time of the marriage. And he adds that he loves us very much all the same. What a confounded scoundrel!"

Monsieur Josserand in his evening dress sank into a chair. Hortense and Berthe also sat down, their legs feeling worn out; and they remained there, the one in blue, the other in pink, in their eternal costumes, altered once again.

"I have always said," murmured the father, "that Bachelard is imposing upon us. He will never give a sou."

Standing up in her flaring dress, Madame Josserand was reading the letter over again. Then, her anger burst out.

"Ah! men! men! That one, one would think him an idiot, he leads such a life. Well! not a bit of it! Though he never seems to be in his right mind, he opens his eye the moment any one speaks to him of money. Ah! men! men!"

She turned towards her daughters, to whom this lesson was addressed.

"It has come to the point, you see, that I ask myself why it is you have such a mania for getting married. Ah! if you had been worried out of your lives by it as I have! Not a fellow who loves you for yourselves and who would bring you a fortune without haggling! Millionaire uncles who, after having been fed for twenty years, will not even give their nieces a dowry! Husbands who are quite incompetent, oh! yes, sir, incompetent!"

Monsieur Josserand bowed his head. Adèle, who was not even listening, was quietly finishing clearing the table. But Madame Josserand suddenly turned angrily upon her.

"What are you doing there, spying upon us? Go into your kitchen and see if I am there!"

And she wound up by saying:

"In short, everything for those wretched beings, the men; and for us, not even enough to satisfy our hunger. Listen! they are only fit for being taken in! Remember my words!"

Hortense and Berthe nodded their heads, as though deeply penetrated by what their mother had been saying. For a long time past she had completely convinced them of man's utter inferiority, his unique part in life being to marry and to pay. A long silence ensued in the smoky dining-room, where the remainder of the things left on the table by Adèle emitted a stuffy smell of food. The Josserands, gorgeously arrayed, scattered on different chairs and overwhelmed, were forgetting the Duveyriers' concert as they reflected on the continual deceptions of life From the depths of the adjoining chamber, one could hear the snoring of Saturnin, whom they had sent to bed early.

At length, Berthe spoke:

"So it is all up. Shall we take our things off?"

But, at this, Madame Josserand's energy at once returned to her. Eh? what? take their things off! and why pray! were they not respectable people, was not an alliance with their family as good as with any other? The marriage should take place all the same, she would die rather. And she rapidly distributed their parts to each: the two young ladies were instructed to be very amiable to Auguste, and not to leave him until he had taken the leap; the father received the mission of overcoming old Vabre and Duveyrier, by agreeing with everything they said, if his intelligence was sufficient to enable him to do such a thing; as for herself, desirous of neglecting nothing, she undertook the women, she would know how to get them all on her side. Then, collecting her thoughts and casting a last glance round the dining-room, as though to make sure that no weapon had been forgotten, she put on the terrible look of a man of war about to lead his daughters to massacre, and uttered these words in a powerful voice:

"Let us go down!"

And down they went. In the solemnity of the staircase,

Monsieur Josserand was full of uneasiness, for he foresaw many disagreeable things for the too narrow conscience of a worthy man like himself.

When they entered, there was already a crush at the Duveyriers'. The enormous grand piano occupied one entire end of the drawing-room, the ladies being seated in front of it on rows of chairs, like at the theatre ; and two dense masses of black coats filled up the doorways leading to the dining-room and the parlour. The chandelier and the candelabra, and the six lamps standing on side-tables, lit up with a blinding light the white and gold room in which the red silk of the furniture and of the hangings showed up vividly. It was very warm, the fans produced a breeze at regular intervals, impregnated with the penetrating odours of bodices and bare shoulders.

Just at that moment, Madame Duveyrier was taking her seat at the piano. With a gesture, Madame Josserand smilingly begged she would not disturb herself; and she left her daughters in the midst of the men, as she accepted a chair for herself between Valérie [and Madame Juzeur. Monsieur Josserand had made for the parlour, where the landlord, Monsieur Vabre, was dozing at his usual place, in the corner of a sofa. There were also Campardon, Théophile and Auguste Vabre, Doctor Juillerat and the Abbé Mauduit, forming a group; whilst Trublot and Octave, who had rejoined each other, had flown from the music to the end of the dining-room. Near them, and behind the stream of black coats, Duveyrier, thin and tall of stature, was looking fixedly at his wife seated at the piano waiting for silence. In the button-hole of his coat he wore the ribbon of the Legion of Honour in a neat little rosette.

"Hush ! hush ! silence !" murmured some friendly voices.

Then, Clotilde Duveyrier commenced one of Chopin's most difficult serenades. Tall and handsome, with magnificent red hair, she had a long face, as pale and cold as snow ; and, in her grey eyes, music alone kindled a flame, an exaggerated passion on which she existed without any other desire either of the flesh or the spirit. Duveyrier continued watching her ; then, after the first bars, a nervous exasperation contracted his lips, he drew aside and kept himself at the farthest end of the dining-room. On his clean-shaven face, with its pointed chin and eyes all askew, large red blotches indicated a bad blood, quite a pollution festering just beneath the skin.

Trublot, who was examining him, quietly observed :

" He does not like music."

" Nor I either," replied Octave.

" Oh ! the unpleasantness is not the same for you. A man, my dear fellow, who was always lucky. Not a whit more intelligent than another, but who was helped along by every one. Belonging to an old middle-class family, the father an ex-presiding judge, called to the bar the moment he had completed his studies, then appointed. deputy judge at Reims, from whence he was removed to Paris and made judge of the Court of First Instance, decorated, and now a counsellor before he is forty-five years of age. It's stiff, isn't it ? But he does not like music, that piano has been the bane of his life. One cannot have everything."

Meanwhile, Clotilde was knocking off the difficult passages with extraordinary composure. She handled her piano like a circus-rider her horse. Octave's attention was solely occupied with the furious working of her hands.

" Just look at her fingers," said he, " it is astonishing ! A quarter of an hour of that must hurt her immensely."

And they both fell to talking of women without troubling themselves any further with what she was playing. Octave felt rather embarrassed on catching sight of Valérie : what line of conduct should he pursue ? ought he to speak to her or pretend not to see her ? Trublot affected a great disdain : there was still not one to take his fancy ; and, as his companion protested, looking about, and saying that there was surely one amongst the number who would suit him, he learnedly declared :

" Well ! take your choice, and you will see afterwards, when the gloss is off. Eh ? not the one with the feathers over there ; nor the blonde in the mauve dress ; nor that old party, though she at least has the merit of being fat. I tell you, my dear fellow, it is absurd to seek for anything of the kind in society. Plenty of airs, but not a particle of pleasure ! "

Octave smiled. He had to make his position in the world ; he could not afford merely to consider his taste, like Trublot, whose father was so rich. The sight of those rows of women set him musing, he asked himself which among them he would have chosen for his fortune and his pleasure, if he had been allowed to take one of them away. As he was weighing them with a glance, one after the other, he suddenly exclaimed :

" Hallo ! my employer's wife ! She visits here then ? "

" Did you not know it ? " asked Trublot. " In spite of the difference in their ages, Madame Hédouin and Madame

TRUBLOT CRITICISING THE FEMALE GUESTS AT THE DUVEYRIERS' RECEPTION.

p. 88.

Duveyrier are two school friends. They used to be inseparable, and were called the polar bears, because they were always fully twenty degrees below freezing point. They are some more of the ornamental class! Duveyrier would be in a sad plight if he had not some other hot water-bottle for his feet in winter time!"

But Octave had now become serious. For the first time, he beheld Madame Hédouin in a low neck dress, her shoulders and arms bare, with her black hair plaited in front; and she appeared in the ardent light as the realisation of his desires: a superb woman, extremely healthy and calmly beautiful, who would be a benefit in every way to a man. Complicated plans were already absorbing him, when an awful din awoke him from his dream.

"What a relief! it is finished!" said Trublot.

Compliments were being showered upon Clotilde. Madame Josserand, who had hastened to her, was pressing her hands; whilst the men resumed their conversation, and the ladies fanned themselves more vigorously. Duveyrier then ventured back into the parlour, where Trublot and Octave followed him. Whilst in the midst of the skirts, the former whispered into the latter's ear:

"Look on your right. The angling has commenced."

It was Madame Josserand who was setting Berthe on to Auguste. He had imprudently gone up to the ladies to wish them good evening. His head was not bothering him so much just then; he merely felt a touch of neuralgia in his left eye; but he dreaded the end of the party, for there was going to be singing, and nothing was worse for him than this.

"Berthe," said the mother, "tell Monsieur Vabre of the remedy you copied for him out of that book. Oh! it is a sovereign cure for headaches!"

And, having started the affair, she left them standing beside a window.

"By Jove! they are going in for chemistry!" murmured Trublot.

In the parlour, Monsieur Josserand, desirous of pleasing his wife, had remained seated before Monsieur Vabre, feeling very embarrassed, for the old gentleman was asleep, and he did not dare awake him to do the amiable. But, when the music ceased, Monsieur Vabre raised his eye-lids. Short and stout, and completely bald, save for two tufts of white hair over his ears, he had a ruddy face, with thick lips, and round eyes almost at the top of his head. Monsieur Josserand having politely inquired after his health, the conversation began. The retired notary, whose four or five ideas always followed the same order, commenced by making an observation about Versailles, where he had practiced during forty years; then, he talked of his sons, once more regretting that neither the one nor the other had shown himself capable of carrying on the practice, so that he had decided to sell it and inhabit Paris; after which, he came to the history of his house, the building of which was the romance of his life.

"I have buried three hundred thousand francs in it, sir. A superb speculation, my architect said. But to-day I have great difficulty in getting the value of my money; more especially as all my children have come to live here, with the idea of not paying me, and I should never have a quarter's rent, if I did not apply for it myself on the fifteenth. Fortunately, I have work to console me."

"Do you still work much?" asked Monsieur Josserand.

"Always, always, sir!" replied the old gentleman with the energy of despair. "Work is life to me."

And he explained his great task. For ten years past, he had every year waded through the official catalogue of the exhibition of paintings, writing on tickets each painter's name, and the paintings exhibited. He spoke of it with an air of weariness and anguish; the whole year scarcely gave him sufficient time, the task was often so arduous, that it sometimes proved too much for him; for instance, when a lady artist married, and then exhibited under her husband's name, how was he to see his way clearly?

"My work will never be complete, it is that which is killing me," murmured he.

"You take a great interest in art, do you not?" resumed Monsieur Josserand, to flatter him.

Monsieur Vabre looked at him, full of surprise.

"No, I do not require to see the paintings. It is merely a matter of statistics. There now! I had better go to bed, my head will be all the clearer to-morrow. Good-night, sir."

He leant on a walking-stick, which he used even in the house, and withdrew, walking painfully, the lower part of his back already succumbing to paralysis. Monsieur Josserand felt perplexed: he had not uderstood very clearly, he feared he had not spoken of the tickets with sufficient enthusiasm.

But a slight hubbub coming from the drawing-room, attracted

Trublot and Octave again to the door. They saw a lady of about fifty enter, very stout, and still handsome, followed by a young man, correctly attired, and with a serious air about him.

"What! they arrive together!" murmured Trublot. "Well! I never!"

The new-comers were Madame Dambreville and Léon Josserand. She had undertaken to find him a wife; then, whilst waiting, she had kept him for her own personal use; and they were now in their full honeymoon, attracting general attention in the middle-class drawing-rooms. There were whisperings amongst the mothers who had daughters to marry. But Madame Duveyrier was advancing to meet Madame Dambreville, who supplied her with young men for her choruses. Madame Josserand at once supplanted her, and overwhelmed her son's friend with all sorts of attentions, reflecting that she might have need of her. Léon coldly exchanged a few words with his mother; yet, she was now beginning to think that he would after all be able to do something for himself.

"Berthe does not see you," said she to Madame Dambreville. "Excuse her, she is telling Monsieur Auguste of some remedy."

"But they are very well together, we must leave them alone," replied the lady, understanding at a glance.

They both watched Berthe maternally. She had ended by pushing Auguste into the recess caused by the window, and was keeping him there with her pretty gestures. He was becoming animated, and running the risk of a bad headache.

Meanwhile, a group of grave men were talking politics in the parlour. There had been a stormy sitting of the Senate the day before, where they were discussing the address respecting the Roman question; and Doctor Juillerat, whose opinions were atheistical and revolutionary, was maintaining that Rome ought to be given to the king of Italy; whilst the Abbé Mauduit, one of the heads of the Ultramontane party prophesied the most awful catastrophes, if Frenchmen did not shed the last drop of their blood in supporting the tempo al power of the pope.

"Perhaps some *modus vivendi* may be found which will prove acceptable to both parties," observed Léon Josserand arriving.

He was just then the secretary of a celebrated ba·rister, one of the deputies of the left. During two years, having nothing to expect from his parents, whose mediocrity moreover exasperated him, he had frequented the students' quarter in the guise of a ferocious demagogue. But, since his acquaintance with the Dambrevilles, at whose expense he was satisfying his first appetites, he was calming down, and drifting into the learned Republican.

"No, no agreement is possible," said the priest. "The Church could not make terms."

"Then, it shall vanish!" exclaimed the doctor.

And, though great friends, having met at the bedsides of all the departing souls of the Saint-Roch district, they seemed irreconcilable, the doctor thin and nervous, the priest fat and affable. The latter preserved a polite smile, even when making his most absolute statements, like a man of the world, tolerant for the short-comings of existence, but also like a Catholic who did not intend to abandon any of his religious belief.

"The Church vanish, pooh!" said Campardon with a furious air, just to be well with the priest, from whom he was expecting a large order.

Besides, it was the opinion of almost all the gentlemen : it could not vanish. Théophile Vabre, who, coughing and spitting, and shaking with fever, dreamed of universal happiness through the organization of a humanitarian republic, alone maintained that, perhaps, it would be transformed.

The priest resumed in his gentle voice :

"The Empire is committing suicide. You will see it is so, next year, when the elections come on."

"Oh! as for the Empire, we permit you to rid us of it," said the doctor boldly. "You will be rendering us a precious service."

Then, Duveyrier, who seemed listening profoundly, shook his head. He belonged to an Orleanist family ; but he owed everything to the Empire and considered he ought to defend it.

"Believe me," he at length declared severely, "do not shake the foundations of society, or everything will collapse. It is we, as sure as fate, who suffer from every catastrophe."

"Very true!" observed Monsieur Josserand, who entertained no opinion, but remembered his wife's instructions.

All spoke at once. None of them liked the Empire. Doctor Juillerat condemned the Mexican expedition, the Abbé Mauduit blamed the recognition of the kingdom of Italy. Yet, Théophile Vabre and even Léon felt anxious when Duveyrier threatened them with another '93. What was the use of those continual revolutions? had not liberty been obtained? and the hatred of new ideas, the fear of the people wishing their share, calmed the

liberalism of those satisfied middle-class men. They all declared, however, that they would vote against the Emperor, for
he was in need of a lesson.

"Ah ! how they bore me ! " said Trublot, who had been trying
to understand for some minutes past.

Octave persuaded him to return to the ladies. In the recess
of the window, Berthe was deafening Auguste with her laughter.
This big fellow, with his pale blood, was forgetting his fear of
women, and was becoming quite red, beneath the attacks of the
lovely girl, whose breath warmed his face. Madame Josserand,
however, probably considered that the affair was dragging, for
she looked fixedly at Hortense ; and the latter obediently went
and gave her sister her assistance.

"Are you quite recovered, madame?" Octave dared to ask Valérie.

" Quite, sir, thank you," replied she coolly, as though she remembered nothing.

Madame Juzeur spoke to the young man about some old lace
which she wished to show him, to have his opinion of it ; and
he had to promise to look in on her for a moment on the morrow.
Then, as the Abbé Mauduit re-entered the drawing-room, she
called him and made him sit beside her with an air of rapture.

The conversation had again resumed. The ladies were discussing their servants.

" Well ! yes," continued Madame Duveyrier, " I am satisfied
with Clémence, she is a very clean and very active girl."

" And your Hippolyte," asked Madame Josserand, " had you
not the intention of discharging him ?"

Just then, Hippolyte, the footman, was handing round some
ices. When he had withdrawn, tall, strong, and with a florid
complexion, Clotilde answered in an embarrassed way :

" We have decided to keep him. It is so unpleasant changing ! You know, servants get used to one another, and I
should not like to part with Clémence."

Madame Josserand hastened to agree with her, feeling that
they were on delicate ground. There was some hope of marrying the two together, some day ; and the Abbé Mauduit, whom
the Duveyriers' had consulted in the matter, slowly wagged his
head, as though to dissemble a state of affairs known to all the
house, but of which no one ever spoke. All the ladies now
opened their hearts : Valérie had sent another servant about
her business that very morning, and that made three in a
week ; Madame Juzeur had decided to take a young girl of
fifteen from the foundling hospital so as to teach her herself ; as

for Madame Josserand, her complaints of Adèle seemed never likely to cease, a slut, a good-for-nothing, whose goings-on were most extraordinary. And they all, feeling languid in the blaze of the candles and the perfume of the flowers, sank deeper into these ante-room stories, wading through greasy account-books, and taking a delight in relating the insolence of a coach-man or of a scullery-maid.

"Have you seen Julie?" abruptly asked Trublot of Octave, in a mysterious tone of voice.

And, as the other looked at him in amazement, he added :

"My dear fellow, she is stunning. Go and see her. Just pretend you want to go somewhere, and then slip into the kitchen. She is stunning!"

He was speaking of the Duveyriers' cook. The ladies' conversation was taking a turn: Madame Josserand was describing, with overflowing admiration, a very modest estate which the Duveyriers had near Villeneuve-Saint-Georges, and which she had merely caught a glimpse of from the train, one day when she was going to Fontainebleau. But Clotilde did not like the country, she lived there as little as possible, merely during the holidays of her son, Gustave, who was then studying rhetoric at the Lycée Bonaparte.

"Caroline is right in not wishing to have any children," declared she, turning towards Madame Hédouin, seated two chairs away from her. "The little things interfere with all your habits!"

Madame Hédouin said that she liked them a good deal. But she was much too busy; her husband was constantly away, and she had everything to look after.

Octave, standing up behind her chair, searched with a side glance the little curly hairs, as black as ink, on the nape of her neck, and the snowy whiteness of her bosom, which—her dress being open very low—disappeared in a mass of lace. She ended by completely confusing him, as she sat there so calm, speaking but rarely and with a continuous smile on her handsome face ; he had never before seen so superb a creature, even at Marseilles. Decidedly, it was worth trying, though it would be a long task.

"Having children robs women of their good looks so quickly!" said he in her ear, leaning over, feeling an absolute necessity to speak to her, and yet finding nothing else to say.

She slowly raised her large eyes, and then replied with the simple air with which she would give him an order at the warehouse.

"Oh! no, Monsieur Octave; with me it is not for that.
One must have the time, that is all."

But Madame Duveyrier intervened. She had merely greeted
the young man with a slight bow, when Campardon had introduced him to her; and now she was examining him, and
listening to him, without seeking to hide a sudden interest.
When she heard him conversing with her friend, she could not
help asking :

"Pray, excuse me, sir. What voice have you?"

He did not understand immediately; but he ended by saying
that his was a tenor voice. Then, Clotilde became quite enthusiastic : a tenor voice, really! what a piece of luck, tenor
voices were becoming so rare! For instance, for the "Blessing
of the Daggers," which they were going to sing by-and-by, she
had never been able to find more than three tenors among her
acquaintances, when at least five were required. And, suddenly
excited, her eyes sparkling, she had to restrain herself from
going at once to the piano to try his voice. He was obliged to
promise to come one evening for the purpose. Trublot, who
was behind him, kept nudging him with his elbow, ferociously
enjoying himself in his impassibility.

"Ah! so you are in for it too!" murmured he, when she had
moved away. "For myself, my dear fellow, she first of all thought
I had a barytone voice; then, seeing that I did not get on 'all
right, she tried me as a tenor; but as I went no better, she has
decided to use me to-night as bass. I am one of the monks."

But he had to leave Octave as Madame Duveyrier was just
then calling him; they were about to sing the chorus, the great
piece of the evening. There was quite a commotion. Some
fifteen men, all amateurs, and all recruited among the guests
of the house, painfully opened a passage for themselves through
the groups of ladies, to form in front of the piano. They were
constantly brought to a standstill, and asked to be excused, in
voices drowned by the hum of conversations; whilst the fans
were moved more rapidly in the increasing heat. At length,
Madame Duveyrier counted them; they were all there, and she
distributed them their parts, which she had copied out herself.
Campardon took the part of Saint-Bris; a young auditor attached to the Council of State was intrusted with De Nevers's
few bars; then came eight nobles, four aldermen, and three
monks, represented by barristers, clerks, and simple householders. She, who accompanied, had also reserved herself the
part of Valentine, passionate cries which she uttered whilst

striking chords; for she would have no lady amongst the gentlemen, the resigned troop of whom she directed with all the severity of a conductor of an orchestra.

The conversations continued, an intolerable noise issued from the parlour especially, where the political discussions were evidently entering on a disagreeable phase. Then Clotilde, taking a key from her pocket, tapped gently with it on the piano. A murmur ran through the room, the voices dropped, two streams of black coats again flowed to the doors; and, looking over the heads, one beheld for a moment Duveyrier's red spotted face wearing an agonised expression. Octave had remained standing behind Madame Hédouin, the glances from his lowered eyes losing themselves in the shadows of her bosom, in the depths of the lace. But when the silence was almost complete, there was a burst of laughter, and he raised his head. It was Berthe, who was amused at some joke of Auguste's; she had heated his poor blood to such a point that he was becoming quite jovial. Every person in the drawing-room looked at them, mothers became grave, members of the family exchanged a glance.

"She has such spirits!" murmured Madame Josserand tenderly, in such a way as to be heard.

Hortense, close to her sister, was assisting her with complaisant abnegation, joining in her laughter, and pushing her up against the young man; whilst the breeze which entered through the partly open window behind them gently swelled the big crimson silk curtains.

But a sepulchral voice resounded, all the heads turned towards the piano. Campardon, his mouth wide open, his beard spread out in a lyrical blast, was giving the first line:

"Yes, we are here assembled by the queen's command."

Clotilde at once ran up a scale and down again; then, her eyes fixed on the ceiling, a look of fright on her face, she uttered the cry:

"I tremble!"

And the whole thing followed, the eight barristers, clerks and householders, their noses on their parts, in the postures of schoolboys humming and hawing over a page of Greek, swore that they were ready to deliver France. This opening was a surprise, for the voices were stifled beneath the low ceiling, one was unable to catch more than a sort of hum, like a noise of passing carts full of paving stones causing the windows to rattle. But when Saint-Bris's melodious line: "For this holy cause—" unrolled the principal theme, some of the ladies recognised it and nodded their heads knowingly. All were warming to the work, the nobles shouted out at random : " We swear it !—We will follow you ! " and, each time, it was like an explosion which caught the guests full in the chest.

"They sing too loud," murmured Octave in Madame Hédouin's ear.

She did not move. Then, as De Nevers's and Valentine's explanations bored him, more especially as the auditor attached to the Council of State was a false barytone, he corresponded by signs with Trublot who, whilst awaiting the entrance of the monks, drew his attention with a wink to the window where Berthe was continuing to keep Auguste imprisoned. Now, they were alone, in the fresh breeze from outside ; whilst, with her ear pricked up, Hortense stood before them, leaning against the curtain and mechanically twisting the loop. No one was watching them now, even Madame Josserand and Madame Dambreville were looking away, after an instinctive exchange of glances.

Meanwhile, Clotilde, her fingers on the keys, carried away and unable to risk a gesture, stretched her neck and addressed to the music stand this oath intended for De Nevers :

" Ah ! from to-day all my blood is yours ! "

The aldermen had made their entrance, a substitute, two attorneys, and a notary. The quartette was well delivered, the line : " For this holy cause—" returned, spread out, supported by half the chorus, in a continuous expansion. Campardon, his mouth opened wider and wider, gave the orders for the combat, with a terrible roll of syllables. And, suddenly, the chant of the monks burst forth : Trublot sang from his stomach, so as to reach the low notes.

Octave, having had the curiosity to watch him singing, was struck with surprise, when he again cast his eyes in the direction of the window. As though carried away by the chorus, Hortense had unfastened the loop, by a movement which might have been unintentional ; and, in falling, the big crimson silk curtain had completely hidden Auguste and Berthe. They were there behind it, leaning against the window bar, without a movement betraying their presence. Octave no longer troubled himself about Trublot, who was just then blessing the daggers : " Holy daggers, by us be blessed." Whatever could they be doing behind that curtain? The fugue was commencing ; to the deep tones of the monks, the chorus replied : "Death ! death ! death !" And still they did not move ; perhaps, feeling the heat too much, they were simply watching the cabs pass. But Saint-Bris's melodious line had again returned, by degrees all the voices uttered it with the whole strength of their lungs, progressively and in a final outburst of extraordinary force. It was like a gust of wind burying itself in the farthest corners of the too narrow room, scaring the candles, making the guests turn pale and their ears bleed. Clotilde furiously strummed away on the piano, carrying the gentlemen along with her with a glance ; then the voices quieted down, almost whispering : "At midnight, let there be not a sound !" and she continued on alone, using the soft pedal, and imitating the cadenced and distant footsteps of some departing patrol.

Then, suddenly, in the midst of this expiring music, of this relief after so much uproar, one heard a voice exclaim :

" You are hurting me !"

All the heads again turned towards the window. Madame Dambreville kindly made herself useful, by going and pulling the curtain aside. And the whole drawing-room beheld Auguste looking very confused and Berthe very red, still leaning against the bar of the window.

" What is the matter, my treasure ?" asked Madame Josserand earnestly.

" Nothing, mamma. Monsieur Auguste knocked my arm with the window. I was so warm !"

She turned redder still. There were affected smiles and scandalized pouts. Madame Duveyrier, who, for a month past, had been trying to keep her brother out of Berthe's way, turned quite pale, more especially as the incident had spoilt the effect of her chorus. However, after the first moment of surprise, the applause burst forth, she was congratulated, and some amiable things were said about the gentlemen. How delightfully they had sung ! what pains she must have taken to get them to sing so well in time ! Really, it could not have been rendered better at a theatre. But, beneath all this praise, she could not fail to hear the whispering which went round the drawing-room : the young girl was too much compromised, a marriage had become inevitable.

" Well ! he is hooked !" observed Trublot as he rejoined Octave. " What a ninny ! as though he could not have pinched her whilst we were all bellowing ! I thought all the while that he was taking advantage of it. You know, in drawing-rooms

CONFUSION OF BERTHE AND AUGUSTE AT THE DUVEYRIERS' RECEPTION.

p. 98.

where they go in for singing, one pinches a lady, and if she cries out it does not matter, no one hears!"

Berthe, now very calm, was again laughing, whilst Hortense looked at Auguste with her crabbed air of a girl who had taken a diploma; and, in their triumph, the mother's lessons reappeared, the undisguised contempt for man. All the gentlemen had now invaded the drawing-room, mingling with the ladies, and raising their voices. Monsieur Josserand, feeling sick at heart through Berthe's adventure, had drawn near his wife. He listened uneasily as she thanked Madame Dambreville for all her kindness to their son Léon, whom she had most decidedly changed to his advantage. But his uneasiness increased when he heard her again refer to her daughters. She pretended to converse in low tones with Madame Juzeur, though speaking all the while for Valérie and Clotilde, who were standing up close beside her.

"Well, yes! her uncle mentioned it in a letter again to-day; Berthe will have fifty thousand francs. It is not much, no doubt, but when the money is there, and as safe as the bank too!"

This lie roused his indignation. He could not help stealthily touching her shoulder. She looked at him, forcing him to lower his eyes before the resolute expression of her face. Then, as Madame Duveyrier turned round quite amiably, she asked her with great concern for news of her father.

"Oh! papa has probably gone to bed," replied the young woman, quite won over. "He works so hard!"

Monsieur Josserand said that Monsieur Vabre had indeed retired, so as to have his ideas clear on the morrow. And he mumbled a few words: a most remarkable mind, extraordinary faculties; asking himself at the same time where he would get that dowry from, and thinking what a figure he would cut, the day the marriage contract had to be signed.

A great noise of chairs being moved now filled the drawing-room. The ladies passed into the dining-room, where the tea was ready served. Madame Josserand sailed victoriously in, surrounded by her daughters and the Vabre family. Soon only the group of serious men remained amidst the vacant chairs. Campardon had button-holed the Abbé Mauduit: there was a question of some repairs to the calvary at Saint-Roch. The architect said he was quite free, for the diocese of Evreux gave him very little to do. All he had in hand there were a pulpit and a heating apparatus, and also some new ranges to be placed in the bishop's kitchen, which work his inspector was quite competent to see after. Then, the priest promised to have the matter definitely settled at the next meeting of the vestry. And they both joined the group where Duveyrier was being complimented on a judgment, of which he admitted himself to be the author; the presiding judge, who was his friend, reserved certain easy and brilliant tasks for him, so as to bring him to the fore.

"Have you read this last novel?" asked Léon, looking through a number of the "Revue des Deux Mondes," lying on a table. "It is well written; but there is another adultery, it is really becoming wearisome!"

And the conversation turned upon morality. Campardon said that there were some very virtuous women. All the others agreed with him. Moreover, according to the architect, one could · always live peacefully at home, if one only went the right way about it. Théophile Vabre observed that it depended on the woman, without explaining himself farther. They wished to have Doctor Juillerat's opinion, but he smiled and begged to be excused: he considered virtue was a question of health. During this, Duveyrier had remained wrapped in thought.

"Dear me!" murmured he at length, "these authors exaggerate; adultery is very rare amongst educated people. A woman who comes from a good family, has in her soul a flower—"

He was for grand sentiments, he uttered the word "ideal" with an emotion which brought a mist to his eyes. And he said that the Abbé Mauduit was right when the latter spoke of the necessity for the wife and mother having some religious belief. The conversation was thus brought back to religion and politics, at the point where these gentlemen had previously left it. The Church would never disappear, because it was the foundation of all families, the same as it was the natural support of governments.

"As a sort of police, perhaps it is," murmured the doctor.

Duveyrier, however, did not like politics being discussed in his house, and he contented himself with severely declaring, as he glanced into the dining-room where Berthe and Hortense were stuffing Auguste with sandwiches:

"There is one fact, gentlemen, which settles everything: religion moralizes marriage."

At the same moment, Trublot, seated on a sofa beside Octave, was bending towards the latter.

"By the way," asked he, "would you like me to get you invited to a lady's where there is plenty of amusement?"

And as his companion desired to know what kind of a lady, he added, indicating the counsellor by a sign:

"His mistress."

"Impossible!" said Octave in amazement.

Trublot slowly opened and closed his eyes. It was so. When one married a woman who was disobliging and disgusted with one's little ailments, and who strummed on her piano to the point of making all the dogs of the neighbourhood ill, one had to go elsewhere and be made a fool of!

"Let us moralize marriage, gentlemen, let us moralize marriage," repeated Duveyrier in his rigid way, with his inflamed face, where Octave now distinguished the foul blood of secret vices.

The gentlemen were being called into the dining-room. The Abbé Mauduit, left for a moment alone in the middle of the empty drawing-room, looked from a distance at the crush of guests. His fat shrewd face bore an expression of sadness. He who heard all those ladies, both old and young, at confession, knew them all in the flesh, the same as Doctor Juillerat, and he had had to end by merely watching over appearances, like a master of the ceremonies throwing the mantle of religion over the corruption of the middle classes, trembling at the certainty of a final downfall, the day when the canker would appear in all its hideousness. At times, in his ardent and sincere faith of a priest, his indignation would overcome him. But his smile returned; he took the cup of tea which Berthe came and offered him, and conversed a minute with her so as to cover, as it were, the scandal of the window, with his sacred character; and he again became the man of the world, resigned to merely insisting upon a decent behaviour from those sinners, who were escaping him, and who would have compromised providence.

"Well, these are fine goings-on!" murmured Octave, whose respect for the house had received another shock.

And seeing Madame Hédouin move towards the ante-room, he wished to reach there before her, and followed Trublot, who was also leaving. His intention was to see her home. She refused; it was scarcely midnight, and she lived so near. Then, a rose having fallen from the bouquet at her breast, he picked it up in spite and made a pretence of keeping it. The young woman's beautiful eyebrows contracted; then, she said in her quiet way:

" Pray open the door for me, Monsieur Octave.   Thank you."

When she had departed, the young man, who was rather confused, looked for Trublot.   But Trublot had disappeared, the same as he had done at the Josserands'.   This time also he must have slipped along the passage leading to the kitchen.

Octave, greatly put out, went off to his room, his rose in his hand.   Upstairs, he beheld Marie leaning over the balustrade, at the place where he had left her ; she had been listening for his footstep, and had hastened to see him come up.   And when she had made him enter her room, she said:

" Jules has not yet come home.   Did you enjoy yourself ? Were there any pretty dresses ? "

But she did not give him time to answer.   She had caught sight of the rose, and was seized with a childish delight.

" Is that flower for me ?   You have thought of me ?   Ah ! how nice of you ! how nice of you ! "

And her eyes filled with tears, she became quite confused and very red.   Then Octave, suddenly moved, kissed her tenderly.

Towards one o'clock, the Josserands withdrew in their turn. Adèle always left a candle and some matches on a chair. When the members of the family, who had not exchanged a word coming upstairs, had entered the dining-room, from whence they had gone down in despair, they suddenly yielded to a mad delirious joy, holding each others' hands, and dancing like savages round the table ; the father himself gave way to the contagion, the mother cut capers, and the daughters uttered little inarticulate cries ; whilst the candle in the middle of them showed up their huge shadows careering along the walls.

" At last, it is settled ! " said Madame Josserand, out of breath, dropping on to a chair.

But she jumped up again at once, in a fit of maternal affection, and ran and imprinted two big kisses on Berthe's cheeks.

" I am very pleased, very pleased indeed with you, my darling.   You have just rewarded me for all my efforts.   My poor girl, my poor girl it is true then, this time ! "

Her voice was choking, her heart was in her mouth.   She succumbed in her flaring dress, beneath the weight of a deep and sincere emotion, suddenly overwhelmed in the hour of her triumph by the fatigues of her terrible campaign which had lasted three winters.   Berthe had to swear that she was not ill; for her mother thought she looked ill, and was full of little attentions, almost insisting on making her a cup of infusion. When the young girl was in bed, she went barefooted and carefully tucked her in, like in the already distant days of her child-hood.

Meanwhile, Monsieur Josserand, his head on his pillow, awaited her. She blew out the light, and stepped over him, to reach the side of the bed nearest the wall. He was wrapped in thought, his uneasiness having returned, his conscience all up-set by that promise of a dowry of fifty thousand francs. And he ventured to mention his scruples aloud. Why make a promise, when one has a doubt of being able to keep it? It was not honest.

"Not honest!" exclaimed Madame Josserand in the dark, her voice resuming its ferocious tone. "It is no thonest to let your daughters become old maids, sir; yes, old maids, such was perhaps your dream! We have plenty of time to turn about, we can talk the matter over, we will end by persuading her uncle. And understand, sir, that in my family, we have always been honest!"

CHAPTER VI.

On the morrow, which was a Sunday, Octave with his eyes open lay thinking for an hour in the warmth of the sheets. He awoke happy, full of the lucidity of the morning laziness. What need was there to hurry? He was very comfortable at "The Ladies' Paradise," he was there losing all his provincial ways, and he had an absolute and profound conviction of one day possessing Madame Hédouin, who would make his fortune; but it was an affair that required prudence, a long series of gallant tactics, which his voluptuous passion for women was already enjoying by anticipation. As he was dozing off again, forming his plans, allowing himself six months to succeed in, Marie Pichon's image resulted in calming his impatience. A woman like that was a real boon; he had merely to stretch out his arm, when he required her, and she did not cost him a sou. Whilst awaiting the other, he could certainly not hope for anything better. In his half-slumber, this bargain and this convenience ended by making him quite tender-hearted: she appeared to him very nice and pretty with all her good-nature, and he promised himself he would behave better to her in future.

"Hang it! nine o'clock!" said he thoroughly roused by his clock striking. "I must get up."

A fine rain was falling. Then, he made up his mind not to go out all day. He would accept an invitation to dine with the Pichons, which he had been refusing for some time past, dreading another meeting with the Vuillaumes; it would please Marie, he would find opportunities of kissing her behind the doors; and, as she was always asking for books, he even thought of giving her the surprise of a quantity which he had, stowed away in one of his boxes in the loft. When he was dressed, he went down to Monsieur Gourd to get the key of this common loft, where all the tenants got rid of whatever things were in their way, or which they had no present use for.

Down below, on that damp morning, it was quite stifling in the heated staircase, the imitation marble, the tall looking-glasses, and the mahogany doors of which were covered with steam. Under the porch, a poorly clad woman, mother Pérou, to whom the Gourds paid four sous an hour for doing the heavy work of the house, was washing the pavement with plenty of water, in face of the icy-cold blast blowing from the court-yard.

"Eh! I say old 'un, just rub that a bit better, that I may not find a spot on it!" called out Monsieur Gourd, warmly covered up, standing on the threshold of his apartment.

And, Octave arriving, he talked to him of mother Pérou with the brutal domineering spirit, the mad mania for revenge, of former servants who were being served in their turn.

"A lazy creature that I can do nothing with! I should like to have seen her at the duke's! Ah well! they stood no nonsense there! I'll send her to the right about, if she doesn't give me my money's worth! That's all I care about. But, excuse me, what is it you require, Monsieur Mouret?"

Octave asked for the key. Then the doorkeeper, without hurrying himself, continued to explain to him that, if they had chosen, Madame Gourd and he, they might have lived respect-ably in their own house, at Mort-la-Ville; only, Madame Gourd adored Paris, in spite of her swollen legs which prevented her getting as far as the pavement; and they were waiting until they had made their income into a round sum, their hearts almost breaking moreover and drawing back, each time that they felt a desire to go and live at last upon the little fortune which they had got together sou by sou.

"No one had better bother me," concluded he, drawing him-self up to the full height of his handsome figure. "I'm no longer working for a living. The key of the loft you said, did you not, Monsieur Mouret? Wherever have we put the key of the loft, my dear?"

Madame Gourd, tenderly seated before a wood fire, the flames of which enlivened the big light room, was drinking her coffee and milk out of a silver cup. She had no idea; perhaps in one of the drawers. And, whilst soaking her toast, she did not take her eyes off the door of the servants' staircase, at the other end of the courtyard, looking barer and severer than ever in the rain.

"Look out! here she is!" said she suddenly, as a woman appeared in the doorway.

Monsieur Gourd at once went and placed himself before his room, so as to prevent the woman from passing, whilst she slackened her footsteps with an air of anxiety.

"We have been on the look-out for her since the first thing this morning, Monsieur Mouret," resumed he, in a low voice. "Last night we saw her pass. You know she comes from that carpenter, upstairs, the only workman we have in the house, thank goodness! And if the landlord only listened to me, he would let the room remain empty, a servant's room which does not go with the other apartments. For one hundred and thirty francs a year, it is really not worth while having such a scum in the place—"

He interrupted himself, to ask the woman roughly :

"Where do you come from?"

"From upstairs, of course!" answered she, walking on.

Then, he exploded.

"We'll have no women here, understand! The man who brings you has already been told so. If you return here to sleep, I'll fetch a policeman, that's what I'll do! and we'll see if you'll continue your goings-on in a respectable house!"

"Oh! don't bother me!" said the woman. "I've a right here ; I shall come if I choose."

And she went off, followed by Monsieur Gourd's indignation, as he talked of going up to fetch the landlord. Had any one ever heard the like! such a creature amongst respectable people, who did not tolerate the least immorality! And it seemed as though that little room occupied by a workman was the abomination of the house, a bad place, the supervision of which offended the doorkeeper's delicacy and spoilt his rest at night.

"And that key!" Octave ventured to observe.

But the doorkeeper, furious at a tenant's having been able to see his authority disputed, fell on mother Pérou, wishing to show that he knew how to make himself obeyed. Did she take him for a fool? She had again splashed the door of his room with her broom. If he paid her out of his own pocket, it was to save him from dirtying his hands, and yet he continually had to clean up after her. Might the devil take him if he was ever again charitable enough to have anything more to do with her! she could go and croak. Without answering, and bent double by the fatigue of this task so much above her strength, the old body continued to scrub with her skinny arms, struggling to keep back her tears, so great was the respectful fright that broad shouldered gentleman in cap and slippers caused her.

"I remember, my darling," called Madame Gourd from her easy chair in which she passed the day, warming her fat person. "It was I who hid the key under the shirts, so that the servants should not be always going into the loft. Come, give it to Monsieur Mouret."

"They're a nice lot, too, those servants!" murmured Monsieur Gourd, who, from his many years in service, had preserved a hatred for menials. "Here is the key, sir; but I must ask you to bring it me back, for no place can be left open, without the servants getting in there and misconducting themselves."

To save crossing the wet courtyard, Octave went back up the principal staircase. It was not till he had reached the fourth floor that he gained the servants' staircase, by taking the door of communication that was close to his room. Up above, a long passage was intersected twice at right angles, it was painted pale yellow with a dado of darker ochre; and the doors of the servants' rooms, also yellow, were uniform and placed at equal distances, the same as in the corridor of a hospital. An icy chill came from the zinc roof. All was bare and clean, with that unsavoury odour of the lodgings of the poor.

The loft overlooking the courtyard was in the right wing, at the further end. But Octave, who had not been there since the day of his arrival, was going along the left wing, when, suddenly, a spectacle which he beheld inside one of the rooms, by the partly open door, brought him to a standstill and filled him with amazement. A gentleman was standing in his shirt sleeves before a little looking-glass, tying his white cravat.

"What! you here?" said he.

It was Trublot. He also, at first, stood as one petrified. No one ever came near there at that hour. Octave, who had walked in, looked at him in that room with its narrow iron bedstead, and its washstand on which a little bundle of woman's hair was floating on the soapy water; and, perceiving the black dress coat hanging up amongst some aprons, he could not restrain himself from saying:

"So you sleep with the cook?"

"Not at all!" replied Trublot, in a fright.

Then, recognising the stupidity of this lie, he began to laugh in his convinced and satisfied way.

"Eh! she is amusing! I assure you, my dear fellow, it is wfully fine!"

Whenever he dined out, he escaped from the drawing-room to go and pinch the cook before her stove ; and when she was willing to trust him with her key, he would take his departure before midnight, and go and wait patiently for her in her room, seated on a trunk, in his black dress coat and white tie. On the morrow, he would leave by the principal staircase towards ten o'clock, and pass before the doorkeeper as though he had been making an early call on one of the tenants. So long as he was pretty punctual at the stockbroker's, his father was satisfied. Moreover, he was now employed in attending the Bourse from twelve to three. It would sometimes happen that on a Sunday he would spend the whole day in some servant's bed, happy, lost, his nose buried in the pillow.

"You, who are going to be so rich some day !" said Octave, his face retaining an expression of disgust.

Then Trublot learnedly declared :

"My dear fellow, you don't know what it is ; don't speak about it."

And he stood up for Julie, a tall Burgundian of forty, with her big face pitted with small-pox, but who had the body of a superb woman. One might disrobe the ladies of the house ; they were all sticks, not one would come up to her knee. Besides that, she was a girl very well to do ; and to prove it he opened her drawers, displayed a bonnet, some jewellery, and some chemises trimmed with lace, no doubt stolen from Madame Duveyrier. Octave, indeed, now noticed a certain coquettishness about the room, some gilded cardboard boxes on the drawers, a chintz curtain hung over the skirts, all the accessories of a cook aping the grand lady.

"There is no denying, you see, that one may own to this one," repeated Trublot. "If they were only all like her !"

At this moment a noise came from the servants' staircase. It was Adèle coming up to wash her ears, Madame Josserand having furiously forbidden her to proceed with her work until she had cleaned them with soap. Trublot peeped out and recognised her.

"Shut the door quick !" said he very anxiously. "Hush ! don't say a word !"

He pricked up his ear, and listened to Adèle's heavy footstep along the passage.

"You sleep with her too, then ?" asked Octave, surprised at his paleness, and guessing that he dreaded a scene.

But this time Trublot was coward enough to deny.

"Oh ! no indeed ! not with that slut !   Whoever do you take me for, my dear fellow ? "

He had seated himself on the edge of the bed, and while waiting to finish dressing, begged Octave not to move ; and both remained perfectly still, whilst that filthy Adèle scoured out her ears, which took at least ten good minutes.   They heard the tempest in her washhand basin.

"There is, however, a room between this one and hers," softly explained Trublot, " a room that is let to a workman, a carpenter who stinks the place out with his onion soup. ·This morning again, it almost made me sick.   And you know, in all houses, the partitions of the servants' rooms are now almost as thin as sheets of paper.   I don't understand the landlords.   It is not very decent, one can scarcely turn in one's bed.   I think it very inconvenient."

When Adèle had gone down again, he resumed his swagger and finished dressing himself, making free use of Julie's combs and pomatum.   Octave having spoken of the loft, he insisted on taking him there, for he knew the most out-of-the-way corner of that floor.   And, as he passed the doors, he familiarly mentioned the servants' names : in this bit of a passage, after Adèle came Lisa, the Campardons' maid, a wench who took her pleasures outside ; then, Victoire, their cook, a stranded whale, seventy years old, the only one he respected ; then, Françoise, who had entered Madame Valérie's service the day before, and whose trunk would perhaps only remain twenty-four hours be· hind the meagre bed upon which such a gallop of maids passed, that it was always necessary to make inquiries before going there and waiting in the warmth of the blanket ; then, a quiet couple, in the service of the people on the second floor ; then, these people's coachman, a strapping fellow of whom he spoke with the jealousy of a handsome man, suspecting him of going from door to door and noiselessly doing some very fine work ; finally, at the other end of the passage, there were Clémence, the Duveyriers' maid, whom her neighbour Hippolyte, the butler, rejoined matrimonially every night, and little Louise, the orphan whom Madame Juzeur had taken on trial, a chit of fifteen, who must hear some very strange things in the small hours, if she were a light sleeper.

"My dear fellow, don't lock the door, do this to oblige me," said he to Octave, when he had helped him to take the books from the box.   "You see, when the loft is open, one can hide there and wait."

Octave, having consented to deceive Monsieur Gourd, returned with Trublot to Julie's room. The young man had left his overcoat there. Then it was his gloves that he could not find; he shook the skirts, overturned the bed-clothes, raised such a dust and such an odour of soiled linen, that his companion, half-suffocated, opened the window. It looked on to the narrow inner courtyard, which gave light to all the kitchens. And he was stretching out his head over this damp well, which exhaled the greasy odours of dirty sinks, when a sound of voices made him hastily withdraw.

"The little morning gossip," said Trublot on all fours under the bed, still searching. "Just listen to it."

It was Lisa, who was leaning out of the window of the Campardons' kitchen to speak to Julie, two storeys below her.

"So it's come off then this time?"

"It seems so," replied Julie, raising her head. "You see, she did all she could to catch him. Hippolyte came from the drawing-room so disgusted, that he almost had an attack of indigestion."

"If we were only to do a quarter as much!" resumed Lisa.

But she disappeared a moment, to drink some broth that Victoire brought her. They got on well together, nursing each other's vices, the maid hiding the cook's drunkenness, and the cook facilitating the maid's outings, from which the latter returned quite worn out, her limbs aching, her eyelids blue.

"Ah! my children," said Victoire leaning out in her turn, her elbows touching Lisa's, "you're young. When you've seen what I've seen! At old Campardon's, there was a niece who had been well brought up, and who used to go and look at the men through the key-hole."

"Pretty goings-on!" murmured Julie with the horrified air of a lady. "Had I been in the place of the little one of the fourth floor, I'd have boxed Monsieur Auguste's ears, if he'd touched me in the drawing-room! He's a fine fellow!"

At these words, a shrill laugh issued from Madame Juzeur's kitchen. Lisa, who was opposite, searched the room with a glance, and caught sight of Louise, whose precocious fifteen years took a delight in listening to the other servants.

"She's spying on us from morning to night, the chit," said she. "How stupid it is to thrust a child upon us! We sha'n't be able to talk at all soon."

She did not finish. The sound of a suddenly opened window chased them away. A profound silence ensued. But they ven-'

tured to look out again.   Eh ! what ! what was the matter ?
They had thought that Madame Valérie or Madame Josserand
was going to catch them.

"No fear!" resumed Lisa.   "They're all soaking in their
washhand basins.   They're too busy with their skins, to think
of bothering us.   It's the only moment in all the day when one
can breathe freely."

"So it still goes on the same at your place ?" asked Julie,
who was paring a carrot.

"Still the same," replied Victoire.   "It's all over, she's
no more use."

"But your big noodle of an architect, what does he do then?"

"Takes up with the cousin, of course ! "

They were laughing louder than ever, when they beheld the
new servant, Françoise, in Madame Valérie's kitchen.   It was
she who had caused the alarm, by opening the window.   At
first there was an exchange of politeness.

" Ah ! it's you, mademoiselle."

"Why, yes, mademoiselle.   I am trying to make myself at
home, but this kitchen is so filthy ! "

Then came scraps of abominable information.

" You will be more than constant, if you remain there long.
The last one had her arms all scratched by the child, and
madame worked her so hard, that we could hear her crying
from here."

" Ah well ! that won't last long with me," said Françoise.
"Thanks all the same, mademoiselle."

" Where is she, your missus ? " asked Victoire curiously.

" She's just gone off to lunch with a lady."

Lisa and Julie stretched their necks, to exchange a glance.
They knew her well, the lady.   A funny sort of lunch, with
her head down and her feet in the air !   Was it possible, to lie
to that extent !   They did not pity the husband, for he deserved
more than that ; only, it was a disgrace to humanity, that a
woman should not behave herself better.

" There's Dish-cloth ! " interrupted Lisa, discovering the Josserands' servant overhead.

Then a host of vulgar expressions were bawled from the
depths of this hole, as obscure and infected as a sewer.   All,
with their faces raised, violently yelled at Adèle, who was their
butt, the dirty awkward creature on whom the entire household
vented their spite.

" Hallo ! she's washed herself, it's evident ! "

"Just throw your fish bones into the yard again, and I'll come up and rub 'em in your face!"

Thoroughly bewildered, Adèle looked down upon them from above, her body half out of the window. She ended by answering:

"Leave me alone, can't you? or I'll water you."

But the yells and the laughter increased.

"You married your young mistress, last night, didn't you? Eh! it's you, perhaps, who teach her how to hook the men?"

"Ah! the heartless thing! she stops in a place where they don't give you enough to eat! On my word, it's that which exasperates me against her! You're such a fool, you should send 'em to blazes!"

Adèle's eyes filled with tears.

"You can only talk nonsense," stammered she. "It's not my fault if I don't get enough to eat."

And the voices swelled, unpleasant words commenced to be exchanged between Lisa and the new servant, Françoise, who stuck up for Adèle, when the latter, forgetting the abuse heaped upon her, and yielding to party instinct, called out:

"Look out! here's madame!"

The silence of the tomb ensued. They all immediately plunged back into their kitchens; and from the dark chasm of the narrow courtyard all that ascended was the stench of the dirty sinks, like the exhalation of the hidden abominations of the families, stirred up there by the spite of the hirelings. It was the sewer of the house, the shames of which it carried off, whilst the masters were still lounging in their slippers, and the grand staircase unfolded the solemnity of its flights, in the silent suffocation· of the hot air stove. Octave recalled the blast of uproar he received full in the face, when entering the Campardons' kitchen, the day of his arrival.

"They are very nice," said he simply.

And, leaning out in his turn, he looked at the walls, as though annoyed at not having at once read through them, behind the imitation marble and the mouldings bright with gilding.

"Where the devil has she stowed them away?" repeated Trublot who had searched everywhere for his white kid gloves.

At length, he discovered them at the bottom of the bed itself, flattened out and quite warm. He gave a last glance in the glass, went and hid the key in the place agreed upon, right at the end of the passage, underneath an old sideboard left behind by some lodger, and led the way downstairs, accompanied by Octave. After passing the Josserands' door, on the grand staircase, he recovered all his assurance, with his overcoat buttoned up to the neck to hide his dress clothes and white tie.

"Good-bye, my dear fellow," said he raising his voice. "I felt anxious, so I just looked in to hear how the ladies were. They passed a very good night. Good-bye."

Octave watched him with a smile as he went downstairs. Then, as it was almost lunch time, he decided to return the key of the loft later on. During lunch, at the Campardons', he particularly watched Lisa, who waited at table. She had her usual clean and agreeable look; but, in his mind, he could still hear her defiling her lips with the most abominable words. His knowledge of women had not deceived him with respect to that girl with the flat chest. Madame Campardon continued to be enchanted with her, surprised that she did not steal anything, which was a fact, for her vice was of a different kind. Moreover, the girl seemed very kind to Angèle, and the mother entirely trusted her.

It so happened, that on that day Angèle disappeared when the dessert was placed on the table, and she could be heard laughing in the kitchen. Octave ventured to make an observation.

"You are perhaps wrong, to let her be so free with the servants."

"Oh! there is not much harm in it," replied Madame Campardon, in her languid way. "Victoire saw my husband born, and I am so sure of Lisa. Besides, how can I help it? the child gives me a headache. I should go crazy, if I heard her jumping about me all day."

The architect gravely chewed the end of his cigar.

"It is I," said he, "who make Angèle pass two hours in the kitchen, every afternoon. I wish her to become a good housewife. It teaches her a great deal. She never goes out, my dear fellow, she is continually under our sheltering wing. You will see what a jewel we shall make of her."

Octave said no more. On certain days, Campardon appeared to him to be very stupid; and as the architect pressed him to go and hear a great preacher at Saint-Roch, he refused, obstinately persisting in remaining indoors. After telling Madame Campardon that he would not dine with them that evening, he was returning to his room, when he felt the key of the loft in his pocket. He preferred to go down and return it at once.

But on the landing an unexpected sight attracted his atten

tion. The door of the room let to the highly distinguished
gentleman, whose name was never mentioned, happened to be
open ; and this was quite an event, for it was invariably shut,
as though barred by the silence of the tomb. His surprise increased : he was looking for the gentleman's work-table, and in
its stead had discovered the corner of a big bedstead, when he
beheld a slim lady dressed in black, her face hidden behind a
thick veil, come out of the room, whilst the door closed noiselessly behind her.

Then, his curiosity being roused, he followed the lady downstairs, to find out if she were pretty. But she hastened along
with an anxious nimbleness, scarcely touching the Wilton carpet with her tiny boots, and leaving no trace in the house, save
a faint odour of verbena. As he reached the vestibule, she disappeared, and he only beheld Monsieur Gourd standing under
the porch, cap in hand and bowing very low to her.

When the young man had returned the doorkeeper his key,
he tried to make him talk.

"She looks very lady-like," said he. "Who is she ?"

" A lady," answered Monsieur Gourd.

And he would add nothing further. But he was more com-
municative regarding the gentleman on the third floor. Oh !
a man belonging to the very best society, who had taken that
room to come and work there quietly, one night a week.

"Ah ! he works !" interrupted Octave. "What at, pray ?"

" He was kind enough to ask me to keep his room tidy for
him," continued Monsieur Gourd, without appearing to have
heard the question. "And, you know, he pays money down.
Ah ! sir, when one waits on people, one soon knows whether
they are decent. He is everything that is most respectable : it
is easily seen by his clothes."

He was obliged to jump on one side, and Octave himself had
to enter the doorkeepers' room for a moment, in order to let
the carriage of the second floor people, who were going to the
Bois, pass. The horses pawed the ground, held back by the
coachman the reins high ; and, when the big closed landau
rolled under the vaulted roof, one beheld through the windows
two handsome children, whose smiling faces almost hid the
vague profiles of the father and mother. Monsieur Gourd
drew himself up, polite, but cold.

"They don't make much noise in the house," observed
Octave.

"No one makes any noise," said the doorkeeper, curtly.

" Each one lives as he thinks best, that's all. There are people who know how to live, and there are people who don't know how to live."

The second floor tenants were judged severely, because they associated with no one. They appeared to be well off, however; but the husband wrote books, and Monsieur Gourd mistrusted him, curling his lip with contempt; more especially as no one knew what the family was up to in there, with its air of requiring nobody, and being always perfectly happy. It did not seem to him natural.

Octave was opening the vestibule door, when Valério returned. He drew politely on one side, to allow her to pass before him.

" Are you quite well, madame ? "

" Yes, sir, thank you."

She was out of breath; and as she went upstairs he looked at her muddy boots, thinking of that lunch, with her head down and her feet in the air, which the servants had spoken of. She had no doubt walked home, not having been able to find a cab. A hot unsavoury odour came from her damp skirts. Fatigue, a placid weariness of all her flesh, made her at times, in spite of herself, place her hand on the balustrade.

" What a disagreeable day, is it not, madame ? "

" Frightful, sir. And, with that, the atmosphere is very close."

She had reached the first-floor landing, and they bowed to each other. But, with a glance, he had seen her haggard face, her eyelids heavy with sleep, her unkempt hair beneath the bonnet tied on in haste ; and as he continued on his way upstairs, he reflected, annoyed and angry. Then, why not with him ? He was neither more stupid nor uglier than the others.

When before Madame Juzeur's door, on the third floor, his promise of the evening before recurred to him. He felt curious about that little woman, so discreet and with eyes like periwinkles. He rang. It was Madame Juzeur herself who answered the door.

" Ah ! dear sir, how kind of you ! Pray walk in."

There was a softness about the lodging which smelt a bit stuffy : carpets and hangings everywhere, seats as yielding as down, with the warm unruffled atmosphere of a chest padded with old rainbow coloured satin. In the drawing-room, to which the double curtains imparted the peacefulness of a church, Octave was invited to seat himself on a broad and very low sofa.

"Here is the lace," resumed Madame Juzeur, reappearing with a sandal-wood box full of finery. "I am going to make a present of it to some one, and I am curious to know its value."

It was a piece of very fine old Brussels. Octave examined it carefully, and ended by valuing it at three hundred francs. Then, without waiting further, as their hands were both handling the lace, he bent forward and kissed her fingers, fingers as delicate as a little girl's.

"Oh! Monsieur Octave, at my age! you cannot think what you are doing!" murmured Madame Juzeur, prettily, without getting angry.

She was thirty-two, and pretended she was quite old. And she made her usual allusion to her misfortunes; good heavens! yes, after ten days of married bliss, the cruel man had gone off one morning and had not returned, nobody had ever discovered why.

"You can understand," continued she, gazing up at the ceiling, "that all is over for the woman who has gone through this."

Octave had kept hold of her little warm hand which seemed to mould itself to his, and he continued kissing it lightly, on the fingers. She turned her eyes towards him, and gazed upon him with a vague and tender look; then, in a maternal way, she uttered this single word:

"Child!"

Thinking himself encouraged, he wished to take her round the waist, and draw her on to the sofa; but she freed herself without any violence, and slipped from his arms, laughing, and with an air of thinking that he was merely playing.

"No, leave me alone, do not touch me, if you wish that we should remain good friends."

"Then, no?" asked he in a low voice.

"What, no? What do you mean? Oh! my hand, as much as you like!"

He had again taken hold of her hand. But, this time, he opened it, kissing it on the palm; and, her eyes half closed, treating the little game as a joke, she opened her fingers like a cat spreads out its claws to be tickled inside its paw. She did not let him go farther than the wrist. The first day, a sacred line was drawn there, where harm began.

"The priest is coming upstairs," Louise suddenly entered and said, on returning from some errand.

The orphan had the yellow complexion, and the squashed features of girls forgotten on doorsteps. She burst into an idiotic laugh on beholding the gentleman eating, as she thought, out of her mistress's hand. But at a glance from the latter, she hastened away.

"I greatly fear I shall never be able to do anything with her," resumed Madame Juzeur. "However, it is only right to try and put one of those poor souls into the straight path. Come this way, if you please, Monsieur Mouret."

She conducted him to the dining-room, so as to leave the drawing-room to the priest, whom Louise ushered in. She invited Octave to come again and have a chat. It would be a little company for her; she was always so sad and so lonely! Happily, religion consoled her.

That evening, towards five o'clock, Octave experienced a real relief in making himself comfortable at the Pichons' whilst waiting for dinner. The house bewildered him somewhat; after having allowed himself to be impressed with a provincial's respect, in the face of the rich solemnity of the staircase, he was gliding to an exaggerated contempt for what he thought he could guess took place behind the high mahogany doors. He was quite at sea; it seemed to him now that those middle-class women, whose virtue had frozen him at first, should yield at a sign; and, when one of them resisted, he was filled with surprise and rancour.

Marie blushed with joy on seeing him place the pile of books which he had fetched for her in the morning on the sideboard. She kept saying,

"How nice of you, Monsieur Octave! Oh! thank you, thank you! And how kind to come early! Will you have a glass of sugar and water with some cognac? It assists the appetite."

He accepted, just to please her. Everything appeared pleasant to him, even Pichon and the Vuillaumes, who conversed round the table, slowly mumbling over again their usual Sunday conversation. Marie, now and again, ran to the kitchen, where she was cooking a boned shoulder of mutton; and he dared in a chaffing way to follow her, seizing hold of her before the stove, and kissing her on the nape of her neck. She, without a cry and without a start, turned round and kissed him in her turn on the mouth, with lips which were always cold. This coolness seemed delicious to the young man.

"Well, and your new Minister?" asked he of Pichon, on returning into the room.

But the clerk gave a start. Ah! there was going to be a new Minister of Public Instruction! He knew nothing of it; no one ever troubled about that at the Ministry.

"The weather is so bad!" he abruptly remarked. "It is quite impossible to keep one's trousers clean!"

Madame Vuillaume talked of a girl at Batignolles who had gone to the bad.

"You will scarcely believe me, sir," said she. "She had been exceedingly well brought up; but she felt so bored at her parents', that she had twice tried to throw herself into the street. It is incredible!"

"They should have put bars on the windows," said Monsieur Vuillaume simply.

The dinner was delightful. This kind of conversation lasted all the time around the modest board lighted by a little lamp. Pichon and Monsieur Vuillaume, having got on to the staff of the Ministry, did nothing but talk of head-clerks and second head-clerks; the father-in-law obstinately alluded to those of his time, then recollected that they were dead; whilst, on his side, the son-in-law continued to speak of the new ones, in the midst of an inextricable confusion of names. The two men, however, as well as Madame Vuillaume, agreed on one point: fat Chavignat, he who had such an ugly wife, had gone in for a great deal too many children. It was absurd for a man of his position. And Octave smiled, feeling happy and at his ease; he had not spent such an agreeable evening for a long time; he even ended by blaming Chavignat with conviction. Marie quieted him with her clear, innocent look, devoid of emotion at seeing him seated beside her husband, helping them both according to their tastes, with her rather tired air of passive obedience.

Punctually at ten o'clock, the Vuillaumes rose to take their departure. Pichon put on his hat. Every Sunday he saw them to the omnibus. Out of deference, he had got into the habit about the time of his marriage, and the Vuillaumes would have been deeply offended had he now tried to give it up. All three made for the Rue de Richelieu, then walked slowly up it, searching with a glance the Batignolles omnibuses which kept passing full, so that Pichon often went thus as far as Montmartre; for he would never have thought of leaving his father and mother-in-law before seeing them into an omnibus. As they could not walk fast, it took him close upon two hours to go there and back.

They exchanged some friendly handshakes on the landing. Octave, on returning to the room with Marie, said quietly,

"It rains; Jules will not get back before midnight."

And, as Lilitte had been put to bed early, he at once took Marie on his knees, and drank the rest of the coffee with her out of the same cup, like a husband glad at having got rid of his guests and at finding himself again in the quiet of his home, excited by a little family gathering, and able to kiss his wife at his ease, with the doors closed. A pleasant warmth filled the narrow room, where some frosted eggs had left an odour of vanilla. He was gently kissing the young woman under the chin, when some one knocked. Marie did not even give a start of affright. It was young Josserand, he who was a bit cracked. Whenever he could escape from the apartment opposite, he would come in this way to chat with her, attracted by her gentleness; and they both got on well together, remaining ten minutes at a time without speaking, exchanging at distant intervals phrases which had no connection with each other.

Octave, very much put out, remained silent.

"They've some people there," stuttered Saturnin. "I don't care a hang for their not letting me dine with them! So I took the lock off and bolted. It serves them right."

"They will be anxious; you ought to go back," said Marie, who noticed Octave's impatience.

But the idiot laughed with delight. Then, with his embarrassed speech, he related what took place in his home. He seemed to come each time for the sake of thus relieving his memory.

"Papa worked all night again. Mamma slapped Berthe. I say, when people get married, does it hurt?"

And, as Marie did not reply, becoming excited, he continued:

"I won't go to the country; I won't. If they only touch her, I'll strangle them; it's easy to do in the night, when they're asleep. The palm of her hand is as soft as note-paper. But, you know, the other is a beast of a girl—"

He recommenced, got more muddled still, and did not succeed in expressing what he had come to say. Marie, at length, made him return to his parents, without his even having noticed Octave's presence.

Then the latter, through fear of being again disturbed, wanted to take the young woman into his own room. But she

refused, her cheeks suddenly becoming scarlet.   He, not understanding this bashfulness, said that they would be sure to hear
Jules coming up, and that she would have time to slip into her
room ; and as he drew her along, she became quite angry, with
the indignation of a woman to whom violence is being offered.

"No, not in your room, never ! It would be too wrong.   Let
us remain here."

And she ran to the farthest end of her room.   Octave was
still on the landing, surprised at this unexpected resistance,
when the sounds of a violent altercation ascended from the
courtyard.   Really, everything seemed to be against him, he
would have done better to have gone off to bed. Such an uproar
was so unusual at that late hour, that he ended by opening a
window, to hear what was going on. Monsieur Gourd, down
below, was shouting out :

"I tell you, you shall not pass ! The landlord has been sent
for.   He will come and turn you out himself."

"What ! turn me out !" replied a thick voice. "Don't I pay
my rent ? Pass, Amélie, and if the gentleman touches you, we'll
have something to laugh at ! "

It was the workman from upstairs, who had returned with
the woman sent away in the morning. Octave leant out ; but,
in the black hole of the courtyard, he could only distinguish
some big moving shadows in a ray of gaslight from the vestibule.

"Monsieur Vabre ! Monsieur Vabre ! " called the doorkeeper
in urgent tones, as the carpenter shoved him aside. "Quick,
quick, she is coming in ! "

In spite of her poor legs, Madame Gourd had gone to fetch
the landlord, who was just then at work on his great task.   He
was coming down.   Octave could hear him furiously repeating :

"It is scandalous ! it is disgraceful ! I will never allow such
a thing in my house ! "

And, addressing the workman, whom his presence seemed at
first to intimidate :

"Send that woman away, at once, at once.   You hear me !
we will have no women brought to the house."

"But she's my wife ! " replied the workman in a scared way.
" She is out at service, she comes once a month, when her people
allow her to.   What a fuss ! It isn't you who'll prevent me
sleeping with my wife, I suppose ! "

At these words, the doorkeeper and the landlord quite lost
their heads.

"I give you notice to quit," stuttered Monsieur Vabre. "And, in the meantime, I forbid you to take my premises for what they are not. Gourd, turn that creature out on to the pavement. Yes, sir, I don't like bad jokes. When a person is married, he should say so. Hold your tongue, do not give me any more of your rudeness!"

The carpenter, who was a jolly fellow, and who had no doubt had a drop too much wine, ended by bursting out laughing.

"It's damned funny all the same. However, as the gentleman objects, you'd better return home, Amélie. We'll wait till some other time. By Jove! I accept your notice with pleasure! I wouldn't stop in such a hole on any account! There are some pretty goings-on in it, one comes across some rare filth. You . won't have women brought here, but you tolerate, on every floor, well-dressed strumpets who lead fine lives behind the doors! You set of mufts! you swells!"

Amélie had gone off so as not to cause her old man any more annoyance; and he, jolly, and without anger, continued his chaff. During this time, Monsieur Gourd protected Monsieur Vabre's retreat, permitting himself to make a few remarks out loud. What a dirty set the lower classes were! One workman in a house was sufficient to pollute it.

Octave closed the window. But, just as he was returning to Marie, an individual who was lightly gliding along the passage, knocked up against him.

"What! it's you again!" said he recognising Trublot.

The latter remained a second taken aback. Then, he wished to explain his presence.

"Yes, it is I. I dined at the Josserands', and I'm going—"

Octave felt disgusted.

"What, with that slut Adèle? You declared it was not so."

Then, Trublot assumed all his swagger, saying with an air of intense satisfaction :

"I assure you, my dear fellow, it's awfully fine. She has such a skin, you've no idea what a skin!"

Then he railed against the workman, who had almost been the cause of his being caught on the servants' staircase, and all his dirty fuss about women. He had been obliged to come round by the grand staircase. And, as he made off, he added :

"Remember, it is next Thursday that I am going to take you to see Duveyrier's mistress. We will dine together."

The house resumed it's peacefulness, lapsing into that religious silence which seemed to issue from its chaste alcoves. Octave

had rejoined Marie in the inner chamber at the side of the conjugal couch, where she was arranging the pillows.   Upstairs,
the chair being littered with the washhand basin and an old
pair of shoes, Trublot sat down on Adèle's narrow bed, and
waited in his dress clothes and his white tie.   When he recognised Julie's step as she came up to bed, he held his breath,
having a constant dread of women's quarrels.   At length Adèle
appeared.   She was in a temper, and went for him at once.

"I say, you! you might treat me a bit better, when I wait
at table !"

"How, treat you better ?"

"Why of course you don't even look at me, you never say if
you please, when you ask for bread.   For instance, this evening
when I handed round the veal, you had a way of disowning me.
I've had enough of it, look you ! All the house badgers me
with its nonsense.   It's too much, if you're going to join the
others !"

Whilst this was taking place, the workman in the next room,
not yet sobered, talked to himself in so loud a voice that every
one on that landing could hear him.

"Well ! it's funny all the same, that a fellow can't sleep with
his wife ! No woman allowed in the house, you fussy old idiot !
Just go now and poke your nose into all the rooms, and see what
you'll see !"

CHAPTER VII.

For a fortnight past, with the view of getting uncle Bachelard to give Berthe a dowry, the Josserands had been inviting him to dinner almost every evening, in spite of his offensive habits.

When the marriage was announced to him, he had contented himself with giving his niece a gentle pat on the cheek, saying :

" What ! you are going to get married ! Ah ! that's very nice, little girl ! "

And he remained deaf to all allusions, exaggerating his air of a silly old boozer who got drunk on liqueurs, the moment money was mentioned before him.

Madame Josserand had the idea to invite him one evening together with Auguste, the bridegroom elect. Perhaps the sight of the young man would decide him. The step was heroical, for the family did not like exhibiting the uncle, always fearing that he would give people a bad impression of them. He had, however, behaved pretty well ; his waistcoat alone had a big syrupy stain, which it had obtained no doubt in some café. But when his sister questioned him, after Auguste had taken his departure, and asked him what he thought of the young fellow, he answered without involving himself :

" Charming, charming."

This would never do. It was a pressing matter. Therefore, Madame Josserand determined to plainly place the position of affairs before him.

" As we are by ourselves," resumed she, " we may as well take advantage of it. Leave us, my darlings ; we want to have some talk with your uncle. You, Berthe, just look after Saturnin, and see that he does not take the lock off the door again."

Saturnin, ever since they had been busy about his sister's marriage, hiding everything from him, had taken to wandering about the rooms, an anxious look in his eyes, and scenting that there was something up ; and he imagined most diabolical things which gave the family awful frights.

" I have obtained every information," said the mother, when she had shut herself in with the father and the uncle. " This is the position of the Vabres."

And she went into long details of figures. Old Vabre had brought half a million with him from Versailles. If the house had cost him three hundred thousand francs, he had two hundred thousand left, which, during the twelve years that had past had been producing interest. Moreover, he received each year twenty-two thousand francs in rent ; and, as he lived with the Duveyriers, scarcely spending anything at all, he must consequently be altogether worth five or six hundred thousand francs, besides the house. Thus, there were some very handsome expectations on that side.

"Has he no vices, then ?" asked uncle Bachelard. " I thought he speculated at the Bourse."

But Madame Josserand cried out. Such a quiet old gentleman, and occupied on such a great task ! That one, at least, had shown himself capable of putting a fortune by ; and she smiled bitterly as she looked at her husband, who bowed his head.

As for Monsieur Vabre's three children, Auguste, Clotilde and Théophile, they had each had a hundred thousand francs on their mother's death. Théophile, after some ruinous enterprises, was living as best he could on the crumbs of this inheritance. Clotilde, with no other passion than her piano, had probably invested her share. And Auguste had purchased the business on the ground floor and gone in for the silk trade with his hundred thousand francs which he had long kept in reserve.

" And the old fellow naturally gives nothing to his children when they marry," observed the uncle.

Well ! he did not much like giving, that was a fact which was unfortunately indisputable. When Clotilde married, he had undertaken to give a dowry of eighty thousand francs; but Duveyrier had never received more than ten thousand, and he did not demand the balance, he even kept his father-in-law, flattering his avarice, no doubt with the hope of one day securing all his fortune. In the same way, after promising Théophile fifty thousand francs at the time of his marriage with Valérie, the old gentleman had commenced by merely paying the interest, then had not forked out even a single sou from his cashbox, and had even got to the point of demanding the rent, which the couple paid him, for fear of being struck out of his will. Therefore, it would not do to count too much on the fifty thousand francs Auguste was to receive in his turn, on the signing of his marriage contract; they would have no reason to complain if his father let him have the warehouse on the ground floor for a few years free of rent.

"Well!" declared Bachelard, "it is always hard on the parents. Dowries are never really paid."

"Let us return to Auguste," continued Madame Josserand. "I have told you his expectations, and the only danger comes from the Duveyriers, whom Berthe will do well to watch very closely, if she enters the family. At the present moment, Auguste, after purchasing the business for sixty thousand francs, has started with the other forty thousand. Only, the sum is not sufficient; besides which, he is single, and requires a wife; that is why he wishes to marry. Berthe is pretty, he already sees her in his counting-house; and as for the dowry, fifty thousand francs are a respectable sum which has decided him."

Uncle Bachelard did not so much as blink his eyes. He ended by saying in a tender-hearted way that he had dreamed of something better. And he commenced to pick the future husband to pieces: a charming fellow, certainly; but too old, a great deal too old, thirty-three years and over; besides which, always ill, his face distorted by neuralgia; in short, a sorry object, not near lively enough for trade.

"Have you another?" asked Madame Josserand, whose patience was wearing out. "I searched all Paris before finding him."

However, she did not deceive herself much. She too picked him to pieces.

"Oh! he is not a phœnix, in fact I think him a bit of a fool. Besides which, I mistrust those men who have never had any youth and who do not risk a stride in life without thinking about it for years beforehand. On leaving college, where his headaches prevented him completing his studies, he remained for fifteen years a mere clerk before daring to touch his hundred thousand francs, the interest of which, it seems, his father was cheating him out of all the time. No, no, he is not up to much."

Monsieur Josserand, who until then had kept silent, ventured an observation.

"But, my dear, why insist so obstinately on this marriage? If the young man's health is so bad—"

"Oh! it is not bad health that need prevent it," interrupted Bachelard. "Berthe would find no difficulty in marrying again."

"However, if he is incapable," resumed the father, "if he is likely to make our daughter unhappy—"

"Unhappy!" cried Madame Josserand. "Say at once that I throw my child at the head of the first-comer! We are among ourselves, we discuss him : he is this, he is that, not young, not handsome, not intelligent. We just talk the matter over, do we not? it is but natural. Only, he is very well, we shall never find a better ; and, shall I tell you? it is a most unexpected match for Berthe. I was about to give up all hope, on my word of honour!"

She rose to her feet. Monsieur Josserand, reduced to silence, pushed back his chair.

"I have only one fear," continued she, making a resolute stand before her brother, "and that is that he may break it off, if he is not paid the dowry on the day the contract is to be signed. It is easy to understand, he is in want of money—"

But at this moment a hot breathing, which she heard behind her, caused her to turn round. Saturnin was there, passing his head round the partly opened door, his eyes glaring like a wolf's as he listened to what was being said. And it created quite a panic, for he had stolen a spit from the kitchen, to spit the geese, said he. Uncle Bachelard, feeling very uneasy at the turn the conversation was taking, availed himself of the general alarm.

"Don't disturb yourselves," cried he from the ante-room. "I'm off, I've an appointment at midnight, with one of my customers, who's come specially from Brazil."

When they had succeeded in getting Saturnin to bed, Madame Josserand, exasperated, declared that it was impossible to keep him any longer. He would end by doing some one an injury, if he was not shut up in a madhouse. Life was unbearable with him always to be kept in hiding. His sisters would never get married, so long as he was there to disgust and frighten people.

"Wait a bit longer," murmured Monsieur Josserand, whose heart bled at the thought of this separation.

"No, no!" declared the mother, "I do not want him to spit me in the end! I had brought my brother to the point, I was about to get him to do something. Never mind! we will go with Berthe to-morrow to his own place, and we will see if he will have the cheek to escape from his promises. Besides, Berthe owes her godfather a visit. It is only proper."

On the morrow, all three, the mother, the father, and the

daughter, paid an official visit to the uncle's warehouses, which occupied the basement and the ground floor of an enormous house in the Rue d'Enghien. Large vans blocked up the entrance. A gang of packers were nailing up cases in the covered courtyard; and, through open bays, one caught glimpses of piles of merchandise, dried vegetables and remnants of silk, stationery and tallow, all the accumulations of the thousand commissions given by the customers, and of the purchases risked in advance at times when prices were low. Bachelard was there with his big red nose, his eye still sparkling from the intoxication of the night before, but with his intelligence clear, his instinct and his luck returning the moment he found himself again before his books.

"Hallo! you here!" said he, greatly annoyed.

And he received them in a little closet, from which he watched his men through a window.

"I have brought Berthe to see you," explained Madame Josserand. "She knows what she owes you."

Then, when the young girl, after kissing her uncle, had, on a glance from her mother, returned to look at the goods in the courtyard, the latter resolutely broached the subject.

"Listen, Narcisse, this is how we are situated. Counting on your kindness of heart and on your promises, I have engaged to give a dowry of fifty thousand francs. If I do not give it, the marriage will be broken off. It would be a disgrace, things having gone as far as they have. You cannot leave us in such an embarrassing position."

But a vacant look had come into Bachelard's eyes; and he stuttered, as though very drunk:

"Eh? what? you've promised. You should never promise; it's a bad thing to promise."

He pleaded poverty. For instance, he had bought a whole stock of horsehair, thinking that the price of horsehair would go up; but not at all, the price had fallen lower still, and he had been obliged to dispatch them at a loss. And he pounced on his books, opened his ledgers, and insisted on showing the invoices. It was ruination.

"Nonsense!" Monsieur Josserand ended by saying, completely out of patience. "I know your business; you make no end of money, and you would be rolling in wealth if you did not squander it in the way you do. I ask you for nothing myself. It was Eléonore who persisted in applying to you. But allow me to tell you, Bachelard, that you have been fooling us.

Every Saturday for fifteen years past, when I come to look over your books for you, you are for ever promising me—"

The uncle interrupted him, and violently slapped himself on the chest.

"I promise? impossible! No, no; let me alone, you'll see. I don't like being asked, it annoys me—it makes me ill. You'll see one day."

Madame Josserand herself could get nothing further out of him. He shook their hands, wiped away a tear, talked of his soul and of his love for the family, imploring them not to worry him any more, and swearing before heaven that they would never repent it. He knew his duty; he would perform it to the uttermost. Later on, Berthe would know how her uncle loved her.

"And what about the dotal insurance," asked he in his natural tone of voice, "the fifty thousand francs you had insured the little one for?"

Madame Josserand shrugged her shoulders.

"It has been dead and buried for fourteen years past. You have been told twenty times already, that when the fourth premium fell due, we were unable to pay the two thousand francs."

"That doesn't matter," murmured he with a wink, "the thing is to talk of this insurance to the family, and then get time for paying the dowry. One never pays a dowry."

Monsieur Josserand rose indignantly.

"What! that is all you can find to say?"

But the uncle mistook his meaning, and went on to show that it was quite a usual thing.

"Never, I tell you! One gives something on account, and then merely pays the interest. Look at Monsieur Vabre himself. Did our father ever pay you Éléonore's dowry? why, no, of course not. Every one sticks to his money; it's only natural!"

"In short, you advise me to commit a most abominable action!" cried Monsieur Josserand. "I should lie, it would be a forgery to produce the policy of that insurance—"

Madame Josserand stopped him. The idea suggested by her brother had rendered her grave. She was surprised she had not thought of it herself.

"Dear me! how excited you become, my dear. Narcisse has not told you to forge anything."

"Of course not," murmured the uncle. "There is no occasion to show any documents."

" It is simply a question of gaining time," continued she. " Promise the dowry, we shall always manage to give it later on."

Then the worthy man's conscience spoke out. No! he refused ; he would not again venture on such a precipice. They were always taking advantage of his complacency, to get him to agree little by little to things which afterwards made him ill, so deeply did they wound his feelings. As he had no dowry to give, he could not promise one.

Bachelard was strumming on the little window with his fingers and whistling a march, as though to show his great contempt for such scruples. Madame Josserand had listened to her husband, her face all pale with an anger which had been slowly rousing, and which suddenly exploded.

" Well ! sir, as this is how you look at it, this marriage shall take place. It was my daughter's last chance. I will cut my hand off sooner than she shall lose it. So much the worse for the others ! One becomes capable of anything at last."

" So, madame, you would commit murder to get your daughter married ? "

She rose to her full height.

" Yes ! " said she furiously.

Then she smiled. The uncle had to quell the storm. What was the use of wrangling ? It was far better to agree together. And, still trembling from the quarrel, bewildered and worn out, Monsieur Josserand ended by promising to talk the matter over with Duveyrier, on whom everything depended, according to Madame Josserand. Only, to get hold of the counsellor when he was in a good humour, the uncle offered to put his brother-in-law in the way of meeting him at a house where he could refuse nothing.

" It is merely to be an interview," declared Monsieur Josserand, still struggling. " I swear that I will not enter into any engagements."

" Of course, of course," said Bachelard. " Eléonore does not wish you to do anything dishonourable."

Berthe just then returned. She had seen some boxes of preserved fruits, and, after some lively caresses, she tried to get one given her. But the uncle's speech again became thick ; impossible, they were counted, and had to leave that very evening for Saint-Petersburg. He slowly got them in the direction of the street, whilst his sister lingered before the activity of the vast warehouses, full to the rafters with every

imaginable commodity, suffering from the sight of that fortune
made by a man without any principles, and bitterly comparing
it with her husband's incapable honesty.

"Well! to-morrow night then, towards nine o'clock, at the
Café de Mulhouse," said Bachelard outside, as he shook
Monsieur Josserand's hand.

It so happened that, on the morrow, Octave and Trublot, who
had dined together before going to see Clarisse, Duveyrier's
mistress, entered the Café de Mulhouse, so as not to call too
early, although she lived in the Rue de la Cerisaie, which was
some distance off. It was scarcely eight o'clock. As they
entered, the sound of a violent quarrel attracted them to a
rather out-of-the-way room at the end. And there they beheld
Bachelard already drunk, enormous in size, and his cheeks
flaring red, having an altercation with a little gentleman, pale
and quarrelsome.

"You have again spat in my beer!" roared he in his voice of
thunder. "I'll not stand it, sir!"

"Go to blazes, do you hear? or I'll give you a thrashing!"
said the little man, standing on the tips of his toes.

Then Bachelard raised his voice very provokingly, without
drawing back an inch.

"If you think proper, sir! As you please!"

And the other having with a blow knocked in his hat, which
he always wore swaggeringly on the side of his head, even in
the cafés, he repeated more energetically still :

"As you please, sir! If you think proper!"

Then, after picking up his hat, he sat himself down with a
superb air, and called to the waiter :

"Alfred, change my beer!"

Octave and Trublot, greatly astonished, had caught sight of
Gueulin seated at the uncle's table, his back against the wall,
smoking with a tranquillity amounting to indifference. As
they questioned him on the cause of the quarrel,

"I don't know," replied he, watching the smoke ascend from
his cigar. "Always a lot of rot! Oh! a mania for getting his
head punched! He never retreats."

Bachelard shook hands with the new-comers. He adored
young people. When he heard that they were going to call on
Clarisse, he was delighted, for he himself was going there with
Gueulin ; only he had to wait for his brother-in-law, Josserand,
whom he had an appointment with. And he filled the little
room with the sounds of his voice, covering the table with every

drink imaginable for the benefit of his young friends, with the insane prodigality of a man who does not care what he spends when out on pleasure. Ill-formed, with his teeth too new and his nose in a blaze beneath his short snow-white hair, he talked familiarly to the waiters and thoroughly tired them out, and made himself unbearable to his neighbours to such a point that the landlord came twice to beg him to leave, if he could not keep quiet. The night before, he had been turned out of the Café de Madrid.

But a girl having put in an appearance, and then gone away, after walking round the room with a wearied air, Octave began to talk of women. This set Bachelard off again. Women had cost him too much money; he flattered himself that·he had had the best in Paris. In his business, one never bargained about such things ; just to show that one had something to fall back upon. Now, he was giving all that up, he wished to be loved. And, in presence of this bawler chucking banknotes about, Octave thought with surprise of the uncle who exaggerated his stuttering drunkenness to escape the family extortions.

"Don't boast, uncle," said Gueulin. "One can always have more women than one wants."

"Then, you silly fool, why do you never have any ?" asked Bachelard.

Gueulin contemptuously shrugged his shoulders.

"Why ? Listen ! Only yesterday I dined with a friend and his mistress. The mistress at once began to kick me under the table. It was an opportunity, wasn't it ? Well ! when she asked me to see her home, I made off, and I haven't been near her since. Oh ! I don't deny that, for the time being, it might have been very agreeable. But afterwards, afterwards, uncle ! Perhaps one of those women a fellow can never get rid of. I'm not such a fool ! "

Trublot nodded his head approvingly, for he also had renounced women of society, through a dread of the troublesome morrows. And Gueulin, coming out of his shell, continued to give examples. One day in the train a superb brunette, whom he did not know, had fallen asleep on his shoulder ; but he had thought twice, what would he have done with her on arriving at the station ? Another day, after a wedding, he had found a neighbour's wife in his room, eh ? that was rather cool ; and he would have made a fool of himself had it not been for the idea that afterwards she would certainly have wanted him to keep her in boots.

"Opportunities, uncle !" said he, coming to an end, "no one has such opportunities as I ! But I keep myself in check. Every one, morever, does the same ; one is afraid of what may follow. Were it not for that, it would, of course, be very pleasant ! Good morning ! good evening ! one would see nothing else in the streets."

Bachelard, become wrapped in thought, was no longer listening to him. His bluster had calmed down, his eyes were wet.

"If you are very good," said he suddenly, "I will show you something."

And, after paying, he led them out. Octave reminded him of old Josserand. That did not matter, they would come back for him. Then, before leaving the room, the uncle, casting a furtive glance around, stole the sugar left by a customer on a neighbouring table.

"Follow me," said he, when he was outside. "It's close by."

He walked along, grave and thoughtful, without uttering a word. He drew up before a door in the Rue Saint-Marc. The three young men were about to follow him, when he appeared to give way to a sudden hesitation.

"No, let us go off, I won't."

But they cried out at this. Was he trying to make fools of them ?

"Well ! Gueulin mustn't come up, nor you 'either, Monsieur Trublot. You're not nice enough, you respect nothing, you'd joke. Come, Monsieur Octave, you're a serious sort of fellow."

He made Octave walk up before him, whilst the other two laughed, and called to him from the pavement to give their compliments to the ladies. On reaching the fourth floor, he knocked, and an old woman opened the door.

"What ! it's you, Monsieur Narcisse ? Fifi did not expect you this evening," said she, with a smile.

She was fat, with the calm, white face of a nun. In the narrow dining-room into which she ushered them, a tall fair young girl, pretty and simple looking, was embroidering an altar cloth.

"Good day, uncle," said she, rising to offer her forehead to Bachelard's thick trembling lips.

When the latter had introduced Monsieur Octave Mouret, a distinguished young man whom he counted amongst his friends, the two women curtsied in an old-fashioned way, and then they all seated themselves round the table, lighted by a petroleum lamp. It was like a quiet country home, two regulated existences, out of sight of all, and living upon next to nothing. As the room overlooked an inner courtyard, one could not even hear the sound of the passing vehicles.

Whilst Bachelard paternally questioned the child on her feelings and·her occupations since the night before, the aunt, Mademoiselle Menu, at once began to tell Octave their history, with the familiarity of a worthy woman who thinks she has nothing to hide.

"Yes, sir, I come from Villeneuve, near Lille. I am well known to Messieurs Mardienne Frères, in the Rue Saint-Sulpice, where I worked as an embroiderer for thirty years. Then, a cousin having left me a house in our part of the country, I was lucky enough to let it as a life interest at a thousand francs a-year, sir, to people who thought they would bury me on the morrow, and who are nicely punished for their wicked idea, for I am still alive, in spite of my seventy-five years."

She laughed, displaying teeth as white as a young girl's.

"I was doing nothing, my eyes being quite worn out," continued she, "when my niece, Fanny, came to me. Her father, Captain Menu, had died without leaving a sou, and no other relation, sir. So, I at once took the child away from her school, and made an embroiderer of her—a very unprofitable craft ; but what could be done ? whether that, or something else, women always have to starve. Fortunately, she met Monsieur Narcisse. Now, I can die happy."

And, her hands clasped on her stomach, in her inaction of an old workwoman who has sworn never again to touch a needle, she looked tenderly at Bachelard and Fifi with tearful eyes. The old man was just then saying to the child :

"Really, you thought of me ! And what did you think ? "

Fifi raised her limpid eyes, without ceasing to draw her golden thread.

"Why, that you were a good friend, and that I loved you very much."

She had scarcely looked at Octave, as though indifferent to the youth of so handsome a fellow. Yet he smiled on her, surprised, and moved by her gracefulness, not knowing what to think ; whilst the aunt, who had grown old in a celibacy and a· chastity which had cost her nothing, continued, lowering her voice :

"I might have married her, might I not ? A workman would have beaten her, a clerk would have given her no end of children. It is better far that she should behave well with Monsieur Narcisse, who looks a very worthy man."

And, raising her voice :

"Ah ! Monsieur Narcisse, it will not have been my fault if she does not please you. I am always telling her: do all you can to please him, show yourself grateful. It is but natural, I am so thankful to know that she is at last provided for. It is so difficult to get a young girl settled in life, when one has no friends ! "

Then Octave abandoned himself to the happy simplicity of this home. In the still atmosphere of the room floated an odour of fruit. Fifi's needle, as it pierced the silk, alone made a slight monotonous noise, like the ticking of a little clock, which might have regulated the placidity of the uncle's amours. Moreover, the old maid was honesty itself; she lived on the thousand francs of her income, never touching Fifi's money, which the latter spent as she chose. Her scruples yielded only to white wine and chestnuts, which her niece occasionally treated her to, after opening the money box in which she collected four sou pieces, given as medals by her good friend.

"My little duck," at length said Bachelard, rising, "we have business to attend to. Good-bye till to-morrow. Now, mind you are very good."

He kissed her on the forehead. Then, after looking at her with emotion, he said to Octave :

"You may kiss her too, she is a mere child."

The young man pressed his lips to her fair skin. She smiled, she was very modest; however, it was merely like a family gathering, he had never seen such sober-minded people. The uncle was going off, when he re-entered the room, exclaiming :

"I was forgetting, I've a little present."

And, turning out his pocket, he gave Fifi the sugar which he had just stolen at the café. She thanked him very heartily, and, as she crunched up a piece, she became quite red with pleasure. Then, becoming bolder, she asked :

"Do you not happen to have some four sou pieces ?"

Bachelard searched his pockets without result. Octave had one, which the young girl accepted as a memorial. She did not accompany them to the door, no doubt out of propriety; and they heard her drawing her needle, having at once resumed her altar-cloth, whilst Mademoiselle Menu saw them to the landing, with her good old woman's aminbility.

"Eh ? it's worth seeing," said uncle Bachelard, stopping on

UNCLE BACHELARD GIVES OCTAVE PERMISSION TO KISS FIFI.

p. 134.

the stairs. "You know, it doesn't cost me five louis a month.
I've had enough of the hussies who almost devoured me. On
my word! what I required was a heart."

But, as Octave laughed, he became mistrustful.

"You're a decent fellow, you won't take advantage of what I
have shown you. Not a word to Gueulin, you swear it on your
honour? I am waiting till he is worthy of her to show her to
him. An angel, my dear fellow! No matter what is said,
virtue is good, it refreshes one. I have always gone in for the
ideal."

His old drunkard's voice trembled, tears swelled his heavy
eyelids. Down below, Trublot chaffed, pretending to take the
number of the house; whilst Gueulin shrugged his shoulders,
asking Octave, who was astounded, what he thought of the little
thing. Whenever the uncle's feelings had been softened by a
booze, he could not resist taking people to see these ladies,
divided between the vanity of showing his treasure and the fear
of having it stolen from him; then, on the morrow, he forgot
all about it, and returned to the Rue Saint-Marc with an air of
mystery.

"Everyone knows Fifi," said Gueulin, quietly.

Meanwhile, Bachelard was looking out for a cab, when Octave
exclaimed:

"And Monsieur Josserand, who is waiting at the café?"

The others had forgotten him entirely. Monsieur Josserand,
very annoyed at wasting his evening, was impatiently waiting at
the entrance, for he never took anything out of doors. At length
they started for the Rue de la Cerisaie. But they had to take
two cabs, the commission agent and the cashier in the one, and
the three young men in the other.

Gueulin, his voice drowned by the jingling noise of the old
vehicle, at first talked of the insurance company where he was
employed. Insurance companies and stockbrokers were equally
unpleasant, affirmed Trublot. Then the conversation turned to
Duveyrier. Was it not unfortunate that a rich man, a magis-
trate, should let himself be fooled by women in that way? He
always wanted them in out-of-the-way neighbourhoods, right at
the end of the omnibus routes: modest little ladies in their
own apartments, playing the parts of widows; unknown mil-
liners, having shops and no customers; girls picked out of
the gutter, clothed, and shut up, as though in a convent, whom
he would go to see regularly once a week, like a clerk trudging
to his office.

Trublot, however, found excuses for him : to begin with, it was the fault of his constitution ; then, it was impossible to put up with a confounded wife like his. On the very first night, so it was said, she could not bear him, affecting to be disgusted at his red blotches, so that she willingly allowed him to have mistresses, whose complaisances relieved her of him, though at times she accepted the abominable burden, with the resignation of a virtuous woman who makes a point of accomplishing all her duties.

"Then, she is virtuous, is she ?" asked Octave, interested.

"Virtuous ? Oh ! yes, my dear fellow ! Every good quality ; pretty, serious, well brought up, learned, full of taste, chaste, and unbearable ! "

A block of vehicles at the bottom of the Rue Montmartre stopped the cab. The young men, who had let down the windows, could hear Bachelard's voice furiously abusing the coachman. Then, when the cab moved on again, Gueulin gave some information about Clarisse. Her name was Clarisse Bocquet, and she was the daughter of a former toy merchant in a small way, who now attended all the fairs with his wife and quite a troop of dirty children. Duveyrier had come across her one night when it was thawing, just as her lover had chucked her out. No doubt, this strapping wench answered to an ideal long sought after, for as early as the morrow he was hooked, he wept as he kissed her eyelids, all shaken by his need to cultivate the little blue flower of romance in his huge masculine appetites. Clarisse had consented to live in the Rue de la Cerisaie, so as not to expose him ; but she led him a fine dance, had made him buy her twenty-five thousand francs' worth of furniture, and was devouring him heartily, in company with some actors of the Montmartre Theatre.

"I don't care a hang !" said Trublot, " so long as one amuses oneself at her place. Anyhow, she doesn't make you sing, and she isn't forever strumming away on a piano like the other. Oh ! that piano ! Listen, when one is deafened at home, when one has had the misfortune to marry a mechanical piano which frightens everybody away, one would be precious stupid not to arrange a pleasant little nest elsewhere, where one could receive one's friends in their slippers."

"Last Sunday," related Gueulin, "Clarisse wanted me to lunch alone with her. I declined. After those sort of lunches one always does something foolish ; and I was afraid of seeing her take up her quarters with me the day she left Duveyrier for

good. You know, she detests him. Oh! her disgust almost
makes her ill. Well! the girl doesn't care much for pimples
either. But she hasn't the resource of sending him elsewhere
like his wife has; otherwise, if she could pass him over to
her maid, I assure you she'd get rid of the job precious
quick."

The cab stopped. They alighted before a dark and silent
house in the Rue de la Cerisaie. But they had to wait for the
other cab fully ten minutes, Bachelard having taken his driver
with him to drink a grog after the quarrel in the Rue Montmartre. On the staircase, as severe-looking as those of the
middle-classes, Monsieur Josserand again asked some questions
respecting Duveyrier's lady friend, but the uncle merely
answered :

"A woman of the world, a very decent girl. She won't eat
you."

It was a little maid, with a rosy complexion, who opened the
door to them. She took the gentlemen's coats with familiar and
tender smiles. For a moment, Trublot kept her in a corner of
the ante-room, whispering things in her ear which almost made
her choke, as though being tickled. But Bachelard had pushed
open the drawing-room door, and he at once introduced Monsieur
Josserand. The latter stood for a moment embarrassed, finding
Clarisse ugly, and not understanding how the counsellor could
prefer this sort of creature—black and skinny, and with a head
of hair like a poodle—to his wife, one of the most beautiful
women of society. Clarisse, however, was charming. She had
preserved the Parisian cackle, a superficial and borrowed wit, an
itch of drollery caught by rubbing up against men, but was able
to put on a grand lady sort of air when she chose.

"Sir, I am charmed. All Alphonse's friends are mine.
Now you are one of us, the house is yours."

Duveyrier, warned by a note from Bachelard, also greeted
Monsieur Josserand very amiably. Octave was surprised at the
counsellor's youthful appearance. He was no longer the severe
and ill-at-ease individual, who never seemed to be in his own
home in the drawing-room of the Rue de Choiseul. The deep
red blotches on his face were turning to a rosy hue, his oblique
eyes shone with a childish delight, whilst Clarisse related in
the midst of a group, how he sometimes hastened to come and
see her during a short adjournment of the court; just time to
jump into a cab, to kiss her, and start back again. Then he
complained of being overworked. Four sittings a week, from

eleven to five ; always the same skein of bickerings to unravel,
it ended by destroying all feeling in one's heart.

"It is true," said he, laughing, "one requires a few roses
amongst all that.   I feel better afterwards."

However, he did not wear his bit of red ribbon, but always took
it off when visiting his mistress ; a last scruple, a delicate distinction, which his sense of decency obstinately persisted in.
Clarisse, without wishing to say so, felt very much hurt at it.

Octave, who had at once shook hands with the young woman
like a comrade, listened and looked about him.   The drawing-
room, with its big floral-pattern carpet, its garnet satin-covered
furniture and hangings, bore a great resemblance to the drawing-room of the Rue de Choiseul ; and, as if to complete this
likeness, a great many of the counsellor's friends, whom Octave
had seen on the evening of the concert, were met with here
likewise, and formed the same groups.   But there was smoking,
and talking in loud tones, much liveliness flying about in
the brilliant light of the candles.   Two gentlemen, stretched
out beside each other, occupied the whole breadth of a divan ;
another, seated astride a chair, was warming his back at the
fire.   It was a pleasant free-and-easy, a liberty which, however,
did not go any farther.   Clarisse never received other women,
out of decency, she said.   When her acquaintances complained
that her drawing-room was in want of a few ladies, she would
answer with a laugh :

"Well ! and I—am I not enough ?"

She had arranged a decent home for Alphonse, very middle-
class in the main, having a mania for what was proper, all
through the ups and downs of her existence.   When she received she would not be addressed familiarly.   When the
guests were gone, however, and the doors closed, all Alphonse's
friends passed in succession, without counting her own, clean-
shaven actors and painters with bushy beards.   It was an old
habit, the need to recruit herself a bit, behind the heels of the
man who paid.   Of all her acquaintances, two alone had not
been willing—Gueulin, dreading what might follow, and
Trublot, whose affections were elsewhere.

The little maid handed round some glasses of punch, with
her agreeable air.   Octave took one ; and, leaning towards his
friend, whispered in his ear,

"The servant is better than the mistress."

"Why, of course ! always!" said Trublot, with a shrug of
the shoulders, full of a disdainful conviction.

Clarisse came and talked with them for a moment. She multiplied herself, going from one to another, casting a word here, a laugh or gesture there. As each new-comer lighted a cigar the drawing-room was soon full of smoke.

"Oh! the horrid men!" exclaimed she prettily, as she went and opened a window.

Without losing any time, Bachelard made Monsieur Josserand comfortable in the recess of this window, to enable him to breathe, said he. Then, thanks to a masterly manœuvre, he brought Duveyrier to an anchor there also, and quickly broached the affair. So the two families were about to be united by a close tie; he felt highly honoured. Then he inquired what day the marriage contract was going to be signed, and that led him up to the matter in hand.

"We intended calling on you to-morrow, Josserand and I, to settle everything, for we are aware that Monsieur Auguste would do nothing without you. It is with respect to the payment of the dowry; and, really, as we are so comfortable here—"

Monsieur Josserand, again suffering the greatest anguish, looked out into the gloomy depths of the Rue de la Cerisaie, with its deserted pavements, and its dark façades. He regretted having come. They were again going to take advantage of his weakness and engage him in some disgraceful affair, which would cause him no end of suffering afterwards. A feeling of revolt made him interrupt his brother-in-law.

"Another time; this is not a fitting place, really."

"But why, pray?" exclaimed Duveyrier, very graciously. "We are better here than anywhere else. You were saying, sir?"

"We give Berthe fifty thousand francs," continued the uncle. "Only, these fifty thousand francs are represented by a dotal insurance at twenty years' date, which Josserand took out for his daughter, when she was four years old. She will therefore only receive the money in three years' time—"

"Allow me!" again interrupted the cashier with a scared look.

"No, let me finish; Monsieur Duveyrier understands perfectly. We do not wish the young couple to wait three years for money they may need at once, and we engage ourselves to pay the dowry in instalments of ten thousand francs every six months, on the understanding that we repay ourselves later on with the insurance money."

A pause ensued. Monsieur Josserand, feeling frozen and

choking, again looked into the dark street. The counsellor seemed to be thinking the matter over for a moment. Perhaps he scented the affair, and was delighted at letting those Vabres be duped, for he hated them in the person of his wife.

"All that seems to me very reasonable," said he, at length. "It is for us to thank you. It is very seldom that a dowry is paid at once in full."

"Never, sir!" affirmed the uncle, energetically. "Such a thing is never done."

And the three men shook hands as they arranged to meet on the Thursday at the notary's. When Monsieur Josserand came back into the light, he was so pale that he was asked if he was unwell. As a matter of fact he did not feel very well, and he withdrew, without being willing to wait for his brother-in-law, who had just gone into the dining-room where the classic tea was represented by champagne.

Gueulin, stretched on a sofa near the window, murmured,

"That scoundrel of an uncle!"

He had overheard some words about the insurance, and he chuckled as he confided the truth of the matter to Octave and Trublot. It had been done at his office; there was not a sou to receive, the Vabres were being taken in. Then, as the two others laughed at this good joke, holding their sides meanwhile, he added, with comical earnestness,

"I want a hundred francs. If the uncle doesn't give me a hundred francs, I'll split."

The voices were becoming louder, the champagne was up-setting the good behaviour established by Clarisse. In her draw-ing-room the conclusion of all the parties was invariably rather lively. She herself would make a mistake sometimes. Trublot drew Octave's attention to her as she stood behind a door with her arms round the neck of a fellow with the build of a peasant, a stone carver just arrived from the South, and whom his native town wished to make an artist of. But Duveyrier having pushed the door, she quickly removed her arms, and recom-mended the young man to him: Monsieur Payan, a sculptor with a very graceful talent; and Duveyrier, delighted, pro-mised to obtain some work for him.

"Work, work," repeated Gueulin, in a low voice; "he has as much here as he can want, the big ninny!"

Towards two o'clock, when the three young men and the uncle left the Rue de la Cerisaie, the latter was completely drunk. They would have liked to have packed him into a cab; but the neighbourhood was asleep in the midst of a solemn silence, without the sound of a wheel, nor even of a belated footstep. Then they decided to support him. The moon had risen, a very bright moon, which whitened the pavements. And in the deserted streets their voices assumed a grave sonorousness.

"Hang it all, uncle! keep yourself up! you're breaking our arms!"

He, with his throat full of sobs, had become very tender-hearted and very moral.

"Go away, Gueulin," stuttered he; "go away! I won't have you see your uncle in such a state. No, my boy, it's not right; go away!"

And as his nephew called him an old rogue:

"Rogue! that's nothing. One must make oneself respected. I esteem women—always decent women; and when there's no feeling it disgusts me. Go away, Gueulin, you're making your uncle blush. These gentlemen are sufficient."

"Then," declared Gueulin, "you must give me a hundred francs. Really, I want them for my rent. They're going to turn me out."

At this unexpected demand, Bachelard's intoxication increased to such an extent that he had to be propped up against the shutters of a warehouse. He stuttered:

"Eh! what! a hundred francs! Don't search me. I've nothing but coppers. You want 'em to squander in bad places! No, I'll never encourage you in your vices. I know my duty; your mother confided you to my care on her death-bed. You know, I'll call out if I'm searched."

He continued, his indignation increasing against the dissolute life led by youth, and returning to the necessity there was for the display of virtue.

"I say," Gueulin ended by saying, "I've not got to the point of taking families in. Ah, you know what I mean! If I were to talk, you'd soon give me my hundred francs!"

But the uncle at once became deaf to everything. He went grunting and stumbling along. In the narrow street where they then were, behind the church of Saint-Gervaise, a white lantern alone burned with the palish glimmer of a night-light, displaying a gigantic number painted on its roughened glass. A stifled trepidation issued from the house, whilst the closed shutters emitted a few narrow rays of light.

"I've had enough of it," declared Gueulin, abruptly. "Excuse me, uncle, I forgot my umbrella up there."

And he entered the house. Bachelard was indignant and full of disgust. He demanded at least a little respect for women. With such morals France was done for. On the Place de l'Hotel-de-Ville, Octave and Trublot at length found a cab, inside which they shoved him like some bundle.

"Rue d'Enghien," said they to the driver. "You must pay yourself. Search him."

The marriage contract was signed on the Thursday before Maitre Renaudin, notary in the Rue de Grammont. At the moment of starting, there had been another awful row at the Josserands', the father having, in a supreme revolt, made the mother responsible for the lie they had forced him to countenance ; and they had once more cast their families in each other's teeth. How did they expect him to earn another ten thousand francs every six months? The obligation was driving him mad. Uncle Bachelard, who was there, kept placing his hand on his heart, full of fresh promises, now that he had so managed that he would not have to part with a sou, and overflowing with affection, and swearing that he would never leave his little Berthe in an awkward position. But the father, in his exasperation, had merely shrugged his shoulders, asking Bachelard if he really took him for a fool.

At the notary's, however, the reading of the contract, drawn up from notes furnished by Duveyrier, slightly calmed Monsieur Josserand. There was no mention of the insurance ; moreover, the first instalment of ten thousand francs was only to fall due six months after the marriage. They would thus have some breathing time. Auguste, who was listening very attentively, allowed some signs of impatience to escape him. He looked at smiling Berthe, at the Josserands, at Duveyrier, and he ended by venturing to speak of the insurance, as a guarantee which he thought it only logical should be mentioned. Then they all looked at him with surprise ; whatever for? it was perfectly understood; and they signed quickly, Maître Renaudin, an amiable young man, holding his tongue as he handed the pen to the ladies. Not till they were outside did Madame Duveyrier express her surprise. No one had ever spoken of an insurance ; the dowry of fifty thousand francs was to have been paid by uncle Bachelard. But Madame Josserand, in the calmest way, denied having mentioned her brother's name in connection with such a trumpery sum. It was his whole fortune that the uncle was going to leave to Berthe.

On the evening of that day, a cab came to fetch Saturnin

away. His mother had declared that it was too dangerous for him to be at the ceremony; one could not cast loose a madman who talked of spitting people in the midst of a wedding-party; and Monsieur Josserand, broken-hearted, had been obliged to apply for the admission of the poor fellow into the Asile des Moulineaux, kept by Doctor Chassagne. The cab was brought under the porch at twilight. Saturnin came down holding Berthe's hand, and thinking he was going with her into the country. But when he was inside the cab, he struggled furiously, breaking the windows and thrusting his bloody fists through them. And Monsieur Josserand returned upstairs weeping, all upset by this departure in the dark, his ears ringing with the wretched creature's yells, mingled with the cracking of the whip and the gallop of the horse.

During dinner, as tears again came to his eyes at the sight of Saturnin's empty chair, his wife, not understanding, exclaimed:

"Come, that is enough, sir, is it not? I trust you are not going to assist at your daughter's marriage with that funereal-looking face. Listen! on all I hold most holy, on my father's grave, her uncle will pay the first ten thousand francs. I will answer for it! He pledged me his oath he would, when we were leaving the notary's."

Monsieur Josserand did not even reply. He passed the night in addressing wrappers. At daylight, in the chill of the morning, he finished his second thousand, and had earned six francs. Several times he had raised his head, as he had a habit of doing, to listen if Saturnin were not moving in his room near by. Then the thought of Berthe renewed his ardour for work. Poor child! she would have liked to have been dressed in white moire. However, with six francs she could add a few more flowers to her bridal bouquet.

CHAPTER VIII.

The marriage before the mayor had taken place on the Thursday. On the Saturday morning, as early as a quarter past ten, some ladies were already waiting in the Josserands' drawing-room, the religious ceremony being fixed for eleven o'clock, at Saint-Roch. There were Madame Juzeur, always in black silk; Madame Dambreville, tightly laced in a costume of the colour of dead leaves; and Madame Duveyrier, dressed very simply in pale blue. All three were conversing in low tones amongst the scattered chairs; whilst Madame Josserand was finishing dressing Berthe in the adjoining room, assisted by the servant and the two bridesmaids, Hortense and little Campardon.

"Oh! it is not that," murmured Madame Duveyrier; "the family is honourable. But, I admit, I rather dreaded on my brother Auguste's account the mother's domineering spirit. One cannot be too careful, can one?"

"No doubt," said Madame Juzeur; "one not only marries the daughter, one often marries the mother as well, and it is very unpleasant when the latter interferes in the home."

At this moment, the door of the inner room opened, and Angèle rushed out, exclaiming:

"A hook, at the bottom of the left hand drawer. Wait a moment."

She flew across the drawing-room, returned and disappeared again, with her white skirt, fastened at the waist by a broad blue ribbon, following her like the foam in the wake of a ship.

"You are mistaken, I think," resumed Madame Dambreville. "The mother is only too happy at being rid of her daughter. Her sole passion is her Tuesdays at home. Besides, she has still another victim."

Madame Valérie now entered in a red costume of provoking singularity. She had come upstairs too quickly, fearing she was late.

"Théophile will never be ready," said she to her sister-in-law. "You know, I sent Françoise about her business this morning, and he is looking everywhere for a tie.   I left him in the midst of such confusion ! "

" The question of health is also a very serious one," continued Madame Dambreville.

" No doubt," replied Madame Duveyrier.   " We discreetly consulted Doctor Juillerat.   It appears that the young girl is perfectly well formed.   As for the mother, she has one of those surprising constitutions ; and that partly helped to decide us, for nothing is more annoying than having infirm relatives to look after.   Healthy relations are far better."

" Especially," said Madame Juzeur in her gentle voice, " when they will not leave anything behind them."

Valérie had seated herself ; but not knowing what the topic of conversation was, she asked, still out of breath :

" Eh ? of whom are you speaking ?"

But the door again opened suddenly, and the sounds of a quarrel issued from the inner room.

" I tell you the box was left on the table."

" It is not true, I saw it here just now."

" Oh ! you obstinate mule ! Go and see for yourself."

Hortense, also in white, and with a broad blue waistband, crossed the drawing-room, looking older, with her hard features and her yellow complexion, amidst the transparent paleness of the muslin.   She returned in a fury with the bridal bouquet, which they had been passionately seeking for five minutes past in the disordered room.

" However, it is no use being too particular," said Madame Dambreville, in conclusion, " one never marries as one would wish.   The wisest thing is to make the best one can of it afterwards."

This time Angèle and Hortense opened the folding-doors wide so that the bride should not catch her dress in anything ; and Berthe appeared in a white silk dress, all gay with white flowers, with a white wreath, a white bouquet, and a white garland, which crossed the skirt, and was lost in the train in a shower of little white buds.   She looked charming amidst all this whiteness, with her fresh complexion, her golden hair, her laughing eyes, and her candid mouth of an already enlightened girl.

" Oh ! delicious !" exclaimed the ladies.

They all embraced her with an air of ecstasy.   The Josserands, at their wits' end, not knowing where to obtain the two thousand francs which the wedding would cost them, five hundred francs for dress, and fifteen hundred francs for their share of the dinner and ball, had been obliged to send Berthe to Doctor Chassagne's to see Saturnin, to whom an aunt had just left three thousand francs ; and Berthe, having obtained permission to take her brother out for a drive, by way of amusing him, had smothered him with caresses in the cab, and had then gone with him for a minute to the notary, who was unaware of the poor creature's condition, and who had everything ready for his signature. The silk dress and the abundance of flowers surprised the ladies, who were reckoning up the cost whilst giving vent to their admiration.

"Perfect! in most exquisite taste !"

Madame Josserand appeared, beaming, in a mauve dress of an unpleasant hue, which made her look taller and rounder than ever, with the majesty of a tower. She fumed about Monsieur Josserand, called to Hortense to find her shawl, and vehemently forbade Berthe to sit down.

"Take care, you will crush your flowers !"

"Do not worry yourself," said Clotilde, in her calm voice. "We have plenty of time. Auguste is coming for us."

They were all waiting in the drawing-room, when Théophile abruptly burst in, his dress-coat askew, his white cravat tied like a piece of cord, and without his hat. His face, with its few hairs and bad teeth, was livid ; his limbs, like an ailing child's, were trembling with fury.

"What is the matter with you?" asked his sister in amazement.

"The matter is—the matter is—"

But a fit of coughing interrupted him, and he stood there for a minute, choking, spitting in his handkerchief, and enraged at being unable to give vent to his anger. Valérie looked at him, confused, and warned by a sort of instinct. At length, he shook his fist at her, without even noticing the bride and the other ladies around him.

"Yes, whilst looking everywhere for my necktie, I found a letter in front of the wardrobe."

He crumpled a piece of paper between his febrile fingers. His wife had turned pale. She realised the situation ; and, to avoid the scandal of a public explanation, she passed into the room that Berthe had just left.

"Ah ! well," said she, simply, "I prefer to leave if he is going mad."

"Let me alone !" cried Théophile to Madame Duveyrier, who was trying to quiet him. "I intend to confound her. This time I have a proof, and there is no doubt, oh, no! It shall not pass off like that, for I know him—”

His sister had seized him by the arm, and squeezing it, shook him authoritatively.

“Hold your tongue! don’t you see where you are? This is not the proper time, understand!”

But he started off again:

“It is the proper time! I don’t care a hang for the others. So much the worse that it happens to-day! It will serve as a lesson to everyone.”

However, he lowered his voice, his strength failing him, he had dropped on to a chair, ready to burst into tears. An uncomfortable feeling had invaded the drawing-room. Madame Dambreville and Madame Juzeur had politely gone to the other end of the apartment, and pretended not to understand. Madame Josserand, greatly annoyed at an adventure, the scandal of which would cast a gloom over the wedding, had passed into the bedroom to cheer up Valérie. As for Berthe, who was studying her wreath before the looking-glass, she had not heard anything. Therefore, she questioned Hortense in a low voice. They whispered together; the latter indicated Théophile with a glance, and added some explanations, whilst pretending to arrange the fall of the veil.

“Ah!” simply said the bride, with a chaste and amused look, her eyes fixed on the husband, without the least sign of confusion in her halo of white flowers.

Clotilde softly asked her brother for particulars. Madame Josserand reappeared, exchanged a few words with her, and then returned to the adjoining room. It was an exchange of diplomatic notes. The husband accused Octave, that counter-jumper, whom he would chastise in church, if he dared to come there. He swore he had seen him the previous day with his wife on the steps of Saint-Roch; he had had a doubt before, but now he was sure of it—everything tallied, the height, the walk. Yes, madame invented luncheons with lady friends, or else she went inside Saint-Roch with Camille, through the same door as everyone, as though to say her prayers; then, leaving the child with the woman who let out the chairs, she would make off with her gentleman by the old way, a dirty passage, where no one would have gone to look for her. However, Valérie had smiled on hearing Octave’s name mentioned; never with that one, she pledged her oath to Madame Josserand, with nobody at all for the matter of that, she added, but less with him than with any-

one else ; and, this time, with truth on her side, she in her turn
talked of confounding her husband, by proving to him that the
note was no more in Octave's handwriting than that Octave
was the gentleman of Saint-Roch.   Madame Josserand listened
to her, studying her with her experienced glance, and solely pre-
occupied with finding some means of helping her to deceive
Théophile.   And she gave her the very best advice.

"Leave all to me, don't move in the matter.   As he chooses,
it shall be Monsieur Mouret, well ! it shall be Monsieur Mouret.
There is no harm in being seen on the steps of a church with
Monsieur Mouret, is there ?   The letter alone is compromising.
You will triumph when our young friend shows him a couple of
lines of his own handwriting.   Above all, say just the same as I
say.   You understand, I don't intend to let him spoil such a
day as this."

When she returned into the room with Valérie, who was
greatly affected, Théophile, on his side, was saying to his sister
in a choking voice :

"I will do so for you, I promise not to disfigure her here, as
you assure me it would scarcely be proper, on account of this
wedding.   But I cannot be answerable for what may take place
at church.   If the counter-jumper comes and beards me there,
in the midst of my own family, I will exterminate them one
after the other."

Auguste, looking very correct in his black dress-coat, his left
eye shrunk up, suffering from a headache which he had been
dreading for three days past, arrived at this moment, accompanied by his father and his brother-in-law, both looking very
solemn, to fetch his bride.   There was a little jostling, for they
had ended by being late.   Two of the ladies, Madame Duveyrier
and Madame Dambreville, had to help Madame Josserand put
on her shawl ; it was an immense tapestry shawl, with a yellow
ground, which she continued to wear on great occasions, though
it had long ago passed out of fashion, and which draped her so
amply and so strikingly that she quite revolutionized the streets
through which she passed.   They had still to wait for Monsieur
Josserand, who was looking under the furniture for a stud swept
away the day before with the dust.   At length he appeared,
stammering excuses, looking bewildered, yet happy, and he led
the way downstairs, tightly pressing Berthe's arm beneath his
own.   Behind them came Auguste and Madame Josserand.
Then followed the rest of the company at hap-hazard, disturbing
the grave silence of the vestibule with the buzz of their conver-

sation. Théophile had seized hold of Duveyrier, whose dignity
he upset with his story; and he poured his complaints into his
ear, requesting advice, whilst in front of them Valérie, quite recovered, and very modest in her attitude, received Madame
Juzeur's tender encouragements without appearing to notice her
husband's terrible looks.

"And your prayer-book!" exclaimed Madame Josserand
suddenly, in a voice of despair.

They were then in the carriages. Angèle was obliged to run
up and fetch the prayer-book bound in white velvet. At last
they started. All the household was there, the servants, the
doorkeepers. Marie Pichon had come down with Lilitte, dressed
as though for a walk; and the sight of the bride, looking so
pretty and so beautifully dressed, brought tears to her eyes.
Monsieur Gourd noticed that the people of the second floor alone
had not come out of their apartments—curious tenants who
always acted differently to others!

At Saint-Roch, the big double doors were opened wide. A
red carpet covered the steps down to the pavement. It was
raining; the May morning was very cold.

"Thirteen steps," said Madame Juzeur in a low voice to
Valérie when they had passed through the doorway. "It is
not a good sign."

As soon as the procession had entered the passage between
the chairs, walking towards the chancel, where the tapers of
the altar were shining like stars, the organs over the couples'
heads broke out into a song of joy. It was a warm pleasant
church, with its big white windows, edged with yellow and pale
blue, its red marble dados ornamenting the walls and pillars,
its gilded pulpit supported by the four evangelists, and its
side-chapels bright with gold and silver plate. Some paintings
enlivened the vaulted roof. Crystal chandeliers hung from the
ends of long cords. When the ladies passed over the broad
gratings of the heating apparatus, the hot air penetrated their
skirts.

"Are you sure you have the ring?" inquired Madame
Josserand of Auguste, who was seating himself with Berthe on
the arm-chairs placed before the altar.

He had a fright, fancying he had forgotten it, then felt it in
his waistcoat pocket. She had, however, not waited for his
answer. Ever since she entered, she had been standing on tiptoe, searching the company with her glance. There were
Trublot and Gueulin, both best men, uncle Bachelard and

Campardon, the bride's witnesses, Duveyrier and Doctor Juillerat, the bridegroom's witnesses, and all the crowd of acquaintances of whom she was proud.   But she had just caught sight of Octave, who was assiduously opening a passage for Madame Hédouin, and she drew him behind a pillar, where she spoke to him in low and rapid tones.   The young man, a look of bewilderment on his face, did not appear to understand. However, he bowed with an air of amiable obedience.

"It is settled," whispered Madame Josserand in Valérie's ear, returning and seating herself in one of the arm-chairs placed for the members of the family, behind those of Berthe and Auguste. Monsieur Josserand, the Vabres, and the Duveyriers were also there.

The organs were now giving forth scales of clear little notes, broken by big pants.   There was quite a crush, the choir was filling up, and men remained standing in the aisles.   The Abbé Mauduit had reserved to himself the joy of blessing the union of one of his dear penitents.   When he appeared in his surplice, he exchanged a friendly smile with the congregation, every face there being familiar to him.   Some voices commenced the *Veni Creator*, the organs resumed their song of triumph, and it was at this moment that Théophile discovered Octave, to the left of the chancel, standing before the chapel of Saint-Joseph.

His sister Clotilde tried to detain him.

"I cannot," stammered he ; "I will never submit to it."

And he made Duveyrier follow him, to represent the family. The *Veni Creator* continued.   A few persons looked round.

Théophile, who had talked of blows, was in such a state of agitation when planting himself before Octave that he was unable at first to say a word, vexed at being short and raising himself up on tiptoe.

"Sir," said he at length, "I saw you yesterday with my wife—"

But the *Veni Creator* was just coming to an end, and he was quite scared on hearing the sound of his own voice.   Moreover, Duveyrier, very much annoyed by the incident, tried to make him understand that the time was badly chosen for an explanation.   The ceremony had now begun before the altar.   After addressing an affecting exhortation to the bride and bridegroom, the priest took the wedding-ring to bless it.

"*Benedic, Domine Deus noster, annulum nuptialem hunc, quem nos in tuo nomine benedicimus—*"

Then Théophile plucked up courage to repeat his words in a low voice:

"Sir, you were in this church yesterday with my wife."

Octave, still bewildered by what Madame Josserand had said to him, and without having thoroughly understood her, related the little story, however, in an easy sort of way.

"Yes, I did indeed meet Madame Vabre, and we went and looked at the repairs of the Calvary which my friend Campardon is directing."

"You admit it," stammered the husband, again overcome by fury, "you admit it—"

Duveyrier was obliged to slap him on the shoulder to calm him. The shrill voice of one of the boy choristers was responding:

"*Amen.*"

"And you no doubt recognise this letter," continued Théophile, offering a piece of paper to Octave.

"Come, not here!" said the counsellor, thoroughly scandalized. "You are going out of your mind, my dear fellow."

Octave unfolded the letter. The emotion had increased amongst the congregation. There were whisperings, and nudgings of elbows, and glancing over the tops of prayer-books; no one was now paying the least attention to the ceremony. The bride and bridegroom alone remained grave and stiff before the priest. Then Berthe, turning her head, caught sight of Théophile getting whiter and whiter as he addressed Octave; and, from that moment, her mind was absent—she kept casting bright side glances in the direction of the chapel of Saint-Joseph.

Meanwhile, the young man was reading in a low voice:

"My duck, what bliss yesterday! Tuesday next, in the confessional of the chapel of the Holy Angels."

The priest, after having obtained from the bridegroom the "yes" of a serious man who signs nothing without reading it, had turned towards the bride.

"You promise and swear to be faithful to Monsieur Auguste Vabre in all things, like a true wife should be to her husband, in accordance with God's commandment?"

But Berthe, having seen the letter, and full of the thought of the blows she was expecting would be given, was not listening, but was following the scene from beneath her veil. There was an awkward silence. At length she became aware that they were waiting for her.

"Yes, yes," she hastily replied, in a happen-what-may manner.

The abbé followed the direction of her glance with surprise; and, guessing that something unusual was taking place in one of the aisles, he in his turn became singularly absent-minded. The story had now circulated; every one knew it. The ladies, pale and grave, did not withdraw their eyes from Octave. The men smiled in a discreetly waggish way. And, whilst Madame Josserand reassured Madame Duveyrier with slight shrugs of her shoulders, Valérie alone seemed to give all her attention to the wedding, beholding nothing else, as though overcome by emotion.

"My duck, what bliss yesterday—"Octave read again, affecting intense surprise.

Then, returning the letter to the husband, he said:

"I do not understand it, sir. That writing is not mine. See for yourself."

And taking from his pocket a note-book in which he wrote down his expenses, like the careful fellow he was, he showed it to Théophile.

"What! not your writing!" stammered the latter. "You are making a fool of me; it must be your writing."

The priest had to make the sign of the cross on Berthe's left hand. His eyes elsewhere, he mistook the hand and made it on the right one.

"*In nomine Patris, et Filii, et Spiritus Sancti.*"

"*Amen,*" responded the boy chorister, also raising himself up to see.

In short, the scandal was prevented. Duveyrier proved to poor, bewildered Théophile that the letter could not have been written by Monsieur Mouret. It was almost a disappointment for the congregation. There were sighs, and a few hasty words exchanged. And when every one, still in a state of excitement, turned again towards the altar, Berthe and Auguste were man and wife, she without appearing to have been aware of what was going on, he not having missed a word the priest had uttered, giving his whole attention to the matter, only disturbed by his headache, which closed his left eye.

"The dear children!" said Monsieur Josserand, absorbed in mind and his voice trembling, to Monsieur Vabre, who ever since the commencement of the ceremony had been busy counting the lighted tapers, always making a mistake, and beginning his calculations over again.

But the organs again resounded in the nave, the Abbé
Mauduit had reappeared in his chasuble, the choristers were
commencing the mass, which was a musical mass of great
pomp. Uncle Bachelard, who was going the round of the
chapels, read the Latin inscriptions on the tombs, without
understanding them; the Duke de Créquy's particularly interested him. Trublot and Gueulin had rejoined Octave, to ascertain the particulars; and all three were chuckling behind
the pulpit. Strains suddenly swelled like tempestuous winds,
boy choristers walked about waving censers; then there were
the sounds of a bell, followed by pauses, during which one
could hear the priest mumbling at the altar.

Théophile could not remain still; he stuck to Duveyrier,
whom he harassed with his mad reflections, having lost ground,
and not understanding how the gentleman of the meeting was
not the gentleman of the letter. The rest of the congregation
continued to watch his every gesture; the entire church, with
its processions of priests, its Latin, its music, and its incense,
excitedly discussed the incident. When, after the *Pater*, the
Abbé Mauduit descended to bestow a final blessing upon the
married couple, he glanced inquiringly at the great agitation of
the faithful, the women's excited faces, the men's sly laughs,
beneath the bright gay light from the windows, and in the
midst of the substantial wealth of the nave and chapels.

"Admit nothing," said Madame Josserand to Valérie, as the
family moved towards the vestry after the mass.

In the vestry, the married couple and their witnesses first of
all wrote their signatures. They were kept waiting, however,
by Campardon, who had taken some ladies to inspect the works
at the Calvary, at the end of the choir, behind a wooden hoarding. He at length arrived, and, apologising, proceeded to
cover the register with a big flourish. The Abbé Mauduit had
wished to honour the two families by handing round the pen
himself, and pointing out with his finger the place where each
one was to sign; and he smiled with his air of amiable, worldly
tolerance in the centre of the grave apartment, the woodwork
of which retained a continual odour of incense.

"Well! mademoiselle," said Campardon to Hortense, "does
not all this make you long to be doing the same?"

Then he regretted his want of tact. Hortense, who was the
elder sister, bit her lips. She was expecting to have a decisive
answer from Verdier that evening at the ball, for she had been
pressing him to choose between her and his creature. Therefore she replied in an unpleasant tone of voice:

"I have plenty of time.   Whenever I think proper."

And, turning her back on the architect, she attacked her brother Léon, who had only just arrived, late as usual.

"You are nice! papa and mamma are very pleased. Not even able to be in time when one of your sisters is being married! We were expecting you at least with Madame Dambreville."

"Madame Dambreville does what she pleases," said the young man curtly, "and I do what I can."

A coolness had arisen between them. Léon considered that she was keeping him too long for her own use, and was weary of a connection the burden of which he had accepted in the sole hope of its leading to some grand marriage; and for a fortnight past he had been requesting her to keep her promises. Madame Dambreville, carried away by a passion of love, had even complained to Madame Josserand of what she termed her son's crotchets. And the latter wished to scold him, reproaching him with having neither affection nor regard for his family, as he made a point of missing the most solemn ceremonies. But he gave some explanations in his young democrat's supercilious voice; spoke of unexpected work for the deputy whose secretary he was, a conference he had had to prepare, all sorts of things he had had to do, as well as visits to pay of the greatest importance.

"Yet a marriage is so soon settled!" said Madame Dambreville, without thinking of her words, and bestowing on him an imploring look to soften him.

"Not always!" retorted he, harshly.

And he went and kissed Berthe, then shook his new brother-in-law's hand, whilst Madame Dambreville turned pale with anguish, drawing herself up in her costume of the colour of dead leaves and smiling vaguely towards the persons who entered.

It was the procession of friends, of simple acquaintances, of all the guests gathered together in the church, which now passed through the vestry. The newly-married couple, standing up, were continually distributing hand-shakes, and invariably with the same embarrassed and delighted air. The Josserands and the Duveyriers were not always able to go through the introductions. At times they looked at each other in surprise, for Bachelard had brought persons whom nobody knew and who talked too loud. Little by little everything gave way to confusion; there was quite a crush, hands were held out over the heads, young girls squeezed between pot-bellied gentlemen, left pieces of their white skirts on the legs of these fathers, these brothers, these uncles, still sweating with some vice, enfranchised in a quiet neighbourhood. Away from the crowd, Gueulin and Trublot were relating to Octave how Clarisse had almost been caught by Duveyrier the night before, and had now resigned herself to smothering him with caresses, so as to shut his eyes.

"Hallo!" murmured Gueulin, "he is kissing the bride; it must smell nice."

The congregation, however, had gradually dispersed. Only the relations and the intimate friends remained. The story of Théophile's misfortune had continued to circulate, amidst the hand-shakes and the compliments; in fact, after the stereotyped phrases exchanged for the occasion, nothing else was talked about. Madame Hédouin, who had just heard the story, looked at Valérie with the surprise of a woman whose virtue is her very health. No doubt the Abbé Mauduit had also been made acquainted with the matter, for his curiosity appeared to be satisfied, and he displayed more unction than usual, amidst the hidden frailties of his flock. Another gaping wound, suddenly bleeding, over which he would have to throw the mantle of religion! And he took Théophile aside for a minute, and talked to him discreetly of forgiving injuries and of the Almighty's impenetrable designs, seeking above all to stifle scandal, enveloping those present in a gesture of pity and despair, as though to hide their shame from heaven itself.

"He is all very fine, the parson! he does not know what it is!" murmured Théophile, whose head was completely upset by the sermon.

Valérie, who kept Madame Juzeur near her to help her to keep her countenance, listened with emotion to the conciliatory words which the Abbé Mauduit also considered it his duty to address to her. Then, as they were at length leaving the church, she paused before the two fathers, to allow Berthe to pass on her husband's arm.

"You ought to be satisfied," said she to Monsieur Josserand, wishing to show how free her mind was. "I congratulate you."

"Yes, yes," declared Monsieur Vabre in his clammy voice, "it is a very great responsibility the less."

And, whilst Trublot and Gueulin rushed about seeing all the ladies to the carriages, Madame Josserand, whose shawl attracted quite a crowd, obstinately insisted on remaining the last on the pavement, publicly to display her maternal triumph.

The repast that evening at the Hotel du Louvre was likewise marred by Théophile's unlucky affair. The latter was quite a. plague, it had been the topic of conversation all the afternoon in the carriages during the drive in the Bois de Boulogne ; and the ladies always came to this conclusion, that the husband ought at least to have waited until the morrow before finding the letter. None but the most intimate friends of both families sat down to table. The only lively episode was a speech from uncle Bachelard, whom the Josserands could not very well avoid inviting, in spite of their terror. He was drunk, indeed, as early as the roast : he raised his glass, and commenced with these words : " I am happy in the joy I feel," which he kept repeating, unable to say anything further. The other guests smiled complacently. Auguste and Berthe, already worn out, looked at each other every now and then, with an air of surprise at seeing themselves opposite one another; and, when they remembered how this was, they gazed in their plates in a confused way.

Nearly two hundred invitations had been issued for the ball. The guests began to arrive as early as half-past nine. Three chandeliers lit up the large red drawing-room, in which only some seats along the walls had been left, whilst at one end, in front of the fire-place, the little orchestra was installed ; moreover, a bar had been placed at the farthest end of an adjoining room, and the two families also had a small apartment into which they could retire.

As Madame Duveyrier and Madame Josserand were receiving the first arrivals, that poor Théophile, who had been watched ever since the morning, was guilty of a most regrettable piece of brutality. Campardon was asking Valérie to grant him the first waltz. She laughed, and the husband took it as a provocation.

" You laugh ! you laugh ! " stammered he. " Tell me who the letter is from ? It must be from somebody, that letter must."

He had taken the entire afternoon to disengage that one idea from the confusion into which Octave's answers had plunged him. Now, he stuck to it : if it was not Monsieur Mouret, it was then some one else, and he demanded a name. As Valérie was walking off without answering him, he seized hold of her arm and twisted it spitefully, with the rage of an exasperated child, repeating the while :

"I'll break it. Tell me, who is the letter from ? "

The young woman, frightened, and stifling a cry of pain, had become quite white. Campardon felt her abandoning herself against his shoulder, succumbing to one of those nervous attacks which would shake her for hours together. He had scarcely time to lead her into the apartment reserved for the two families, where he laid her on a sofa. Some ladies had followed him, Madame Juzeur, Madame Dambreville, who unlaced her, whilst he discreetly retired.

However, only three or four people at most in the drawing-room had noticed this brief display of violence. Madame Duveyrier and Madame Josserand continued to receive the guests, the stream of whom gradually filled the vast apartment with light costumes and black dress suits. A murmur of amiable words arose, and faces continually smiled around the bride : the broad countenances of fathers and mothers, the skinny profiles of young girls, the fine and compassionate heads of young women. At the end of the room a violinist was tuning his first string, which sent forth little plaintive cries.

"Sir, I beg your pardon," said Théophile, going up to Octave, whose eyes he had encountered when twisting his wife's arm. "Every one in my place would have suspected you, is it not so ? But I wish to shake hands with you, to prove to you that I admit myself to have been in the wrong."

He shook hands with him, and led him on one side, tortured by a necessity to unbosom himself, to find a confidant for the outpourings of his heart.

"Ah ! sir, if I were to tell you—"

And he talked for a long while of his wife. When a young girl, she was delicate, it was said jokingly that marriage would set her right. She had not sufficient air in her parents' shop, where every evening for three months she had appeared to him very nice, obedient, of a rather sad disposition, but charming.

"Well ! sir, marriage did not set her right, far from it. After a few weeks she became terrible, we could no longer agree together. There were quarrels about nothing at all. Changes of temper at every minute, laughing, crying, without my knowing why. And absurd sentiments, ideas that would knock a person down, a perpetual mania for making people wild. In short, sir, my home has become a hell."

"It is very remarkable," murmured Octave, who felt a necessity for saying something.

Then, the husband, ghastly pale, and drawing himself up on

his short legs, to override the ridiculous, came to what he called
the wretched woman's bad behaviour.   Twice he had suspected
her; but he was too honourable, he could not retain such an
idea in his head.   This time, though, he was obliged to yield to
evidence.   It was not possible to doubt, was it?   And, with his
trembling fingers, he felt the pocket of his waistcoat which contained the letter.

"If she did it for money, I might understand it," added he.
"But they never give her any, I am sure of that, I should know
it.   Then, tell me what it can be that she has in her skin?   I
am very nice myself, she has everything at home, I cannot
understand it.   If you can understand it, sir, explain it to me,
I beg of you."

"It is very curious, very curious," repeated Octave, embarrassed by all these disclosures, and trying to make his escape.

But the husband, in a state of fever, and tormented by a want
of certitude, would not let him go.   At this moment, Madame
Juzeur reappearing, went and whispered a word to Madame Josserand, who was greeting the arrival of a big jeweller of the
Palais-Royal with a grand curtsey; and she, quite upset, hastened
to follow her.

"I think that your wife has a very violent attack," observed
Octave to Théophile.

"Never mind her!" replied the latter in a fury, vexed at not
being ill so as to be coddled up also, "she is only too pleased to
have an attack!   It always puts everyone on her side.   My
health is no better than hers, yet I have never deceived her!"

Madame Josserand did not return.   The rumour circulated
among the intimate friends that Valérie was struggling in frightful convulsions.   There should have been men present to hold
her down; but, as they had been obliged to half undress her,
they declined Trublot's and Gueulin's offers of assistance.   The
orchestra was now playing a quadrille, and Berthe was opening
the ball with Duveyrier, who danced like a judge, whilst, not
having been able to discover Madame Josserand, Auguste faced
them with Hortense.   The attack was kept a profound secret
from the young married couple for fear of dangerous emotions.
The ball was becoming lively, peals of laughter resounded in the
brilliant light of the chandeliers.   A polka, which the violins
next gave out in a sprightly style, whirled the couples round
the vast drawing-room, amidst an endless string of long trains.

"Doctor Juillerat! where is Doctor Juillerat?" asked Madame
Josserand, rushing back into the room.

The doctor had been invited, but no one had as yet seen him. Then she no longer strove to hide the slumbering rage which had been collecting within her since the morning. She spoke out before Octave and Campardon, without mincing her words.

"I am beginning to have enough of it. It is not very pleasant for my daughter, all this cuckoldom paraded before us!"

She looked about for Hortense, and at length caught sight of her talking to a gentleman, of whom she could only see the back, but whom she recognised by its breadth. It was Verdier. This increased her ill-humour. She sharply called the young girl to her, and, lowering her voice, told her that she would do better to remain at her mother's disposal on such a day as that. Hortense did not listen to the reprimand. She was triumphant, Verdier had just fixed their marriage at two months from then, in June.

"Shut up!" said the mother.

"I assure you, mamma. He already sleeps out three nights a week so as to accustom the other to it, and in a fortnight he will stop away altogether. Then it will be all over, and I shall have him."

"Shut up! I have already had more than enough of your romance! You will just oblige me by waiting near the door for Doctor Juillerat, and by sending him to me the moment he arrives. And, above all, not a word of all this to your sister!"

She returned to the adjoining room, leaving Hortense muttering that, thank goodness! she required no one's approbation, and that they would all be nicely caught one day, when they saw her make a better marriage than the others. Yet, she went to the door, and watched for the doctor's arrival.

The orchestra was now playing a waltz. Berthe was dancing with one of her husband's young cousins, so as to dispose of the relations in turn. Madame Duveyrier had been unable to refuse uncle Bachelard, who inconvenienced her a great deal by breathing in her face. The heat increased, the refreshment bar was already crowded with gentlemen wiping their foreheads. Some little girls were jumping together in a corner; whilst several mothers sat musing away from the dancers, thinking of the marriages their daughters had so often missed. Congratulations were showered upon the two fathers, Monsieur Vabre and Monsieur Josserand, who did not leave each other a moment, without their exchanging, however, a word. All the guests had an air of amusing themselves immensely, and expatiated before them on the liveliness of the ball.   It was, according to Campardon, a liveliness of a good standard.

The architect, with an effusion of gallantry, concerned himself a great deal about Valérie's condition, without, however, missing a dance.   He had the idea to send his daughter Angèle for news in his name.   The child, whose fourteen years had been burning with curiosity since the morning around the lady that everyone was talking about, was delighted at being able to penetrate into the little room.   And, as she did not return, the architect was obliged to take the liberty of slightly opening the door and thrusting his head in.   He beheld his daughter standing up beside the sofa, deeply absorbed by the sight of Valérie, whose bosom, shaken by spasms, had escaped from the unhooked bodice.   Protestations arose, the ladies called to him not to come in ; and he withdrew, assuring them that he merely wished to know how she was getting on.

"She is no better, she is no better," said he, in a melancholy way to the persons who happened to be near the door.   "There are four of them holding her.   How strong a woman must be, to be able to bound about like that without hurting herself ! "

A small group had formed there.   They discussed, in an undertone, the slightest phases of the attack.   Some ladies, hearing of what was taking place, would come between two quadrilles, enter the little room with an air of pity, and then return in a few minutes and give the gentlemen the latest particulars, and go and rejoin the dance.   It was a regular corner of mystery, words whispered in each other's ears, glances exchanged, in the midst of the increasing hubbub.   And, alone and abandoned, Théophile walked up and down before the door, rendered quite ill by the fixed idea that he was being made a fool of, and that he ought not to suffer it.

But Doctor Juillerat quickly crossed the ballroom, accompanied by Hortense, who was explaining matters to him. Madame Duveyrier followed them.   Some persons showed their surprise, more rumours circulated.   Scarcely had the doctor disappeared than Madame Josserand left the little room with Madame Dambreville.   Her rage was increasing ; she had just emptied two water bottles over Valérie's head ; never before had she seen a woman as nervous as that.   Then she had decided to make the round of the ballroom, so as to stop all remarks by her presence.   Only, she walked with such a terrible step, she distributed such sour smiles, that everyone behind her was let into the secret.

VALÉRIE IN HYSTERICS AT THE WEDDING BALL.

Madame Dambreville did not leave her. Ever since the morning she had been speaking to her of Léon, making vague complaints, trying to bring her to speak to her son, so as to patch up their connection. She drew her attention to him, as he was conducting a tall, scraggy girl back to her place, and to whom he made a show of being very assiduous.

"He abandons us," said she, with a slight laugh, trembling with suppressed tears. "Scold him now, for not so much·as 'ooking at us."

"Léon !" called Madame Josserand.

When he came to her, she added roughly, not being in the temper to choose her words :

"Why are you angry with madame? She bears you no ill-will. Make it up with her. It does no good being ill-tempered."

And she left them embarrassed before each other. Madame Dambreville took Léon's arm, and they went and conversed in the recess of a window ; then they tenderly left the ballroom together. She had sworn to arrange his marriage in the autumn.

Madame Josserand, who continued distributing smiles, was overcome by emotion when she found herself before Berthe, who was out of breath at having danced so much, and looked quite rosy in her white dress, which was becoming rumpled. She clasped her in her arms, and almost fainted away at a vague association of ideas, recalling, no doubt, the other one, whose face was so frightfully convulsed :

"My poor darling, my poor darling ! " murmured she, giving her two big kisses.

Then Berthe calmly asked :

"How is she ?"

At this, Madame Josserand at once became very sour again. What ! Berthe knew it ! Why of course she knew it, everyone knew it. Her husband alone, whom she pointed out conducting an old lady to the refreshment bar, was still ignorant of the story. She even intended to get some one to tell him everything, for it made him appear too stupid to be always behind everyone else, and never to know anything.

"And I, who have been slaving to hide the catastrophe ! " said Madame Josserand, beside herself. "Ah, well ! I shall not put myself out any more, it must be put a stop to. I will not tolerate their making you ridiculous."

Everyone did indeed know it. Only, so as not to cast a gloom over the ball, it was not talked about. The orchestra had smothered the first words of sympathy ; now, in the greater freedom of the couples, everyone proceeded to smile at the affair. It was very hot, night was drawing on apace. Waiters handed round refreshments. On a sofa, two little girls, overcome by fatigue, had fallen asleep in each other's arms, their faces close together. Near the orchestra, in the deep tones of a double bass, Monsieur Vabre had brought himself to talk to Monsieur Josserand of his great task, with respect to a doubt which, for a fortnight past, he had felt concerning the real works of two painters of the same name ; whilst, close by, Duveyrier, in the centre of a group, was energetically blaming the Emperor for having authorised the production of a piece attacking society at the Comédie-Française. But, whenever a waltz or a polka was struck up, the men had to vacate their position, couples whirled round the room, trains swept the floor, raising in the bright light a fine dust amidst the musky odour of the costumes.

"She is better," Campardon, who had taken another peep, hastened to say. "One can go in."

A few male friends ventured to enter. Valérie was still lying down, only, the attack was passing off ; and, out of decency, they had covered her bosom with a napkin, found lying on a sideboard. Madame Juzeur and Madame Duveyrier were standing before the window listening to Doctor Juillerat, who was explaining that the attacks sometimes yielded to hot water applications to the neck. But the invalid, having seen Octave enter with Campardon, called him to her by a sign, and spoke a few incoherent words to him in a final hallucination. He had to sit down beside her, at the doctor's express order, who was desirous above all not to thwart her ; and thus the young man listened to her disclosures, he who, during the evening, had already heard the husband's. She trembled with fright, she took him for her lover, and implored him to hide her. Then she recognised him, and burst into tears, thanking him for his lie of the morning during the mass. Octave thought of that other attack, of which he had wished to take advantage, with the greedy desire of a schoolboy. Now, he was her friend, and she would tell him everything, perhaps it would be better.

At this moment, Théophile, who had continued to wander up and down before the door, wished to enter. Other men were there, so he could very well be there himself. But his appearance created a regular panic. On hearing his voice, Valérie was again seized with a fit of trembling, everyone thought she was about to have another attack. He, imploring, and struggling amongst the ladies, whose arms thrust him back, kept obstinately repeating :

"I only ask her for the name. Let her tell me the name."

Then, Madame Josserand arriving, gave vent to her wrath. She drew Théophile into the little room, to hide the scandal, and said to him furiously :

"Look here! will you shut up? Ever since this morning you have been badgering us with your stupidities. You have no tact, sir; yes, you have absolutely no tact at all! One should not harp on such things on a wedding-day."

"Excuse me, madame," murmured he, "this is my business, and does not concern you!"

"What! it does not concern me? but I form part of your family now, sir, and do you think your affair amuses me on account of my daughter? Ah! you have given her a pretty wedding! Not another word, sir, you are deficient in tact!"

He stood bewildered, looking around him, seeking some one who would take his part. But the ladies all showed by their coldness that they judged him with equal severity. It was that exactly, he had no tact; for there are occasions when one should be able to restrain one's passions. Even his own sister would have nothing to do with him. As he still protested, he raised a general revolt. No, no, there was no answer possible, such behaviour was unheard of!

This cry closed his mouth. He was so scared, so feeble looking, with his slender limbs, and his face like a girl's, that the ladies smiled slightly. When one had not the facilities for making a woman happy, one ought not to marry. Hortense weighed him with a disdainful glance; little Angèle, whom they had forgotten, hovered round him, with her sly air, as though she had been looking for something; and he drew back embarrassed, and blushed when he saw them all, so big and plump, hemming him in with their sturdy hips. But they felt the necessity of patching up the matter. Valérie had started off sobbing again, whilst the doctor continued to bathe her temples. Then they understood one another with a glance, a common feeling of defence drew them together. They puzzled their brains, trying to explain the letter to the husband.

"Pooh!" murmured Trublot, who had just rejoined Octave, "it is easy enough; they have only to say the letter was addressed to the servant."

Madame Josserand heard him. She turned round and looked

at him with a glance full of admiration.   Then, turning towards
Théophile :

"Does an innocent woman lower herself to give explanations,
when accused with such brutality?   Still, I may speak.   The
letter was dropped by Françoise, that maid whom your wife had
to pack off on account of her bad conduct.   There, are you satisfied? do you not blush with shame?"

At first, the husband shrugged his shoulders.   But the ladies
all remained serious, answering his objections with very strong
reasoning.   He was shaken, when, to complete his discomfiture,
Madame Duveyrier got angry, telling him that his conduct had
been abominable, and that she disowned him.   Then, vanquished,
and feeling a longing to be kissed, he threw his arms round
Valérie's neck, and begged her pardon.   It was most touching.
Even Madame Josserand was deeply affected.

"It is always best to come to an understanding," said she,
with relief.   "The day will not end so badly after all."

When they had dressed Valérie again, and she appeared in
the ballroom on Théophile's arm, the joy seemed to be redoubled.
It was close upon three o'clock, the guests were beginning to
leave ; but the orchestra continued to get through the quadrilles
with great gusto.   Some of the men smiled behind the backs
of the reconciled couple.   A medical remark of Campardon's,
respecting that poor Théophile, quite delighted Madame Juzeur.
The young girls hastened to stare at Valérie ; then they put on
their stupid looks before their mothers' scandalized glances.
Berthe, who was at length dancing with her husband, must
have whispered a word or two in his ear ; for Auguste, made
aware of what had been taking place, turned his head round,
and, without getting out of step, looked at his brother Théophile
with the surprise and the superiority of a man to whom such
things cannot happen.   There was a final gallop, the guests were
getting more free in the stifling heat and the reddish light of
the candles, the vacillating flames of which caused the pendants
of the chandeliers to sparkle.

"You are very intimate with her?" asked Madame Hédouin,
as she whirled round on Octave's arm, having accepted his invitation to dance.

The young man fancied he felt a slight quiver in her frame,
so erect and so calm.

"Not at all," said he.   "They mixed me up in the matter,
which annoys me immensely.   The poor devil swallowed everything."

"It is very wrong," declared she, in her grave voice.

No doubt Octave was mistaken. When he withdrew his arm from her waist, Madame Hédouin was not even panting, her eyes were clear, and her hair not the least disarranged. But a scandal upset the end of the ball. Uncle Bachelard, who had finished himself off at the refreshment bar, ventured on a lively idea. He had suddenly been seen dancing a most indecent step before Gueulin. Some napkins rolled round, and stuffed in the front of his buttoned-up coat, gave him the bosom of a wet-nurse ; and two big oranges placed on the napkins, behind the lapels, displayed their roundness, in the sanguineous redness of an excoriated skin. This time everyone protested : though one may earn heaps of money, yet there are limits which a man who respects himself should never go beyond, especially before young persons. Monsieur Josserand, ashamed, and in despair, drew his brother-in-law away. Duveyrier displayed the greatest disgust.

At four o'clock, the newly-married couple returned to the Rue de Choiseul. They brought Théophile and Valérie back in their carriage. As they went up to the second floor, where an apartment had been prepared for them, they came across Octave, who was also retiring to rest. The young man wished to draw politely on one side, but Berthe made a similar movement, and they knocked up against each other.

"Oh ! excuse me, mademoiselle," said he.

The word "mademoiselle" amused them immensely. She looked at him, and he recalled the first glance exchanged between them on that same staircase, a glance of gaiety and daring, the charming welcome of which he again beheld. They understood each other perhaps, she blushed, whilst he went up alone to his room, in the midst of the death-like peacefulness of the upper floors.

Auguste, with his left eye closed up, half mad with the headache which had been clinging to him since the morning, was already in the apartment, where the other members of the family were arriving. Then, at the moment of quitting Berthe, Valérie yielded to a sudden fit of emotion, and pressing her in her arms, and completing the rumpling of her white dress, she kissed her, saying in a low voice :

"Ah ! my dear, I wish you better luck than I have had !"

CHAPTER IX.

Two days later, towards seven o'clock, as Octave arrived at the Campardons' for dinner, he found Rose by herself, dressed in a cream-colour dressing-gown, trimmed with white lace.

"Are you expecting anyone?" asked he.

"No," replied she, rather confused. "We will have dinner directly Achille comes in."

The architect was abandoning his punctual habits, was never there at the proper time for his meals, arrived very red in the face, with a wild expression, and cursing business. Then he went off again every evening, on all kinds of pretexts, talking of appointments at cafés, inventing distant meetings. Octave, on these occasions, would often keep Rose company till eleven o'clock, for he had understood that the husband had him there to board to amuse his wife, and she would gently complain, and tell him her fears : ah ! she left Achille very free, only she was so anxious when he came home after midnight !

"Do you not think he has been rather sad lately?" asked she, in a tenderly frightened tone of voice.

The young man had not noticed it.

"I think he is rather worried, perhaps. The works at Saint-Roch cause him some anxiety."

But she shook her head, without saying anything further about it. Then she was very kind to Octave, questioning him with a motherly and sisterly affection as to how he had employed the day. During nearly nine months that he had been boarding with them, she had always treated him thus as a child of the house.

At length, the architect appeared.

"Good evening, my pet ; good evening, my duck," said he, kissing her with his doting air of a good husband. "Another fool has been detaining me in the street !"

Octave had moved away, and he heard them exchange a few words in a low voice.

" Will she come ? "

" No, what is the good ? and, above all, do not worry yourself."

" You declared to me that she would come."

" Well ! yes, she is coming. Are you pleased ? It is for your sake that I have done it."

They took their seats at the table. During the whole of dinner-time they talked of the English language, which little Angèle had been learning for a fortnight past. Campardon had suddenly upheld the necessity for a young lady knowing English ; and, as Lisa had come to them from an actress who had been to London, each meal was employed in discussing the names of the dishes that she brought in. That evening, after long and fruitless endeavours to pronounce the words "rump steak," they had to send the dish away, Victoire having left it too long at the fire, and the meat being as tough as leather.

They were taking their dessert, when a ring at the bell caused Madame Campardon to start.

"It is madame's cousin," Lisa returned and said, in the wounded tone of a servant whom one has omitted to let into a family secret.

And it was indeed Gasparine who entered. She wore a black woollen dress, looking very quiet, with her thin face, and her air of a poor shop-girl. Rose, tenderly enveloped in her dressing-gown of cream-colour silk, and plump and fresh, rose up so moved, that tears filled her eyes.

"Ah ! my dear," murmured she, "you are good. We will forget everything, will we not ? "

She took her in her arms, and gave her two hearty kisses. Octave discreetly wished to retire. But they grew angry : he could remain, he was one of the family. So he amused himself by looking on. Campardon, at first greatly embarrassed, turned his eyes away from the two women, puffing about, and looking for a cigar ; whilst Lisa, who was roughly clearing the table, exchanged glances with surprised Angèle.

"It is your cousin," at length said the architect to his daughter. "You have heard us speak of her. Come, kiss her now."

She kissed her with her sullen air, troubled by the sort of governess glance with which Gasparine took stock of her, after asking some questions respecting her age and education. Then, when the others passed into the drawing-room, she preferred to follow Lisa, who slammed the door, saying, without even fearing that she might be heard :

" Ah, well ! it'll become precious funny here now ! "

In the drawing-room, Campardon, still restless, began to excuse himself.

" On my word of honour ! the happy idea was not mine. It is Rose who wished to be reconciled. Every morning, for more than a week past, she has been saying to me : ' Now, go and fetch her.' So I ended by fetching you."

And, as though he had felt the necessity of convincing Octave, he took him up to the window.

" Well ! women are women. It bothered me, because I have a dread of rows. One on the right, the other on the left, there was no squabbling possible. But I had to give in. Rose says we shall be far happier thus. Anyhow, we will try. It depends on these two, now, to make my life comfortable."

Meanwhile, Rose and Gasparine had seated themselves side by side on the sofa. They were talking of the past, of the days lived at Plassans, with good papa Domergue. Rose's complexion was then livid, and she had the slender limbs of a young girl sickly from her birth ; whilst Gasparine, who was a woman at fifteen, was tall and crummy, with beautiful eyes. Looking at each other now, they seemed different people, the one so freshly plump in her enforced chastity, the other dried up by the life of nervous passion which was consuming her. For a moment, Gasparine suffered from her yellow face and her poor dress in the presence of Rose, arrayed in silk, and hiding beneath folds of lace the delicate softness of her white neck. But she mastered this twinge of jealousy, she at once accepted the position of a poor relation on her knees before her cousin's elegance and grace.

" And your health ? " asked she in a low voice. " Achille spoke to me about it. Is it no better ? "

" No, no," replied Rose in a melancholy tone. " You see, I eat, I look very well. But it gets no better, it will never get any better."

As she began to cry, Gasparine, in her turn, took her in her arms, and pressed her against her flat and ardent breast, whilst Campardon hastened to console them.

" Why do you cry ? " asked she maternally. " The main thing is that you do not suffer. What does it matter, if you have always people about you to love you ? "

Rose was becoming calmer, and already smiling amidst her tears. Then the architect, carried away by his feelings, clasped

THE ARCHITECT CLASPS ROSE AND GASPARINE IN THE SAME EMBRACE.

p. 168.

them both in the same embrace, kissing them alternately, and stammering :

"Yes, yes, we will love each other very much, we will love you such a deal, my poor little duck. You will see how well everything will go, now that we are united."

And, turning towards Octave, he added :

"Ah! my dear fellow, people may talk, there is nothing after all like family ties!"

The end of the evening was delightful. Campardon, who usually fell asleep on leaving the table if he remained at home, recovered all his artist's gaiety, the old jokes and the broad songs of the School of Fine Arts. When, towards eleven o'clock, Gasparine prepared to leave, Rose insisted on accompanying her to the door, in spite of the difficulty she experienced in walking that day ; and, leaning over the balustrade, in the grave silence of the staircase, she called after her :

"Come and see us often!"

On the morrow, Octave, feeing interested, tried to make the cousin talk at "The Ladies' Paradise," whilst they were receiving a consignment of linen goods together. But she answered curtly, and he felt that she was hostile, annoyed at his having been a witness the evening before. Moreover, she did not like him; she even displayed a sort of rancour towards him in their business relations. For a long time past she had seen through his game in connection with the mistress, and she assisted at his assiduous courtship with black looks and a contemptuous curl of the lips, which at times troubled him. Whenever that tall devil of a girl thrust her skinny hands between them, he experienced the decided and disagreeable sensation that Madame Hédouin would never be his.

Octave had given himself six months, however, and though scarcely four had passed, he was becoming impatient. Every morning he asked himself whether he should not hurry matters forward, seeing the little progress he had made in the affections of this woman, always so icy and gentle. She had ended, however, by showing a real esteem for him, won over by his enlarged ideas, his dreams of vast modern warehouses discharging millions of merchandise into the streets of Paris. Often, when her husband was not there, and she opened the correspondence with the young man of a morning, she would detain him beside her and consult him, profiting a great deal by his advice, and a sort of commercial intimacy was thus gradually established between them. Their hands met amidst bundles of

invoices, their breaths mingled as they added up columns of
figures, and they yielded to moments of emotion before the open
cash-box after some extra fortunate receipts. He even took
advantage of these occasions, his tactics being now to reach her
heart through her good trader's nature, and to conquer her on
a day of weakness, in the midst of the great emotion occasioned
by some unexpected sale. So he remained on the watch for
some surprising occurrence which should deliver her up to him.
The moment he no longer kept her talking of business, she at
once resumed her quiet authoritative way, politely giving him
his instructions, the same as she did to the shopmen ; and she
managed the establishment with her beautiful woman's frigidity,
wearing a man's little necktie round her throat resembling an
ancient statue's, and a quiet, tight-fitting dress invariably black.

About this time, Monsieur Hédouin, having fallen ill, went
to pass a season at Vichy to take the waters. Octave, to speak
frankly, was delighted. Though as cold as marble, Madame
Hédouin would become more tender-hearted during her enforced
widowhood. But he fruitlessly awaited a quiver, a languidness
of desire. Never had she been so active, her head so free, her
eye so clear. Up at break of day, she received the consign-
ments herself in the basement, her pen behind her ear, in the
busy manner of a clerk. She was everywhere, upstairs and
down, in the linen department and in the silk one, superintend-
ing the display and the sales ; and she moved peacefully about,
without even catching so much as a speck of dust, amidst those
piles of bales with which the too small warehouse was bursting.
When he met her in the middle of some narrow passage,
between a wall of woollens and a pile of napkins, Octave would
stand in an awkward way on one side, that she might be pressed
for a second against his breast ; but she passed by so occupied
that he scarcely felt her dress touch him. He was greatly
troubled, too, by Mademoiselle Gasparine's eyes, the harsh look
of which he always found fixed upon them at such moments.

At heart, though, the young man did not despair. At times
he thought he had reached the goal, and was already arranging
his mode of living for the near day when he would be the lover
of his employer's wife. He had kept up his connection with
Marie to help him to wait patiently ; only, though she was convenient and cost him nothing, she might perhaps one day
become irksome, with her faithfulness of a beaten cur. Therefore, at the same time that he took her in his arms on the
nights when he felt dull, he would be thinking of a way of

breaking off with her. To do so abruptly seemed to him to be worse than foolish. One holiday morning, when about to rejoin his neighbour's wife, the neighbour himself having gone out early, the idea had at length come to him of restoring Marie to Jules, of sending them in a loving way into each other's arms, so that he might withdraw with a clear conscience. It was moreover a good action, the touching side of which relieved him of all remorse. He waited a while, however, not wishing to find himself without a female companion of some kind.

At the Campardons' another complication was occupying Octave's mind. He felt that the moment was arriving when he would have to take his meals elsewhere. For three weeks past, Gasparine had been making herself quite at home there, with an authority daily increasing. At first she had began by coming every evening; then she had appeared at lunch; and, in spite of her work at the shop, she was commencing to take charge of everything, of Angèle's education and of the household affairs. Rose was for ever repeating in Campardon's presence :

"Ah ! if Gasparine only lived with us !"

But each time the architect, blushing with conscientious scruples, and tormented with shame, cried out :

"No, no ; it cannot be. Besides, where would you put her to sleep ?"

And he explained that they would have to give his study as a bedroom to their cousin, whilst he would move his table and plans into the drawing-room. It would certainly not inconvenience him in the least ; he would perhaps decide to make the alteration one day, for he had no need of a drawing-room, and his study was becoming too cramped for all the work he had in hand. Only, Gasparine might very well remain as she was. What need was there to live all in a heap ?

"When one is comfortable," repeated he to Octave, "it is a mistake to wish to be better."

About that time, he was obliged to go and spend two days at Evreux. He was worried about the work in hand at the bishop's palace. He had yielded to the bishop's desires without a credit having been opened for the purpose, and the construction of the range for the new kitchens and of the heating apparatus threatened to amount to a very large figure, which it would be impossible to include in the cost of repairs. Besides that, the pulpit, for which three thousand francs had been granted, would come to ten thousand at the least. He wished to talk the matter over with the bishop, so as to take certain precautions.

Rose was only expecting him to return on the Sunday night. He arrived in the middle of lunch, and his sudden entrance caused quite a scare. Gasparine was seated at the table, between Octave and Angèle. They pretended to be all at their ease; but there reigned a certain air of mystery. Lisa had closed the drawing-room door at a despairing gesture from her mistress; whilst the cousin kicked beneath the furniture some pieces of paper that were lying about. When Campardon talked of changing his things, they stopped him.

"Wait a while. Have a cup of coffee, as you lunched at Evreux."

At length, as he noticed Rose's embarrassment, she went and threw her arms round his neck.

"My dear, you must not scold me. If you had not returned till this evening, you would have found everything straight."

She tremblingly opened the doors, and took him into the drawing-room and the study. A mahogany bedstead, brought that morning by a furniture dealer, occupied the place of the drawing-table, which had been moved into the middle of the adjoining room; but as yet nothing had been put straight, portfolios were knocking about amongst some of Gasparine's clothes, the Virgin with the Bleeding Heart was lying against the wall, kept in position by a new wash-stand.

"It was a surprise," murmured Madame Campardon, her heart bursting, as she hid her face in her husband's waistcoat.

He, deeply moved, looked about him. He said nothing, and avoided encountering Octave's eyes. Then, Gasparine asked in her sharp voice:

"Does it annoy you, cousin? It is Rose who pestered me. But if you think I am in the way, it is not too late for me to leave."

"Oh! cousin!" at length exclaimed the architect. "All that Rose does is well done."

And the latter having burst out sobbing on his breast, he added:

"Come, my duck, how foolish of you to cry! I am very pleased. You wish to have your cousin with you, well! have your cousin with you. Everything suits me. Now do not cry any more! See! I kiss you like I love you, so much! so much!"

He devoured her with caresses. Then, Rose, who melted

into tears for a word, but who smiled at once, in the midst of her sobs, was consoled. She kissed him in her turn, on his beard, saying to him gently:

"You were harsh. Kiss her also."

Campardon kissed Gasparine. They called Angèle, who had been looking on from the dining-room, her eyes bright and her mouth wide open; and she had to kiss her also. Octave had moved away, having arrived at the conclusion that they were becoming far too loving in that family. He had noticed with surprise Lisa's respectful attitude and smiling attentiveness towards Gasparine. She was decidedly an intelligent girl, that hussy with the blue eyelids!

Meanwhile, the architect had taken off his coat, and whistling and singing, as lively as a boy, he spent the afternoon in arranging the cousin's room. The latter helped him, pushing the furniture with him into its place, unpacking the bed linen, and shaking the clothes; whilst Rose sitting down through fear of tiring herself, gave them advice, such as placing the washstand here and the bed there, as being more convenient for every one. Then, Octave understood that his presence interfered with the free expansion of their hearts; he felt he was one too many in such an united family, so he mentioned that he was going to dine out that evening. Moreover, he had made up his mind: on the morrow, he would thank Madame Campardon for her kind hospitality, and invent some story for no longer trespassing upon it.

Towards five o'clock, as he was regretting that he did not know where to find Trublot, he had the idea to go and ask the Pichons for some dinner, so as not to pass the evening alone. But, on entering their apartments, he found himself in the midst of a deplorable family scene. The Vuillaumes were there, trembling with rage and indignation.

"It is disgraceful, sir!" the mother was saying, standing up with her arm thrust out towards her son-in-law, who was sitting on a chair in a state of collapse. "You gave me your word of honour."

"And you," added the father, causing his daughter to draw back tremblingly as far as the sideboard, "do not try to defend him, you are quite as guilty. Do you wish to die of hunger!"

Madame Vuillaume had put on her bonnet and shawl again.

"Good-bye!" uttered she in a solemn tone. "We will at least not encourage your dissoluteness by our presence. As you no

longer pay the least attention to our wishes, we have nothing
to detain us here.   Good-bye ! "

And, as through force of habit her son-in-law rose to accompany them she added :

"Do not trouble yourself, we shall be able to find the omnibus
very well without you.   Pass first, Monsieur Vuillaume.
Let them eat their dinner, and much good may it do them, for
they won't always have one ! "

Octave, thoroughly bewildered, drew on one side.   When
they had gone, he looked at Jules who was still in a state of
collapse on his chair, and at Marie leaning against the sideboard and looking very pale.   Neither of them said a word.

" What is the matter ? " asked he.

But, without answering him, the young woman commenced
scolding her husband in a doleful voice.

" I told you how it would be.   You should have waited, and
let them learn the thing by degrees.   There was no hurry, it
does not show as yet."

" What is the matter ? " repeated Octave.

Then, without even turning her head, she said bluntly, in the
midst of her emotion !

" I am in the family way."

" I have had enough of them !" cried Jules rising indignantly.
"I thought it right to tell them at once of this bother.   I wonder
if they think it amuses me !   I am more taken in by it all than
they are.   More especially, by Jove ! as it is through no fault of
mine.   Is it not true, Marie, that we have no idea how it has
come about ? "

" That is so, indeed," affirmed the young woman.

It quite affected Octave ; aud he felt a violent desire to do
something nice for the Pichons.   Jules continued to grumble :
they would receive the child all the same, only it would have
done better to have remained where it was.   On her side, Marie,
generally so gentle, became angry, and ended by agreeing with
her mother, who never forgave disobedience.   And the couple
were coming to a quarrel, throwing the youngster from one to
the other, accusing each other of being the cause of it, when
Octave gaily interfered.

" It is no use quarrelling, now that it is there.   Come, we
won't dine here ; it would be too sad.   I will take you to a restaurant, if you are agreeable."

The young woman blushed.   Dining at a restaurant was her
delight.   She spoke however of her little girl, who invariably

prevented her from having any pleasure. But it was decided that, for this once, Lilitte should go too. And they spent a very pleasant evening. Octave took them to the "Bœuf à la Mode," where they had a private room, to be more at their ease, as he said. There, he overwhelmed them with food, with an earnest prodigality, without thinking of the bill, happy at seeing them eat. He even at dessert, when they had laid Lilitte down between two of the sofa cushions, called for champagne ; and they sat there, their elbows on the table, their eyes dim, all three full of heart, and feeling languid from the suffocating heat of the room. At length, at eleven o'clock, they talked of going home ; but they were very red, and the fresh air of the street intoxicated them. Then, as the child, heavy with sleep, refused to walk, Octave, to do things handsomely until the end, insisted on hailing a cab, though the Rue de Choiseul was close by. In the cab, he was scrupulous to the point of not pressing Marie's knees. Only, upstairs, whilst Jules was tucking Lilitte in, he imprinted a kiss on the young woman's forehead, the farewell kiss of a father parting with his daughter to a son-in-law. Then, seeing them very loving and looking at each other in a drunken sort of way, he left them to themselves, wishing them a good-night and many pleasant dreams as he closed the door.

"Well ! " thought he, as he jumped all alone into bed, "it has cost me fifty francs, but I owed them quite that. After all, my only wish is that her husband may make her happy, poor little woman ! "

And, with his heart full of emotion, he resolved, before falling asleep, to make his grand attempt on the following evening.

Every Monday, after dinner, Octave assisted Madame Hédouin to examine the orders of the week. For this purpose they both withdrew to the little closet at the back, a narrow apartment which merely contained a safe, a desk, two chairs, and a sofa. But it so happened that on the Monday in question the Duveyriers were going to take Madame Hédouin to the Opéra-Comique. So, towards three o'clock, she sent for the young man. In spite of the bright sunshine, they were obliged to burn the gas, for the closet only received a pale light from an inner courtyard. He bolted the door, and, as she looked at him in surprise, he murmured :

"No one can come and disturb us."

She nodded her head approvingly, and they set to work. The new summer goods were going splendidly, the business of the house continued increasing. That week especially the sale of the little woollens seemed so promising that she heaved a sigh.

"Ah! if we only had enough room!"

"But," said he, commencing the attack, "it depends upon yourself. I have had an idea for some time past, which I wish to lay before you."

It was the stroke of audacity he had been waiting for. His idea was to purchase the adjoining house in the Rue Neuve-Saint-Augustin, to give notice to an umbrella-dealer and to a toy-merchant, and then to enlarge the warehouses, to which they could add several other vast departments. And he warmed up as he spoke, showing himself full of disdain for the old way of doing business in the depths of damp, dark shops, without any display, evoking a new commerce with a gesture, piling up in palaces of crystal all the luxury pertaining to woman, turning over millions in the light of day, and illuminating at night-time in a princely style.

"You will crush the other drapers of the Saint-Roch neighbourhood," said he; "you will secure all the small customers. For instance, Monsieur Vabre's silk warehouse does you a good deal of harm at present; well! increase your shop front, have a special department for silks, and you will force him into bankruptcy before five years are past. Besides, there is still a question of opening that new street, the Rue du Dix-Décembre, which is to lead from the new Opera-House to the Bourse. My friend Campardon alludes to it every now and then. It may increase the business of the neighbourhood tenfold."

Madame Hédouin listened to him, her elbow on a ledger, her beautiful, grave head buried in her hand. She was born at "The Ladies' Paradise," which had been founded by her father and her uncle; she loved the house, she could see it expanding, swallowing up the neighbouring houses, and displaying a royal frontage; and this dream suited her active intelligence, her upright will, her woman's delicate intuition of the new Paris.

"Uncle Deleuze would never give his consent," murmured she. "Besides, my husband is too unwell."

Then, seeing her wavering, Octave assumed his most seductive voice—an actor's voice, soft and musical. At the same time he looked tenderly at her, with his eyes the colour of old gold, which some women thought irresistible. But, though the gas-jet flared close to the nape of her neck, she remained as cool as ever; she merely fell into a reverie, half stunned by the young man's inexhaustible flow of words. He had come to studying the affair from the money point of view, already making an estimate with the impassioned air of a romantic page declaring a long pent up love. When she suddenly awoke from her reflections, she found herself in his arms. He was thinking that she was at length yielding.

"Dear me! so this is what it all meant!" said she in a sad tone of voice, freeing herself from him as from some tiresome child.

"Well! yes, I love you," cried he. "Oh! do not repel me. With you I will do great things—"

And he went on thus to the end of the tirade, which had a false ring about it. She did not interrupt him; she was standing up and again scanning the pages of the ledger. Then, when he had finished, she replied:

"I know all that—I have already heard it before. But I thought you were more sensible than the others, Monsieur Octave. You grieve me, really you do, for I had counted upon you. However, all young men are foolish. We need a great deal of order in such a house as this, and you begin by desiring things which would disturb us from morning to night. I am not a woman here, I have too much to occupy me. Come, you who are so well organized, how is it you did not comprehend that it could never be, because in the first place it is stupid, in the second useless, and, moreover, luckily for me, I do not care the least about it!"

He would have preferred her to have been indignantly angry, displaying grand sentiments. Her calm tone of voice, her quiet reasoning of a practical woman, sure of herself, disconcerted him. He felt himself becoming ridiculous.

"Have pity, madame," stammered he, before losing all hope. "See how I suffer."

"No, you do not suffer. Anyhow, you will get over it. Hark! there is some one knocking, you would do better to open the door."

Then he had to draw the bolt. It was Mademoiselle Gasparine, who wished to know if any lace-trimmed chemises were expected. The bolted door had surprised her. But she knew Madame Hédouin too well; and, when she saw her with her cold air standing in front of Octave, who was full of uneasiness, a slight mocking smile played about her lips as she looked at him. It exasperated him, and in his own mind he accused her of having been the cause of his ill-success.

"Madame," declared he abruptly, when Gasparine had withdrawn, "I leave your employment this evening."

This was a surprise for Madame Hédouin. She looked at him.

"Why so ? I do not discharge you. Oh ! it will not make any difference ; I have no fear."

These words decided him. He would leave at once ; he would not endure his martyrdom a minute longer.

"Very good, Monsieur Octave," resumed she as serenely as ever. "I will settle with you directly. However, the firm will regret you, for you were a good assistant."

Once out in the street, Octave perceived that he had behaved like a fool. Four o'clock was striking, the gay spring sun covered with a sheet of gold a whole corner of the Place Gaillon. And, angry with himself, he wandered at hap-hazard down the Rue Saint-Roch, discussing the way in which he ought to have acted. To begin with, why had he not pinched that Gasparine's hips ? That perhaps was what she wanted ; but, unlike Campardon, he did not care for women dried up to such a point ; besides, he might perhaps have made a mistake there also, for she seemed to be one of those who are rigidly virtuous with Sunday gentlemen, having a week-day friend to count upon from the Monday to the Saturday. And how absurdly green too of him to wish to become the mistress's lover in spite of her ! Could he not have made his money in the house without requiring at the same time both bread and bed ? For a moment, scarcely knowing what to do, he was on the point of returning to " The Ladies' Paradise," and admitting himself to have been in the wrong. Then the thought of Madame Hédouin, so calmly superb, awakened his suffering vanity, and he went towards Saint-Roch. So much the worse ! it was done now. He would go and see if Campardon happened to be in the church, and take him to the café to have a glass of Madeira. It would help to divert his thoughts. He entered by the vestibule into which the vestry door opened, a dark dirty passage such as is to be met with in houses of ill-repute.

"You are perhaps looking for Monsieur Campardon ?" said a voice close beside him, as he stood hesitating, scrutinizing the nave with his glance.

It was the Abbé Mauduit, who had just recognised him. The architect being away, he insisted on showing the works, about which he was most enthusiastic, to the young man. He took him behind the chancel, and first of all showed him the chapel of the Virgin, with its white marble walls and its altar surmounted by the group in the manger, the infant Jesus between Joseph and the Virgin Mary, executed in an old-fashioned style; then, still farther back, he took him across to the chapel of Perpetual Adoration, with its seven golden lamps, its golden candelabra, its golden altar shining in the dim reddish light of the aureate stained-glass windows. But there, on the right and the left, wooden hoardings shut off the farthest portion of the apsis; and, in the midst of the chilly silence, above the kneeling black shadows, muttering prayers, resounded the strokes of picks, the voices of masons, all the deafening uproar of a work-yard.

"Walk in," said the Abbé Mauduit, gathering up his cassock. "I will explain everything to you."

On the other side of the planks there was a continual shower of old plaster, a corner of the church open to the outside air, white with the lime flying about, and damp with the spilt water. On the left one could still see the Tenth Station, Jesus being nailed to the cross, and on the right, the Twelfth, the women around Jesus. But, in the middle, the group of the Eleventh Station, Jesus on the cross, had been removed, and laid against a wall; and it was there that the men were at work.

"Here we are," continued the priest. "I had the idea of lighting the central group of the Calvary from above by means of an opening in the cupola. You can fancy what an effect it will have."

"Yes, yes," murmured Octave, whose thoughts were diverted by this stroll amidst building materials.

The Abbé Mauduit, speaking in a loud voice, had the air of a stage-carpenter directing the placing of some gorgeous scenery.

"There will naturally be only the most rigid bareness, nothing but stone walls, without a touch of paint or a fillet of gold. One must fancy oneself in a crypt in some desolate chamber underground. But the great effect will be the Christ on the Cross, with the Virgin Mary and Mary Magdalene at his feet. I shall place the group on the top of a rock, detaching the white statues by means of a grey background; and the light from the cupola, like some invisible ray, will light them up with a brightness that will bring them forward and animate them with a supernatural life. You will see, you will see!"

And he turned round to call out to a workman:

"Move the Virgin on one side ; you will be breaking her leg directly."

The workman called a comrade. Between them they got hold of the Virgin round the small of her back and carried her to a place of safety, like some tall white girl who had fallen down under a nervous attack.

"Be careful !" repeated the priest, following them through the rubbish, "her dress is already cracked. Wait a while !"

He gave them a hand, seizing Mary round the waist, and then, all covered with plaster, withdrew from the embrace.

"Then," resumed he, returning to Octave, "just imagine that the two bays of the nave there before us are open, and go and stand in the chapel of the Virgin. Over the altar, and through the chapel of Perpetual Adoration, you will behold the Calvary right at the back. Just fancy the effect : these three enormous figures, this bare and simple drama in this tabernacle recess, beyond the dim mysterious light of the stained-glass windows, the lamps and the gold candelabra. Eh ? I think it will be irresistible !"

He was waxing eloquent, and, proud of his idea, he laughed joyfully.

"The most sceptical will be moved," observed Octave to please him.

"That is what I think !" cried he. "I am impatient to see everything in place."

On returning to the nave he forgot himself, retaining his loud tone of voice and his mason's bearing, and he spoke of Campardon in the highest terms—a fellow who, in the middle ages, said he, would have had a very remarkable religious feeling. He let Octave out by the little door at the back, detaining him a minute or two longer in the courtyard of the vicarage, whence one can see the apsis of the church buried amidst the neighbouring buildings. It was there that he lived, on the second floor of a tall house with a mildewed frontage, occupied entirely by the clergy of Saint-Roch. A discreet priestly odour, the whispering hush of the confessional, issued from the vestibule surmounted by a statue of the Virgin, and from the tall windows veiled by thick curtains.

"I am going to see Monsieur Campardon this evening," at length said the Abbé Mauduit. "Ask him to wait in for me. I wisk to speak to him about an improvement without being disturbed."

And he bowed with his worldly air. Octave was calmed

now. Saint-Roch, with its cool vaults, had unbraced his nerves. He looked curiously at this entrance to a church through a private house, at the doorkeeper's room from whence at night-time the door was often opened for the cause of the faith, at all that corner of a convent lost amidst the black conglomeration of the neighbourhood. Out in the street, he again raised his eyes; the house displayed its bare frontage, with its barred and curtainless windows; but boxes of flowers were fixed by iron supports to the windows of the fourth floor; and, down below, in the thick walls, were narrow shops, which helped to fill the coffers of the clergy—a cobbler's, a clock-maker's, an embroiderer's, and even a wine-shop, where the mutes congregated whenever there was a funeral. Octave, who from his rebuff was in a mood to renounce the world, regretted the quiet lives which the priests' servants led up there in those rooms enlivened with verbenas and sweet peas.

That evening, at half-past six, as he entered the Campardons' apartments without ringing, he came suddenly upon the architect and Gasparine kissing each other in the anteroom. The latter, who had just come from the warehouse, had not even given herself time to close the door. Both stood stock-still.

"My wife is combing her hair," stammered the architect for the sake of saying something. "Go in and see her."

Octave, feeling as embarrassed as themselves, hastened to knock at the door of Rose's room, where he usually entered like a relation. He really could no longer continue to board there, now that he caught them behind the doors.

"Come in!" cried Rose's voice. "So it is you, Octave. Oh! there is no harm."

She had not, however, donned her dressing-gown, and her arms and shoulders, as white and delicate as milk, were bare. Sitting attentively before the looking-glass, she was rolling her golden hair in little curls. Every day she thus passed hours together in the most minute details of her toilet; her sole care was a continuous study of the pores of her skin, a perpetual adornment of her person, and then to go and stretch herself out in an easy-chair in all the beauty and luxury of a sexless idol.

"So you are making yourself beautiful again to-night," said Octave, smiling.

"Yes, for it is the only amusement I have," replied she. "It occupies me. You know I have never been a good house-wife; and, now that Gasparine will be here—Eh? don't you think that curl suits me ?   It consoles me a little when 1 am well dressed and I feel that I look pretty."

As the dinner was not ready, he told her of his having left "The Ladies' Paradise."   He invented a story about some other situation he had long been on the look-out for ; and thus reserved to himself a pretext for explaining his intention of taking his meals elsewhere.   She was surprised that he could give up a berth which held out great promises for the future. But she was busy at her glass, and did not catch all he said.

"Look at this red place behind my ear.   Is it a pimple ?"

He had to examine the nape of her neck, which she held towards him with her grand tranquillity of a sacred woman.

"It is nothing," said he.   "You must have dried yourself too roughly."

And, when he had assisted her to put on her dressing-gown of blue satin embroidered with silver, they passed into the dining-room.   As early as the soup, Octave's departure from the Hédouins' was discussed.   Campardon did not repress his surprise, whilst Gasparine smiled faintly; they were quite at their ease together.   The young man even ended by being touched by the tender attentions they showered upon Rose. Campardon poured out her wine, whilst Gasparine selected the best pieces from the dish for her.   Was she pleased with the bread ? if not they would change the baker ; would she like a pillow for her back ?   And Rose, full of gratitude, begged them not to disturb themselves.   She ate a good deal, throning her-self between them, with her beautiful blonde's delicate neck, arrayed in her queenly dressing-gown, having on her right her puffing husband, who was becoming thin, and on her left her dark dried-up cousin, whose shoulders were confined in a gloomy black dress, and whose flesh was melting away in the warmth of her desires.

At dessert Gasparine sharply rated Lisa, who had answered her mistress rudely respecting a piece of cheese that was miss-ing.   The maid became very humble.   Gasparine had already taken the household arrangements in hand, and had mastered the servants ; with a word, she could make Victoire herself quake amongst her saucepans.   So that Rose looked at her gratefully with moist eyes ; she was respected, now that her cousin was there, and her longing was to get her also to leave "The Ladies' Paradise," and take charge of Angèle's education.

"Come," murmured she caressingly, "there is quite enough

to occupy you here.   Angèle, implore your cousin, tell her how
pleased you will be."

The young girl implored her cousin, whilst Lisa nodded her
head approvingly.   But Campardon and Gasparine remained
grave; no, no, they must wait, one should not take a leap in
life without having something to hold on to.

The evenings in the drawing-room were now delightful.   The
architect had altogether given up going out.   That evening he
had arranged to hang some engravings, which had come back
from the framer, in Gasparine's room : Mignon supplicating
Heaven, a view of the fountain of Vaucluse, and several others.
And he was full of a stout man's jollity, with his yellow beard
flying about, his cheeks red through having eaten too much,
and feeling happy and contented in all his appetites.   He called
to the cousin to light him, and they heard him mount a chair
and commence knocking in the nails.   Then, Octave, finding
himself alone with Rose, resumed his story, and explained that
at the end of the month he would be obliged to take his meals
away from them.   She seemed surprised, but her thoughts were
elsewhere; she returned at once to her husband and her cousin
whom she heard laughing.

"Ah ! how it amuses them to hang those pictures !   What
would you have !   Achille no longer stays out; for a fortnight
pas the has not left me of an evening.   No, no more going to the
café, no more business meetings, no more appointments; and
you remember how anxious I used to be, when he was out after
midnight !   Ah ! it is a great ease to my mind now !   I at least
have him by me."

" No doubt, no doubt," murmured Octave.

And she continued speaking of the economy of the new arrangement.   Everything went on better in the house, they laughed
from morning to night.

"When I see Achille pleased," resumed she, "I am satisfied."

Then, returning to the young man's affairs, she added :

"So you are really going to leave us ?   You should stay
though as we are all going to be so happy."

He recommenced his explanations.   She comprehended, and
lowered her eyes : the young fellow would indeed interfere with
their family effusions, and she herself felt a certain relief at his
departure, no longer requiring him moreover to keep her company of an evening.   He had to promise to come and see her
very often.

" There you are, Mignon supplicating Heaven !" cried Campardon joyously. " Wait a moment, cousin ; I will help you down."

They heard him take her in his arms and place her somewhere.' There was a short silence, and then a faint laugh. But the architect was already entering the drawing-room ; and he held his hot cheek to his wife.

" It is done, my duck. Kiss your old pet for working so well."

Gasparine came with some embroidery and seated herself near the lamp. Campardon commenced cutting out a gilt cross of the Legion of Honour which he had found on some label ; and he turned very red, when Rose persisted in pinning this paper cross on to his breast : some one had promised him the decoration, but they all made a great mystery about it. On the other side of the lamp, Angèle, who was learning some scripture history, raised her head now and then and darted a glance here and there, with her enigmatical air of a well-brought up young lady, taught to say nothing, and whose real thoughts are hidden. It was a peaceful evening, a very homely patriarchal corner.

But the architect suddenly became virtuously indignant. He had just noticed that instead of studying her scripture history, the child was reading the " Gazette de France," lying on the table.

" Angèle," said he severely, " what are you doing ? This morning, I crossed out that article with a red pencil. You know very well that you are not to read what is crossed out."

" I was reading beside it, papa," replied the young girl.

All the same, he took the paper away from her, complaining in low tones to Octave of the demoralization of the press. That number contained the report of another abominable crime. If families could no longer admit the "Gazette de France," then what paper could they take in ? And he was raising his eyes to heaven, when Lisa announced the Abbé Mauduit.

" Ah ! yes," observed Octave, " he asked me to tell you he was coming."

The priest entered smiling. As the architect had forgotten to take off his paper cross, he stammered in the presence of that smile. The Abbé Mauduit happened to be the person whose name was kept a secret and who had the matter in hand.

"The ladies did it," murmured Campardon, preparing to take the cross off. " They are so fond of a joke.

" No, no, keep it," exclaimed the priest very amiably. " It is well where it is, and we will replace it by a more substantial one."

He at once asked after Rose's health, and greatly approved Gasparine's coming to live with one of her relations. Single young ladies ran so many risks in Paris! He said these things with all his good priest's unction, though fully aware of the real state of affairs. Then, he talked of the works, suggesting a rather happy alteration. And he seemed to have come to bless the good union of the family and thus save a delicate situation, which might otherwise be talked about in the neighbourhood. The architect of the Calvary should be sure of all honest persons' respect.

When the Abbé Mauduit appeared, Octave had wished the Campardons good evening. As he crossed the anteroom, he heard Angèle's voice in the now dark dining-room she having also made her escape.

" Was it about the butter that she was kicking up such a row ? " asked she.

" Of course," answered another voice, which was Lisa's. "She's as spiteful as can be. You saw how she went on at me at dinner-time. But I don't care a fig ! One must pretend to obey, with a person of that sort, but that doesn't prevent our amusing ourselves all the same ! "

Then, Angèle must have thrown her arms round Lisa's neck, for her voice was drowned in the servant's bosom.

"Yes, yes. And, afterwards, so much the worse ! it's you I love ! "

Octave was going up to bed, when a desire for fresh air brought him down again. It was not more than ten o'clock, he would stroll as far as the Palais-Royal. Now, he was single again : both Valérie and Madame Hédouin had declined to have anything to do with his heart, and he had been too hasty in restoring Marie to Jules, the only woman he had succeeded in conquering, and without having done anything for it. He tried to laugh, but he felt sad ; he bitterly recalled his successes at Marseilles and beheld a bad omen, a regular blow at his fortunes, in the rout that his seductions had experienced. A chill seemed to come over him when he had no skirts about him. Even Madame Campardon, who allowed him to go without shedding a tear ! It was a terrible revenge to take. Was Paris going to refuse herself?

As he was placing his foot on the pavement, a woman's voice called to him ; and he recognised Berthe at the door of the silk warehouse, the shutters of which were being put up by the porter.

"Is it true, Monsieur Mouret ?" asked she, "have you really left 'The Ladies' Paradise ?'"

He was surprised that it was already known in the neighbourhood. The young woman had called her husband. As he intended speaking to Monsieur Mouret on the morrow, he might just as well do so then. And Auguste abruptly offered Octave in a sour way a berth in his employ. The young man, taken unawares, hesitated and was on the point of refusing, thinking of the small importance of the house. But he caught sight of Berthe's pretty face, as she smiled at him with her air of welcome, with the gay glance he had already twice encountered, on the day of his arrival and the day of the wedding.

"Well ! yes," said he resolutely.

CHAPTER X.

THEN, Octave found himself brought into closer contact with the Duveyriers. Often, when Madame Duveyrier returned from a walk, she would come through her brother's shop, and stop to talk a minute with Berthe; and, the first time that she saw the young man behind one of the counters, she amiably reproached him for not keeping his word, reminding him of his long standing promise to come up and see her one evening, and try his voice at the piano. She wished to give a second performance of the "Benediction of the Daggers," at one of her first Saturdays at home of the coming winter, but with two extra tenors, something very complete.

"If it does not interfere with your arrangements," said Berthe one day to Octave, "you might go up to my sister-in-law's after dinner. She is expecting you."

She maintained towards him the attitude of a mistress simply polite.

"The fact is," he observed, "I intended arranging these shelves this evening."

"Do not trouble about them," resumed she, "there are plenty of people here to do that. I give you your evening."

Towards nine o'clock, Octave found Madame Duveyrier awaiting him in her grand white and gold drawing-room. Everything was ready, the piano open, the candles lit. A lamp placed on a small round table beside the instrument only imperfectly lighted the room, one half of which remained in shadow. Seeing the young woman alone, he thought it proper to ask after Monsieur Duveyrier. She replied that he was very well; his colleagues had selected him to report on a very grave affair, and he had just gone out to obtain certain information respecting it.

"You know, the affair of the Rue de Provence," said she simply.

"Ah! he has that in hand!" exclaimed Octave.

It was a scandal which was the talk of all Paris, quite a

clandestine prostitution, young girls of fourteen procured for high personages. Clotilde added :

"Yes, it gives him a great deal of work. For a fortnight past all his evenings have been taken up with it."

He looked at her, knowing from Trublot that uncle Bachelard had invited Duveyrier to dinner that day, and that afterwards they were to finish the evening at Clarisse's. But she was very serious, she still talked gravely of her husband, relating with her highly respectable air some most extraordinary stories, in which she explained how it was he was so seldom seen beneath the conjugal roof.

"No doubt! for he too has the cure of souls," murmured he, embarrassed by her clear glance.

She seemed to him very beautiful, all alone in that room. Her red hair gave a certain paleness to her rather long face, which had the obstinate immobility of a woman absorbed in her duty ; and, dressed in grey silk, her waist and shoulders tightly encompassed in a bodice plentifully supplied with whalebones, she treated him with an amiability devoid of all warmth, as though separated from him by a triple coat of mail.

"Well! sir, shall we begin ?" resumed she. "You will excuse my importunity, will you not ? And open your lungs, display all your powers, as Monsieur Duveyrier is not here. You perhaps heard him boast that he did not like music."

She put such contempt into the words, that he thought it right to risk a faint laugh. Moreover, it was the sole bitter feeling which at times escaped her before other people with respect to her husband, when exasperated by his jokes on her piano, she who was strong enough to hide the hatred and the physical repulsion with which he inspired her.

"How can one help liking music?" remarked Octave with an air of ecstasy, so as to make himself agreeable.

Then, she seated herself on the music-stool. A collection of old tunes was open on the piano. She had already selected an air out of "Zémire and Azor," by Grétry. As the young man could only just manage to read his notes, she made him go through it first in a low voice. Then, she played the prelude, and he sang the first verse.

"Perfect !" cried she with delight, "a tenor, there is not the least doubt of it, a tenor ! Pray continue, sir."

Octave, feeling highly flattered, gave out the two other verses. She was beaming. For three years past she had been seeking for one ! And she told him of all her vexations, Monsieur Tru-

blot for instance ; for, it was a fact, the causes of which were
worth studying, that there were no longer any tenors among
the young men of society : no doubt it was owing to tobacco.

"Be careful, now !" resumed she, " we must put some expression into it.   Begin it boldly."

Her cold face assumed a languid expression, her eyes turned
towards him with an expiring air.   Thinking that she was
warming, he became more animated also, and considered her
charming.   Not a sound came from the adjoining rooms, the
vague shadow of the grand apartment seemed to envelop them
in a drowsy voluptuousness; and, bending behind her, touching
her chignon with his chest, the better to see the music, he sighed
out in a quaver the two lines :

> " And I am myself
> More trembling than you."

But, the melodious phrase ended, she let her impassioned
expression fall like a mask.   Her frigidity was beneath it.
He drew back, feeling anxious, and not caring for another adventure like that with Madame Hédouin.

"You will get along very well," said she. " Only, accentuate
the time more.   See, like this."

And she herself sang, repeating quite twenty times : " More
trembling than you," bringing out the notes with the rigour of
a sinless woman, whose passion for music was not more than
skin deep in her mechanism.   Her voice rose little by little,
filling the room with shrill cries, when they both suddenly
heard some one exclaiming loudly behind their backs :

"Madame ! madame !"

She started, and, recognising her maid Clémence, exclaimed :
"Eh ? what ?"

"Madame, your father has fallen with his face in his papers,
and he doesn't move.   We are so frightened."

Then, without exactly understanding, and greatly surprised,
she quitted the piano and followed Clémence.   Octave, who
was uncertain whether to accompany her, remained walking
about the drawing-room.   However, after a few minutes of
hesitation and embarrassment, as he heard people rushing
about and calling out distractedly, he made up his mind, and,
crossing a room that was in darkness, he found himself in
Monsieur Vabre's bedchamber.   All the servants had hastened
to the spot—Julie with her kitchen apron on, Clémence and
Hippolyte, their minds still full of a game at dominos they had
just left ; and, standing up with bewildered looks, they sur-

rounded the old man, whilst Clotilde, leaning close to his ear,
called to him, and implored him to say a word, just one word.
But still he did not move, his nose remained buried in his tickets.
His forehead had struck the ink-stand. A splash of ink covered
his left eye, and trickled slowly down to his lips.

"He is in a fit," said Octave. "He must not be left there.
We must get him on to his bed."

But Madame Duveyrier was losing her head. Emotion
was little by little seizing upon her cold nature. She kept repeating :

"Do you think so, do you think so ? O good heavens ! O my
poor father !"

Hippolyte, a prey to an uneasy feeling, to a visible repugnance
to touch the old man, who might go off in his arms, did not
hurry himself. Octave had to call to him to help. Between
them they laid him on the bed.

"Bring some warm water !" resumed the young man, addressing Julie. "Wipe his face."

Now Clotilde became angry with her husband. Ought he to
have been away ? What would become of her if anything
happened ? It was just as though it were done on purpose ; he
was never at home when he was wanted ; and, gracious goodness ! that was not often ! Octave interrupted her to advise
her to send for Doctor Juillerat. No one had thought of it.
Hippolyte started off at once, delighted at the chance of getting
away.

"To leave me alone like this !" continued Clotilde. "I
don't know, but there must be all sorts of affairs to settle. O
my poor father !"

"Would you like me to inform the other members of the
family ?" asked Octave. "I can fetch your brothers. It would
be prudent."

She did not answer. Two big tears swelled her eyes, whilst
Julie and Clémence tried to undress the old man. Then she
stopped Octave ; her brother Auguste was out, having an appointment that evening ; and as for Théophile, he would do
well not to come, for the mere sight of him would be their
father's death-blow. Then she related that the latter had
called on his children for some overdue rent ; but they had
received him most brutally, especially Valérie, who refused to
pay, and demanded the sum he promised at the time of their
marriage ; and that scene was no doubt the cause of the fit,
for he had come back in a most pitiable state.

OLD MONSIEUR VABRE DISCOVERED IN A FIT

p. 190.

"Madame," observed Clémence, "one side of him is already quite cold."

This increased Madame Duveyrier's anger. She no longer spoke, for fear of saying too much before the servants. Her husband did not apparently care a button for their interests ! Had she only been acquainted with the law ! And she could not remain still, she kept walking up and down before the bed. Octave, whose attention was diverted by the sight of the tickets, looked at the formidable apparatus which covered the table; it was a big oak box, filled with a series of cardboard tickets, scrupulously sorted, the stupid work of a lifetime. Just as he was reading on one of these tickets: " 'Isidore Charbotel;' Exhibition of 1857, 'Atalanta ;' Exhibition of 1859, 'The Lion of Androcles ;' Exhibition of 1861, 'Portrait of Monsieur P——,' " Clotilde went and stood before him and said resolutely, in a low voice :

"Go and fetch him."

And, as he evinced his surprise, she seemed, with a shrug of her shoulders, to cast off the story about the report of the affair of the Rue de Provence, one of those eternal pretexts which she invented for her acquaintances. She let out everything in her emotion.

"You know, Rue de la Cerisaie. All our friends know it."

He wished to protest.

"I assure you, madame—"

"Do not stand up for him !" resumed she. "I am only too pleased ; he can stay there. Ah ! good heavens ! if it were not for my poor father !"

Octave bowed. Julie was wiping Monsieur Vabre's eye with the corner of a towel ; but the ink had dried, and the smudge remained in the skin, which was marked with livid streaks. Madame Duveyrier told her not to rub so hard ; then she returned to the young man, who was already at the door.

"Not a word to any one," murmured she. "It is needless to upset the house. Take a cab, call there, and bring him back in spite of everything."

When he had gone, she sank on to a chair beside the patient's pillow. He had not recovered consciousness ; his breathing alone, a deep and painful breathing, troubled the mournful silence of the chamber. Then, the doctor not arriving, finding herself alone with the two servants, who stood by with frightened looks, she burst out into a terrible fit of sobbing, in a paroxysm of deep grief.

It was at the Café Anglais that uncle Bachelard had invited
Duveyrier to dine, without any one knowing why, perhaps for
the pleasure of treating a counsellor, and of showing him that
tradespeople knew how to spend their money. He had also
invited Trublot and Gueulin, four men and no women, for
women do not know how to eat ; they interfere with the truffles,
and spoil digestion. The uncle, too, was known all along the
Boulevards for his gorgeous dinners, whenever a customer
called on him from the most remote parts of India or Brazil,
dinners at three hundred francs a head, by which he nobly
upheld the honour of French commission agents. He was
seized with a mania for spending money ; he demanded the
most extravagant articles, gastronomic curiosities, often uneatable, sterlets from the Volga, eels from the Tiber, grouse from
Scotland, bustards from Sweden, bears' feet from the Black
Forest, bison humps from America, turnips from Teltow,
gourds from Greece ; and he also ordered things most out
of season, such as peaches in December and partridges in July,
besides an abundance of flowers, of silver plate, and of crystal
glass, and an attendance which quite upset the restaurant,
without mentioning the wines, for which he had the cellar
turned topsy-turvy, requiring unknown vintages, considering
nothing old enough or rare enough, dreaming of unique bottles
at two louis the glass.

That evening, as it was summer-time—a season when everything is in abundance—he had not found it so easy to run up
the bill. The fare, decided upon the day before, was, however,
remarkable—asparagus cream soup, then some little *timbales à
la Pompadour;* two *relevés,* a trout in the Genevese style and a
fillet of beef *à la Chateaubriand;* two *entrées,* ortolans *à la
Lucullus* and a crayfish salad ; and, finally, a haunch of venison
in the way of roast, and artichoke hearts *à la jardinière* for
vegetable, followed by a chocolate *soufflé* and some fruit. It
was simple and grand, and swelled, moreover, by a truly royal
selection of wines—old Madeira with the soup, Château-Filhot
'58 with the side-dishes, Johannisberger and Pichon-Longueville
with the *relevés,* Château-Lafite '48 with the *entrées,* Sparkling
Moselle with the roast, and iced Rœderer with the dessert.
He deeply regretted a bottle of Johannisberger a hundred and
five years old, which had been sold to a Turk for ten louis three
days before.

" Drink away, drink away, sir," he kept saying to
Duveyrier ; " when wines are good, they never intoxicate.

UNCLE BACHELARD'S DINNER AT THE CAFÉ ANGLAIS.

p. 192.

It's the same with food ; it never does one harm so long as it's delicate."

He, however, was careful. On this occasion he was posing for the gentleman, shaved and brushed up, and with a rose in his buttonhole, restraining himself from breaking the crockery, which he was in the habit of doing. Trublot and Gueulin eat of everything. The uncle's theory seemed the right one, for Duveyrier, who suffered a great deal from his stomach, had drank considerably, and had returned to the crayfish salad, without feeling the least indisposed, the red blotches on his face merely assuming a purple hue.

At nine o'clock, the dinner was still in full swing. The breeze from an open window fanned the flames of the candles as they lit up the silver plate and the glass ; and, in the midst of the confusion of the table, four superb baskets of flowers were fading. Besides the two butlers, each guest had a waiter behind his chair, specially charged with supplying him with bread and wine, and changing his plates. It was close in spite of the breeze from the Boulevard. A feeling of repletion was taking possession of all, in the spicy fumes of the dishes and the vanilla-like bouquet of the grand wines.

Then, when the coffee had been served, with some liqueurs and cigars, and all the attendants had withdrawn, uncle Bachelard suddenly leant back in his chair and heaved a sigh of satisfaction.

"Ah !" declared he, "one is comfortable."

Trublot and Gueulin, also leaning back in their chairs, opened their arms.

"Completely !" said the one.

"Up to the eyes !" added the other.

Duveyrier, who was puffing, nodded his head and murmured :

"Oh ! the crayfish !"

All four looked at each other and chuckled. Their skins were well-nigh bursting, and they were digesting in the slow and selfish way of four worthy citizens who had just had a tuck-out away from the worries of their families. It had cost a great deal ; no one had partaken of it with them ; there was no girl there to take advantage of their emotion ; and they unbuttoned their waistcoats, and laid their stomachs as it were on the table. With eyes half-closed, they even avoided speaking at first, each one absorbed in his solitary pleasure. Then, free and easy, and whilst congratulating themselves that there were no women present, they placed their elbows on the table, and, with their excited faces close together, they did nothing but talk incessantly of them.

"As for myself, I am disabused," declared uncle Bachelard. "It is after all far preferable to be virtuous."

Duveyrier nodded his head approvingly.

"So I have said good-bye to pleasure. Ah! I have wallowed in it, I own. Rue Godot-de-Mauroy, for instance, I know every one of them. There are blondes and brunettes, and red-haired ones, and who sometimes, though not often, are very well shaped. Then, there are the dirty holes, you know, furnished lodgings at Montmartre, dark alleys in my neighbourhood, where one meets some most astonishing creatures, very ugly, and most extraordinarily made."

"Oh! prostitutes!" interrupted Trublot in his supercilious way, "what rot! I keep clear of all such goods!"

This smutty conversation tickled Duveyrier's fancy. He was sipping kummel, whilst sharp twinges of sensuality kept shooting across his stiff magisterial face.

"For my part," said he, "I cannot bear vice. It shocks me. Now, to be able to love a woman, one must esteem her, is it not so? It would be impossible for me to have anything to do with one of those unfortunates, unless, of course, she showed some repentance, and she had been extricated from her life of shame for the purpose of making a respectable woman of her. Love could not have a nobler mission. In short, a virtuous mistress, you understand me? Then, I do not deny I might succumb."

"Virtuous mistresses! but I have had no end of them!" cried Bachelard. "They are a far greater nuisance than the others; and such sluts too! Wenches who, behind your back, lead a life fit to give you every possible ailment! Take, for instance, my last, a very respectable-looking little lady, whom I met at a church door. I set her up in business at Les Ternes as a milliner, just to give her a position. She never had a single customer though. Well, sir, believe me or not as you like, but she had the whole street to sleep with her."

Gueulin was chuckling, whilst his carroty hair bristled more than usual, and his forehead was bathed in perspiration from the heat of the candles. He murmured, as he sucked his cigar:

"And the other, the tall one at Passy, who had a sweet-stuff shop. And the other, she who had a room over there, with her outfits for orphan children. And the other, the captain's widow, you surely remember her ! she used to show the mark of a sword thrust on her body. All, uncle, all of them played the fool with you ! Now, I may tell you, may I not? Well ! I had to defend myself one night against the one with the sword thrust. She wanted to, but I was not such a fool ! One never knows where such women may lead one to !"

Bachelard seemed annoyed. He recovered his good humour, however, and, blinking his heavy eyelids, said :

" My little fellow, you can have them all; I have something far better."

And he refused to explain himself further, delighted at having awakened the others' curiosity. Yet he was burning to be indiscreet, to let them imagine what a treasure he possessed.

" A young girl," said he at length, "and a genuine one, on my word of honour."

" Impossible !" cried Trublot. "Such things no longer exist."

" Of good family ?" asked Duveyrier.

" Of most excellent family," affirmed the uncle. "Imagine something stupidly chaste. A mere chance. She submitted quite innocently. She has no idea of anything even now."

Gueulin listened to him in surprise ; then, making a sceptical gesture, he murmured :

" Ah ! yes, I know."

" What ? you know !" said Bachelard, angrily. "You know nothing at all, my little fellow ; no one knows anything. She is for yours truly. She is neither to be seen nor touched. Hands off !"

And, turning to Duveyrier, he added :

" You will understand, sir, you who have feeling. It affects me so much going there, that when I come away I feel quite young again. In short, it is a cosy little nook for me, where I can recruit myself after all those hussies. And, if you only knew, she is so polite and so fresh, with a skin like a flower, and a figure not in the least thin, sir, but as round and firm as a peach !"

The counsellor's red blotches were almost bleeding through the rush of blood to his face. Trublot and Gueulin looked at the uncle ; and they felt a desire to slap him as they beheld him with his set of false teeth, which were too white, and at the corners of which the saliva trickled. What! that old carcass of an uncle, that wreck of the dirtiest bacchanals of Paris, whose big flaming nose alone retained its place

between the hanging flesh of his cheeks, had an innocent little
thing stowed away in some room, regular flesh in the bud,
which he soiled with his old vices, concealed behind his pretended simplicity of a palsied senile drunkard !

Bachelard became quite tender-hearted, and resumed, licking
the brim of his liqueur glass with the tip of his tongue :

"After all, my sole dream is to make the child happy ! But
there, my pot-belly tells me I'm getting old, I'm like a father
to her. I give you my word ! if I found a very good young
fellow, I'd give her to him, oh ! in marriage, not otherwise."

"You would make two happy ones," murmured Duveyrier
sentimentally.

It was almost stifling in the small apartment. A glass of
chartreuse that had been upset had made the tablecloth all
sticky, it was also covered with cigar ash. The gentlemen were
in want of some fresh air.

"Would you like to see her ?" abruptly asked the uncle rising from his seat.

They consulted one another with a glance. Well ! yes, they
were willing, if it could afford him any pleasure ; and their
affected indifference hid a gluttonous satisfaction at the thought
of going and finishing their dessert with the old fellow's little
one. Duveyrier merely observed that Clarisse was expecting
them. But Bachelard who, since his proposal, had become pale
and agitated, swore that they would not even sit down there ;
the gentlemen would see her, and then go off at once, at once.
They went down and waited some minutes on the Boulevard
whilst he settled the score. When he reappeared, Gueulin pretended not to know where the young person lived.

"Let's get along, uncle ! Which is the way ?"

Bachelard became quite grave again, tortured by his ridiculously vain longing to exhibit Fifi and by his terror of being
robbed of her. For a moment he looked to the left, then to
the right, in an anxious way. At length, he boldly said :

"Well ! no, I won't."

And he obstinately adhered to his determination, without
caring a straw for Trublot's chaff, nor even deigning to explain
by some pretext his sudden change of mind. They therefore
had to turn their steps in Clarisse's direction. As it was a
splendid evening, they decided to walk all the way, with the
hygienic idea of hastening their digestion. Then, they started
off down the Rue de Richelieu, pretty steady on their legs, but
so full that they considered the pavements far too narrow.

Gueulin and Trublot walked first. Behind them came Bachelard and Duveyrier, deep in fraternal confidences. The first was swearing to the second that it was not him whom he mistrusted: he would have shown her to him, for he knew he was a man of delicacy; but it was always imprudent to expect too much of youth, was it not? And the other approved, confessing also the fears he once entertained respecting Clarisse: at first, he had kept all his friends away; then, he had had the pleasure of receiving them, and had thus made himself a delightful abode, when she had given him the most extraordinary proofs of fidelity. Oh! quite a strong-minded woman, incapable of forgetting herself, and with plenty of heart, and most sound ideas! No doubt, one might reproach her with some little matters in connection with her past, which had occurred through want of proper guidance; only, since she had loved him, she had returned to the path of honour. The counsellor kept on thus all along the Rue de Rivoli; whilst the uncle, annoyed at being unable to put in another word about his little one, did his utmost to restrain himself from telling the other of Clarisse's goings-on with everybody.

"Yes, yes, no doubt," murmured he. "But rest assured, dear sir, the best thing after all is virtue."

The house in the Rue de la Cerisaie seemed asleep amidst the solitude and the silence of the street. Duveyrier was surprised at not seeing any lights in the third floor windows. Trublot said, with a serious air, that Clarisse had no doubt gone to bed to wait for them; or perhaps, Gueulin added, she was playing a game of bézique in the kitchen with her maid. They knocked. The gas on the staircase was burning with the straight and immovable flame of a lamp in some chapel. Not a sound, not a breath. But, as the four men passed before the room of the doorkeeper, the latter hastily came out.

"Sir, sir, the key!"

Duveyrier stood stock-still on the first step.

"Is madame not there then?" asked he.

"No, sir. And, wait a moment, you must take a candle with you."

As he handed him the candlestick, the doorkeeper allowed quite a chuckle of ferocious and vulgar jocosity to pierce through the exaggerated respect depicted on his pallid countenance. Neither of the two young men nor the uncle had said a word. It was in the midst of this silence, and with bent backs, that they ascended the stairs in single file, the interminable noise of their

footsteps resounding up each mournful flight.   At their head,
Duveyrier, who was puzzling himself trying to understand,
lifted his feet with the mechanical movement of a somnambulist ;
and the candle, which he held with a trembling hand, cast their
four shadows on the wall, resembling in their strange ascent a
procession of broken puppets.

On the third floor, a faintness came over him, and he was
quite unable to find the key-hole.   Trublot did him the service
of opening the door.   The key turned in the lock with a sonorous and reverberating noise, as though beneath the vaulted roof
of some cathedral.

"Jupiter !" murmured he, "it doesn't seem as if the place
was inhabited."

"It sounds empty," said Bachelard.

"A little family vault," added Gueulin.

They entered.   Duveyrier passed first, holding high the
candle.   The anteroom was empty, even the hat-pegs had disappeared.   The drawing-room and the parlour were also empty:
not a stick of furniture, not a curtain at the windows, not
even a brass rod.   Duveyrier stood as one petrified, first looking down at his feet, then raising his eyes to the ceiling, and
then searchingly gazing at the walls, as though he had been
seeking the hole through which everything had disappeared.

"What a clear out !" Trublot could not help exclaiming.

"Perhaps the place is going to be done up," observed Gueulin
without so much as a smile.   "Let us see the bedroom.   The
furniture may have been moved in there."

But the bedroom was also bare, with that ugly and chilly
bareness of plaster walls from which the paper has been torn off.
Where the bedstead had stood, the iron supports of the canopy,
also removed, left gaping holes; and, one of the windows having
been left partly open, the air from the street filled the apartment with the humidity and the unsavouriness of a public
square.

"My God ! my God !" stuttered Duveyrier, at length able to
weep, unnerved by the sight of the place where the friction of
the mattresses had rubbed the paper off the wall.

Uncle Bachelard became quite paternal.

"Courage, sir !" he kept repeating.   "The same thing
happened to me and I did not die of it.   Honour is safe, damn
it all !"

The counsellor shook his head and went into the dressing-
room, and then into the kitchen.   The evidence of the disaster

increased. The piece of American cloth behind the washstand in tho dressing-room had been taken down and the hooks had been removed from the kitchen.

"No, that is too much, it is pure capriciousness!" said Gueulin in amazement. "She might have left the hooks."

Trublot, who was very tired after the dinner and the walk, commenced to find this solitude far from amusing. But Duveyrier, who did not let go of the candle, continued to wander about, as though seized by a necessity to dive deeper into his abandonment; and the others were obliged to follow him. He again went through each room, wishing to have another look at the drawing-room, the parlour and the bed-chamber, carefully casting the light into every corner; whilst the gentlemen behind him continued the procession of the staircase, with their big dancing shadows, which strangely peopled the naked walls. The noise of their footsteps on the boards assumed a sad sonorousness in the mournful atmosphere. And, to complete tho melancholy, the whole place was scrupulously clean, without a scrap of paper or a straw, as spotless as a well-washed porringer, for the doorkeeper had had the cruelty to give a thorough good sweep all round.

"I can't stand this any longer, you know," Trublot ended by declaring, as they visited the drawing-room for the third time "Really! I would give ten sous for a chair."

All four came to a halt, standing.

"When did you see her last?" asked Bachelard.

"Yesterday, sir!" exclaimed Duveyrier.

Gueulin wagged his head. By Jove! it had not taken long, it had been neatly done. But Trublot uttered an exclamation. He had just caught sight of a dirty collar and a damaged cigar on the mantelpiece.

"Do not complain," said he laughing, "she has left you a keepsake. It is always something."

Duveyrier looked at the collar with sudden emotion. Then, he murmured :

"Twenty-five thousand francs' worth of furniture, there was twenty-five thousand francs' worth! Well! no, no, it is not that which I regret!"

"You will not have the cigar?" interrupted Trublot. "Then, allow me to. It has a hole in it, but I can stick a cigarette paper over that."

He lighted it at the candle which the counsellor was still holding, and letting himself drop down against the wall he added:

"So much the worse! I must sit down a while on the floor.
My legs will not bear me any longer."

"I beg of you," at length said Duveyrier, "to explain to me
where she can possibly be."

Bachelard and Gueulin looked at each other. It was a delicate matter. However, the uncle came to a manly decision,
and he told the poor fellow everything, all Clarisse's goings-on,
her continual escapades, the lovers she picked up behind his
back, at each of their parties. She had no doubt gone off with
the last one, big Payan, that mason of whom a Southern town
wished to make an artist. Duveyrier listened to the abominable story with an expression of horror. He allowed this cry of
despair to escape him :

"There is then no honesty left on earth !"

And suddenly opening his heart, he told them all he had
done for her. He talked of his soul, he accused her of having
shaken his faith in the best sentiments of existence, naïvely
hiding beneath this sentimental pain the derangement of his
gross appetites. Clarisse had become necessary to him. But
he would find her again solely to make her blush for her behaviour, so he said, and to see if her heart had lost all noble-
ness.

"Leave her alone !" exclaimed Bachelard delighted with the
counsellor's misfortune, "she will humbug you again. There
is nothing like virtue, understand ! It is far better to take a
little one devoid of malice, as innocent as the child just born.
Then, there is no danger, one may sleep in peace."

Trublot meanwhile was smoking leaning against the wall with
his legs stretched out. He was gravely reposing, the others
had forgotten him.

"If you particularly want it, I can find the address for you,"
said he. "I know the maid."

Duveyrier turned round, surprised at that voice which seemed
to issue from the boards ; and, when he beheld him smoking all
that remained of Clarisse, puffing big clouds of smoke, in which
he fancied he beheld the twenty-five thousand francs' worth of
furniture evaporating, he made an angry gesture and replied :

"No, she is unworthy of me. She must beg my pardon on
her knees."

"Hallo ! here she is coming back !" said Gueulin listening.

And someone was indeed walking in the anteroom, whilst a
voice said : "Well ! what's up ? is every one dead ?" And
Octave appeared. He was quite bewildered by the open doors

and the empty rooms. But his amazement increased still more,
when he beheld the four men in the midst of the denuded drawing-room, one sitting on the floor and the other three standing
up, and only lighted by the meagre candle which the counsellor was holding like a taper at church. A few words sufficed to
inform him of what had occurred.

"It isn't possible!" cried he.

"Did they not tell you anything then downstairs?" asked
Gueulin.

"No, nothing at all ; the doorkeeper quietly watched me come
up. Ah ! so she's gone ! It does not surprise me. She had
such queer hair and eyes !"

He asked some particulars, and stood talking a minute, forgetful of the sad news which he had brought. Then turning
abruptly towards Duveyrier, he said :

"By the way, it's your wife who sent me to fetch you. Your
father-in-law is dying."

"Ah!" simply observed the counsellor.

"Old Vabre!" murmured Bachelard. "I expected as much."

"Pooh ! when one gets to the end of one's reel !" remarked
Gueulin philosophically.

"Yes, it's best to take one's departure," added Trublot, in
the act of sticking a second cigarette paper round his cigar.

The gentlemen at length decided to leave the empty apartment. Octave repeated he had given his word of honour that
he would bring Duveyrier back with him at once, no matter
what state he was in. The latter carefully shut the door,
as though he had left his dead affections there ; but, downstairs, he was overcome with shame, and Trublot had to
return the key to the doorkeeper. Then, outside on the pavement, there was a silent exchange of hearty hand-shakes ; and,
directly the cab had driven off with Octave and Duveyrier,
uncle Bachelard said to Gueulin and Trublot as they stood in
the deserted street :

"Jove's thunder ! I must show her to you."

For a minute past he had been stamping about, greatly excited by the despair of that big noodle of a counsellor, bursting
with his own happiness, with that happiness which he considered due to his own deep malice, and which he could no
longer contain.

"You know, uncle," said Gueulin, "if it's only to take us as
far as the door again and then to leave us—"

"No, Jove's thunder! you shall see her. It will please me.

True it's nearly midnight; but she shall get up if she's in bed. You know, she's the daughter of a captain, Captain Menu, and she has a very respectable aunt, born at Villeneuve, near Lille, on my word of honour! Messieurs Mardienne Brothers, of the Rue Saint-Sulpice, will give her a character. Ah! Jove's thunder! we're in need of it; you'll see what virtue is!"

And he took hold of their arms, Guculin on his right, Trublot on his left, putting his best foot forward as he started off in quest of a cab to arrive there the sooner.

Meanwhile, Octave briefly related to the counsellor all he knew of Monsieur Vabre's attack, without hiding that Madame Duveyrier was acquainted with the address of·the Rue de la Cerisaie. After a pause, the counsellor asked in a doleful voice:

" Do you think she will forgive me?"

Octave remained silent. The cab continued to roll along, in the obscurity lighted up every now and then by a ray from a gas-lamp. Just as they were reaching their destination, Duveyrier, tortured with anxiety, put another question:

"The best thing for me to do for the present is to make it up with my wife again, do you not think so?"

"It would perhaps be wise," replied the young man, obliged to answer.

Then, Duveyrier felt the necessity of regretting his father-in-law. He was a man of great intelligence, with an incredible capacity for work. However, they would very likely be able to set him on his legs again In the Rue de Choiseul, they found the street-door open, and quite a group gathered before Monsieur Gourd's room. Julie, who had come down to go to the chemist's, was abusing the masters who allow one another to die without help when ill; it was only workpeople who take each other a bowl of broth, or anything needful; during the two hours he had been dying up there, the old fellow might have swallowed his tongue twenty times, before his children would have taken the trouble to put a lump of sugar into his mouth. They were a hard-hearted lot, said Monsieur Gourd, people who did not know how to make use of their ten fingers, who would have thought themselves dishonoured if they had had to give their father an enema; whilst Hippolyte, trying to surpass the others, told them about madame upstairs, how stupid she looked, with her arms dangling by her sides in front of the poor gentleman, around whom the servants were vying with each other to do all they could. But they held their tongues, directly they caught sight of Duveyrier.

" Well ? " inquired the latter.

" The doctor is applying mustard poultices to Monsieur Vabre," replied Hippolyte.   " Oh ! I had such difficulty to find him ! "

Upstairs in the drawing-room, Madame Duveyrier came forward to meet them. She had cried a great deal, her eyes sparkled beneath the swollen lids. The counsellor, full of embarrassment, opened his arms ; and he embraced her as he murmured :

" My poor Clotilde ! "

Surprised at this unusual display of affection, she drew back. Octave had kept behind ; but he heard the husband add in a low voice :

" Forgive me, let us forget our grievances on this sad occasion. You see, I have come back to you, and for always. Ah ! I am well punished ! "

She did not reply, but disengaged herself. Then, resuming in Octave's presence her attitude of a woman who desires to ignore everything, she said :   .

" I should not have disturbed you, my dear, for I know how important that inquiry respecting the Rue de Provence is. But I was all alone, I felt that your presence was necessary. My poor father is lost. Go and see him ; you will find the doctor there."

When Duveyrier had gone into the next room, she drew near to Octave, who, so as not to appear to be listening to them, was standing in front of the piano. The instrument was still open, and the air from " Zémire and Azor " remained there just as they had left it ; and he was pretending to be studying it. The soft light from the lamp continued to illuminate only a portion of the vast apartment. Madame Duveyrier looked at the young man a minute without speaking, tormented by an uneasiness which ended by forcing her to cast off her habitual reserve.

" Was he there ? " asked she briefly.

" Yes, madame."

" Then what has happened, what is the matter with him ? "

" The person has left him, madame, and taken all the furniture away with her. I found him with nothing but a candle between the bare walls."

Clotilde made a gesture of despair. She understood. An expression of repugnance and discouragement appeared on her beautiful face. It was not enough that she had lost her father, it seemed as though this misfortune was also to serve as a pretext for a reconciliation with her husband ! She knew him well, he would be forever after her, now that there would be nothing elsewhere to protect her ; and, in her respect for every duty, she trembled at the thought that she would be unable to refuse to submit to the abominable service. For an instant, she looked at the piano. Bitter tears came to her eyes, as she simply said to Octave :

"Thank you, sir."

They both passed in turn into Monsieur Vabre's bed-chamber. Duveyrier, looking very pale, was listening to Doctor Juillerat, who was giving him some explanations in a low voice. It was an attack of serous apoplexy ; the patient might last till the morrow, but there was not the slightest hope of his recovery. Clotilde just at that moment entered the room ; she heard this giving over of the patient, and dropped into a chair, wiping her eyes with her handkerchief, already soaked with tears, and twisted up, and almost reduced to a pulp. She, however, found the strength to ask the doctor if her poor father would recover consciousness. The doctor had his doubts ; and, as though he had penetrated the object of the question, he expressed the hope that Monsieur Vabre had long since put his affairs in order. Duveyrier, whose mind seemed to have remained behind in the Rue de la Cérisaie, now appeared to wake up. He looked at his wife, and then remarked that Monsieur Vabre confided in no one. He therefore knew nothing, he had merely received some promises in favour of their son, Gustave, whom his grandfather often talked of bettering, to reward them for having taken him to live with them. In any case, if a will existed, it would be found.

"I presume the family knows what has happened," said Doctor Juillerat.

"Well ! no," murmured Clotilde. "I received such a shock ! My first thought was to send Monsieur Mouret for my husband."

Duveyrier gave her another glance. Now, they understood each other. He slowly approached the bed, and examined Monsieur Vabre, stretched out in his corpse-like stiffness, and whose immovable face was streaked with yellow blotches. One o'clock struck. The doctor talked of withdrawing, for he had tried all the usual remedies, and could do nothing more. He would call again early on the morrow. At length, he was going off with Octave, when Madame Duveyrier called the latter back.

"We will wait till to-morrow," said she, " you can send Berthe to me under some pretext ; I will also get Valérie to come, and they shall break the news to my brothers. Ah ! poor things, let them sleep in peace this night ! There is quite enough with our having to watch in tears."

And she and her husband remained alone with the old man, whose death rattle chilled the chamber.

CHAPTER XI.

When Octave went down on the morrow at eight o'clock, he was greatly surprised to find the entire house acquainted with the attack of the night before, and the desperate condition of the landlord. The house, however, was not concerned about the patient: it was solely interested in what he would leave behind him.

The Pichons were seated before some basins of chocolate in their little dining-room. Jules called Octave in.

"I say, what a fuss there will be if he dies like that! We shall see something funny. Do you know if he has made a will?"

The young man, without answering, asked them where they had heard the news. Marie had learnt it at the baker's; moreover, it crept from storey to storey, and even to the end of the street by means of the servants. Then, after slapping Lilitte, who was soaking her fingers in her chocolate, the young woman observed in her turn:

"Ah! all that money! If he only thought of leaving us as many sous as there are five franc pieces. But there is no fear of that!"

And as Octave took his departure, she added:

"I have finished your books, Monsieur Mouret. Will you please take them when convenient?"

He was hastening downstairs, feeling anxious, as he recollected having promised Madame Duveyrier to send Berthe to her before anything was known of the matter, when, on the third floor, he came in contact with Campardon, who was going out.

"Well!" said the latter, "so your employer is coming in for something. I have heard that the old fellow has close upon six hundred thousand francs, besides this property. You see, he spent nothing at the Duveyriers', and he had a good deal left of what he brought from Versailles, without counting the twenty and odd thousand francs received in rent from the house. Eh!

it is a fine cake to share, when there are only three to partake of
it ! ”

Whilst talking thus, he continued to go down behind Octave.
But, on the second floor, they met Madame Juzeur, who was
returning from seeing what her little maid, Louise, could be
doing of a morning, taking over an hour to fetch four sous’
worth of milk. She entered naturally into the conversation,
being very well informed.

“ It is not known how he has settled his affairs,” murmured
she in her gentle way. “ There will perhaps be some bother.”

“ Ah, well ! ” said the architect, gaily, “ I should like to be
in their shoes. It would not take long. One makes three equal
shares, each takes his own, and there you are ! ”

Madame Juzuer leant over the balusters, then raised her head,
and made sure that no one else was on the stairs. At length,
lowering her voice, she observed :

“ And if they did not find what they expected ? There are
rumours about.”

The architect opened his eyes wide with amazement. Then
he shrugged his shoulders. Pooh ! mere gossip ! Old Vabre
was a miser who hid his savings in worsted stockings. And he
went off, as he had an appointment at Saint-Roch with the Abbé
Mauduit.

“ My wife complains of you,” said he to Octave, looking back,
after going down three stairs. “ Call in and have a chat with
her now and then.”

Madame Juzeur detained the young man a moment.

“ And I, how you neglect me ! I thought you loved me a
little. When you come, I will let you taste a liqueur from the
West Indies, oh ! something delicious ! ”

He promised to call on her, and hastened to reach the
vestibule. But, before arriving at the little door communicating
between the shop and the porch, he was again obliged to pass
through a whole group of servants, who were distributing
the dying man’s belongings. So much for Madame Clotilde, so
much for Monsieur Auguste, so much for Monsieur Théophile.
Clémence boldly gave the figures ; she knew the amount for
certain, for Hippolyte had told it to her, and he had seen the
money in a drawer. Julie however disputed it. Lisa related
how her first master, an old gentleman, had bilked her by dying
without even leaving her his dirty linen ; whilst Adèle, her
mouth wide open and swinging her arms, was listening to all
these stories of inheritances, which tumbled down gigantic piles

of five franc pieces before her. And, out on the pavement,
Monsieur Gourd, looking very solemn, was talking with the
stationer opposite. In his eyes, the landlord was already dead.

"What interests me," said he, "is to know who will have
the house. They have divided everything, very good! but the
house, they cannot cut it into three."

Octave at length entered the warehouse. The first person he
beheld, seated at the cashier's desk, was Madame Josserand
under arms, polished up and laced, and her hair already done.
Close beside her, Berthe, who had no doubt come down in haste,
in the charming deshabille of a dressing-gown, appeared to be
very excited. But they stopped talking on catching sight of
him, and the mother looked at him with a terrible eye.

"So, sir," said she, "it is thus that you love the firm? You
enter into the plots of my daughter's enemies."

He wished to defend himself, and state the facts of the case.
But she prevented him from speaking, she accused him of
having spent the night with the Duveyriers, looking for the will,
to insert all sorts of things in it. And, as he laughed, asking
what interest he could have had in doing such a thing, she
resumed :

"Your own interest, your own interest. In short! sir, you
should have hastened to inform us, as God was good enough to
make you a witness of the occurrence. When one thinks that,
had it not been for me, my daughter would still have been in
ignorance of it! Yes, she would have been despoiled, had I
not rushed downstairs the moment I heard the news. Eh!
your interest, your interest, sir, who knows? Though Madame
Duveyrier is very faded, yet some people not over particular
may still find her good enough perhaps."

"Oh! mamma!" said Berthe, "Clotilde who is so virtuous!"

But Madame Josserand shrugged her shoulders pityingly.

"Pooh! you know very well people will do anything for
money!"

Octave was obliged to relate to them all the circumstances of
the attack. They exchanged glances : as the mother said, there
had evidently been manœuvres. Clotilde was really too kind to
wish to spare her relations emotions! However, they let the
young man start on his work, though still having their doubts
as to his conduct in the matter. Their lively explanation continued.

"And who will pay the fifty thousand francs agreed upon in

the contract?" said Madame Josserand, "We are not likely to
see a single one of them when he is dead and buried."

"Oh! the fifty thousand francs!" murmured Berthe in an
embarrassed way. "You know he only agreed as we did to pay
ten thousand francs every six months. The time is not up yet,
the best thing is to wait."

"Wait! wait till he comes back and brings them to you, I
suppose! You great blockhead, do you want to be robbed?
No, no! you must demand them at once out of the estate. As
for us, we are still alive, thank goodness! It is not known
whether we shall pay or not; but with him it is another thing,
as he is dead he must pay."

And she made her daughter swear not to yield, for she had
never given any one the right to take her for a fool. Whilst
fanning her anger, she now and again turned an ear towards the
ceiling, as though she wished to overhear what was taking place
at the Duveyriers' on the first floor, in spite of the "entresol"
floor which intervened. The old fellow's bed-chamber was, as
nearly as possible, just over her head. Auguste had at once
gone up to his father, on learning from her what had taken
place. But that did not ease her, she longed to be there herself, imagining the most complicated plots.

"Go up too!" she ended by exclaiming, in a cry from her
heart. "Auguste is too weak, they are sure to be taking him
in again!"

Then, Berthe went off upstairs. Octave, who was arranging
the display in the window, had listened to what they said.
When he found himself alone with Madame Josserand, and saw
her moving in the direction of the door, he asked her, in the
hope of a holiday, whether it would not be proper to close the
warehouse.

"Whatever for?" inquired she. "Wait till he is dead. It
is not worth while losing a day's sale."

Then, as he folded a remnant of poppy-coloured silk, she
added, to soften the harshness of her words:

"Only, you may as well, I think, not put any red in the
window."

Up on the first floor, Berthe found Auguste with his father.
The room had in no way changed since the day before; it was
still dampish, and silent, save for the same long and painful
death rattle. The old man on the bed continued perfectly rigid,
in a complete annihilation of all feeling and movement. The
oak box filled with tickets still littered the table; not an article

of furniture seemed to have been moved, or even opened. 'The Duveyriers, however, appeared to be more dejected, tired out by a sleepless night, an anxious twinge in their eyelids, their minds a prey to a continuous pre-occupation. As early as seven o'clock, they had sent Hippolyte to fetch their son Gustave from the Lycée Bonaparte; and the youngster, a thin and precocious youth of sixteen, was there, in all the flutter of that unexpected holiday to be spent in the company of a dying man.

"Ah! my dear, what a frightful visitation!" said Clotilde, going up to and embracing Berthe.

"Why not have informed us of it?" asked the latter, with her mother's affected pout. "We were there to help you to bear it."

Auguste, with a glance, begged her to keep silent. The moment for quarrelling had not arrived. They could wait. Doctor Juillerat, who had already been once, was to call again; but he still gave no hope, the patient would not live through the day. Auguste was informing his wife of this, when Théophile and Valérie entered in their turn. Clotilde at once advanced to meet them, and repeated as she embraced Valérie:

"What a frightful visitation, my dear!"

But Théophile was in a state of great excitement. "So, now," said he, without even lowering his voice, "when one's father is dying one only hears of it through the charcoal-dealer. Did you then require time to rifle his pockets?"

Duveyrier rose up indignantly. But Clotilde motioned him aside, whilst she answered her brother very gently:

"Unhappy man! is our father's death agony not even sacred to you? Look at him, behold your work; yes, it is you who have brought him to this, by refusing to pay your overdue rent."

Valérie burst out laughing.

"Come," said she, "you are not speaking seriously."

"What! not speaking seriously!" resumed Clotilde, filled with indignation. "You know how much he liked to collect his rents. Had you really wished to kill him, you could not have acted in a better way."

And they came to high words, they reciprocally accused one another of wishing to lay hands on the estate, when Auguste, still sullen and calm, requested them to recollect where they were.

"Keep quiet! You have plenty of time. It is not decent at such a moment."

Then the others, admitting the justice of this observation, settled themselves around the bed. A deep silence ensued; again nothing but the death-rattle was heard in the moist atmosphere of the room. Berthe and Auguste were at the dying man's feet; Valérie and Théophile, being the last comers, had been obliged to seat themselves at the table, some distance off; whilst Clotilde was at the head of the bed, with her husband behind her; and she had pushed her son Gustave, whom the old man adored, close up against the edge of the mattresses. They now all looked at one another, without exchanging a word. But the bright eyes, the tightly-compressed lips, told of the hidden thoughts, the surmises full of anxiety and irritation, which were passing in the pale-faced heads of those next-of-kin, with their red and swollen eyelids. The sight of the collegian, so close to the bed, especially exasperated the two young couples; for it was self-evident that the Duveyriers were counting on Gustave's presence to influence the grandfather's affections if he recovered consciousness.

Moreover, this manœuvre was a proof that in all probability no will existed; and the Vabres glanced covertly at the old iron safe which the retired notary had brought with him from Versailles and had had fixed in the wall of his bed-chamber. He had a mania for shutting up all sorts of things inside it. No doubt, the Duveyriers had hastened to ransack this safe during the night. Théophile had the idea of laying a trap for them to compel them to speak.

"I say," he at length went and whispered in the counsellor's ear, "suppose we send for the notary. Papa may wish to alter his will."

Duveyrier did not at first hear. As he felt excessively bored in that room, he had allowed his thoughts all through the night to revert to Clarisse. The wisest thing would decidedly be to make it up with his wife; but then the other was so funny, when she threw her chemise over her head, with the gesture of a street-arab; and with his vague glance fixed on the dying man, he still had visions of her, and would have given everything to have had her with him again. Théophile was obliged to repeat his question.

"I have questioned Monsieur Renaudin," at length answered the counsellor in a bewildered way. "There is no will."

"But here?"

"No more here than at the notary's."

Théophile looked at Auguste ; was it not sufficiently evident ? the Duveyriers had searched everything. Clotilde saw the glance, and was greatly irritated with her husband. What was the matter with him ? was grief sending him to sleep ? And she added :

"Papa has no doubt done what he thought right. We shall learn it only too soon, heaven knows !"

She burst into tears. Valérie and Berthe, affected by her grief, also started off, sobbing gently. Théophile had returned to his chair on tip-toe. He knew what he wished to know. If his father regained consciousness, he would certainly not allow the Duveyriers to take advantage of their hobbledehoy of a son to get the lion's share. But as he sat down, he saw his brother Auguste wipe his eyes, and this affected him so much that he also nearly choked : the thought of death came to him, he would perhaps die of the same illness, it was abominable. Then the whole family wept, except Gustave, who could not cry. He was struck with consternation, he looked on the ground, and tried to make his breathing keep time with the rattle, for the sake of doing something, the same as he was made to walk in step at his gymnastic lessons.

Meanwhile, the hours passed away. At eleven o'clock they had a diversion, Doctor Juillerat again calling. The patient's condition was becoming worse and worse, it was now even doubtful whether he would be able to recognize his children before dying. And the sobbing started afresh, when Clémence announced the Abbé Mauduit. Clotilde, who rose to meet him, was the first to receive his consolations. He appeared to be deeply affected by the family visitation ; he had an encouraging word for each. Then, with much tact, he talked of the rights of religion, insinuating that they should not let that soul pass away without the succour of the Church.

"I had thought of it," murmured Clotilde.

But Théophile raised objections. Their father was not at all religious ; he had at one time very advanced ideas, for he was a reader of Voltaire's works ; in short, the best thing was to do nothing, as they were unable to consult him. In the heat of the discussion, he even added :

"It is as though you brought the sacrament to that piece of furniture."

The three women compelled him to leave off. They were all trembling with emotion, and said that the priest was right, whilst they excused themselves for not having sent for him before, through the confusion in which the catastrophe had plunged them. Monsieur Vabre would certainly have consented had he been able to speak, for he had a horror of acting different to other people. Moreover, the ladies would take the responsibility on their own shoulders.

"It should be done if only on account of the neighbours," repeated Clotilde.

"No doubt," said the Abbé Mauduit, who hastened to give his approval. "A man of your father's position should set a good example."

Auguste had no opinion either way. But Duveyrier, aroused from his recollections of Clarisse, whose way of putting on her stockings with one leg in the air he was just then thinking of, energetically demanded the sacraments. They were absolutely necessary; not a member of the family should die without them. Doctor Juillerat, who had discreetly moved on one side, hiding his freethinker's disdain, then went up to the priest, and said familiarly to him, in a whisper, the same as to a colleague often encountered under similar circumstances:

"Be quick; you have no time to lose."

The priest hastened to take his departure. He announced that he would bring the sacrament and the extreme unction, so as to be prepared for every emergency. And Théophile, in his obstinacy, murmured:

"Ah, well! so dying people are now made to receive the communion in spite of themselves!"

But they all at once experienced a great emotion. On regaining her place, Clotilde had found the dying man with his eyes wide open. She could not repress a faint cry; the others hastened to the bedside; and the old fellow's glance slowly wandered round the circle, without the least movement of his head. Doctor Juillerat, with an air of surprise, came and bent over his patient, to follow this last crisis.

"Father, it is us; do you know us?" asked Clotilde.

Monsieur Vabre looked at her fixedly; then his lips moved, but not a sound came from them. They were all pushing one another, wishing to secure his last word. Valérie, who found herself right at the rear, and obliged therefore to stand on tiptoe, said harshly:

"You are stifling him. Do move away from him. If he desired anything, no one would be able to know."

The others had to draw on one side. And Monsieur Vabre's eyes were indeed looking round the room.

"He wants something, that is certain," murmured Berthe.

"Here's Gustave," said Clotilde. "You see him, do you not? He has come expressly from school to embrace you. Kiss your grandfather, my child."

As the youngster drew back frightened, she kept him there with her arm, whilst she awaited a smile on the dying man's distorted features. But Auguste, who had been watching his eyes, declared that he was looking at the table ; no doubt he wished to write. This caused quite a shock. All tried to be first. They brought the table to the bedside, and fetched some paper, an inkstand, and a pen. Then they raised him, propping him up with three pillows. The doctor gave his consent to all this with a simple blink of the eyes.

"Give him the pen," said Clotilde, quivering, and without leaving go of Gustave, whom she continued to hold towards him.

Then came a solemn moment. The relations, pressed round the bed, awaited anxiously. Monsieur Vabre, who did not appear to recognise any one, had let the penholder drop from his fingers. For a moment his eyes wandered over the table, on which was the oak box full of tickets. Then, slipping from off his pillows, and falling forward like a piece of rag, he stretched out his arm in a final effort, and, plunging his hand amongst the tickets, he dabbled about, in the happy manner of a baby playing with something dirty. He brightened up, and wished to speak, but he could only lisp one syllable, ever the same, one of those syllables into which brats in swaddling-clothes put a whole host of sensations.

"Ga—ga—ga—ga—"

It was to the work of his life, to his great statistical study, that he was bidding good-bye. Suddenly his head rolled over. He was dead.

"I expected as much," murmured the doctor, who, seeing how scared the relations were, carefully laid him out, and closed his eyes.

Was it possible ? Auguste had removed the table, they all remained chilled and dumb. Soon their sobs burst forth. Well ! as there was nothing more to hope for, they would manage all the same to share the fortune. And Clotilde, after hastening to send Gustave away, to spare him the frightful spectacle, gave free vent to her tears, her head leaning against Berthe, who was sobbing the same as Valérie. Standing at the window, Théophile and Auguste were roughly rubbing their eyes. But Duveyrier especially exhibited a most extraordinary amount of grief, stifling heart-rending sobs in his handkerchief. No, really, he could not live without Clarisse, he would rather die at once, like the other one there; and the loss of his mistress, coming in the midst of all this mourning, caused him immense bitterness.

"Madame," announced Clémence, "here are the sacraments."

Abbé Mauduit appeared on the threshold. Behind his shoulder, one caught a glimpse of the face full of curiosity of a boy chorister. On beholding the display of grief, the priest questioned the doctor with a glance, whilst the latter extended his arms, as though to say it was not his fault. So, after mumbling a few prayers, Abbé Mauduit withdrew with an air of embarrassment, taking his paraphernalia along with him.

"It is a bad sign," said Clémence to the other servants, standing in a group at the door of the anteroom. "The sacraments are not to be brought for nothing. You will see they will be back in the house before another year goes by."

Monsieur Vabre's funeral did not take place till the day after the morrow. Duveyrier, all the same, had inserted in the circulars announcing his demise, the words, "provided with the sacraments of the Church."

As the warehouse did not open on that day, Octave was free. This holiday delighted him, as, for a long time past, he had wished to put his room straight, alter the position of some of the furniture, and arrange his few books in a little bookcase he had bought second-hand. He had risen earlier than usual, and was just finishing what he was about towards eight o'clock on the morning of the funeral, when Marie knocked at the door. She had brought him back a heap of books.

"As you do not come for them," said she, "I am obliged to take the trouble to return them to you."

But she blushingly refused to enter, shocked at the idea of being in a young man's room. Their intimate relations had, moreover, completely ceased, in quite a natural manner, because he had not returned to her. And she remained quite as affectionate with him, always greeting him with a smile whenever they met.

Octave was very merry that morning. He wished to tease her.

"So it is Jules who won't let you come into my room?" he kept saying. "How do you get on with Jules now? Is he amiable? Yes, you know what I mean. Answer now!"

She laughed, and was not at all scandalized.

"Why, of course! whenever you take him out, you treat him to vermouth, and tell him things which send him home like a madman. Oh! he is too amiable. You know, I don't ask for so much. Still, I prefer it should take place, at home than elsewhere, that's very certain."

She became serious again, and added :

"Here, I have brought you back your Balzac, I was not able to finish it. It's too sad. That gentleman has nothing but disagreeable things to tell one !"

And she asked him for stories with a great deal of love in them, and travels and adventures in foreign lands. Then she talked of the funeral, she would attend the service in the church, and Jules was going to follow the corpse to the cemetery. She had never been afraid of dead people ; when twelve years old, she had remained a whole night beside an uncle and an aunt who had been carried off by the same fever. Jules, on the contrary, hated talking of death to such a point that he had forbidden her since the day before to speak of the landlord stretched out on his back downstairs ; but she could find nothing to say about anything else, nor he either, so that they did not exchange ten words an hour, but sat thinking of the poor gentleman all the while. It was becoming wearisome, she would be glad when he was taken away, for Jules's sake. And, happy at being able to discuss the subject to her heart's content, she satisfied her inclination, harassing the young man with questions : had he seen him? was he very much altered? was she to believe what was related about an abominable accident which occurred whilst he was being put in his coffin? as for the relations, were they not pulling the mattresses to pieces, so as to search everything? So many idle stories circulated in a house like theirs, where there was such a number of servants ! Death was death : everyone was interested in it.

"You're giving me another Balzac," resumed she, looking at the books he was again lending her. "No, take it back, it is too realistic."

As she held the volume out to him, he caught hold of her by the wrist, and tried to draw her into the room. She amused him with all her curiosity about death ; he thought her comic and more lively, and on a sudden she became an object to be desired. But she comprehended, and turned very red, then, disengaging herself, she hastened away, saying :

"Thank you, Monsieur Mouret.   I shall see you by-and-by at the funeral."

When Octave was dressed, he remembered his promise to go and see Madame Campardon.   He had two good hours to·while away, the funeral being timed for eleven o'clock, and he thought of utilizing his morning in making a few calls in the house. Rose received him in bed ; he apologized, fearing that he disturbed her; but she herself called him in.   They saw so little of him, and she was so delighted at having some one to talk to.

"Ah ! my dear child," declared she at once, "it is I who ought to be below, nailed up between four planks ! "

Yes, the landlord was very lucky, he had finished with existence.   And Octave, surprised at finding her a prey to such melancholy, asked her if she felt worse.

"No, thank you.   It is always the same.   Only there are times when I have had enough of it.   Achille has been obliged to have a bed put up in his workroom, because it annoyed me whenever he moved in the night.   And you know that Gasparine has yielded to our entreaties, and has left the drapery establishment.   I am very grateful to her, she nurses me so tenderly ! Ah ! I could no longer live were it not for all these kind affections around me ! "

Just then, Gasparine, with her submissive air of a poor relation, fallen to the rank of a servant, brought her a cup of coffee and some bread and butter.   She helped her to raise herself, propping her up against some cushions, and served her on a little tray covered with a napkin.   And Rose, dressed in a little loose embroidered jacket, ate with a hearty appetite, amidst the linen, edged with lace.   She was quite fresh, looking younger than ever, and very pretty, with her white skin, and short fair curly hair.

"Oh ! the stomach is all right, it is not the stomach that is ailing," she kept saying, as she soaked her slices of bread and butter.

Two tears dropped into her coffee.   Then Gasparine scolded her.

"If you cry, I shall call Achille.   Are you not pleased ? are you not sitting there like a queen ? "

When Madame Campardon had finished, and she again found herself alone with Octave, she was quite consoled.   Out of coquetry, she again returned to the subject of death, but with the gentle gaiety of a woman idling away the morning between her warm sheets.   Well ! she would go off all the same, when her turn came ; only, they were right, she was not unhappy, she could let herself live ; for, in point of fact, they spared her all the main cares of life.

Then, as the young man rose to leave, she added :

"Now do try and come oftener? Amuse yourself well, don't let the funeral make you too sad. One dies a trifle every day, the thing is to get used to it."

It was the little maid Louise who opened the door to Octave at Madame Juzeur's, on the same landing. She ushered him into the drawing-room, looked at him a moment as she laughed in her bewildered sort of way, and then ended by stating that her mistress was just finishing dressing. Madame Juzeur appeared almost at once, dressed in black, and looking gentler and more refined than ever in her mourning.

"I felt sure you would call this morning," sighed she with a weary air. "All night long I have been dreaming and seeing you. It is impossible to sleep, you understand, with that corpse in the house !"

And she admitted that she had got up three times in the night to look under the furniture.

"But you should have called me !" said the young man gallantly. "Two in a bed are never frightened."

She assumed a charming air of shame.

"Hold your tongue, it's naughty ! "

And she held her open hand over his lips. He was naturally obliged to kiss it. Then, she spread the fingers out, laughing the while as though being tickled. But he, excited by this play, sought to push matters farther. He had caught hold of her, and was pressing her against his breast, without her making the least attempt to free herself; then, in a very low voice, he whispered in her ear:

"Come now, why won't you ? "

"Oh ! in any case, not to-day ! "

"Why not to-day ? "

"What! with that corpse below. No, no, it's impossible."

He was holding her tighter, and she was abandoning herself. Their warm breaths were heating one another's faces.

"Then, when ? to-morrow ? "

"Never."

"But you are free, your husband behaved so badly, that you owe nothing to him."

And he was forcibly seizing her. But she, very supple, glided from him. Then taking him in her arms, and holding him so that he could not move, she murmured in her caressing voice :

"Anything you like except that!   You understand me, never that, never, never !   I would sooner die.   It's an idea of mine, that's all?   I have taken an oath, however there is no necessity for you to know.   You are then like other men, who are never satisfied, so long as anything is refused them.   Yet, I love you a great deal.   Anything you like, except that, my love ! "

In her determination, there was a sort of jesuitical reserve, a fear of the confessional, a certainty of having her minor sins forgiven, whilst the great one would cause her no end of unpleasantness with her spiritual director.   Then, there were other unavowed sentiments, her honour and self-esteem blended together, the coquetry of always having the advantage of men by never satisfying them, and a shrewd personal enjoyment in being smothered with kisses, without any after consequences. She liked this better, and she stuck to it, not a man could flatter himself of having succeeded with her, since her husband's cowardly desertion.   And she was a respectable woman !

" No, sir, not one !   Ah ! I can hold up my head, I can ! What a number of wretched women, in my position, would have misconducted themselves ! "

She pushed him gently aside and rose from the sofa.

" Leave me.   It worries me so much, does that corpse downstairs.   It seems to me that the whole house smells of it."

Meanwhile, the time for the funeral was approaching.   She wished to be at the church beforehand, so as not to see all the funeral trappings.   But, while escorting him to the door, she recollected having mentioned her liqueur ; she therefore made him come in again, and fetched the bottle and a couple of glasses herself.   It was a very sweet cream, with a perfume of flowers.   When she had drank of it, a greediness like that of a little girl gave an air of languid delight to her face.   She could have lived on sugar ; vanilla and rose-scented sweeties had the same effect on her as an amorous caress.

" It will sustain us," said she.

And, when he kissed her on the mouth in the anteroom, she closed her eyes.   Their sugary lips seemed to be melting like sweetmeats.

It was close upon eleven o'clock.   The coffin had not been brought down for exhibition, as the undertaker's men, after wasting their time at a neighbouring wine-shop, had not finished putting up the hangings.   Octave went to have a look out of curiosity.   The porch was already closed in at the back by a large black curtain, but the men had still to fix the hangings over the door.   And outside on the pavement, a group of maid-servants were gossiping with their noses in the air ; whilst Hippolyte, dressed in deep mourning, hastened on the work with a diguified air.

"Yes, madame," Lisa was saying to a dried-up woman, a widow, who had been with Valérie for a week, "it will have benefitted her nothing.   The story's well known in the neighbourhood.   To make sure of her share of what the old fellow left behind him, she went and had a child by a butcher of the Rue Sainte-Anne, because her husband looked as though he were going to die right off.   But the husband's still jogging along, and it's the old chap who's gone.   A fat lot of good she's done herself with her dirty brat !"

The widow, highly disgusted, nodded her head.

"It serves her right!" rejoined she.   "She's had all her piggishness for nothing.   I sha'n't stay with her, you may take my word.   I gave her a week's notice this morning. Her little monster Camille went messing all over my kitchen !"

But Lisa ran to question Julie, who came down to give Hippolyte some instructions.   Then, after a few minutes' conversation, she returned to Valérie's servant.

"It's an affair no one can understand.   I think your mistress might have spared herself the trouble of getting her child and have let her husband die all the same, for it seems they're still searching after the old fellow's fortune.   The cook says they're making such funny faces up there, the faces of people who'll be fighting together before the day's over."

Adèle now arrived, with four sous' worth of butter under her apron, Madame Josserand having requested her never to show anything that she was sent to fetch.   Lisa insisted on seeing, and then abused her and called her a fool.   Whoever heard of anyone going out for four sous' worth of butter !   Ah, well ! she would have made those skinflints feed her better, or else she would have fed herself before them ; yes, with the butter, the sugar, the meat, everything.   For some time past the other servants had been thus inciting Adèle to rebel.   She was becoming perverted.   She took up a small piece of the butter and eat it at once without any bread, just to show the others how brave she was.

"Shall we go up now ?" asked she.

" Not I," said the widow, " I want to see him brought down.
I've been keeping an errand back on purpose for it."

" And I also," added Lisa.　" I've heard he weighs twelve
stone.　If they drop him on their beautiful staircase, won't it
just knock it about !"

"Well, I'm going up, I'd rather not see him," resumed Adèle.
" I don't want to dream again like I did last night, that he's
pulling my feet and abusing me because of the mess I make."

And she went off, followed by the jokes of the other two.
All night long, on the servants' floor, they had been amused by
Adèle's nightmares.　Moreover, so as not to be alone, the servants had left their doors open ; and, a funny coachman having
played at being a ghost, little cries and smothered laughter had
been heard along the passage up till daylight.　Lisa said in an
affected way that she was not likely to forget it.　It was a fine
bit of fun, all the same !

But Hippolyte's angry voice brought their attention back to
the hangings.　He was shouting out, forgetful of his dignified
air :

" You damned drunkard ! you're putting it on upside down !"

It was true, the workman was hooking on the escutcheon
bearing the deceased's monogram wrong side up.　The black
hangings edged with silver lace were now fixed ; there remained
nothing but a few curtain-rests to put up, when a truck filled
with some poor person's furniture appeared at the door.　A
youngster was drawing it along, whilst a tall, pale girl followed,
pushing behind.　Monsieur Gourd, who was talking with his
friend, the stationer opposite, rushed up to them and, in spite
of the solemnity of his mourning, exclaimed :

" Well ! well ! what's he up to ?　Can't you see, you fool ?"

The tall girl interposed.

"I am the new lodger, sir, you know.　This is my furniture."

" Impossible ! to-morrow !" shouted the doorkeeper in a
rage.

She looked at him, and then at the funeral hangings, in a
stupefied sort of a way.　This door walled up with black
evidently bewildered her.　But she recovered herself, and explained that she could not leave her furniture out in the street.
Then Monsieur Gourd treated her roughly.

" You're the boot-stitcher, aren't you ?　You've taken the
small room upstairs.　Another piece of the landlord's obstinacy !
All this for the sake of a hundred and thirty francs, and in spite
of the bother we had with the carpenter !　Yet he promised me

he would never let to work-people any more.   Ah ! bosh, now it's going to begin again, and with a woman this time ! "

Then he recollected that Monsieur Vabre was dead.

" Yes, you may look ; it just happens that it's the landlord who's dead, and if he'd gone off a week ago you'd not be here, that's very certain !   Come, look sharp ; get it over before they bring him down ! "

And, in his exasperation, he himself gave a shove to the truck, pushing it through the hangings, which opened and then slowly closed again.   The tall, pale girl disappeared behind the black mass.

" She comes at a nice time ! " observed Lisa.   " How lively it is to move into a lodging in the middle of a funeral !   Had I been in her place, I'd have given the doorkeeper a bit of my mind ! "

But she held her tongue when Monsieur Gourd, who was the terror of the servants, reappeared.   His ill-temper arose from the fact of its being rumoured that the house was going to fall to Monsieur Théophile and his wife as their share of the inheritance.   He would have given a hundred francs out of his own pocket to have had Monsieur Duveyrier for landlord—a man who belonged to the magistracy.   It was this that he was explaining to the stationer.   However, some of the people now began to come out.   Madame Juzeur passed and smiled at Octave, who had found Trublot waiting on the pavement. Then Marie appeared, and she, deeply interested, stood watching the men arrange the trestles for the coffin.

" The people on the second floor are extraordinary," said Monsieur Gourd, raising his eyes to the closed shutters of that storey.   " One could almost fancy that they made their arrangements to avoid acting like every one else.   Yes, they went away on a journey three days ago."

At this moment Lisa hid herself behind the widow, as she caught sight of cousin Gasparine, who was bringing a wreath of violets, a delicate attention on the part of the architect, desirous of keeping on good terms with the Duveyriers.

" By Jove ! " declared the stationer, " she makes herself smart, does the other Madame Campardon ! "

He innocently called her thus by the name all the tradespeople of the neighbourhood gave to her.   Lisa suppressed a laugh.   But there was a great disappointment.   The servants suddenly learnt that the coffin had been brought down.   It was really too stupid for them to have remained in the street looking at the black cloth !

They hastened indoors ; and the coffin, borne by four men, was indeed just coming out of the vestibule. The hangings darkened the porch ; one could catch a glimpse of the white light of the courtyard beyond, which had been well washed that morning. Little Louise, who had followed Madame Juzeur, was there alone, standing on tiptoe, her eyes wide open and her face pale with curiosity. The men who had carried down the coffin were puffing and blowing at the foot of the stairs, the gildings and imitation marble of which looked coldly solemn beneath the faint light from the ground glass windows.

"He's gone off without his last quarter's rent !" murmured Lisa, with the waggish hatred of a Paris girl for landlords.

Then Madame Gourd, who had remained in her armchair on account of her poor legs, rose painfully on her feet. As she was quite unable to get even as far as the church, Monsieur Gourd had told her to be sure and salute the landlord's corpse when it passed their room. It was a matter of duty. She went to the door with a mourning cap on her head, and curtsied as the coffin went by.

At Saint-Roch, Doctor Juillerat made a show of not going inside during the ceremony. There was, moreover, a tremendous crowd, and quite a group of men preferred to remain on the steps. The weather was very mild, a superb June day. And, as they were unable to smoke, their conversation turned upon politics. The principal door was left open, and at moments the sound of the organs issued from the church, which was draped in black and filled with lighted tapers, looking like so many stars.

"You know that Monsieur Thiers will stand for our district next year," announced Léon Josserand in his grave way.

"Ah !" said the doctor. "Of course you will not vote for him—you who are a Republican ?"

The young man, whose opinions cooled down the more Madame Dambreville introduced him into good society, curtly answered :

"Why not ? He is the declared adversary of the Empire."

Then a heated discussion ensued. Léon talked of tactics, whilst Doctor Juillerat stuck to principles. According to the latter, the middle classes had had their day ; they were an obstacle in the road of the Revolution ; now that they had acquired property, they barred the future with greater obstinacy and blindness than the old nobility.

"You are afraid of everything; you go in for the very worst reaction the moment you fancy yourselves threatened !"

At this Campardon flew into a passion.

"I, sir, have been a Jacobin and an atheist like you. But, thank heaven ! reason came to me. No, I will not even stoop to your Monsieur Thiers. A blunderhead—a man who amuses himself with chimeras !"

However, all the Liberals present—Monsieur Josserand, Octave, Trublot even, who did not care a straw, declared that they would vote for Monsieur Thiers. The official candidate was a great chocolate manufacturer of the Rue Saint-Honoré, Monsieur Dewinck, whom they chaffed immensely. . This Monsieur Dewinck had not even the support of the clergy, who were uneasy at his relations with the Tuileries. Campardon, decidedly gone over to the priests, greeted his name with reserve. Then, suddenly changing the subject, he exclaimed :

"Look here ! the bullet which wounded your Garibaldi in the foot ought to have pierced his heart !"

And, so as not to be seen any longer in the company of these gentlemen, he entered the church, where the Abbé Mauduit's shrill voice was responding to the lamentations of the chanters.

"He sleeps there now," murmured the doctor, shrugging his shoulders. "Ah ! what a clean sweep ought to be made of it all !"

The Roman question interested him immensely. Then, as Léon reminded them of the words of the Cabinet Minister to the Senate that the Empire had sprung from the Revolution, only in order to keep it within bounds, they returned to the coming elections. All were agreed upon the necessity of giving the Emperor a lesson ; but they were beginning to be troubled with anxiety, they were already divided respecting the candidates, whose names gave rise to visions of the red spectre at night-time. Close to them, Monsieur Gourd, dressed as correctly as a diplomatist, listened with supreme contempt to what they were saying; he was for the powers that be, pure and simple.

The service was drawing to a close, a long melancholy wail which issued from the depths of the church, silenced them.

"*Requiescat in pace !*"

"*Amen !*"

Whilst the body was being lowered into the grave at the Père-Lachaise cemetery, Trublot, who had not let go of Octave's arm, saw him exchange another smile with Madame Juzeur.

" Ah ! yes," murmured he, "the very unhappy little woman. Anything you like except that ! "

Octave started. What ! Trublot also ! The latter·made a gesture of disdain : no, not he, one of his friends. And, moreover, everybody who cared for that kind of thing.

" Excuse me," added he. " As the old fellow's now stowed away, I will go and render Duveyrier an account of something which I undertook to see after for him."

The relations were retiring, silent and doleful. Then, Trublot detained the counsellor behind the others, to tell him that he had seen Clarisse's maid; but he did not know the new address, the maid having left Clarisse the day before she moved out, after a battle royal. It was the last hope which had flown. Duveyrier buried his face in his handkerchief and rejoined the other relations.

That very evening, quarrels commenced. The family found itself in the presence of a disaster. Monsieur Vabre, with that sceptical carelessness which notaries occasionally display, had not left any will. All the furniture was ransacked in vain, and the worst was that there was not a rap of the expected six or seven hundred thousand francs, neither money, title-deeds nor shares ; they discovered merely seven hundred and thirty-four francs in ten sou pieces, the hoard of a silly paralytic old man. And undeniable traces, a note-book covered with figures, letters from stockbrokers, opened the eyes of the next-of-kin, pale with passion, to the old fellow's secret vice, an ungovernable passion for gambling, an unskilful and desperate craving for stock-jobbing, which he hid behind the innocent mania for his great statistical work. All had been engulfed, the money he had saved at Versailles, the rents of his house, even the sous he had sneaked from his children ; and during the latter years, he had gone to the point of mortgaging the house for one hundred and fifty thousand francs, at three different periods. The family stood thunder-stricken before the famous safe, in which it thought the fortune was locked up, but which simply contained a host of singular things, broken scraps picked up in the various rooms, pieces of old iron, fragments of glass, ends of ribbon, jumbled amidst wrecked toys stolen from young Gustave in bygone days.

Then, the most violent recriminations were indulged in. They called the old fellow a swindler. It was disgraceful, to fritter away his money thus, like a sly person who does not care a straw for anyone and who acts an infamous comedy in order to get people to continue to coddle him. The Duveyriers were inconsolable at having boarded him for twelve years, without once asking him for the eighty thousand francs of Clotilde's dowry, of which they had only had ten thousand francs. It was always ten thousand francs, rejoined Théophile, who had not had a sou of the fifty thousand promised him at the time of his marriage. But Auguste, in his turn, complained more bitterly still, reproaching his brother with having at least secured the interest of the money during three months; whilst he would never have a shadow of the fifty thousand francs, inserted in his contract. And Berthe, incited by her mother, said some very unpleasant things with an indignant air at having entered a dishonest family. And Valérie, bemoaning the rent she had so long been stupid enough to pay the old chap, for fear of being disinherited, could not stomach it, regretting the money as though it had been used for an immoral purpose, employed in supporting debauchery.

For fully a fortnight, all these stories formed an exciting topic of conversation to the occupants of the house. The long and short of it was that there remained nothing but the building, estimated to be worth three hundred thousand francs; when the mortgage had been paid off, there would be about half that sum to divide between Monsieur Vabre's three children. It was fifty thousand francs for each; a meagre consolation, but they would have to make the most of it. Théophile and Auguste had already decided what they would do with their shares. It was settled that the building should be sold. Duveyrier undertook all the arrangements in his wife's name. To begin with, he persuaded the two brothers not to have the sale by auction before the court; if they were all agreed, it could take place at his notary's, Maître Renaudin, a man whom he could answer for. Then, he gave them the idea, on the notary's advice, he said, of putting up the house at a low figure, at a hundred and forty thousand francs merely: it was very cunning, people would flock to the sale, the bids would mount up, and they would realise even more than they expected. Théophile and Auguste laughed confidently. Then, on the day of the sale, after five or six bids, Maître Renaudin abruptly knocked the house down to Duveyrier, for the sum of one hundred and forty-nine thousand francs. There was not even sufficient to pay the mortgage. It was the final blow.

One never knew the particulars of the terrible scene which was enacted that same evening at the Duveyriers'. The solemn

walls of the house stifled the sounds. Théophile most probably
called his brother-in-law a scoundrel : he publicly accused him
of having bought over the notary, by promising to get him appointed a justice of the peace. As for Auguste, he simply
talked of the assize-court, where he wished to drag Maître Renaudin, whose rogueries were the talk of the neighbourhood.
But though one always ignored how it was that the relatives
got to the point of knocking each other about, as rumour said
they did, one heard the last words exchanged on the threshold,
words which had an unpleasant ring in the respectable severity
of the staircase.

"Dirty scoundrel!" shouted Auguste. "You sentence
people to penal servitude who have not done nearly as much!"

Théophile, who came out last, held the door, whilst he almost
choked with rage and coughing.

"Robber! robber! Yes, robber! And you too, Clotilde, do
you hear? robber!"

He swung the door to so roughly, that all the other doors on the
staircase shook. Monsieur Gourd, who was listening, was quite
alarmed. He darted a searching glance at the different floors ;
but he merely caught sight of Madame Juzeur's sharp profile.
Arching his back, he returned on tiptoe to his room, where he
resumed his dignified demeanour. One could deny everything.
He, delighted, considered the new landlord in the right.

A few days later, there was a reconciliation between Auguste
and his sister. The whole house was amazed. Octave had
been seen to go to the Duveyriers'. The counsellor, feeling anxious, had agreed not to charge any rent for the warehouse for
five years, thus shutting one of the grumbler's mouths. When
Théophile learnt this, he went with his wife and had another
row this time with his brother. So he had sold himself, he had
gone over to the bandits! But Madame Josserand happened
to be in the shop, and he was soon shut up. She plainly advised Valérie not to sell herself any more than her daughter
had sold herself. And Valérie had to beat a retreat, exclaiming:

"Then, we're the only ones who get nothing? May the
devil take me if I pay my rent! I've a lease. The convict
won't dare to turn us out. And as for you, my little Berthe,
we'll see one day what it'll cost to have you!"

The doors banged again. The two families were sworn
enemies for life. Octave, who had rendered some services, was
present, and entered into the private affairs of the family.
Berthe almost fainted in his arms, whilst Auguste was ascertain-

ing whether the customers had overheard anything. Even
Madame Josserand confided in the young man. She, moreover,
continued to judge the Duveyriers very severely.

"The rent is something," said she. "But I want the fifty
thousand francs."

"Of course, if you paid yours," Berthe ventured to observe.

The mother did not appear to understand.

"You hear me, I want them ! No, no, he must be laughing
too much in his grave, that old scoundrel Vabre, I will not let
him boast of having taken me in. What rascals there are in
the world ! to promise money one does not possess ! Oh ! they
will pay you, my daughter, or I will dig him up again and spit
in his face !"

CHAPTER XII

One morning that Berthe happened to be at her mother's, Adèle came and said with a scared look that Monsieur Saturnin was there with a man. Doctor Chassagne, the director of the Asile des Moulineaux, had already warned the parents several times that he would be unable to keep their son, for he did not consider him sufficiently mad. And, hearing of the signature which Berthe had obtained from her brother for the three thousand francs, dreading being compromised in the matter, he suddenly sent him home to his family.

It created quite a scare. Madame Josserand, who was afraid of being strangled, wished to argue with the man. But all she could get out of him was:

"The director told me to inform you that when one is sufficiently sensible to give money to one's parents, one is sensible enough to live with them."

"But he is mad, sir! he will murder us."

"Anyhow, he is not too mad to sign his name!" answered the man going off.

However, Saturnin came home very quietly, with his hands in his pockets, just as though he had returned from a stroll in the Tuileries gardens. He did not even allude to where he had been staying. He embraced his father who was crying, and likewise heartily kissed his mother and his sister Hortense, whilst they both trembled tremendously. Then, when he caught sight of Berthe, he was indeed delighted, and caressed her with all the pretty ways of a little boy. She at once took advantage of his affected and confused condition to inform him of her marriage. He displayed no anger, not appearing at first to understand, as though he had forgotten his former fits of passion. But when she wished to return to her home downstairs, he began to howl: he did not mind whether she was married or not, so long as she remained where she was, always with him and close to him. Then, seeing her mother's frightened looks as she ran and locked herself in another room, it occurred to Berthe to take Saturnin to live with her. They would be able to find him something to do in the basement of the warehouse, though it were only to tie up parcels.

That same evening, Auguste, in spite of his evident repugnance, acceded to Berthe's desire. They had scarcely been married three months and a secret disunion was already cropping up between them, it was the collision of two different constitutions and educations, a surly, fastidious and passionless husband, and a lively woman who had been reared in the hothouse of false Parisian luxury, who played fast and loose with existence, so as to enjoy it all alone like a spoiled and selfish child. Therefore he could not understand her need of movement, her constant goings-out on visits, on errands and for walks, her gallop through the theatres, exhibitions, and other entertainments. Two and three times a week, Madame Josserand would call for her daughter, and keep her until dinner-time, delighted at going about in her company, and of thus taking advantage of her daughter's handsome dresses which she no longer paid for.

The husband's main revolts were on account of these too glaring costumes, the usefulness of which he was unable to see. Why dress oneself thus above one's means and position in life? What need was there to spend in such a manner the money which was so necessary for his business? He generally said that when one sold silks to other women, one should wear woollens oneself. But then Berthe put on her mother's ferocious airs, asking him if he expected her to go about naked; and she discouraged him still more by the doubtful whiteness of her petticoats, by her disdain of all linen which is not displayed, having stock phrases with which to shut him up always ready in case he persisted in his complaints :

"I prefer to excite envy rather than pity. Money is money, and when I have only had twenty sous, I have always pretended I had forty."

As a result of matrimony, Berthe was gradually acquiring her mother's build. She was growing fatter, and resembled her more than she had ever done before. She was no longer the girl who did not seem to care about anything and who quietly submitted to the maternal cuffs ; she had grown into a woman, who was rapidly becoming more obstinate every day, and who had formed the intention of making everything bow to her pleasure. Auguste looked at her at times, astounded at such a sudden change. At first, she had felt a vain joy in throning herself at the cashier's desk, in a studied costume of elegant simplicity. Then, she had soon wearied of trade, suffering from constant want of exercise, threatening to fall ill, yet resigning herself to it all the same, but with the attitude of a victim who sacrifices her life to the prosperity of her home. And, from that moment, a struggle at every hour of the day had commenced between her and her husband. She shrugged her shoulders behind his back, the same as her mother did behind her father's; she went again through all the family quarrels which had disturbed her youth, treating her husband as the gentleman who had simply got to pay, overwhelming him with that contempt for the male sex, which was, so to say, the basis of her education.

"Ah! mamma was right!" she would exclaim after each of their quarrels.

Yet, in the early days, Auguste had tried to please her. He liked peace, he longed for a quiet little home, he already had his whims like an old man, and had got thoroughly into the habits of his chaste and economical bachelor life. His old lodging on the "entresol" no longer sufficing, he had taken the suite of apartments on the second floor, overlooking the courtyard, and thought himself sufficiently insane in spending five thousand francs on furniture. Berthe, at first delighted with her room upholstered in thuja and blue silk, had shown the greatest contempt for it, after visiting a friend who had just married a banker. Then quarrels arose with respect to the servants. The young woman, used to the waiting of poor semi-idiotic girls, who had their bread even cut for them, insisted on their doing things which set them crying in their kitchens for afternoons together. Auguste, not particularly tender-hearted as a rule, having imprudently gone and consoled one, had to turn her out of the place an hour later on account of madame's tears, and her request that he should choose between her and that creature. Afterwards, a wench had come who appeared to have made up her mind to stop. Her name was Rachel, and she was probably a Jewess, but she denied it, and let no one know whence she had sprung. She was about twenty-five years old, with harsh features, a large nose, and very black hair. At first, Berthe declared that she would not allow her to stop two days; then, in presence of her dumb obedience, her air of understanding and saying nothing, she had little by little allowed herself to be satisfied, as though she had yielded in her turn, and was keeping her for her good qualities, and also through an unavowed fear. Rachel, who submitted without a murmur to the hardest tasks, accompanied by dry bread, took possession of the establishment, with her eyes open and her mouth shut, like a servant of foresight biding the fatal and foreseen hour when her mistress would be able to refuse her nothing.

Meanwhile, from the ground floor of the house to the servants' storey, a great calm had succeeded to the emotions caused by Monsieur Vabre's sudden death. The staircase had again become as peaceful as a church; not a breath issued from behind the mahogany doors, which were for ever closed upon the profound respectability of the various homes. There was a rumour that Duveyrier had become reconciled with his wife. As for Valérie and Théophile, they spoke to no one, but passed by stiff and dignified. Never before had the house exhaled a more strict severity of principles. Monsieur Gourd, in his cap and slippers, wandered about it with the air of a solemn beadle.

One evening, towards eleven o'clock, Auguste continued going to the door of the warehouse, stretching his head out, and glancing up and down the street. An impatience which had increased little by little was agitating him. Berthe, whom her mother and sister had fetched away during dinner, without even giving her time to finish her dessert, had not returned home after an absence of more than three hours, and in spite of her distinct promise to be back by closing time.

"Ah! good heavens! good heavens!" he ended by saying, clasping his hands together, and making his fingers crack.

And he stood still before Octave, who was ticketing some remnants of silk on a counter. At that late hour of the evening, no customer ever appeared in that out-of-the-way end of the Rue de Choiseul. The shop was merely kept open to put things straight.

"Surely you know where the ladies have gone?" inquired Auguste of the young man.

The latter raised his eyes with an innocent and surprised air.

"But, sir, they told you. To a lecture."

"A lecture, a lecture," grumbled the husband. "Their lecture was over at ten o'clock. Respectable women should be home at this hour!"

Then he resumed his walk, casting side glances at his assistant, whom he suspected of being an accomplice of the ladies, or at least of excusing them. Octave, also feeling anxious, slyly observed him. He had never before seen him so nervously excited.   What was it all about?   And, as he turned his head, he caught sight of Saturnin at the other end of the shop cleaning a looking-glas with a sponge dipped in spirit.   Little by little, the family set the madman to do house-work, so that he might at least earn his food.   But that evening Saturnin's eyes sparkled strangely.   He crept behind Octave, and said in a very low voice :

"Beware of him.   He has found a paper.   Yes, he has a paper in his pocket.   Look out, if it's anything of yours ! "

And he quickly resumed rubbing his glass.   Octave did not understand.   For some time past the madman had been displaying a singular affection for him, like the caress of an animal yielding to an instinct.   Why did he speak to him of a paper? He had written no letter to Berthe, as yet he only ventured to look at her with tender glances, watching for an opportunity of making her some trifling present.   It was a tactic he had adopted after deep reflection.

"Ten minutes past eleven !—damnation ! damnation ! " suddenly exclaimed Auguste, who never swore.

But at that very moment the ladies returned.   Berthe had on a delicious dress of pink silk, embroidered over with white jet ; whilst her sister, always in blue, and her mother, always in mauve, still wore their glaring and laboriously obtained costumes, altered every season.   Madame Josserand, broad and imposing, entered first, so as at once to nip in the bud the reproaches which all three had just foreseen, at a council held at the end of the street, her son-in-law would begin to make.   She even deigned to explain that they were late through having loitered before the shop-windows.   But Auguste, who was very pale, did not utter a single complaint ; he answered curtly ; it was evident he was keeping it in and waiting.   For a moment longer, the mother, who felt the coming storm through her great knowledge of domestic broils, tried to intimidate him ; then she was obliged to go upstairs, merely adding :

"Good night, my child.   And sleep well, you know, if you wish to live long."

Directly she had gone, Auguste, losing all patience, forgetting that Octave and Saturnin were present, withdrew a crumpled paper from his pocket, and thrust it under Berthe's nose, whilst he stammered out :

" What's that ? "

Berthe had not even had time to take her bonnet off.   She turned very red.

"That?" said she, "why, it's a bill!"

"Yes, a bill! and for false hair, too! Is it possible? for hair! as though you had none left on your head! But that's not all. You've paid the bill; tell me, what did you pay it with?"

The young woman, becoming more and more confused, ended by replying:

"With my own money, of course!"

"Your money! but you haven't any. Some one must have given you some, or else you have taken it from here. And, listen! I know all: you're in debt. I will tolerate what you like; but no debts, understand me, no debts!—never!"

And he put into these words all the horror of a prudent fellow, all his commercial integrity, which consisted in never owing anything. For a long while he relieved his pent-up feelings, reproaching his wife with her constant goings-out, her visits all over Paris, her dresses, her luxury, which he could not provide for. Was it sensible for people in their position to stop out till eleven o'clock at night, with pink silk dresses embroidered with white jet? When one had such tastes as those, one should bring five hundred thousand francs as a marriage portion. Moreover, he knew who was the guilty one; it was the silly mother who brought up her daughters to squander fortunes, without even being able to give them so much as a chemise on their wedding-day.

"Don't say a word against mamma!" cried Berthe, raising her head and thoroughly exasperated at last. "No one can reproach her with anything; she has done her duty. And your family, it's a nice one! People who killed their father!"

Octave had buried himself in his tickets, and pretended not to hear. But he followed the quarrel from out of the corner of his eye, and especially watched Saturnin, who was all in a tremble, and had left off rubbing the glass, his fists clenched, his eyes glaring, ready to spring at the husband's throat.

"Let us leave our families alone," resumed the latter. "We have quite enough with our own home. Listen! you must alter your ways, for I will not give another sou for all this tomfoolery. Oh! I have quite made up my mind. Your place is here at the till, in a quiet dress, like a woman who has some respect for herself. And if you incur any more debts, we'll see."

Berthe was almost stifling, in presence of that brutal husband's foot set down upon her habits, her pleasures, and her dresses. It was the extinction of all she loved, of all she had dreamed of when marrying. But, with a woman's tactics, she hid the wound from which her heart was bleeding ; she gave a pretext to the passion which was swelling her face, and repeated more violently than ever :

"I will not permit you to insult mamma !"

Auguste shrugged his shoulders.

"Your mother ! Listen ! you're like her, you're quite ugly, when you put yourself in that state. Yes, I scarcely know you ; it is she herself. On my word, it quite frightens me !"

At this, Berthe calmed down, and, looking him full in the face, exclaimed :

"Only go and tell mamma what you were saying just now, and see how quickly she'll show you the door."

"Ah ! she'll show me the door !" yelled the husband, in a fury. "Well, then ! I'll go up and tell her at once."

And he did indeed move towards the door. It was time he went, for Saturnin, with his wolf-like eyes, was treacherously advancing to strangle him from behind. The young woman had dropped into a chair, where she was murmuring in a low voice :

"Ah ! good heavens ! I'd take care not to marry him, if I had my choice over again !"

Upstairs, Monsieur Josserand, greatly surprised, answered the door, Adèle having just gone up to bed. As he was then preparing to pass the night in addressing wrappers, in spite of the ill-health he had lately been complaining of, it was with a certain embarrassment, a shame at being found out, that he ushered his son-in-law into the dining-room ; and he spoke of some pressing work, a copy of the last inventory of the Saint-Joseph glass factory. But, when Auguste deliberately accused his daughter, reproaching her with running into debt, relating all the quarrel brought about by the matter of the false hair, the poor old man's hands were seized with a nervous trembling. Struck to the heart, he could only manage to stammer out a few words, whilst his eyes filled with tears. His daughter in debt, living as he had lived himself, in the midst of constant matrimonial squabbles ! All the unhappiness of his life was then going to be gone through again in the person of his daughter ! And another fear almost froze him on his chair : he dreaded every minute to hear his son-in-law broach the money question, demand the dowry, and call him a thief. No doubt the young man knew everything, as he burst in upon them at past eleven o'clock at night.

"My wife is going to bed," stammered he, his head in a whirl. "It is useless to disturb her, is it not? I am really amazed at the things you have told me! Poor Berthe is not wicked though, I assure you. Be indulgent. I will speak to her. As for ourselves, my dear Auguste, we have done nothing, I think, which can displease you."

And he sounded him, so to speak, with his glance, already reassured, as he saw that he could know nothing as yet, when Madame Josserand appeared on the threshold of the bedroom. She was in her night-gown, all white and terrible. Auguste, though greatly excited, drew back. No doubt she had been listening at the door, for she commenced with a direct thrust.

"It's not your ten thousand francs you've come for, I suppose? There are still two months before the time they become due. And in two months time we will pay them to you, sir. We don't die to get out of our engagements."

This superb assurance completely overwhelmed Monsieur Josserand. However, Madame Josserand continued dumbfounding her son-in-law by the most extraordinary declarations, without allowing him time to speak.

"You're by no means smart, sir. When you've made Berthe ill, you'll have to call in the doctor, and that will occasion some expense at the chemist's, and it will still be you who'll have to pay. A little while ago, I went off, when I saw that you were bent on making a fool of yourself. Do as you like! Beat your wife, my maternal heart is easy, for God is watching, and retribution is never long in coming!"

At length, Auguste was able to state his grievances. He returned to the constant goings-out, the dresses, and was even so bold as to condemn the way in which Berthe had been brought up. Madame Josserand listened to him with an air of supreme contempt. Then when he had finished, she retorted:

"What you say is so absurd that it does not deserve an answer, my dear fellow! I've my conscience, and that suffices me. A man to whom I confided an angel! I'll have nothing more to do with the matter, as I'm insulted. Settle it between yourselves."

"But your daughter will end by deceiving me, madame!" exclaimed Auguste, again overcome with passion.

Madame Josserand, who was going off, turned round, and looked him full in the face.

"You're doing all you can to bring such a thing about, sir."

And she retired into her room, with the dignity of a colossal triple-breasted Ceres draped in white.

The father kept Auguste a few minutes longer. He was conciliatory, giving him to understand that with women it was best to put up with everything, and finally sent him off calmed, and resolved to forgive. But when the poor old man found himself alone again in the dining-room, seated in front of his little lamp, he burst into tears. It was all over; there was no longer any happiness; he would never have time enough of a night to address sufficient wrappers to enable him to assist his daughter clandestinely. The thought that his child might run into debt crushed him like some personal fault. And he felt ill; he had just received another blow; strength would fail him one of those nights. At length, restraining his tears, he painfully recommenced his work.

Downstairs in the shop, her face buried in her hands, Berthe had remained for a while immovable. After putting up the shutters, the porter had returned to the basement. Then Octave thought he might approach the young woman. Ever since the husband's departure, Saturnin had been making signs to him over his sister's head, as though inviting him to console her. Now, he was beaming and multiplied his winks; fearing that he was not understood, he emphasised his advice by blowing kisses into space, with a child's overflowing effusion.

"What! you want me to kiss her?" asked Octave by signs.

"Yes, yes," replied the madman, with an enthusiastic nod of the head.

And, when he beheld the young man smiling before his sister, who had noticed nothing, he seated himself on the floor, behind a counter, hiding, so as not to be in their way. In the profound silence of the closed warehouse the gas-jets were still burning with tall flames. There reigned a death-like peacefulness, a closeness of atmosphere mingled with the unsavoury odour of the dressed silk.

"Do not take it so much to heart, madame, I beg of you," said Octave, in his caressing tones.

She started at finding him so close to her.

"Excuse me, Monsieur Octave. It is not my fault that you assisted at this painful scene. And I must ask you to excuse my husband, for he could not have been very well this evening. You know that in all families there are little unpleasantnesses—"

Sobs choked her utterance. The mere idea of extenuating

her husband's faults before the world had brought on a copious flood of tears, which quite unnerved her.   Saturnin raised his anxious face on a level with the counter ; but he dived down again directly he saw Octave take hold of his sister's hand.

"I beg of you, madame, summon up a little courage," said the assistant.

"No, I cannot help it," stammered she.   "You were there —you heard everything.   For ninety-five francs' worth of hair ! As though all women did nor wear false hair now ! But he knows nothing—he understands nothing.   He knows no more about women than the Grand Turk ; he has never had anything to do with them, no never, Monsieur Octave !   Ah ! I am very miserable !"

She said all this in her feverish spite.   A man whom she pretended she had married for love, and who would soon allow her to go without a chemise !   Did she not fulfil her duties ?   Had he the least negligence to reproach her with ?   If he had not flown into a passion on the day when she asked him for some hair, she would never have been reduced to the necessity of paying for it out of her own pocket !   And for the least thing there was the same story over again ; she could never express a wish, desire the most insignificant article of dress, without coming into contact with his ferocious sullenness.   She naturally had her pride, so she no longer asked for anything, preferring to go without necessaries rather than humiliate herself to no purpose.   Thus, for a fortnight past, she had been ardently longing for a fancy set of ornaments which she had seen with her mother in a jeweller's window in the Palais-Royal.

"You know, three stars in paste for the hair.   Oh ! a mere trifle—a hundred francs, I think.   Well ! although I spoke of them from morning till night, don't imagine that my husband understood !'

Octave would never have dared to hope for such an opportunity.   He hastened matters.

"Yes, yes, I know.   You mentioned the subject several times in my presence.   And, dear me ! madame, your parents received me so well ; you yourself have welcomed me so kindly, that I thought I might venture—"

As he spoke he withdrew from his pocket an oblong box, in which the three stars were sparkling on some cotton wool. Berthe had risen from her seat, deeply affected.

"But it is impossible, sir.   I will not—you were very wrong indeed."

He pretended to be very simple, inventing various pretexts. In the South such things were done constantly. And, besides, the ornaments were of no value whatever. She had turned quite rosy, and was no longer weeping, whilst her eyes, fixed on the box, acquired a fresh lustre from the sparkling of the imitation gems.

"I beg of you, madame. Just to show me that you are satisfied with my work."

" No really, Monsieur Octave ; do not insist. You pain me."

Saturnin had reappeared, and he looked at the jewels in ecstasy, as though he were beholding some reliquary. But his sharp ear heard Auguste's returning footsteps. He warned Berthe by making a slight noise with his tongue. Then the latter came to a decision just as her husband was about to enter.

"Well ! listen," murmured she rapidly, popping the box into her pocket, " I'll say that my sister Hortense made me a present of them."

Auguste gave orders for the gas to be turned out, and then went up with her to bed, without saying a word about the quarrel, delighted at heart at finding her all right again and very lively, as though nothing had taken place between them. The warehouse became wrapped in intense darkness ; and, just as Octave was also retiring, he felt hot hands squeezing his own almost sufficient to crush them in the obscurity. It was Saturnin, who slept in the basement.

" Friend—friend—friend," repeated the madman, with an outburst of wild tenderness.

Disconcerted in his expectations, Octave little by little became seized with a young and passionate desire for Berthe. If he had at first been merely following his old plan of seduction, his wish to succeed by the aid of women, he now no longer beheld in her the employer simply whose possession would place the whole establishment in his hands ; he desired above all the Parisian, that adorable creature of luxury and grace, which he had never had an opportunity of tasting at Marseilles ; he felt a sudden hunger for her little gloved hands, her tiny feet encased in high-heeled boots, her delicate neck hidden by gewgaws, even for the questionable unseen, the make-shifts which he suspected were covered by her gorgeous costumes ; and this sudden attack of passion went so far as to get the better of his shrewd economical nature, to the extent of causing him to squander in presents and all sorts of other expenses the five thousand francs which he had brought with him from the South, and had already doubled by financial operations which he never mentioned to anybody.

But what mainly put him out was that he had become timid at the same time that he had fallen in love. He no longer possessed his former determination, his hurry to reach the goal, enjoying, on the contrary, a lazy delight in hastening nothing. Moreover, in this passing weakness of his usually so practical mind, he ended by considering Berthe's conquest to be a campaign of extreme difficulty, which required delays and the caution of high diplomacy. No doubt his two failures with Valérie and Madame Hédouin filled him with the dread of being once more foiled. But, besides this, there lurked beneath his hesitating uneasiness a fear of the adored one, an absolute belief in Berthe's virtue, all that blindness of love paralysed by desire, and which causes one to despond.

On the morrow of the quarrel, Octave, delighted at having prevailed on the young woman to accept his present, thought that it would be well for him to ingratiate himself with the husband. Therefore, as he took his meals at his employer's table—the latter being in the habit of feeding his assistants, so as always to have them at hand—he showed him the utmost attention, listened to him at dessert and warmly approved all he said. He even went so far in private as to appear to sympathize with his complaints against his wife, pretending, too, to watch her, and making him little reports. Auguste felt greatly touched ; he admitted one night to the young man that he had been on the point of discharging him, under the idea that he was conniving with his mother-in-law. Octave, turning icy cold, at once expressed the utmost horror of Madame Josserand, which had the effect of binding them together in a complete communion of opinions. Moreover, the husband was a decent fellow at heart, simply disagreeable, but willingly resigned, so long as no one upset him by spending his money or interfering with his moral code. He even swore that he would never again fly into a passion, for after the quarrel he had had an abominable headache, which had driven him crazy for three days.

"You understand me, you do ! " he would say to the young man. " I merely want peace. Beyond that I don't care a hang, virtue excepted of course, and providing my wife doesn't carry off the cash-box. Eh ? am I not reasonable ? I don't ask her for anything extraordinary ? "

And Octave lauded his wisdom, and they celebrated together

the sweetness of an uneventful existence, year after year always
the same, passed in measuring off silk. One evening, he had
alarmed Auguste, by reverting to his dream of vast modern
bazaars, and by advising him, as he had advised Madame
Hédouin, to purchase the adjoining house, so as to enlarge his
premises. Auguste, whose head was already splitting between his four counters, had looked at him with the frightened
air of a tradesman accustomed to dividing farthings into
four, that he had hastened to withdraw his suggestion
and to go into raptures over the honest security of small
dealings.

Days passed by, Octave was making his little nest in the
place, a cosy nest lined with wool which would keep him nice
and warm. The husband esteemed him, Madame Josserand
herself, with whom however he avoided being too polite, looked
at him encouragingly. As for Berthe, she was becoming charmingly familiar with him. But his great friend was Saturnin,
whose dumb affection he felt was increasing daily, a faithful dog's
devotion which grew as his longing for the young woman became more intense. Towards every one else the madman displayed a gloomy jealousy ; a man could not approach his sister,
without his becoming at once uneasy, curling up his lips, and
preparing to bite. But if, on the contrary, Octave leant
freely towards her, and caused her to laugh with the soft and
tender laughter of a happy mistress, he laughed himself with
delight, and his face reflected a little of their sensual joy. The
poor creature seemed to feel a gratitude full of happiness for
the chosen lover. He would detain the latter in all the corners, casting mistrustful glances about, then if he found they
were alone, he would speak to him of her, always repeating the
same stories in broken phrases.

"When she was little, she had tiny limbs as large as that;
and already plump, and quite rosy, and so gay—Then, she used
to sprawl about on the floor. It amused me, I would go down
on my knees and watch her—Then, bang ! bang ! bang ! she
would kick me in the stomach—And I used to be so pleased,
oh ! so pleased ! "

Octave thus learnt all about Berthe's childhood, with its little
ailments, its playthings, its growth of a charming uncontrolled
little creature. Saturnin's empty brain treasured up unimpor-
tant matters, which he alone remembered : the day when she
had pricked herself and he had sucked the blood ; one morning
when she had fallen into his arms on trying to get on to the

Q

table. But he invariably returned to the great event, the young
girl's serious illness.

"Ah ! if you had only seen her ! At night-time, I was alone
beside her. They used to beat me to make me go to bed. And
I would creep back, with nothing on my feet. All alone. It
made me cry, she was so white. I used to touch her to see if
she was turning cold. Then, they left me there. I nursed her
better than they, I knew all about the medicines, she took
whatever I gave her. At times, when she complained a great
deal, I laid her head on my breast. We were so nice together.
Then, she got well, and I wished· to return, and they beat me
again."

His eyes lighted up, he laughed and cried, just as though
these events had occurred the day before. From his broken
sentences the history of this strange affection could be spun together : his poor half-witted devotion at the little patient's bed-
side, when she had been given up by the doctors|; his heart and
body devoted to the dying darling, whom he nursed in her
nudity with all the tenderness of a mother ; his affection and
his desires had been arrested there, checked for evermore by
this drama of suffering, from the shock of which he never recovered ; and, from that time, in spite of the ingratitude which
followed the recovery, Berthe remained everything to him, a
mistress before whom he trembled, a child and a sister whom
he had saved from death, an idol which he worshipped with a
jealous adoration. So that he pursued the husband with the
furious hatred of a displeased lover, never at a loss for ill-natured
remarks as he opened his heart to Octave.

"He's got his eye bunged up again. His headache's becoming
a nuisance !—You heard him dragging his feet about yesterday
—Look, there he is squinting into the street. Eh ? isn't he a
fool ?—Dirty beast, dirty beast ! "

And Auguste could scarcely move without angering the madman. Then would come the disquieting proposals.

"If you like, we'll bleed him like a pig between us."

Octave would calm him. Then, on his quiet days, Saturnin
would go from Octave to the young woman, with an air of delight, repeating what one had said about the other, doing their
errands, and acting like a continual bond of tenderness between
them. He would have thrown himself on the floor at their feet,
to serve them as a carpet.

Berthe had not again alluded to the present. She did not
seem to notice Octave's trembling attentions, but treated him

as a friend, without the least confusion. He had never before
been so careful in his dress, and he was ever caressing her with
his eyes of the colour of old gold, and whose velvety softness he
deemed irresistible. But she was only grateful to him for his
lies, on the occasions when he helped her to hide some freak.
A complicity was thus established between them : he favoured
the young woman's goings-out with her mother, putting the
husband off the scent, at the least suspicion. She even ended
by giving a free vent to her mania for excursions and visits, re-
lying entirely upon his intelligence. And if, on her return,
she found him behind a pile of wares, she thanked him with a
good friendly shake of the hand.

One day, however, she experienced a great emotion. On returning from a dog-show, Octave beckoned to her to descend to the
basement ; and there handed her a bill, amounting to sixty-two
francs, for some embroidered stockings which had been brought
during her absence. She turned quite pale, and in a cry that
came from her heart at once asked :

" Good heavens ! has my husband seen this ? "

He hastened to set her mind at rest, telling her what trouble
he had had to get hold of the bill under Auguste's very nose.
Then in an embarrassed way, he was obliged to add in a low
voice :

" I paid it."

Then she made a show of feeling in her pockets, and, finding
nothing, said simply :

" I will pay you back. Ah! what thanks I owe you, Monsieur
Octave ! It would have killed me, if Auguste had seen this."

And, this time, she took hold of both his hands, and for a
moment held them pressed between her own. But the sixty-
two francs were never again mentioned.

With her it was an increasing appetite for liberty and pleasure, all that in her girlhood she had looked for after marriage,
all that her mother had taught her to exact from man. She
brought with her so to say an old unappeased appetite, she
avenged herself for the needy youth passed at her parents', for
the inferior meat cooked without butter in order to be able to
buy boots, for the laboriously acquired dresses remade up at
least twenty times, for the lie of their position in life kept up
at the price of black misery and filth. But she especially made
up for the three winters she had spent in floundering through
the Paris mud in dancing shoes, seeking for a husband ; evenings dead with weariness, during which she gorged herself with

syrup on a empty stomach; burdensome with smiles and modest graces directed towards silly young men ; and filled with secret exasperations at being obliged to pretend to ignore everything, when she knew all. Then, there were the returns home in the pouring rain and without a cab ; next, the chill of her icy cold bed and the maternal cuffs which kept her cheeks warm. At twenty-two years old, she was still despairing, and had become as humble as a cripple, looking at herself in her chemise at night-time, to see if she was deficient of anything. And now she had secured a husband at last, and like the sportsman who finishes off the hare which he has lost his breath in chasing with a brutal blow of his fist, she showed herself without mercy for Auguste, and treated him like a fallen foe.

Thus, little by little, the breach between the couple widened, in spite of the husband's efforts, he being desirous of having no disturbance in his existence. He desperately defended his desire for a somnolent and idiotic peacefulness, he closed his eyes to small faults, and even stomached some big ones, with the constant dread of discovering something abominable which would drive him into a furious passion. He, therefore, tolerated Berthe's lies, by which she attributed to her sister's or her mother's affection a host of little things, the purchase of which she could not have otherwise explained ; he even no longer grumbled overmuch when she went out of an evening, thus enabling Octave to take her twice privately to the theatre, accompanied by Madame Josserand and Hortense ; delightful outings, after which these ladies agreed together that the young man knew how to live.

Up till then, moreover, at the least word, Berthe threw her virtue in her husband's teeth. She lived respectably, he ought to deem himself lucky ; for, to her mind, as to her mother's, a husband only had a legitimate right to complain when he caught his wife in the flagrant act of seriously misbehaving herself. This chaste behaviour, which was genuine during the earlier days when she was gluttonously satisfying her appetites, was not, however, much of a sacrifice to her. She was cold by nature, and selfishly rebellious to all the worries of passion ; preferring to take her pleasures alone and utterly devoid of virtue. The court that Octave paid her simply flattered her, after the repulses she had experienced when a girl seeking for a husband, believing herself to be abandoned by men ; and she profited from it in many ways, of which she serenely took advantage, having grown up with a mad longing for money. One day, she had allowed the assistant to pay five hours' cab hire for her ; another day, when on the point of going out, she had made him lend her thirty francs, behind her husband's back, pretending she had forgotten her purse. She never repaid anything. The young man was of no consequence, she had no design upon him, she merely made use of him, always without thinking, just as her pleasure or circumstances required. And, meanwhile, she gloried in her martyrdom of an ill-used woman, who strictly fulfilled all her duties.

It was on a Saturday that a frightful quarrel occurred between the husband and wife, with respect to twenty sous which were deficient in Rachel's accounts. While Berthe was balancing up the book, Auguste brought, according to his custom, the money necessary for the household expenses of the ensuing week. The Josserands were to dine there that evening, and the kitchen was littered with things: a rabbit, a leg of mutton, and some cauliflowers. Saturnin, squatting on the tiled floor beside the sink, was blacking his sister's shoes and his brother-in-law's boots. The quarrel began with long arguments respecting the twenty sou piece. What had become of it? How could one mislay twenty sous? Auguste would go over all the additions again. During this time, Rachel, always pliant in spite of her harsh looks, her mouth closed but her eyes on the watch, was quietly spitting the leg of mutton. At length, he gave fifty francs, and was on the point of going downstairs again when he returned, worried by the thought of the missing coin.

"It must be found though," said he. "Perhaps you borrowed it of Rachel, and have forgotten doing so."

Berthe felt greatly hurt at this.

"Accuse me of cooking the accounts ! Ah ! you are nice !"

Everything started from that, and they soon came to high words. Auguste, in spite of his desire to purchase peace at a dear price, became aggressive, excited by the sight of the rabbit, the leg of mutton and the cauliflowers, beside himself before that pile of food, which she was going to thrust all at once under her parents' noses. He looked through the account-book expressing astonishment at almost every item. It was incredible! she must be in league with the servant to make something on the marketing.

"I ! I !" exclaimed the young woman thoroughly exasperated ; "I in league with the servant ! But it's you, sir, who pay her to spy upon me ! Yes, I am for ever feeling her about me, I can't move a step without encountering her eyes. Ah !

she may watch me through the key-hole, when I'm changing
my underlinen. I do no harm, and I don't care a straw for
your system of police. Only, don't you dare to reproach me
with being in league with her."

This unexpected attack quite dumbfounded the husband for
a moment. Rachel turned rouud still holding the leg of
mutton; and, placing her hand upon her heart, she protested.

"Oh! madame, how can you think so? I who respect
madame so much!"

"She's mad!" said Auguste shrugging his shoulders. "Don't
take the trouble to defend yourself, my girl. She's mad!"

But a noise behind his back caused him some anxiety. It
was Saturnin who had violently thrown down one of the half
polished shoes to fly to his sister's assistance. With a terrible
expression in his face and his fists clenched, he stuttered out
that he would strangle the dirty rascal, if he again called her
mad. Thoroughly frightened, Auguste sought refuge behind
the filter, calling out:

"It's really become unbearable; I can no longer make a remark to you without his thrusting himself in between us! I
allowed him to come here, but he must leave me alone! He's
another nice present of your mother's! She was frightened to
death of him, and so she saddled him on me, preferring to see
me murdered in her stead. Thanks for nothing! He's got a
knife now. Do make him desist!"

Berthe disarmed her brother and calmed him with a look, whilst
Auguste, who had turned very pale, continued to mumble angry
words. Always knives being caught up! An injury is so soon
done; and, with a madman, one could do nothing, justice would
even refuse to avenge it! In short, it was not proper to make
a body-guard of such a brother, rendering a husband powerless,
even in circumstances of the most legitimate indignation, and
going as far as forcing him to submit to his shame.

"You've no tact, sir," declared Berthe disdainfully. "A
gentleman would not discuss such matters in a kitchen."

And she withdrew to her room, slamming the doors behind
her. Rachel had returned to the roaster, as though no longer
hearing the quarrel between her master and mistress. Through
an excess of discretion, like a girl who kept herself in her place
even when she knew everything, she did not follow madame
with her eyes when the latter left the room; and she allowed
her master to stamp about for a full minute, without venturing
on the least change of features. Besides, her master hastened

SATURNIN THREATENING AUGUSTE.

p. 246.

off after her mistress almost directly.   Then, Rachel, still un-
moved, was able to put the rabbit on the fire.

"Do understand, my dear," said Auguste to Berthe, whom
he had rejoined in the bedroom, " it was not in reference to you
that I spoke, it was for that girl who robs us.   Those twenty
sous ought certainly to be found."

The young woman trembled nervously with exasperation.
She looked him full in the face, very pale and resolute.

" Will you leave off bothering me about your twenty sous?
It's not twenty sous I want, it's five hundred francs a month.
Yes, five hundred francs for my dress.   Ah! you discuss money
matters in the kitchen, before the servant!   Well! that has
decided me to discuss them also!   I've been restraining myself
for a long time past.   I want five hundred francs."

He stood aghast at such a demand.   And she commenced
the grand quarrel which, during twenty years, her mother had
picked with her father, regularly every fortnight.   Did he expect to see her walk about barefoot?   When one married a
woman, one should at least arrange to clothe and feed her
decently.   She would sooner beg than resign herself to such a
pauper existence!   It was not her fault, if he proved incapable
of managing his business properly; oh! yes, incapable, without
ideas or initiative, only knowing how to split farthings into
four.   A man who ought to have made it his glory to acquire
a fortune quickly, so as to dress her like a queen, and make the
people of "The Ladies' Paradise" die with rage!   But no!
with such a poor head as his, bankruptcy was sure to come
sooner or later.   And from this flow of words emerged the
respect, the furious appetite for money, all that worship of
wealth, the adoration of which she had learnt in her own family,
when beholding the mean tricks to which one stoops, merely to
appear to possess it.

"Five hundred francs!" said Auguste at length.   " I would
sooner shut up the shop."

She looked at him coldly.

"You refuse.   Very well, I will run up bills."

"More debts, you wretched woman!"

In a sudden violent movement, he seized her by the arms,
and pushed her against the wall.   Then, without a cry, choking
with passion, she ran and opened the window, as though to
throw herself out; but she retraced her steps, and pushing him
in her turn towards the door, turned him out of the room
gasping:

"Go away, or I shall do you an injury!"

And she noisily pushed the bolt behind his back. For a moment he listened and hesitated. Then, he hastened to go down to the warehouse, again seized with terror, as he beheld Saturnin's eyes gleaming in the shadow, the noise of the short struggle having brought him from the kitchen.

Downstairs, Octave, who was selling silk handkerchiefs to an old lady, at once noticed his agitated appearance. The assistant looked at him out of the corner of his eye as he feverishly paced up and down before the counters. When the customer had gone, Auguste's heart quite overflowed.

"My dear fellow, she's going mad," said he, without naming his wife. "She has shut herself in. You ought to oblige me by going up and speaking to her. I fear an accident, on my word of honour, I do!"

The young man pretended to hesitate. It was such a delicate matter! Finally, he agreed to do so out of pure devotion. Upstairs, he found Saturnin keeping guard before Berthe's door. On hearing footsteps, the madman uttered a menacing grunt. But, when he recognised the assistant, his face brightened.

"Ah! yes, you," murmured he. "You're all right. She mustn't cry. Be nice, say something to her. And you know, stop there. There's no danger. I'm here. If the servant tries to peep, I'll settle her."

And he squatted down on the floor, guarding the door. As he still held one of his brother-in-law's boots, he commenced to polish it, to pass away the time.

Octave made up his mind to knock. No answer, not a sound. Then, he gave his name. The bolt was at once drawn. And, opening the door slightly, Berthe begged him to enter. Then, she closed and bolted it again with a nervous hand.

"I don't mind you," said she; "but I won't have him!"

She paced the room, carried away by passion, going from the bedstead to the window, which still remained open. And she muttered disconnected sentences: he might entertain her parents at dinner, if he liked; yes, he could account to them for her absence, for she would not appear at the table; she would sooner die! Besides, she preferred to go to bed. With her feverish hands, she already began to tear off the quilt, shake up the pillows, and turn down the sheet, forgetful of Octave's presence to the extent that she was about to unhook her dress. Then, she jumped to another idea.

"Just fancy! He beat me, beat me, beat me! And only

because, ashamed of always going about in rags, I asked him for five hundred francs ! "

Octave, standing up in the middle of the room, tried to find some conciliating words. She was wrong to allow it to upset her so much. Everything would come right again. And he ended by timidly offering her assistance.

"If you are worried about any bill, why not apply to your friends? I should be so pleased! Oh! simply a loan. You could return it to me some other time."

She looked at him. After a pause, she replied :

"Never! it cannot be. What would people think, Monsieur Octave ? "

Her refusal was so decided, that there was no further question of money. But her anger seemed to have left her. She breathed heavily, and bathed her face ; and she looked quite pale, very calm, rather wearied, with large resolute eyes. Standing before her, he felt himself overcome by that timidity of love, which he held in such contempt. Never before had he loved so ardently ; the strength of his desire communicated an awkwardness to his charms of a handsome assistant. Whilst continuing to advise a reconciliation in vague phrases, he was reasoning clearly in his own mind, asking himself if he ought not to take her in his arms ; but the fear of being again repulsed made him hesitate. She, without uttering a word, continued to look at him with her decided air, her forehead contracted by a faint wrinkle.

"Really ! " he stammeringly continued, " you must be patient. Your husband is not a bad fellow. If you only go the right way to work with him, he will give you whatever you ask for."

And beneath the emptiness of these words, they both felt the same thought take possession of them. They were alone, free, safe from all surprise, with the door bolted. This security, the close warmth of the room, exercised its influence on them. Yet he did not dare ; the feminine side of his nature, his womanly feeling refined him in that moment of passion to the point of making him the woman in their encounter. Then, as though recollecting one of her former lessons, Berthe dropped her handkerchief.

"Oh ! thank you," said she to the young man who picked it up.

Their fingers touched, they were drawn closer together by that momentary contact. Now, she smiled tenderly, and gave an easy suppleness to her form, as she recollected that men détest sticks. It would never do to act the simpleton, one must permit a little playfulness without seeming to do so, if one would hook one's fish.

"Night is coming on," resumed she, going and pushing the window to.

He followed her, and there, in the shadow of the curtains, she allowed him to take her hand. She laughed louder, bewildering him with her ringing tones, enveloping him with her pretty gestures; and, as he at length became bolder, she threw back her head, displaying her neck, her young and delicate neck all quivering with her gaiety. Distracted by the sight, he kissed her under the chin.

"Oh! Monsieur Octave!" said she in confusion, making a pretence of prettily putting him back into his place.

His moment of triumph had come, but it was no sooner over than all the ferocious disdain of woman, which was hidden beneath his air of wheedling adoration, returned. And when Berthe rose up, without strength in her wrists, and her face contracted by a pang, her utter contempt for man was thrown into the dark glance which she cast upon him. The room was wrapped in complete silence. One only heard Saturnin, on the other side of the door, polishing the husband's boot with a regular movement of the brush.

Octave's thoughts reverted to Valérie and Madame Hédouin. At last, he was something more than little Pichon's lover! It seemed like a rehabilitation in his own eyes. Then, encountering Berthe's uneasy glance, he experienced a slight sense of shame, and kissed her with extreme gentleness. She was resuming her air of resolute recklessness, and with a gesture, seemed to say: "What's done can't be undone." But she afterwards experienced the necessity of giving expression to a melancholy thought.

"Ah! If you had only married me!" murmured she.

He felt surprised, almost uneasy; but this did not prevent him from replying, as he kissed her again:

"Oh! yes, how nice it would have been!"

That evening, the dinner with the Josserands was most delightful, Berthe had never shown herself so gentle. She did not say a word of the quarrel to her parents, she received her husband with an air of submission. The latter, delighted, took Octave aside to thank him; and he imparted so much warmth into the proceeding, pressing his hands and displaying such a lively gratitude, that the young man felt quite embarrassed. More-

over, they one and all overwhelmed him with marks of their affection. Saturnin, who behaved very well at table, looked at him
with approving eyes. Hortense on her part deigned to listen
to him, whilst Madame Josserand, full of maternal encouragement, kept filling his glass.

"Dear me! yes," said Berthe at dessert, "I intend to resume
my painting. For a long time past I have been wanting to
decorate a cup for Auguste."

The latter was deeply moved at this loving conjugal thought.
Ever since the soup, Octave had kept his foot on the young
woman's under the table; it was like a taking of possession in
the midst of this little middle-class gathering. Yet, Berthe
was not without a secret uneasiness before Rachel, whose eyes
she always found looking her through and through. Was it
then visible? The girl was decidedly one to be sent away or
else to be bought over.

Monsieur Josserand, who was near his daughter, finished
soothing her by passing her nineteen francs done up in paper
under the tablecloth. He bent down and whispered in her
ear:

"You know, they come from my little work. If you owe
anything, you must pay it."

Then, between her father who nudged her knee, and her lover
who gently rubbed her boot, she felt quite happy. Life would
now be delightful. And they united in throwing aside all reserve, enjoying the pleasure of a family gathering, unmarred by
a single quarrel. In truth, it was hardly natural, something
must have brought them luck. Auguste, alone, had his eyes
half closed, suffering from a headache, which he had moreover
expected after so many emotions. Towards nine o'clock he was
even obliged to retire to bed.

CHAPTER XIII.

For some time past, Monsieur Gourd had been prowling about
with an uneasy and mysterious air. He was met gliding noiselessly along, his eyes open, his ears pricked up, continually ascending the two staircases, where lodgers had even encountered
him going his rounds in the dead of night. The morality of
the house was certainly worrying him; he felt a kind of breath
of shameful things which troubled the cold nakedness of the
courtyard, the calm peacefulness of the vestibule, the beautiful
domestic virtues of the different storeys.

One evening, Octave had found the doorkeeper standing
motionless and without a light at the end of his passage, close
to the door which opened on to the servants' staircase. Greatly
surprised, he questioned him.

"I wish to ascertain something, Monsieur Mouret," simply
answered Monsieur Gourd, deciding to go off to bed.

The young man was very much frightened. Did the doorkeeper suspect his relations with Berthe? He was perhaps
watching them. Their attachment encountered continual ob-
stacles in that house where there was always someone prying
about and the inmates of which professed the most strict principles. Thus he could only rarely approach his mistress, his
sole joy being, if she went out in the afternoon without her
mother, to leave the warehouse on some pretext and join her in
one of the more out of the way Passages, where he would stroll
about with her on his arm for an hour or so. Since the end of
July, however, Auguste had been in the habit of going every
Tuesday night to Lyons; for he had been foolish enough to
take a share in a silk manufactory which was in difficulties.
But until then, Berthe had refused to profit by this night of
liberty. She trembled at the thought of her maid, she feared
that some forgetfulness on her part, might place her in the girl's
power.

It happened to be a Tuesday night when Octave discovered

Monsieur Gourd watching close to his room. This increased his uneasiness. For a week past, he had been imploring Berthe to come up and join him in his apartment, when all the house would be asleep. Had the doorkeeper guessed this? Octave went back to his room dissatisfied, tormented with fear and desire. His love was chafing, becoming a mad passion, and he angrily saw himself falling into all the stupidities of which the heart is capable. As it was, he could never join Berthe in a Passage, without buying her whatever attracted her attention in a shop window. Thus, the day before in the Passage de la Madeleine, she had looked so greedily at a little bonnet, that he had made her a present of it : chip straw, and nothing more than a garland of roses, something deliciously simple, but costing two hundred francs ; he thought the price rather stiff.

The night was a close one, and overcome by the heat, Octave had dosed off in an easy chair, when towards midnight he was roused by a gentle knocking.

"It's I," faintly whispered a woman's voice.

It was Berthe. He opened the door and clasped her in his arms in the obscurity. But she had not come up for that; when he had lighted his candle, he saw that she was deeply troubled about something. The day before, not having sufficient money in his pocket, he had been unable to pay for the bonnet at the time ; and as in her delight she had so far forgotten herself as to give her name, they had sent her the bill that evening. Then, trembling at the thought that they might call on the morrow when her husband was there, she had dared to come up, gathering courage from the great silence of the house, and confident that Rachel was asleep.

"To-morrow morning, you will be sure to pay it to-morrow morning, won't you?" implored she, trying to escape.

But he again clasped her in his arms.

"Stay !"

She remained. The clock slowly struck the hours in the voluptuous warmth of the room ; and, at each sound of the bell, he begged her so tenderly to stay, that her strength seemed to desert her and she yielded to his entreaties. Then, towards four o'clock, just as she had at length determined to go, they both dropped off to sleep locked in each other's arms. When they again opened their eyes, the bright daylight was entering at the window, it was nine o'clock. Berthe uttered a cry.

"Good heavens ! I'm lost !"

Then ensued a moment of confusion. With her eyes half

closed with sleep and fatigue, feeling vaguely about with her hands scarcely able to distinguish anything, she gave vent to stifled exclamations of regret. He, seized with a similar despair, had thrown himself before the door, to prevent her from going out, at such an hour. Was she mad? people might meet her on the stairs, it was too risky; they must think the matter over, and devise a way for her to go down without being noticed. But she was obstinate, simply wishing to get away; and she again made for the door, which he defended. Then, he thought of the servants' staircase. Nothing could be more convenient; she could go quickly through her own kitchen into her apartment. Only, as Marie Pichon was always in the passage of a morning, Octave considered it prudent to divert her attention, whilst the other young woman made her escape.

He went out in his ordinary quiet way, and was surprised to find Saturnin making himself at home at Marie's, and calmly watching her do her house work. The madman loved thus to seek refuge beside her as in former days, delighted with the manner in which she left him to himself, and certain of not being jostled. Moreover, he was not in her way, and she willingly tolerated him, though his conversational powers were not great. It was company all the same, and she would still sing her ballad in a low and expiring voice.

"Hallo! so you're with your lover?" said Octave, manœuvring so as to keep the door shut behind his back.

Marie turned crimson. Oh! that poor Monsieur Saturnin! Was it possible? He who seemed to suffer even when any one touched his hand by accident! And the madman also got angry. He would not be any one's lover—never, never! Whoever told his sister such a lie would have him to deal with. Octave, amazed at his sudden irritation, felt it necessary to calm him.

Meanwhile, Berthe made her way to the servants' staircase. She had two flights to descend. At the first step a shrill laugh, issuing from Madame Juzeur's kitchen below, caused her to stop; and she tremblingly stood against the landing window, opened wide on to the narrow courtyard. Then the sound of voices broke forth, the flow of morning filth ascended from the pestiferous hole. It was the servants who were all furious with little Louise, accusing her of looking through their keyholes when they were going to bed. Not yet fifteen, a mere chit, something decent! Louise laughed, and laughed louder than ever. She did not deny it. She knew all about Adèle's plumpness.   Oh ! it was a sight worth seeing ! Lisa was precious skinny, Victoire's stomach was staved in like an old barrel ; and to silence her the others retorted with the most abominable language.   Then, annoyed at having been thus undressed before each other, tormented by the necessity of defending themselves, they took their revenge on their mistresses by undressing them in their turn.   Thank you for nothing ! Lisa might be skinny, but she was not as bad as the other Madame Campardon, a fine shark's skin, a regular treat for an architect ; Victoire contented herself with wishing all the Vabres, the Duveyriers, and the Josserands in the world as well preserved stomachs as her own, if ever they reached her age ; as for Adèle, she would certainly not have exchanged her plumpness with madame's young ladies, who had next to nothing at all ! And Berthe, frightened and immovable, never having even suspected the existence of that common sewer, assisted for the first time at the washing of the domestics' dirty linen, at the moment when the masters and mistresses were washing themselves.

Suddenly a voice exclaimed :

" Here's master coming for his hot water ! "

And windows were quickly closed, and doors slammed.   The silence of death ensued, yet Berthe did not at first dare to move. When she at length went down the thought came to her that Rachel was probably in her kitchen, waiting for her.   This caused her fresh anguish.   She now dreaded to enter, she would have preferred to reach the street and fly away in the distance for ever.   She nevertheless pushed the door ajar, and felt relieved on beholding that the servant was not there. Then, seized with a childish joy on finding herself at home again and safe, she hurried to her room.   But there was Rachel standing before the bed, which had not even been opened.   She looked at the bed and then at her mistress with her expressionless face.   In her first moment of fright the young woman lost her head to the point of trying to excuse herself, and talked of an illness of her sister's.   She stammered out the words, and then, frightened at the poorness of her lie, understanding that denial was utterly useless, she suddenly burst into tears. Dropping on to a chair she continued crying.

This lasted a good while.   Not a word was exchanged, sobs alone disturbed the perfect quiet of the room.   Rachel, exaggerating her habitual discretion, maintaining her cold manner of a girl who knows everything, but who says nothing, had turned her back and was making a pretence of beating up the pillows, as though she was just finishing arranging the bed. At length, when madame, more and more upset by this silence, was giving too loud a vent to her despair, the maid, who was then dusting, said simply, in a respectful tone of voice:

"Madame is wrong to take on so, master is not so very pleasant."

Berthe left off crying. She would pay the girl, that was all. Without waiting further she gave her twenty francs. Then, not thinking that sufficient, and already feeling uneasy, having fancied she saw her curl her lip disdainfully, she rejoined her in the kitchen, and brought her back to make her a present of an almost new dress.

At the same moment Octave, on his part, was again in a state of alarm on account of Monsieur Gourd. On leaving the Pichons', he had found him standing immovable the same as the night before, listening behind the door communicating with the servants' staircase. He followed him without even daring to speak to him. The doorkeeper gravely went back again down the grand staircase. On the floor below he took a key from his pocket and entered the room which was let to the distinguished individual who came there to work one night every week. And through the door, which remained open for a moment, Octave obtained a clear view of that room which was always kept as closely shut as a tomb. It was in a terrible state of disorder that morning, the gentleman having no doubt worked there the night before. A huge bed, with the sheets stripped off, a wardrobe with a glass door, empty save for the remnants of a lobster and two partly filled bottles, two dirty hand-basins lying about, one beside the bed and the other on a chair. Monsieur Gourd, with his calm air of a retired judge, at once occupied himself with emptying and rinsing out the basins.

As he hurried to the Passage de la Madeleine to pay for the bonnet, the young man was tormented by a painful uncertainty. Finally, he determined to engage the doorkeepers in conversation on his return. Madame Gourd, reclining in her commodious arm-chair, was getting a breath of fresh air between the two pots of flowers at the open window of their room. Standing up beside the door, old mother Pérou was waiting in an humble and frightened manner.

"Have you a letter for me?" asked Octave, as a commencement.

Monsieur Gourd just then came down from the room on the third floor. Seeing after that was the only work that he now condescended to do in the house; and he showed himself highly flattered by the confidence of the gentleman, who paid him well on condition that his basins should not pass through any other hands.

"No, Monsieur Mouret, nothing at all," answered he.

He had seen old mother Pérou perfectly well, but he pretended not to be aware of her presence. The day before he had got into such a rage with her for upsetting a pail of water in the middle of the vestibule, that he had sent her about her business on the spot. And she had called for her money, but the mere sight of him made her tremble, and she almost sank into the ground with humility.

However, as Octave remained some time doing the amiable with Madame Gourd, the doorkeeper roughly turned towards the poor old woman.

"So, you want to be paid. What's owing to you?"

But Madame Gourd interrupted him.

"Look, darling, there's that girl again with her horrible little beast."

It was Lisa who, a few days before, had found a spaniel in the street. And this occasioned continual disputes with the doorkeepers. The landlord would not allow any animals in the house. No, no animals and no women! The little dog was even forbidden to go into the courtyard; the street was quite good enough for him. As it had been raining that morning, and the little beast's paws were sopping wet, Monsieur Gourd rushed forward, exclaiming:

"I will not have him walk up the stairs, you hear me! Carry him in your arms."

"So that he shall make me all in a mess!" said Lisa insolently. "What a great misfortune it'll be, if he wets the servants' staircase a bit! Up you go, doggie."

Monsieur Gourd tried to seize hold of her, and almost slipped, so he fell to abusing those sluts of servants. He was always at war with them, tormented with the rage of a former servant who wishes to be waited on in his turn. But Lisa turned upon him, and with the verbosity of a girl who had grown up in the gutters of Montmartre she shouted out:

"Eh! just you leave me alone, you miserable old flunkey! Go and empty the duke's jerries!"

It was the only insult capable of silencing Monsieur Gourd, and the servants all took advantage of it. He returned to his room quivering with rage and mumbling to himself, saying that he was certainly very proud of having been in service at the duke's, and that she would not have stayed there two hours even, the baggage! Then, he assailed mother Pérou, who almost jumped out of her skin.

"Well! what is it you're owed? Eh! you say twelve francs sixty-five centimes. But it isn't possible? Sixty-three hours at twenty centimes the hour. Ah! you charge a quarter of an hour. Never! I warned you, I only pay the hours that are completed."

And he did not even give her her money then, he left her perfectly terrified, and joined in the conversation between his wife and Octave. The latter was cunningly alluding to all the worries that such a house must cause them, hoping thus to get them to talk about the lodgers. Such strange things must sometimes take place behind the doors! Then, the doorkeeper chimed in, as grave as ever.

"What concerns us, concerns us, Monsieur Mouret, and what doesn't concern us, doesn't concern us. Over there, for instance, is something which quite puts me beside myself. Look at it, look at it!"

And, stretching out his arm, he pointed to the boot-stitcher, that tall pale girl who had arrived at the house in the middle of the funeral. She walked with difficulty; she was evidently in the family way, and her condition was exaggerated by the sickly skinniness of her neck and legs.

With his arm tragically thrust out, the doorkeeper continued to point at her, whilst she went towards the servants' staircase. It seemed to him that this woman's condition cast a gloom over the chilly cleanliness of the courtyard, and even over the imitation marble and the gilded zinc work of the vestibule. In his eyes it gave a disgraceful character to the building, making even the very walls feel uncomfortable, and causing an unpleasant perturbation in the morality of the different storeys.

"On my word of honour! sir, if this sort of thing was likely to continue, we would prefer to retire to our home, at Mort-ia-Ville; would we not, Madame Gourd? for thank heaven! we have sufficient to live on, we are dependent on no one. A house like this to be made the talk of the place by such a creature! for so it is, sir!"

"She seems very ill," said Octave following her with his eyes, not daring to pity her too much. "I always see her looking so sad, so pale, so forlorn. But of course she has a lover."

At this, Monsieur Gourd gave a violent start.

"Now we have it ! Do you hear, Madame Gourd ? Monsieur Mouret is also of opinion that she has a lover. It's clear, such things don't come of themselves. Well ! sir, for two months past I've been on the watch, and I've not yet seen the shadow of a man. How full of vice she must be ! Ah ! if I only found her chap, how I would chuck him out ! But I can't find him, and it's that which worries me."

"Perhaps no one comes," Octave ventured to observe.

The doorkeeper looked at him with surprise.

"That would not be natural. Oh ! I'm determined, I'll catch him. I've still six weeks before me, for I got the landlord to give her notice to quit in October. Just fancy her being confined here ! And, you know, though Monsieur Duveyrier showed his indignation by insisting upon her going elsewhere for that event, I can scarcely sleep at night, for she is capable of playing us the trick of not waiting till then. In short, all these sort of accidents would have been avoided had it not been for that curmudgeon, old Vabre. Just to make a hundred and thirty francs a year more, and against my advice ! The carpenter ought to have been a sufficient lesson for him. Not at all, he must needs go and let to a boot-stitcher. Go it, rot your house with labourers, lodge a lot of dirty people who work ! When you have the lower classes in your house, sir, that's the sort of thing you have to expect !"

And, with his arm still thrust out, he pointed to the young woman who was painfully wending her way up the servants' staircase. Madame Gourd was obliged to calm him : he took the respectability of the house too much to heart, he would end by making himself ill. Then, mother Pérou having dared to manifest her presence by a discreet cough, he returned to her, and coolly deducted the sou she had charged for the odd quarter of an hour. She was at length going off with her twelve francs sixty centimes, when he offered to take her back, but at three sous an hour only. She burst into tears, and accepted.

"I shall always be able to get some one," said he. "You're no longer strong enough, you don't even do two sous' worth."

Octave felt his mind relieved as he returned to his room for a minute. On the third floor, he caught up Madame Juzeur who was also going to her apartments. She was obliged now to run down every morning after Louise, who loitered at the different shops.

"How proud you are becoming," said she with her sharp

smile. "One can see very well that you are being spoilt elsewhere."

These words once more aroused all the young man's anxiety. He followed her into her drawing-room, pretending to joke with her the while. Only one of the curtains was slightly drawn back, and the carpet and the hangings before the doors subdued still more this alcove-like light; and the noise of the street did not penetrate more than to the extent of a faint buzz in this room as soft as down. She made him seat himself beside her on the low wide sofa. But as he did not take her hand and kiss it, she asked him archly:

"Do you then no longer love me?"

He blushed and protested that he adored her. Then she gave him her hand of her own accord with a little stifled laugh; and he was obliged to raise it to his lips, so as to dispel her suspicions, if she had any. But she almost immediately withdrew it again.

"No, no, though you pretend to excite yourself, it gives you no pleasure. Oh, I feel it does not, and, besides, it is only natural!"

What? what did she mean? He seized her round the waist, and pressed her with questions. But she would not answer; she abandoned herself to his embrace, and kept shaking her head. At length, to oblige her to speak, he commenced tickling her.

"Well, you see," she ended by murmuring, "you love another."

She named Valérie, and reminded him of the evening at the Josserands' when he devoured her with his eyes. Then, as he declared that Valérie was nothing to him, she retorted with another laugh that she knew that very well, and had been only teasing him. Only there was another; and this time she named Madame Hédouin, laughing more than ever, and amused at his protestations, which were very energetic. Who then? was it Marie Pichon? Ah! he could not deny that one. Yet he did do so; but she shook her head. She assured him that her little finger never told stories. And to draw each of these women's names from her, he was obliged to redouble his caresses.

But she had not named Berthe. He was loosening his hold of her, when she resumed:

"Now, there's the last one."

"What last one?" inquired he, anxiously.

Screwing up her mouth, she again obstinately refused to say

anything more, so long as he had not opened her lips with a
kiss. Really, she could not name the person, for it was she
who had thrown out the first idea of her marriage ; and she
gave Berthe's history without mentioning her name. Then,
with his lips pressed close to her delicate neck, he admitted
everything, feeling a cowardly enjoyment in the avowal. How
ridiculous he was to hide anything from her ! Perhaps he
thought she would be jealous. Why should she be ? She had
granted him nothing, had she ? Nothing more than mere
playfulness as at present. In short, she was a virtuous woman,
and almost quarrelled with him for having fancied she would
be jealous.

He continued to hold her reclining in his arms. She
languishingly alluded to the cruel being who had deserted her
after having only been married a week. A miserable woman
like her knew too much of the tempests of the heart ! For a
long time past, she had guessed what she styled Octave's
" little games ; " for not a kiss could be exchanged in the house
without her hearing it. And, in the depths of the wide sofa,
they had quite a cosy little chat, interrupted now and then
with all sorts of delightful caresses. She called him a big
ninny, for he had missed fire with Valérie entirely through his
own fault. She would have put him in the way of overcoming
her, if he had merely looked in and asked her for her advice.
Then she questioned him about little Pichon. But she kept
returning to Berthe ; she thought her charming ; a superb skin;
the foot of a marchioness. However, she soon had to repel
him, and eventually sent him away, after making him solemnly
swear to come often and confess himself, without hiding anything whatever from her, if he wished her to assume the
direction of his affairs of the heart.

When Octave left her he felt more at ease. She had restored
his good humour, and she amused him with her complicated
principles of virtue. Downstairs, directly he entered the warehouse, he reassured Berthe with a sign, as her eyes questioned
him with reference to the bonnet. Then all the terrible
adventure of the morning was forgotten. When Auguste returned, a little before lunch-time, he found them both looking
the same as usual, Berthe very much bored at the pay-desk,
and Octave gallantly measuring off some silk for a lady.

But, after that day, the lovers' private meetings became
rarer still. He, who was very ardent, was in despair, and
followed her into every corner with continual entreaties and

prayers for assignations, whenever she liked, and no matter
where. She, on the contrary, with the indifference of a girl
who had grown up in a hot-house, seemed only to enjoy her
guilty passion for the sake of the secret outings, the presents,
the forbidden pleasures, and the expensive hours passed in
cabs, at the theatres and the restaurants. All her early education was cropping up again, her desire for money, for dress, and
for wasted luxury; and she had soon reached the point of being
tired of her lover the same as of her husband, thinking him too
exacting for what he gave, and trying, with a quiet unconscious-
ness, not to render him his full weight of love. So that, exaggerating her fears, she constantly refused him; never again
would she venture in his room, she would die of fright! to receive him in hers was impossible, they might be surprised;
then, when he implored her to make some assignation out of
doors, she would burst into tears, and say that he could really
have little respect for her. However, the expenses continued,
and her caprices increased; after the bonnet, she had desired a fan
covered with Alençon lace, without counting the innumerable
costly little nothings which took her fancy in the shop-windows.
Though he did not yet dare refuse, his avarice was aroused by
the rapid sweep made of his savings. As a practical fellow, he
ended by thinking it stupid to be always paying, when she, on her
side, only gave him her foot under the table. Paris had decidedly
brought him ill-luck; at first, repulses, and then this silly
passion, which was fast emptying his purse. He could certainly
not be accused of succeeding through women. He now found a
certain honour in it by way of consolation, in his secret rage at
the failure of his plan so clumsily carried out up till then.

Yet Auguste was not much in their way. Ever since the bad
turn affairs had taken at Lyons, he had suffered more than ever
with his headaches. On the first of the month, Berthe had experienced a sudden joy on seeing him, in the evening, place three
hundred francs under the bedroom timepiece for her dress; and,
in spite of the reduction on the amount which she had demanded,
as she had given up all hope of ever seeing a sou of it, she threw
herself into his arms, all warm with gratitude. On this occasion the husband had a night of hugging such as the lover
never experienced.

September passed away in this manner, in the great calm of
the house emptied of its occupants by the summer months.
The people of the second floor had gone to the seaside in Spain,
which caused Monsieur Gourd, full of pity, to shrug his

shoulders; what a fuss! as though the most distinguished people were not satisfied with Trouville! The Duveyriers, since the beginning of Gustave's holidays, had been at their country house at Villeneuve-Saint-Georges. Even the Josserands went and spent a fortnight at a friend's, near Pontoise, spreading a rumour beforehand that they were going to some watering-place.

This clearance, these deserted apartments, the staircase slumbering in a greater silence than ever, seemed to Octave to offer less danger; and he argued and so wearied Berthe that she at last received him in her room one evening whilst Auguste was away at Lyons. But this meeting also nearly took a bad turn. Madame Josserand, who had returned home two days before, was seized with such an attack of indigestion after dining out, that Hortense, filled with anxiety, went downstairs for her sister. Fortunately, Rachel was just finishing scouring her saucepans, and she was able to let the young man out by the servants' staircase. On the following days, Berthe availed herself of that alarm to again refuse him everything.

Besides, they were so foolish as not to reward the servant. She attended to them in her cold way, and with her superior respect of a girl who hears and sees nothing; only, as madame was for ever crying after money, and as Monsieur Octave already spent too·much in presents, she curled her lip more and more in that wretched establishment, where the mistress's lover did not even present her with ten sous when he stayed there. If they fancied they had bought her for evermore, with a dress and twenty francs, ah! no, they made a mistake; she put a higher price on herself than that! Thenceforward she became less obliging, no longer shutting the doors behind them, without their being conscious of her ill-humour; for one does not think of bestowing gratuities when, furious at not knowing where to go to exchange a kiss, one comes to quarrelling about it. And the silence of the house increased, and Octave, always on the lookout for some safe nook, encountered Monsieur Gourd everywhere, watching for the disreputable things which made the walls shudder, gliding noiselessly along, haunted by visions of pregnant women.

Meanwhile, Madame Juzeur wept with that lovesick darling who could only gaze on his mistress from a distance; and she gave him the very best advice. Octave's passion reached such a pitch that he thought one day of imploring her to lend him her apartment; no doubt she would not have refused, but he feared rousing Berthe's indignation by his indiscretion. He also had the idea of utilising Saturnin; perhaps the madman would watch over them like a faithful dog in some out of the way room; only, he displayed such a fantastical humour, at one time overwhelming his sister's lover with the most awkward caresses, at another, sulking with him and casting suspicious glances gleaming with a sudden hatred. One could almost have thought him jealous, with the nervous and violent jealousy of a woman. He had been like this especially since Octave had met him at times of a morning, laughing with little Pichon. In point of fact, Octave never passed Marie's door now without going in, seized again with a singular fancy, a fit of longing, which he would not even admit to himself; he adored Berthe, he madly desired her, and this longing to possess her gave birth to an infinite tenderness for the other one, to a love which had never appeared so sweet at the time of their former intimate connection. There was a continual charm in looking at her and in touching her, coupled with jokes and teasings, all the playfulness of a man who wishes to regain possession of a woman and is secretly bothered by the fact of his loving elsewhere. And, on those days, when Saturnin found him hanging about Marie's skirts, the madman would threaten him with his wolf-like eyes, his teeth ready to bite, and would neither forgive him nor come and kiss his fingers, like some cowed animal, until he beheld him again faithful and loving with Berthe.

Just as September was drawing to a close, and the lodgers were on the point of returning home, a wild idea came to Octave in the midst of his torment. Rachel had asked permission to sleep out on one of the Tuesdays that her master would be at Lyons, in order to enable her to attend the wedding of one of her sisters in the country; and it was merely a question of passing the night in the servant's room, where no one in the world would think of seeking them. Berthe, feeling deeply hurt at the suggestion, at first displayed the greatest repugnance; but he implored her with tears in his eyes; he talked of leaving Paris where he suffered too much; he confused and wearied her with such a number of arguments, that, scarcely knowing what she did, she ended by consenting. All was settled. The Tuesday evening, after dinner, they took a cup of tea at the Josserands', so as to dispel any suspicions. Trublot, Gueulin, and uncle Bachelard were there; and, very late in the evening, Duveyrier, who occasionally came to sleep at the Rue de Choiseul, on account of business which he pretended he had to attend to early in the morning, even put in an appearance. Octave made a show of joining freely in the conversation of these gentlemen; then, when midnight struck, he withdrew, and went and locked himself in Rachel's room, where Berthe was to join him an hour later when all the house was asleep.

Upstairs, the arrangement of the room occupied him during the first half hour. He had provided himself with clean bed linen, and he proceeded to remake the bed, awkwardly, and occupying a long while over it through fear of being overheard. Then, like Trublot, he sat down on a box and tried to wait patiently. The servants came up to bed, one by one; and through the thin partitions the sounds of women undressing themselves could be heard. One o'clock struck, then the quarter, then the half hour past. He began to feel anxious; why was Berthe so long in coming? She must have left the Josserands' about one o'clock at the latest; and it could not take her more than ten minutes to go to her rooms and come out again by the servants' staircase. When two o'clock struck, he imagined all sorts of catastrophes. At length, he heaved a sigh of relief, on fancying he recognised her footstep. And he opened the door, in order to light her. But surprise rooted him to the spot. Opposite Adèle's door, Trublot, bent almost double, was looking through the key-hole, and jumped up, frightened by that sudden light.

"What! it's you again!" murmured Octave with annoyance.

Trublot began to laugh, without appearing the least surprised at finding him there at such a time of night.

"Just fancy," explained he very softly, "that fool Adèle hasn't given me her key, and she has gone and joined Duveyrier in his room. Eh? what's the matter with you? Ah! you didn't know Duveyrier slept with her. It is so, my dear fellow. He really is reconciled with his wife, who, however, only resigns herself to him now and then; so he falls back upon Adèle. It's convenient, whenever he comes to Paris."

He interrupted himself, and stooped down again, then added between his clenched teeth.

"What a confounded brainless girl that Adèle is! If she had only given me her key, I could have made myself comfortable here."

Then, he returned to the loft where he had been previously waiting, taking Octave with him, who, moreover, desired to question him respecting the finish of the evening at the Josserands'. But, for some time, Trublot would not allow him to open his mouth. He was highly irate with Duveyrier, and in the obscurity, black as ink, and the close atmosphere beneath the low-lying beams, he was continually recurring to him. Yes, the dirty animal had at first wanted Julie ; only she had taken a fancy to little Gustave down in the country. So that, snuffed out on this side, and not daring to take Clémence, because of Hippolyte, the counsellor had no doubt thought it preferable to pick up with some one outside his own home. And no one knew where or how he had jumped upon Adèle—behind some door no doubt, in a draught ; and that big slut would certainly never have dared to have been impolite to the landlord.

"For a month past, he has not missed a single one of the Josserands' Tuesdays at home," said Trublot. "It's very awkward. I must discover Clarisse for him, so that he may leave us in peace."

Octave was at length able to question him as to the wind-up of the party. It seemed that Berthe had left her mother's shortly after midnight, looking very composed. No doubt, she was now in Rachel's room. But Trublot, delighted at the meeting, would not let him go.

"It's idiotic, keeping me waiting so long," continued he. "Besides, I'm almost asleep as it is. My governor has put me into the liquidation department, and I'm up all night three times a week, my dear fellow. If Julie were only there, she would make room for me. But Duveyrier only brings Hippolyte up from the country. And, by the way, you know Hippolyte, that tall ugly chap ! Well ! I just saw him going to join Louise, that frightful brat of a foundling whose soul Madame Juzeur wishes to save. Eh ? it's a fine success for Madame ! 'Anything you like except that ! ' An abortion of fifteen, a dirty bundle picked up on a doorstep, a fine morsel for that bony fellow with damp hands and the shoulders of a bull ! As for me, I don't care a button, and yet it disgusts me all the same."

That night, Trublot, who was greatly bored, was full of philosophical reflections. He added almost in a whisper :

"Well you know ! like master, like man. When landlords set the example, its scarcely surprising if the servants' tastes are not exactly refined. Ah ! everything's decidedly going to the dogs in France ! "

"Good-bye," said Octave, "I'm off."

But Trublot still detained him, enumerating the servants'

rooms where he might have slept, as the summer had emptied nearly the whole of them; only the worst was that they all double-locked their doors, even when they were merely going to the end of the passage, they had such a fear of being robbed by each other. There was nothing to be done with Lisa. As for Victoire, ten years ago she might have been passable. And he especially deplored Valérie's mania for changing her cook. He counted the last half-dozen she had had on his fingers. There was a regular string of them : one who had insisted on chocolate of a morning; one who had left because her master did not eat cleanly; one whom the police had come for, just as she was putting a piece of veal to the fire; one who could not touch a thing without breaking it, she was so strong; one who engaged a maid to wait upon her; one who went out in madame's dresses, and who slapped madame's face, the day when madame ventured to allude to the matter. All those in a month! Not giving one sufficient time to pinch them in their kitchen!

"And then," added he, "there was Eugénie. You must have noticed her, a fine tall girl, a regular Venus, my dear fellow! and no joking this time: people turned round in the street to look at her. So that for ten days, the house was quite topsy-turvy. The ladies were furious. The men could scarcely contain themselves : Campardon's tongue hung out; Duveyrier had the idea of coming up here every day to see if the roof leaked. A real revolution, a flame which blazed in the confounded house from the cellars to the loft. As for me, I mistrusted her. She was too stylish! It ended by Eugénie being sent about her business the day when madame found out, by means of her sheets, which were as black as soot, that she was joined every morning by the charcoal-dealer of the Place Gaillon; regular nigger's sheets, the washing of which cost an awful sum!"

At length, Octave was able to get free. He was on the point of leaving Trublot in the profound obscurity of the loft, when the latter suddenly expressed his surprise.

"But you, what are you doing amongst the maids? Ah! rascal, you come here too!"

And he laughed with delight, and promising to keep Octave's secret, sent him off, wishing him a pleasant night of it.

When Octave found himself back in Rachel's room, he experienced a fresh deception. Berthe was not there. Anger got the better of him now : Berthe had humbugged him, she had promised him merely to get rid of his importunities. Whilst he was chafing there, she was sleeping, happy at being alone, occupying the whole breadth of the conjugal couch. Then, instead of returning to his room and going to sleep himself, he obstinately waited, throwing himself all·dressed as he was on the bed, and passing the night in forming projects of revenge. Three o'clock chimed out in the distance. The snores of robust maid-servants arose on his left; while on his right there was a continual wail, a woman moaning with pain in the fever of a sleepless night. He ended by recognising the boot-stitcher's voice. The wretched woman was lying suffering all alone in one of those poverty-stricken closets next to the roof.

Just as day was breaking, Octave fell asleep. A profound silence reigned ; even the boot-stitcher no longer moaned, but lay like one dead. The sun was peering through the narrow window, when the door opening abruptly awoke the young man.

It was Berthe who, urged by an irresistible desire, had come up to see if he was still there ; she had at first scouted the idea, then she had furnished herself with pretexts, the need for going to the room and putting everything straight, in case he had left it anyhow in his rage. Moreover she no longer expected to find him there. When she beheld him rise from the little iron bedstead, ghastly pale and menacing, she stood dumbfounded ; and she listened with bowed head to his furious reproaches. He pressed her to answer, to give him at least some explanation. At length, she murmured :

"At the last moment, I could not do it. It was too indelicate. I love you, oh ! I swear it. But not here, not here !"

And, seeing him approach her, she drew back, afraid that he might wish to take advantage of the opportunity. Eight o'clock was striking, the servants had all gone down, even Trublot had departed. Then, as he tried to take hold of her hands, saying that when one loves a person, one accepts everything, she complained that the closeness of the room made·her feel unwell, and she slightly opened the window. But he again tried to draw her towards him, overpowering her with his importunities. At this moment a turbid torrent of foul words ascended from the inner courtyard.

"Pig ! slut ! have you done? Your dish-cloth's again fallen on my head."

Berthe, turning ghastly pale, and quivering from head to foot, released herself, murmuring :

"Do you hear those girls ? They make me shiver all over. The other day, I thought I should have been ill. No, leave me alone, and I promise to see you, on Tuesday next, in your room."

The two lovers, standing up and not daring to move, were compelled to hear everything.

"Show yourself a moment," continued Lisa, who was furious, "so that I may shy it back in your ugly face!"

Then, Adèle went and leant out of her kitchen window.

"There's a fuss about a bit of rag! To begin with, I only used it for washing-up with yesterday. And then it fell out by accident."

They made peace together, and Lisa asked her what they had had for dinner at her place the day before. Another stew! What misers! She would have ordered chops for herself, if she had been in such a hole! She was for ever inciting Adèle to sneak the sugar, the meat, the candles, just to show that she could do as she liked; as for herself, never being hungry, she left Victoire to rob the Campardons, without even taking her share.

"Oh!" said Adèle, who was gradually becoming corrupted, "the other night I hid some potatoes in my pocket. They quite burnt my leg. It was jolly, it was jolly! And, you know, I like vinegar, I do. I don't care, I drink it out of the cruet now."

Victoire came and leant out in her turn, as she finished drinking some cassis mixed with brandy, which Lisa treated her to now and then of a morning, to pay her for concealing her day and night escapades. And, as Louise thrust out her tongue at them, from the depths of Madame Juzeur's kitchen, Victoire was at once down upon her.

"Wait a bit! you street foundling; I'll shove your tongue somewhere for you!"

"Come along then, old swiller!" retorted the little one. "I saw you yesterday bringing it all up again in your plate."

At this, the rush of foul words again rebounded from wall to wall of the pestiferous hole. Adèle herself, who was mastering the Paris gift of the gab, called Louise a filthy drab, whilst Lisa yelled out:

"I'll make her shut up, if she bothers us. Yes, yes, little strumpet, I'll tell Clémence. She'll settle you. But, hush! here's the man. He's a nice dirty beast, he is!"

Hippolyte just then appeared at the Duveyriers' window, blacking his master's boots. The other servants, in spite of everything, were very polite to him, for he belonged to the aristocracy, and he despised Lisa, who in her turn despised Adèle, with more haughtiness than rich masters show to masters

in difficulties. They asked him for news of Mademoiselle
Clémence and Mademoiselle Julie. Well ! really, they were
almost bored to death there ; but they were pretty well. Then,
jumping to another subject, he asked :

"Did you hear that girl, last night, wriggling about with her
stomach-ache ? Wasn't it annoying ? Luckily she's going to
leave soon. I had half a mind to call out to her."

This allusion to the boot-stitcher's condition caused them to
pass all the ladies of the house in review.

At first they talked of Madame Campardon, who at least had
nothing more to fear ; then of Madame Juzeur, who took her
precautions ; next of Madame Duveyrier, who was disgusted
with her husband ; and of Madame Valérie, who went and got
her children away from home. And at each recital bursts of
laughter arose in blasts from the squalid hole.

Berthe had again turned pale. She waited, no longer even
daring to leave the room, her eyes cast down with shame, like
one to whom violence was being offered in Octave's presence.
He, exasperated with the servants, felt that they were becoming
too filthy, and that he could not again take her in his arms ;
his desire was giving place to a weariness and a great sadness.
But suddenly the young woman started. Lisa had just uttered
her name.

"Talking of enjoying oneself, there's one who seems to me
to go in for a rare dose of it ! Eh ! Adèle, isn't it true that
your Mademoiselle Berthe was up to all manner of tricks at the
time you used to wash her petticoats ?"

"And now," said Victoire, "she gets her husband's assistant
to give her a dusting !"

"Hush !" exclaimed Hippolyte softly.

"What for ? Her jade of a servant isn't there to-day. A
sly hussy who'd eat you, when one speaks of her mistress ! You
know she's a Jewess, and she murdered some one once. Perhaps the handsome Octave dusts her also, in the corners. The
governor must have engaged him just to increase the family, the
big ninny !"

Then Berthe, suffering indescribable anguish, raised her eyes
to her lover. And, cast down, imploring some aid, she
stammered in a painful voice :

"My God ! my God !"

Octave took her hand and squeezed it tightly ; he was choking
with impotent rage. What was to be done ? he could not show
himself and force those women to leave off. The foul words

continued, words which the young woman had never heard before, all the overflow of a sewer which every morning found an outlet there, close to her, and of which she had never had the least suspicion. Their love, so carefully hidden as they thought, was now being dragged amidst the vegetable parings and the kitchen slops. These women knew all, without any-one having spoken. Lisa related how Saturnin held the candle. Victoire was highly amused by the husband's headaches, and said that he would do well to get himself another eye and have it placed somewhere ; even Adèle had a fling at her mistress's young lady, whose ailments, private habits, and toilet secrets she ruthlessly exposed. And a filthy chaff soiled all that remained that was good and tender in their love.

"Look out below !" suddenly exclaimed Victoire, "here's some of yesterday's carrots which stink enough to poison one ! They'll do for that crapulous old Gourd !"

The servants, out of spite, threw all the filth they could into the inner courtyard, so that the doorkeeper should have it to sweep up.

"And here's a bit of mouldy kidney !" said Adèle in her turn.

All the scrapings of the saucepans, all the muck from the washing-up basins, found their way there, whilst Lisa continued to pull Berthe and Octave to pieces. The pair remained stand-ing, hand in hand, face to face, unable to turn away their eyes ; and their hands became as cold as ice, and their looks acknowledged the impurity of their intimacy. This was what their love had come to, this fornication beneath a downpour of putrid meat and stale vegetables !

"And you know," said Hippolyte, "the young gentleman doesn't care a damn for the missis. He merely took her to help him along in the world. Oh ! he's a miser at heart in spite of his airs, an unscrupulous fellow, who, with his pre-tensions of loving women, is not above slapping them ! "

Berthe, her eyes on Octave, saw him turn pale, his face so upset, so changed, that he frightened her.

"On my word ! the two make a nice pair," resumed Lisa. " I wouldn't give much for her skin either. Badly brought up, with a heart as hard as a stone, caring for nothing except her own pleasure, and sleeping with fellows for the sake of their money, yes, for their money ! for I know the sort of woman."

The tears streamed from Berthe's eyes. Octave beheld her features all distorted. It was as if they had been flayed before

each other, laid utterly bare, without any possibility of pro-
testing. Then, the young woman, suffocated by this open
cesspool which discharged its exhalations full in her face,
wished to fly. He did not detain her, for disgust with themselves made their presence a torture, and they longed for the
relief of no longer seeing each other.

"You promise to come, next Tuesday, to my room ?"

"Yes, yes."

And she hurried away, quite distracted. Left alone, he
walked about the room, fumbling with his hands, putting the
linen he had brought, into a bundle. He was no longer listening to the servants, when their last words attracted his attention.

"I tell you that Monsieur Hédouin died last night. If
handsome Octave had foreseen that, he would have continued
to cultivate Madame Hédouin, who's worth a lot."

This news learnt there, amidst those surroundings, re-echoed
in the innermost recesses of his being. Monsieur Hédouin was
dead ! And he was seized with an immense regret. He
thought out loud, he could not restrain himself from saying :

"Ah ! yes, by Jove ! I've been a fool !"

When Octave at length went down, with his bundle, he met
Rachel coming up to her room. Had she been a few minutes
sooner, she would have caught them there. Downstairs, she
had again found her mistress in tears ; but, this time, she had
not got anything out of her, neither an avowal, nor a sou.
And furious, understanding that they took advantage of her
absence to see each other and thus to do her out of her little
profits, she stared at the young man with a look black with
menace. A singular schoolboy timidity prevented Octave from
giving her ten francs ; and, desirous of displaying perfect ease
of mind, he went in to joke with Marie a while, when a grunt
proceeding from a corner caused him to turn round : it was
Saturnin who rose up saying, in one of his jealous fits :

"Take care ! we're mortal enemies !"

That morning was the 8th of October, and the boot-stitcher
had to clear out before noon. For a week past, Monsieur
Gourd had been watching her with a dread that increased hourly.

The boot-stitcher had implored the landlord to let her stay a
few days longer, so as to get over her confinement ; but had
met with an indignant refusal. Pains were seizing her at every
moment ; during the last night, she had fancied she would be
brought to bed all alone. Then, towards nine o'clock, she had

begun her moving, helping the youngster whose little truck was
in the courtyard, leaning against the furniture or sitting down
on the stairs, whenever a formidable spasm doubled her up.

Monsieur Gourd, however, had discovered nothing. Not a
man! He had been regularly humbugged. So that, all the
morning, he prowled about in a cold rage. Octave, who met
him, shuddered at the thought that he also must know of their
intimacy. Perhaps the doorkeeper did know of it, but he
bowed to him as politely as ever; for what did not concern
him, did not concern him, as he was in the habit of saying.
That morning, he had also taken his cap off to the mysterious
lady, as she glided from the room of the gentleman on the third
floor, leaving nothing belonging to her in the staircase but an
evaporated odour of verbena; he had also bowed to Trublot, to
the other Madame Campardon, and to Valérie. They were all
ladies and gentlemen, neither the young men seen coming from
the maid-servants' bedrooms, nor the ladies met on the stairs
in incriminating dressing-gowns concerned him. But what did
concern him, did concern him, and he did not lose sight of the
few poor sticks of furniture belonging to the boot-stitcher, as
though the man so long sought for was about to make off in
one of the drawers.

At a quarter to twelve, the work-girl appeared, with her
wax-like face, her perpetual sadness, her mournful despondency.
She could scarcely move along. Monsieur Gourd trembled
until she was safe out in the street. Just as she handed him
her key, Duveyrier issued from the vestibule, so heated by his
night's work that the red blotches on his forehead seemed almost bleeding. He put on a haughty air, an implacable moral
severity, when the creature passed before him. Ashamed and
resigned, she bowed her head; and, following the little truck,
she went off with the same despairing step as she had come,
the day when she had been engulfed by the undertaker's black
hangings.

Then, only, did Monsieur Gourd triumph. As though this
woman had carried off with her all the uneasiness of the house,
the disreputable things with which the very walls shuddered,
he called out to the landlord:

"A good riddance, sir! One will be able to breathe now,
for, on my word of honour! it was becoming disgusting. It
has lifted a hundredweight from off my chest. No, sir, you
see, in a house which is to be respected, there should be no
single women, and especially none of those women who work!"

CHAPTER XIV.

On the following Tuesday, Berthe did not keep her promise to Octave. This time, she had warned him not to expect her, in a rapid explanation they had had that evening, after the warehouse closed ; and she sobbed ; she had been to confession the day before, feeling a want of religious comfort, and was still quite upset by Abbé Mauduit's grievous exhortations. Since her marriage, she had thrown aside all religion ; but, after the foul words with which the servants had sullied her, she had suddenly felt so sad, so abandoned, so unclean, that she had returned for an hour to the belief of her childhood, inflamed with a hope of purification and salvation. On her return, the priest having wept with her, her sin quite horrified her. Octave, impotent and furious, shrugged his shoulders.

Then, three days later, she again promised for the following Tuesday. At a meeting with her lover, in the Passage des Panoramas, she had seen some Chantilly lace shawls ; and she was incessantly alluding to them, whilst her eyes were filled with desire. So that, on the Monday morning, the young man laughingly said to her, in order to soften the brutal nature of the bargain, that, if she at last kept her word, she would find a little surprise for herself up in his room. She understood him, and again burst into tears. No ! no ! she would not go now, he had spoilt all the pleasure she had anticipated from their being together. She had spoken of the shawl thoughtlessly, she no longer wanted it, she would throw it on the fire if he gave it her. However, on the morrow, they made all their arrangements : she was to knock three times at his door very softly, half an hour after midnight.

That day, when Auguste started for Lyons, he struck Berthe as being rather peculiar. She had caught him whispering with Rachel, behind the kitchen door ; besides which, he was quite yellow, and shivering, with one eye closed up ; but as he complained a good deal of his headache she thought he was ill, and told him that the journey would do him good. Directly he had left, she returned to the kitchen, still feeling slightly uneasy, and tried to sound the servant. The girl continued to be discreet and respectful, and maintained the stiff attitude of her early days. The young woman, however, felt that she was vaguely dissatisfied ; and she thought that she had been very foolish to give her twenty francs and a dress, and then to stop all further gratuities, although compelled to do so, for she was for ever in want of a five franc piece herself.

"My poor girl," said she to her, " I have not been very generous, have I ? But it is not my fault. I have not forgotten you, and I shall recompense you by-and-by."

"Madame owes me nothing," answered Rachel in her cold way.

Then Berthe went and fetched two of her old chemises, wishing at least to show her good nature. But the servant, on receiving them, observed that they would do for rags for the kitchen.

" Thank you, madame, calico irritates my skin, I only wear linen."

Berthe, however, found her so polite, that she became more easy. She made herself very familiar with her, told her she was going to sleep out, and even asked her to leave a lamp alight, in case she required it. The door leading on to the grand staircase could be bolted, and she would go out by way of the kitchen, the key of which she would take with her. The servant received these instructions as coolly as if it had been a question of cooking a piece of beef for the morrow's dinner.

By a refinement of discretion, as his mistress was to dine with her parents that evening, Octave accepted an invitation to the Campardons'. He counted on staying there till ten o'clock, and then going and shutting himself up in his room, and waiting for half-past twelve with as much patience as possible.

The dinner at the Campardons' was quite patriarchal. The architect, seated between his wife and her cousin, lingered over the dishes, regular family dishes, abundant and wholesome, as he described them. That evening, they had a fowl and rice, a joint of beef and stewed potatoes. Since the cousin had been managing everything, the household had been living in a continuous state of indigestion, she knew so well how to buy things, paying less and bringing home twice as much meat as any one else. And Campardon had three helps of fowl, whilst Rose stuffed herself with rice. Angèle reserved herself for the

underdone beef; she liked blood, Lisa sometimes brought her
spoonfuls of it on the sly. And Gasparine alone scarcely
touched anything, her stomach having shrunk, so she said.

"Eat away," cried the architect to Octave, "you may be
eaten yourself some day."

Madame Campardon, bending towards the young man's ear,
was once more congratulating herself on the happiness which
the cousin had brought the household: an economy of quite
cent. per cent., the servants made to be respectful, Angèle looked
after properly and receiving good examples.

"In short," murmured she, "Achille continues to be as happy
as a fish in water, and as for me I have absolutely nothing
whatever left to do, absolutely nothing. Listen! she even
washes me, now. I can live without moving either arms or
legs, she has taken all the cares of the household on her own
shoulders."

Then, the architect related how "he had settled those jokers
of the Ministry of Public Instruction."

"Just fancy, my dear fellow, they made no end of a fuss about
the work I've done at Evreux. You see, I wished above all to
please the bishop. Only, the range for the new kitchens and
the heating apparatus have come to more than twenty thousand
francs. No credit was voted for them, and it is not easy to get
twenty thousand francs out of the small sum allowed for repairs. Besides that, the pulpit, for which I had received three
thousand francs, came to close upon ten thousand : making another seven thousand francs to provide somehow or other. So
that they sent for me to the Ministry this morning, where a
great stick of a fellow commenced by giving me a fine blowing
up. Ah! but it was no go! I don't care for that sort of thing!
So I quietly shut him up by threatening to send for the bishop
to explain the matter himself. And he at once became so
polite, oh! so polite! see, it even makes me laugh now! You
know they've an awful fear of the bishops just at present. When
I've a bishop with me, I might demolish Notre-Dame and build
it up again, I don't care a straw for the government!"

They laughed all round the table, without the least respect
for the Ministry, of which they spoke with disdain, their mouths
full of rice. Rose declared that it was best to be on the side of
religion. Ever since the works at Saint-Roch, Achille was
overwhelmed with orders : the greatest families would employ
no one else, it was impossible for him to attend to them all, he
would have to work all night as well as all day. God wished

them well, most decidedly, and the family returned thanks to Him, both night and morning.

They were having dessert, when Campardon exclaimed :

" By the way, my dear fellow, you know that Duveyrier has found—"

He was about to name Clarisse. But he recollected that Angèle was present, so, casting a side glance towards his daughter, he added :

" He has found his relative, you know."

And, biting his lip and winking his eye, he at length made himself understood by Octave, who at first did not in the least catch what he meant.

" Yes, Trublot whom I met, told me so. The day before yesterday, when it was pouring in torrents, Duveyrier stood up inside a doorway, and who do you think he saw there? why his relative shaking out her umbrella. Trublot had been seeking her for a week past, so as to restore her to him."

Angèle had modestly lowered her eyes on to her plate, and began swallowing enormous mouthfuls. The family rigorously excluded all indecent words from their conversation.

" Is she good looking?" asked Rose of Octave.

"That's a matter of taste," replied the latter. "Some people may think so."

" She had the audacity to come to the shop one day," said Gasparine, who, in spite of her own skinniness, detested thin people. " She was pointed out to me. A regular bean-stalk."

"All the same," concluded the architect, "Duveyrier's hooked again. His poor wife—"

He intended saying that Clotilde was probably relieved and delighted. Only, he remembered a second time that Angèle was present, and put on a doleful air to declare :

" Relations do not always agree together. Yes! every family has its worries.

Lisa, on the other side of the table, with a napkin on her arm, looked at Angèle, and the latter, seized with a mad fit of laughter, hastened to take a long drink, and hide her face in her glass.

A little before ten o'clock, Octave pretended to be very fatigued, and retired to his room. In spite of Rose's affectionate ways, he was ill at ease in that family circle, where he felt Gasparine's hostility to him to be ever on the increase. Yet he had never done anything to her. She detested him for being a handsome man, she suspected him of having overcome all the women of the house, and that exasperated her, though she did not desire him the least in the world, but merely yielded, at the thought of his happiness, to the instinctive anger of a woman whose beauty had faded too soon.

Directly he had left, the family talked of retiring for the night. Before getting into bed, Rose spent an hour in her dressing-room every evening. She proceeded to wash and scent herself all over, then did her hair, examined her eyes, her mouth, her ears, and even placed a tiny patch under her chin. At night-time, she replaced her luxury of dressing-gowns by a luxury of night-caps and chemises. On that occasion, she selected a chemise and a cap trimmed with Valenciennes lace. Gasparine had assisted her, handing her the basins, wiping up the water she spilt, drying her with a soft towel, little things which she did far better than Lisa.

"Ah! I do feel comfortable!" said Rose at length, stretched out in her bed, whilst the cousin tucked in the sheets and raised the bolster.

And she laughed with delight, all alone in the middle of the big bed. With her soft, delicate, and spotless body, reclining amidst the lace, she looked like some beautiful creature, awaiting the idol of her heart. When she felt herself pretty, she slept better, she used to say. Besides, it was the only pleasure left her.

"Is it all right?" asked Campardon, entering the room. "Well! good-night, little duck."

He pretended he had some work to do. He would have to sit up a little longer. But she grew angry, she wished him to take some rest: it was foolish to work himself to death like that!

"You hear me, now go to bed. Gasparine, promise me to make him go to bed."

The cousin, who had just placed a glass of sugar and water, and one of Dickens's novels on the night table, looked at her. Without answering, she bent over and said:

"You are so nice, this evening!"

And she kissed her on both cheeks, with her dry lips and bitter mouth, in the resigned manner of a poor and ugly relation. Campardon, his face very red, and suffering from a difficult digestion, also looked at his wife. His moustache quivered slightly as he kissed her in his turn.

"Good-night, my little duck."

"Good-night, my darling. Now, mind you go to bed at once."

"Never fear!" said Gasparine. "If he's not in bed asleep at eleven o'clock, I'll get up and put his lamp out."

Towards eleven o'clock, Campardon, who was yawning over a Swiss cottage, the fancy of a tailor of the Rue Rameau, rose from his seat and undressed himself slowly, thinking of Rose, so pretty and so clean; then, after opening his bed, on account of the servants, he went and joined Gasparine in hers. It was so narrow that they slept very uncomfortably in it, and their elbows were constantly digging into each other's ribs. He especially always had one leg quite stiff in the morning, through his efforts to balance himself on the edge of the mattress.

At the same time, as Victoire had gone to her room, having finished her washing up, Lisa came, in accordance with her usual custom, to see if mademoiselle required anything more. Angèle was waiting for her comfortably in bed; and thus, every evening, unknown to the parents, they had endless games at cards, on a corner of the counterpane which they spread out for the purpose. They played at beggar-my-neighbour, while abusing cousin Gasparine, a dirty creature, whom the maid coarsely pulled to pieces before the child. They both avenged themselves for their hypocritical submission during the day, and Lisa took a low delight in this corruption of Angèle, and in satisfying the curiosity of this sickly girl, agitated by the crisis of her thirteen years. That night, they were furious with Gasparine who, for two days past, had taken to locking up the sugar, with which the maid filled her pockets, to empty them afterwards on the child's bed. What a bear she was! now they were not even able to get a lump of sugar to suck, when going to sleep!

"Yet your papa gives her plenty of sugar!" said Lisa, with a sensual laugh.

"Oh! yes!" murmured Angèle laughing also.

"What does your papa do to her? Come, show me."

Then, the child caught the maid round the neck, pressed her in her bare arms, and kissed her violently on the mouth, saying as she did so:

"See! like this. See! like this."

Midnight struck. Campardon and Gasparine were moaning in their over narrow bed, whilst Rose, stretching herself out in the middle of hers, and extending her limbs, was reading Dickens, with tears of emotion. A profound silence followed, the chaste night cast its shadow over the respectability of the family.

On going up to his room, Octave found that the Pichons had company. Jules called him in, and persisted on his taking a glass of something. Monsieur and Madame Vuillaume were there, having made it up with the young couple, on the occasion of Marie's churching, she having been confined in September. They had even agreed to come to dinner one Tuesday, to celebrate the young woman's recovery, which only fully dated from the day before. Anxious to pacify her mother, whom the sight of the child, another girl, annoyed, she had sent it out to nurse, not far from Paris. Lilitte was sleeping on the table, overcome by a glass of pure wine, which her parents had forced her to drink to her little sister's health.

"Well! two may still be put up with!" said Madame Vuillaume, after clinking glasses with Octave. "Only don't do it again, son-in-law."

The others all laughed. But the old woman remained perfectly grave.

"There is nothing laughable in that," she continued. "We accept this child, but I swear to you that if another were to come—"

"Oh! if another came," finished Monsieur Vuillaume, "you would have neither heart nor brains. Dash it all! one must be serious in life, one should restrain oneself, when one has not got hundreds and thousands to spend in pleasures."

And, turning towards Octave, he added :

"You see, sir, I am decorated. Well! I may tell you that, so as not to dirty too many ribbons, I don't wear my decoration at home. Therefore, if I deprive my wife and myself of the pleasure of being decorated in our own home, our children can certainly deprive themselves of the pleasure of having daughters. No, sir, there are no little economies."

But the Pichons assured him of their obedience. They were not likely to be caught at that game again !

"To suffer what I've suffered !" said Marie still quite pale.

"I would sooner cut my leg off," declared Jules.

The Vuillaumes nodded their heads with a satisfied air. They had their word, so they forgave them that time. And, as ten was striking by the clock, they tenderly embraced all round ; and Jules put on his hat to see them to the omnibus. This resumption of the old ways affected them so much that they embraced a second time on the landing. When they had taken their departure, Marie, who stood watching them go down, leaning over the balustrade, beside Octave, took the latter back to the dining-room, saying :

" Ah ! mamma is not unkind, and she is quite right : children are no joke ! "

She had shut the door, and was clearing the table of the glasses which still lay about. The narrow room, with its smoky lamp, was quite warm from the little family jollification. Lilitte continued to slumber on a corner of the American cloth.

" I'm off to bed," murmured Octave.

But he sat down, feeling very comfortable there.

" What ! going to bed already ! " resumed the young woman. "You don't often keep such good hours. Have you something to see to then early to-morrow ? "

" No," answered he. " I feel sleepy, that is all. Oh ! I can very well stay another ten minutes or so."

He just then thought of Berthe. She would not be coming up till half-past twelve : he had plenty of time. And this thought, the hope of having her with him for a whole night, which had been consuming him for weeks past, no longer had the same effect on him. The fever of the day, the torment of his desire counting the minutes, evoking the continual image of approaching bliss, gave way beneath the fatigue of waiting.

" Will you have another small glass of brandy ? " asked Marie.

" Well ! yes, I don't mind."

He thought that it would set him up a bit. When she had taken the glass from him, he caught hold of her hands, and held them in his, whilst she smiled, without the least alarm. He thought her charming, with her paleness of a woman who had recently gone through a deal of suffering. All the hidden tenderness with which he felt himself again invaded, ascended with sudden violence to his throat, and to his lips. He had one evening restored her to her husband, after placing a father's kiss upon her brow, and now he felt a necessity to take her back again, an acute and immediate longing, in which all desire for Berthe vanished, like something too distant to dwell upon.

" You are not afraid then, to-day ? " asked he, squeezing her hands tighter.

" No, since it has now become impossible. Oh ! we shall always be good friends ! "

And she gave him to understand that she knew everything. Saturnin must have spoken. Moreover, she always noticed when Octave received a certain person in his room. As he turned pale with anxiety, she hastened to ease his mind : she would never say a word to any one, she was not angry, on the contrary she wished him much happiness.

"Come," repeated she, "I'm married so I can't bear you any ill-will."

He took her on his knees and exclaimed :

"But it's you who I love !"

And he spoke truly.   At that moment he loved her and only her and with an absolute and infinite passion.   All his new intrigue, the two months spent in pursuing another, were as naught.   He again beheld himself in that narrow room, coming and kissing Marie on the neck, behind Jules's back, ever finding her willing, with her passive gentleness.   This was true happiness, how was it that he had disdained it ? . Regret almost broke his heart.   He still wished for her, and he felt that if he had her no more he would be eternally miserable.

"Let me be," murmured she, trying to release herself. "You are not reasonable, you will end by grieving me.   Now that you love another what is the use of continuing to torment me ? "

She defended herself thus, in her gentle and irresolute way, merely feeling a certain repugnance for what did not amuse her much.   But he was getting crazy, he squeezed her tighter, he kissed her throat through the coarse material of her woollen dress.

"It's you who I love, you cannot understand—Listen ! on what I hold most sacred, I swear to you I do not lie.   Tear my heart open and see.   Oh ! I implore you, be kind ! "

. Marie paralysed by the will of this man made a movement as though to take slumbering Lilitte into the next apartment; but he prevented her, fearing that she would awaken the child. The peacefulness of the house, at that hour of the night, filled the little room with a sort of buzzing silence.   Suddenly, the lamp went down, and they were about to find themselves in the dark, when Marie, rising, was just in time to wind it up again.

"Are you angry with me ? " asked Octave with tender gratitude.

She left off attending to the lamp, and returned him a last kiss with her cold lips as she replied :

"No.   But it is not right all the same, on account of that other person."

Tears filled her eyes, and she remained sad, though still without anger.   When he left her, he felt dissatisfied, he would have liked to have gone to sleep.   His gratified passion had

OCTAVE RENEWING HIS VOWS OF LOVE TO MARIE.

p. 282.

left an unpleasant after taste, of which his mouth retained all
the bitterness.   But the other one would be there shortly, he
must wait for her, and this thought weighed terribly on him ;
after having spent feverish nights in concocting extravagant
plans for getting her to visit him in his room, he longed for
something to happen which would prevent her from coming up.
Perhaps she would once again fail to keep her word.   It was a
hope with which he scarcely dared delude himself.

Midnight struck.   Octave, quite tired out, stood listening,
fearing to hear the rustling of her skirts along the narrow
passage.   At half past twelve, he was seized with real anxiety ;
at one o'clock, he thought himself saved, but a secret irritation
mingled with his relief, the annoyance of a man made a fool of by
a woman.   But, just as he made up his mind to undress himself, yawning for want of sleep, there came three gentle taps at
the door.   It was Berthe.   He felt both annoyed and flattered,
and advanced to meet her with open arms, when she motioned
him aside, and stood trembling and listening against the door,
which she had hastily shut after her.

" What is the matter ? " asked he in a low voice.

" I don't know, I was frightened," stammered she.   " It is
so dark on the stairs, I thought that somebody was following
me.   Dear me ! how stupid all this is !   Some harm is sure to
happen to us."

This chilled them both.   They did not even kiss each other.
Yet she was charming in her white dressing-gown, and with her
golden hair rolled up on the back of her head.   He looked at
her, and thought her much prettier than Marie ; but he no
longer desired her ; it was a nuisance.   She had dropped on to
a chair to take breath ; and she suddenly affected to be angry
on beholding a box on the table, which she at once guessed contained the lace shawl she had been talking about for a week
past.

" I am going back," said she without leaving her chair.

" What, you are going ? "

" Do you think I sell myself ?   You are always hurting my
feelings ; you have again spoilt all my pleasure to-night.   Why
did you buy it, when I forbade you to do so ? "

She got up, and at length consented to look at it.   But,
when she opened the box, she experienced such a disappointment, that she could not restrain this indignant exclamation :

" What ! it is not Chantilly at all, it is llama ! "

Octave, who was reducing his presents, had yielded to a

miserly idea. He tried to explain to her that there was some
superb llama, quite equal to Chantilly; and he praised up the
article, just as though he had been behind his counter, making
her feel the lace, and swearing that it would last her for ever.
But she shook her head, and silenced him by observing contemptuously,

"The long and short of it is, this costs one hundred francs,
whereas the other would have cost three hundred."

And, seeing him turn pale, she added, so as to soften her words,

"You are very kind all the same, and I am much obliged to
you. It is not the value which makes the present, when one's
intention is good."

She sat down again, and a pause ensued. She was still quite
upset by her silly fright on the stairs! And she returned to
her misgivings with respect to Rachel, relating how she had
found Auguste whispering with the maid behind a door. Yet,
it would have been so easy to have bought the girl over by
it giving her a five franc piece from time to time. But to do this
was necessary to have some five franc pieces; she never had one,
she had nothing. Her voice became harsh, the llama shawl
which she no longer alluded to was working her up to such a
pitch of rancour and despair, that she ended by picking the
quarrel with her lover which had already existed so long between her and her husband.

"Come, now, is it a life worth living? never a sou, always at
any one's mercy for the least thing! Oh! I've had enough of
it, I've had enough of it!"

Octave, who was pacing the room, stopped short to ask her:
"But why do you tell me all this?"

"Eh? sir, why? But there are things which delicacy alone
ought to tell you, without my being made to blush by having
to discuss such matters with you. Ought you not, long ere
now, and without having to be told, to have made me easy by
bringing this girl to our feet?"

She paused, then she added in a tone of disdainful irony,

"It would not have ruined you."

There was another silence. The young man, who was again
pacing the room, at length replied,

"I am not rich, and I regret it for your sake."

Then matters went from bad to worse, the quarrel assumed
quite conjugal violence.

"Say that I love you for your money!" cried she, with all
the bluntness of her mother, whose very words seemed to come

to her lips. "I am a money-loving woman, am I not? Well! yes, I am a money-loving woman, because I am a sensible woman. It is no use your pretending the contrary; money will ever be money in spite of everything. As for me, whenever I have had twenty sous, I have always pretended that I had forty, for it is better to create envy than pity."

He interrupted her to say in a weary voice, like a man who only desires peace,

"Listen, if it annoys you so much that it's a llama shawl, I will give you one in Chantilly."

"Your shawl!" continued she in a regular fury, "why, I've already forgotten all about your shawl! The other things are what exasperate me, understand! Oh! moreover, you're just like my husband. You wouldn't care a bit if I hadn't a pair of boots to go out in. Yet when one loves a woman, good-nature alone should prompt one to feed and dress her. But no man will ever understand that. Why, between the two of you, you would soon let me go out with nothing on but my chemise, if I was agreeable!"

Octave, tired out by this domestic squabble, decided not to answer, having noticed that Auguste sometimes got rid of her in that way. He let pass the flow of words, and thought of the ill-luck of his amours. Yet he had ardently desired this one, even to the point of upsetting all his calculations; and, now that she was in his room, it was to quarrel with him, to make him pass a sleepless night, as though they had already left six months of married life behind them.

"Let's go to bed," said he at length. "We promised ourselves so much happiness! It is excessively stupid to waste time in saying disagreeable things to one another."

And, full of conciliation, without desire, but polite, he tried to kiss her. She pushed him away, and burst into tears. Then, despairing of winning her round, he took off his boots in a rage, decided on going to bed without her.

"Go on, reproach me also with my outings," stammered she in the midst of her sobs. "Accuse me of being too great an expense to you. Oh! I see clearly now; it's all on account of that wretched present. If you could shut me up in a box, you would do so. I have lady friends; I go to call on them; that is no crime. And as for mamma—"

"For heaven's sake leave your mamma alone," interrupted Octave; "and allow me to tell you that she has given you a precious bad temper."

She mechanically commenced to undress herself, and becoming more and more excited, she raised her voice.

"Mamma has always done her duty. It's not for you to speak of her here. I forbid you to mention her name. It only remained for you to attack my family!"

Finding a difficulty in undoing the string of her petticoat, she broke it. Then, seating herself on the edge of the bed, her bosom heaving with anger in the midst of the surrounding lace of her chemise, she continued :

"Ah! how I regret my weakness, sir! how one would reflect, if one could only foresee everything!"

Octave, who had made a show of lying with his face to the wall, suddenly bounced round, exclaiming,

"What! you regret having loved me?"

"Most certainly, a man incapable of understanding a woman's heart!"

And they looked at each other close together, with hardened faces, quite devoid of love.

"Ah! good heavens! if it were only to come over again!" added she.

"You would take another, wouldn't you?" said he brutally and in a very loud voice.

She was about to answer in the same exasperated tone, when there came a sudden hammering at the door. Not understanding at first what it meant, they remained immovable and their blood seemed to freeze in their veins. A hollow voice said,

"Open the door, I can hear you at your dirty tricks. Open, or I will burst it in!"

It was the husband's voice. Still the lovers did not move, their heads were filled with such a buzzing that they could think of nothing ; and they felt very cold, just like corpses. Berthe at length jumped from the bed, with an instinctive desire to fly from her lover, whilst, on the other side of the door, Auguste repeated :

"Open! open I say!"

Then ensued a terrible confusion, an inexpressible anguish. Berthe turned about the room in a state of distraction, seeking for some outlet, with a fear of death which made her turn ghastly pale. Octave, whose heart jumped to his mouth at each blow, had gone and mechanically leant against the door, as though to strengthen it. The noise was becoming unbearable, the fool would wake the whole house up, he would have to open the door. But, when she understood his determination, she hung on to his arms, imploring him with terrified eyes : no, no, mercy ! the other would rush upon them with a pistol or a knife. He, as pale as herself, and partly overcome by her fright, slipped on his trousers and beseeched her to dress herself. Still bewildered, she only managed to put on her stockings. All this time, the husband continued his uproar.

"You won't, you don't answer. Very well, you'll see."

Ever since he had last paid his rent, Octave had been asking his landlord for some slight repairs, two new screws in the staple of his lock, which scarcely held to the wood. Suddenly the door cracked, the staple yielded, and Auguste, unable to stop himself, rolled into the middle of the room.

"Damnation !" swore he.

He simply held a key in his hand, which was bleeding through becoming grazed in his fall. When he got up, livid, and filled with rage and shame at the thought of his ridiculous entry, he hit out into space, and wished to spring upon Octave. But the latter, in spite of the awkwardness of being barefooted and having his trousers all awry, seized him by the wrists, and, being the stronger of the two, mastered him, at the same time exclaiming :

"Sir, you are violating my domicile. It is disgraceful, you should act like a gentleman."

And he almost beat him. During their short struggle, Berthe had made off in her chemise by the door which had remained wide open ; she fancied she beheld a kitchen knife in her husband's bleeding fist, and she seemed to feel the cold steel between her shoulders. As she rushed along the dark passage, she thought she heard the sound of blows, without being able to make out who had dealt them, or who received them. Voices which she no longer recognised were saying :

"I am at your service, whenever you please."

"Very well, you will hear from me."

With a bound, she gained the servants' staircase. But when she had rushed down the two flights, as though there had been the flames of a conflagration behind her, she found the kitchen door locked, and remembered she had left the key upstairs in the pocket of her dressing-gown. Moreover, there was no lamp, not the least glimmer of a light beneath the door : it was evidently the servant who had sold them. Without stopping to take breath, she tore upstairs again, passing once more before the passage leading to Octave's room, where the two men's voices still continued in violent altercation.

They were going on abusing each other, she would have time perhaps. And she rapidly descended the grand staircase, with the hope that her husband had left their outer door open. She would bolt herself in her 100m, and open to nobody. But there for the second time she encountered a locked door. Then, shut out from her home, with scarcely a covering to her body, she lost her head, and scampered from floor to floor, like some hunted animal which knows not where to take earth. She would never have the courage to knock at her parents' door. At one moment, she thought of taking refuge with the door-keepers; but shame drove her upstairs again. She listened, raised her head, bent over the handrail, her ears deafened by the beating of her heart in the profound silence, her eyes blinded by lights which seemed to shoot out from the dense obscurity. And it was always the knife, the knife in Auguste's bleeding fist, the icy cold point of which was about to pierce her. Suddenly, there was a noise, she fancied he was coming, and she shivered to her very marrow; and, as she was opposite the Campardons' door, she rang desperately, furiously, almost breaking the bell.

"Good heavens! is the house on fire?" asked an agitated voice inside.

The door opened at once. It was Lisa, who was only then leaving mademoiselle, walking softly, and with a candlestick in her hand. The mad ringing of the bell had made her start, just as she was crossing the anteroom. When she caught sight of Berthe in her chemise, she stood rooted to the spot.

"What's the matter?" asked she.

The young woman had entered, violently slamming the door behind her; and, panting and leaning against the wall, she stammered out:

"Hush! keep quiet! He wants to kill me."

Lisa was trying to get a sensible explanation from her, when Campardon appeared, looking very anxious. This incomprehensible uproar had disturbed Gasparine and him in their narrow bed. He had simply slipped on his trousers, and his fat face was swollen and covered with perspiration, whilst his yellow beard was quite flaccid and full of the white down of the pillow. He was all out of breath, and endeavouring to assume the assurance of a husband who sleeps alone.

"Is that you, Lisa?" called he from the drawing-room. "It's absurd! How is it you're not upstairs?"

"I was afraid I had not fastened the door properly, sir; I

BERTHE'S FLIGHT DOWN THE GRAND STAIRCASE.

p. 288.

could not sleep for thinking of it, so I came down to make sure. But it's madame—"

The architect, seeing Berthe leaning against the wall of his anteroom with nothing but her chemise on, stood lost in amazement also. Berthe forgot how scantily she was clad.

"Oh ! sir, keep me here," repeated she. "He wants to kill me."

"Who does ?" asked he.

"My husband."

The cousin now put in an appearance behind the architect. She had taken time to don a dress ; and, her hair all untidy and also full of down, her breast flat and hanging, her bones almost protruding through her garment, she brought with her the rancour arising from her interrupted repose. The sight of the young woman, of her plump and delicate nudity, only increased her ill-humour.

"Whatever have you done then to your husband?" she asked.

At this simple question Berthe was overcome by a great shame. She remembered she was half-naked, and blushed from head to foot. In this long thrill of shame, she crossed her arms over her bosom, as though to escape the glances directed at her. And she stammered out :

"He found me—he caught me—"

The two others understood, and looked at each other with indignation in their eyes. Lisa, whose candle lighted up the scene, pretended to share her master's reprehension. At this moment, however, the explanation was interrupted by Angèle also hastening to the spot; and she pretended to have just woke up, rubbing her eyes heavy with sleep. The sight of the lady with nothing on her but a chemise suddenly brought her to a standstill, with a jerk, a quivering of her precocious young girl's slender body.

"Oh !" she simply exclaimed.

"It's nothing, go back to bed !" cried her father.

Then, understanding that some sort of story was necessary, he related the first that came into his head ; but it was really too ludicrous.

"Madame sprained her ankle coming downstairs, so she's come here for assistance. Go back to bed, you'll catch cold !"

Lisa choked back a laugh on encountering Angèle's wide open eyes, as the latter returned to her bed, all rosy and quite delighted at having seen such a sight. For some minutes past,

Madame Campardon had been calling from her room. She had not put her light out, being so interested in her Dickens, and she wished to know what had happened. What did it all mean? who was there? why did not some one come to set her mind at rest?

"Come, madame," said the architect, taking Berthe with him. " And you, Lisa, wait a minute."

In the bedroom, Rose was still spread out in the middle of the big bed. She throned there with her queenly luxury, her quiet serenity of an idol. She was deeply affected by what she had read, and she had placed the book on her breast, with the heavings of which it gently rose and fell. When the cousin in a few words had made her acquainted with what had taken place, she also appeared to be scandalized. How could one go with a man who was not one's husband? and she was filled with disgust for that which was denied to her. But the architect now cast confused glances at the young woman; and this ended by making Gasparine blush.

"It is shocking !" cried she. "Cover yourself up, madame, for it is really shocking ! Pray cover yourself up ! "

And she herself threw a shawl of Rose's over Berthe's shoulders, a large knitted woollen shawl which was lying about. It did not reach to her knees, however, and in spite of himself, the architect's eyes wandered over the young woman's person.

Berthe was still trembling. Though she was in safety, she kept starting and looking towards the door. Her eyes were full of tears, and she beseeched this lady who seemed so calm and comfortable as she lay in bed :

" Oh ! madame, keep me, save me. He wants to kill me."

A pause ensued. The three were consulting one another with their eyes, without hiding their disapproval of such culpable conduct. Besides, it was not proper to come in a state of nudity and wake people up after midnight, and perhaps put them to great inconvenience. No, such a thing was not right ; it showed a want of discretion, besides placing them in a very awkward position.

" We have a young girl here," said Gasparine at length. " Think of our responsibility, madame."

" You would be better with your parents," insinuated the architect, "and if you will allow me to see you to their door—"

Berthe was again seized with terror.

" No, no, he is on the stairs, he would kill me."

And she implored him to let her remain : a chair was all she needed to wait on till morning ; on the morrow, she would go quietly away. The architect and his wife would have consented, he won over by such tender charms, she interested by the drama of this surprise in the middle of the night. But Gasparine remained inflexible. Yet she had her curiosity to satisfy, and she ended by asking :

"Wherever were you ?"

"Upstairs, in the room at the end of the passage, you know."

At this, Campardon held up his arms and exclaimed :

"What ! with Octave, it isn't possible ! "

With Octave, with that bean-stalk, such a pretty plump little woman ! He was annoyed. Rose, also, felt vexed, and was now inclined to be severe. As for Gasparine, she was quite beside herself, stung to the heart by her instinctive hatred of the young man. He again ! she knew very well that he had them all ; but, she was certainly not going to be so stupid as to keep them warm for him in her home.

"Put yourself in our place," resumed she harshly. "I tell you again we have a young girl here."

"Besides," said Campardon in his turn, "there is the house to be considered, there is your husband, with whom I have always been on the best of terms. He would have a right to be surprised. It will never do for us to appear to publicly approve your conduct, madame, oh ! a conduct which I do not permit myself to judge, but which is rather—what shall I say?—rather indiscreet, is it not ?"

"We are certainly not going to cast stones at you," continued Rose. "Only, the world is so wicked ! People will say that you had your meetings here. And, you know, my husband works for some very strait-laced people. At the least stain on his morality, he would lose everything. But, allow me to ask you, madame : how is it you were not restrained by religion ? The Abbé Mauduit was talking to us of you quite paternally, only the day before yesterday."

Berthe turned her head about between the three of them, looking at the one who spoke, in a bewildered sort of way. In the midst of her fright, she was beginning to understand, she felt surprised at being there. Why had she rang, what was she doing amongst these people whom she disturbed ? She saw them clearly now, the wife occupying the whole width of the bed, the husband in his drawers and the cousin in a thin skirt, the pair of them white with the feathers of the same pillow. They were right, it was not proper to tumble amongst people in that way. And, as the architect pushed her gently towards the anteroom, she went off without even answering Rose's religious regrets.

"Shall I accompany you as far as your parents' door?" asked Campardon. "Your place is with them."

She refused, with a terrified gesture.

"Then wait a moment, I will take a look up and down the stairs, for I should deeply regret if the least harm happened to you."

Lisa had remained in the middle of the anteroom, with her candle. He took it, went out on to the landing, and returned almost immediately.

"I assure you there is no one. Run up quick."

Then Berthe, who had not again opened her lips, hastily took off the woollen shawl, and threw it on the floor saying :

"Here! this is yours. It's no use keeping it as he's going to kill me!"

And she went out into the darkness, with nothing on but her chemise, the same as when she came. Campardon double locked the door in a fury, murmuring the while :

"Eh! go and get tumbled elsewhere!"

Then, as Lisa burst out laughing behind him, he added :

"It's true, they'd be coming every night, if one received them. Every one for himself. I would have given her a hundred francs, but my reputation! no, by Jove!"

In the bedroom, Rose and Gasparine were recovering themselves. Had any one ever seen such a shameless creature? to walk about the staircase with nothing on! Really! there were women who respected nothing, at certain times! But it was close upon two o'clock, they must get to sleep. And they embraced again : good-night my darling, good-night my duck. Eh? was it not nice to love each other, and to always agree together, when one beheld such catastrophes occurring in other families? Rose again took up her Dickens; he supplied all her requirements; she would read a few more pages, then let the book slip into the bed, the same as she did every night, and fall off asleep, weary with emotion. Campardon followed Gasparine, made her get into bed first, and then laid himself down beside her. They both grumbled : the sheets had become cold again, they were not at all comfortable, it would take them another half hour to get warm.

And Lisa, who before going upstairs had returned to Angèle's room, was saying to her :

"The lady has sprained her ankle. Come, show me how she sprained it."

"Why! like this!" replied the child, throwing herself on the maid's neck, and kissing her on her lips.

Berthe was on the stairs shivering. It was cold, the heating apparatus was not lighted till the beginning of November. Her fright had at length abated. She had gone down and listened at her door: nothing, not a sound. Then she had gone up, not daring to venture as far as Octave's room, but listening from a distance: there was a death-like silence, unbroken by a murmur. Then, she had squatted down on her parents' mat, where she vaguely thought of waiting for Adèle, for the idea of confessing everything to her mother upset her as much as if she had still been a little girl. But, by degrees, the solemnity of the staircase filled her with a fresh anguish. It was black, it was severe. No one saw her, and yet she was seized with confusion at having nothing on but her chemise amidst the gilded zinc and the imitation marble. From behind the tall mahogany doors, the conjugal dignity of the alcoves seemed to exhale a reproach. Never before had the house breathed with so virtuous a breath. Then, a moonbeam glided through the windows of the landings, and one might have thought the place a church: a peacefulness ascended from the vestibule to the servants' rooms, all the virtues of the middle-classes smouldered in the shadow of the different storeys, whilst her semi-nakedness shone out all white in the pale light. She felt she was a scandal to the walls, she gathered her chemise around her, dreading to see the ghost of Monsieur Gourd appear in his velvet cap and slippers.

Suddenly, a noise affrighted her, causing her to jump up, and she was about to hammer with both her fists on her mother's door, when some one calling out stopped her.

It was a voice almost as faint as a zephyr.

"Madame—madame—"

She looked downstairs, but saw nothing.

"Madame—madame—it's I."

And Marie showed herself in her chemise also. She had heard all the disturbance, and had slipped out of bed, leaving Jules asleep, whilst she remained listening in her little dining-room without a light.

"Come in. You are in trouble. I am a friend."

She gently reassured her, and told her all that had taken place. The men had not hurt each other: he had cursed and swore, and pushed the chest of drawers up against his door, to shut himself in ; whilst the other had gone downstairs with a bundle in his hand, the things she had left behind, her shoes and petticoat, which he must have rolled up mechanically in her dressing-gown, on seeing them lying about. In short, it was all over. It would be easy enough to prevent them fighting on the morrow.

But Berthe remained standing on the threshold with a remnant of fear and shame at thus entering the abode of a lady whom she did not habitually frequent. Marie was obliged to lead her in by the hand.

"You will sleep there, on that sofa. I will lend you a shawl, and I will go and see your mother. Good heavens ! what a misfortune ! When one is in love, one does not stop to think."

"Ah ! for the little pleasure we had ! " said Berthe, with a sigh, which was full of the cruelty and stupidity of her unprofitable night. "He does right to swear. If he's like me, he's had more than enough of it !"

They were on the point of speaking of Octave. They said nothing further, but suddenly fell sobbing into each other's arms in the dark. Their limbs clasped with a convulsive passion, their bosoms, hot with tears, were pressed close together beneath their crumpled chemises. It was a final weariness, an immense sadness, the end of everything. They did not say another word, whilst their tears flowed, flowed without ceasing, in the midst of the darkness and of the profound slumber of that house so full of decency.

CHAPTER XV.

THAT morning, the house awoke with a great middle-class dignity. Nothing of the staircase preserved a trace of the scandals of the night, neither the imitation marble which had reflected that gallop of a woman in her chemise, nor the Wilton carpet from which all the odour of her semi-nudity had evaporated. Monsieur Gourd alone, when he went upstairs owards seven o'clock to give his look round, sniffed at the walls; but what did not concern him, did not concern him; and as, on going downstairs again, he saw two of the servants in the courtyard, Lisa and Julie, who were no doubt discussing the catastrophe, for they seemed deeply interested, he stared at them so fixedly that they at once separated. Then he went outside to make sure of the tranquillity of the street. It was calm. Only, the servants must already have been talking, for some of the neighbours' wives stopped, tradespeople came to their shop doors, looking up in the air, examining and searching the different floors, in the gaping way in which the crowd scrutinizes houses where a crime has been committed. In the presence of the rich frontage, however, people held their tongues and politely passed on.

At half-past seven, Madame Juzeur appeared in a dressing-gown, to look after Louise, she said. Her eyes sparkled, and her hands were feverishly hot. She stopped Marie, who was going up with her milk, and endeavoured to get her to talk; but she could draw nothing out of her, and did not even learn how the mother had received her guilty daughter. Then, under the pretence of waiting a minute for the postman, she entered the Gourds' room, and ended by asking why Monsieur Octave did not come down; perhaps he was ill. The doorkeeper replied that he did not know; moreover, Monsieur Octave never came down before ten minutes past eight. At this moment, the other Madame Campardon, pale and erect, passed by; every one bowed to her. And Madame Juzeur, obliged to go upstairs again, had the luck, on reaching her landing, to meet the architect just starting off and putting on his gloves. At first, they both looked at each other in a dejected sort of way ; then he shrugged his shoulders.

"Poor things ! " murmured she.

"No, no, it serves them right ! " said he ferociously. "An example must be made of them. A fellow whom I introduce into a respectable house, beseeching him not to bring any women there, and who, to humbug me, goes and sleeps with the landlord's sister-in-law ! I look like a fool in it all ! "

No more was said. Madame Juzeur entered her apartments, whilst Campardon continued on his way downstairs, in such a state of fury that he tore one of his gloves.

Just as eight o'clock was striking, Auguste, looking very dejected, his features contracted by an atrocious headache, crossed the courtyard to go to his warehouse. Filled with shame, and dreading to meet any one, he had come down by way of the servants' staircase. However, he could not leave his business to take care of itself. When in the midst of his counters, and before the pay-desk where Berthe usually sat, his emotion almost choked him. The porter was taking down the shutters, and Auguste was giving the orders for the day, when the abrupt appearance of Saturnin coming up from the basement gave him an awful fright. The madman's eyes were like flames of fire, his white teeth resembled a famished wolf's. He went straight up to the husband, clenching his fists.

"Where is she ? If you touch her, I'll bleed you to death like a pig ! "

Auguste drew back, exasperated.

"Here's this one, now ! "

"Shut up, or I'll bleed you ! " repeated Saturnin, making a rush at him.

Then the husband preferred to beat a retreat. He had a horror of madmen ; one could not reason with such people. But, as he went out into the porch, calling to the porter to shut Saturnin up in the basement, he found himself face to face with Valérie and Théophile. The latter, who had caught a frightful cold, was wrapped up in a big red comforter, and coughed and moaned. They must both have known everything, for they stopped before Auguste with an air of condolence. Since the quarrel about the inheritance, the two couples had been sworn enemies, and were no longer on speaking terms.

"You still have a brother," said Théophile, shaking him by

the hand, when he had finished coughing. " I wish you to
remember it in your misfortune."

" Yes," added Valérie, " this ought to avenge me, for she
said some filthy things to me, did she not? But we pity you
all the same, for we are not quite heartless."

Auguste, deeply touched by their kind manner, led them to
the end of his warehouse, keeping an eye on Saturnin, who was
prowling about. And, there, their reconciliation became complete. Berthe's name was not mentioned; only, Valérie
allowed it to be understood that all the unpleasantness arose
from that woman, for there had never been a disagreeable word
said in the family till she had entered it to dishonour them.
Auguste, his eyes cast on the ground, listened and nodded his
head approvingly. And a certain gaiety gleamed beneath
Théophile's commiseration, for he was delighted at no longer
being the only one, and he examined his brother's face to see
how a person looks when in that awkward position.

" Now, what have you decided to do?" inquired he.

" To challenge him, of course!" firmly replied the husband.

Théophile's joy was spoilt. His wife and he became cooler,
in the presence of Auguste's courage. The latter related to
them the frightful scene of the night—how, having been foolish
enough to hesitate purchasing a pistol, he had been forced to
content himself with merely slapping the gentleman's face; and
to tell the truth, the gentleman had done the same to him, but
that did not prevent his having received a pretty good hiding!
A scoundrel who had been making a fool of him for six months
past, by pretending to take his part against his wife, and whose
impudence had gone as far as making reports respecting her on
the days she went out! As for her, the creature, as she had
gone to her parents, she could remain with them; he would
never take her back.

" Would you believe that last month I allowed her three
hundred francs for her dress!" cried he. " I who am so kind,
so tolerant, who had decided to put up with everything, sooner
than make myself ill! But one cannot put up with that—no!
no! one cannot!"

Théophile was thinking of death. He trembled feverishly,
and almost choked as he said:

" It's absurd, you will get spitted. I would not fight."

And, as Valérie looked at him, he added in an embarrassed
manner:

" If such a thing happened to me."

"Ah! the wretched woman!" then murmured his wife, "when one thinks that two men are going to kill each other on account of her! In her place, I could never sleep again."

Auguste remained firm. He would fight. Moreover, his plans were settled. As he particularly wished Duveyrier to be his second, he was going up to inform him of what had taken place, and to send him at once to Octave. Théophile should be his other second, if he would consent. The latter was obliged to do so; but his cough suddenly seemed to become much worse, and he put on his peevish air of a sick child who wants to be pitied. He, however, offered to accompany his brother to the Duveyriers'. Though they might be robbers, yet one forgot everything in certain circumstances; and both he and his wife appeared to be desirous of a general reconciliation, they having, no doubt, reflected that it was not their interest to sulk any longer. Valérie, who was most obliging to Auguste, ended by offering to attend at the pay-desk, to give him time to find a suitable person.

"Only," added she, "I must take Camille to the Tuileries gardens towards two o'clock."

"Oh! it does not matter for once in a way!" said her husbad. "It's raining, too."

"No, no, the child wants air. I must go out."

At length the two brothers went up to the Duveyriers'. But an abominable fit of coughing obliged Théophile to stop on the very first stair. He held on to the hand-rail, and when he was able to speak, though still with a slight rattle in his throat, he stammered:

"You know, I'm very happy now; I'm quite sure of her. No, I've not the least thing to reproach her with, and she has given me proofs."

Auguste stared at him without comprehending, and saw how yellow and half dead he looked with the scanty hairs of his beard drying up in his flabby flesh. This look completed Théophile's annoyance, whilst he felt quite embarrassed by his brother's valour.

"I am speaking of my wife," he resumed. "Ah! poor old fellow, I pity you with all my heart! You recollect my stupidity on your wedding-day. But with you there can be no mistake, as you saw them."

"Bah!" said Auguste doing the brave, "I'll spit him like a lark. On my word, I shouldn't care a hang if I hadn't such a headache!"

Just as they rang at the Duveyriers' door, Théophile suddenly thought that very likely the counsellor would not be in, for since the day he had found Clarisse, he had been drifting into bad habits, and had now even got to the point of sleeping out. Hippolyte, who opened the door to them, avoided answering with respect to his master ; but he said that the gentlemen would find madame playing her scales. They entered. Clotilde, tightly laced up from the moment she got out of bed, was seated at her piano, practising with a regular and continuous movement of her hands ; and, as she went in for this kind of exercise for two hours every day, so as not to lose the lightness of her touch, she occupied her mind in another way, by reading the "Revue des deux Mondes," which stood open on the piano before her, without the agility of her fingers being in any way hampered.

"Why ! it's you !" said she, when her brothers had drawn her from the volley of notes, which isolated and enveloped her like a storm of hail.

And she did not even show her surprise when she caught sight of Théophile. The latter, moreover, kept himself very stiff, like a man who had come on another's account. Auguste, filled with shame at the thought of telling his sister of his misfortune, and afraid of terrifying her with his duel, had a story all ready. But she did not give him time to lie, she questioned him in her quiet way, after looking at him intently.

"What do you intend doing now ?"

He started and blushed. So every one knew it then ? And he answered in the brave tone which had already closed Théophile's mouth :

"Why, fight, of course ! "

"Ah !" said she, greatly surprised this time.

However, she did not disapprove. It would increase the scandal, but yet honour had to be satisfied. She contented herself with recalling that she had at first opposed the marriage. One could expect nothing of a young girl who appeared to be ignorant of all a woman's duties. Then, as Auguste asked her where her husband was :

"He is travelling," answered she, without the least hesitation.

Then he was quite distressed, for he did not wish to do anything before consulting Duveyrier. She listened to him, without mentioning the new address, unwilling to acquaint her family with her home troubles. At length she hit on an expedient : she advised him to go to Monsieur Bachelard in the

Rue d'Enghien ; perhaps he would be able to tell him something. And she returned to her piano.

"It's Auguste who asked me to come up," Théophile, who had not spoken until then, thought it necessary to declare. "Will you let me kiss you, Clotilde ? We are all in trouble."

She presented her cold cheek, and said :

"My poor fellow, only those are in trouble who choose to be. As for me, I forgive every one. And take care of yourself, you seem to me to have a very bad cough."

Then, calling to Auguste, she added :

"If the matter does not get settled, let me know, for I shall then be very anxious."

The storm of notes recommenced, enveloping and drowning her ; and, whilst her nimble fingers practised the scales in every key, she gravely resumed her reading of the " Revue des deux Mondes," in the midst of it all.

Downstairs, Auguste for a moment discussed the question whether he should go to Bachelard's or not. How could he say to him : "Your niece has deceived me ?" At length, he decided to obtain Duveyrier's address from the uncle, and to tell him nothing. Everything was settled : Valérie would look after the warehouse, whilst Théophile would watch the home, until his brother's return. The latter had sent for a cab, and he was just going off, when Saturnin, who had disappeared a moment before, came up from the basement with a big kitchen knife, which he flourished about, as he cried :

"I'll bleed him ! I'll bleed him ! "

This created another scare. Auguste, turning very pale, jumped precipitately into the cab, and pulled the door to, saying :

"He's got another knife ! Wherever does he find all those knives ! I beseech you, Théophile, send him away, try and arrange that he shall no longer be here when I come back. As though what has already happened were not bad enough for me!"

The porter had hold of the madman by his shoulders. Valérie told the driver the address. But he, a fat and filthy looking man, with a face the colour of bullock's blood, and still drunk from the night before, did not hurry himself, but took his time to gather up the reins and make himself comfortable on the box.

"By distance, governor ? " asked he in a hoarse voice.

"No, by the hour, and quickly please. There will be something handsome for yourself."

The cab started off. It was an old landau, both big and dirty, and shaking alarmingly on its worn-out springs. The horse, an enormous white carcass, ambled along with an extraordinary waste of strength, jogging his neck, and lifting his hoofs high off the ground. Auguste looked at his watch: it was nine o'clock. The duel might be settled by eleven. At first, the slowness of the vehicle irritated him. Then, little by little, he began to get drowsy; he had not closed his eyes all night, and that lamentable cab saddened him. When he found himself alone, rocked inside the rickety vehicle, and half deafened by the rattling of the cracked windows, the fever which had kept him up before his relations, began to calm down. What a stupid adventure it was all the same! And his face became ashy grey as he pressed his aching head between his hands.

In the Rue d'Enghien, he met with another vexation. To begin with, the commission agent's doorway was so blocked up with vans that he almost got crushed; then, he found himself in the courtyard with the glass roof, amidst a crowd of packers all violently nailing up cases, and not one of whom could tell him where Bachelard was. The hammering seemed to split his skull. He was however making up his mind to wait for the uncle, when an apprentice, pitying his suffering look, came and whispered an address in his ear: Mademoiselle Fifi, Rue Saint-Marc, third floor. Old Bachelard was most likely there.

"Where do you say?" asked the driver who had fallen asleep.

" Rue Saint-Marc, and a little faster, if it's possible."

The cab resumed its funereal crawl. On the boulevards, the wheel caught in an omnibus. The panels cracked, the springs uttered plaintive cries, a gloomy melancholy more and more overcame the husband in search of his second. However, they at last reached the Rue Saint-Marc.

On the third floor, the door was opened by a little old woman, plump and white. She seemed suffering from some strong emotion, and she admitted Auguste directly he asked for Monsieur Bachelard.

"Ah! sir, you are one of his friends, surely. Pray try to calm him. Something happened to vex him a little while ago, the poor dear man. You know me no doubt, he must have spoken to you of me: I am Mademoiselle Menu."

Auguste, feeling quite scared, found himself in a ·narrow room overlooking the courtyard, and as clean and peaceful as a country home. One could almost detect the odour of order and work, the purity of the happy existence of people in a quiet way. Seated before an embroidery frame, on which a priest's stole was stretched, a fair young girl, pretty and having a candid air, was weeping bitterly ; whilst uncle Bachelard, standing up, his nose inflamed, his eyes bloodshot, was drivelling with rage and despair. He was so upset, that Auguste's entry did not appear to surprise him in the least. He immediately called upon him to bear witness, and the scene continued.

"Come now, you, Monsieur Vabre, who are an honest man, what would you say in my place? I arrived here this morning, a little earlier than usual ; I entered her room with the sugar from the café and three four sou pieces, just for a surprise for her, and I find her in bed with that pig Gueulin! No, there, frankly what would you say?"

Auguste, greatly embarrassed, turned very red. He at first thought that the uncle knew of his misfortune and was making a fool of him. But the other added, without even waiting for a reply :

"Ah ! listen, mademoiselle, you don't know what it is you have done! I who was becoming young again, who felt so delighted at having found a nice quiet little nook, where I was once more beginning to believe in happiness! Yes, you were an angel, a flower, in short something fresh which helped me to forget a lot of dirty women. And here you go and sleep with that pig Gueulin!"

A genuine emotion contracted his throat, his voice choked in accents of profound suffering. Everthing was crumbling away, and he wept for the loss of the ideal, with the hiccoughs of a remnant of drunkenness.

"I did not know, uncle," stammered Fifi, whose sobs redoubled in presence of this pitiful spectacle; "no, I did not know it would cause you so much grief."

And indeed she did not look as if she did know. She retained her ingenuous eyes, her odour of chastity, the naivete of a little girl unable as yet to distinguish a gentleman from a lady. Aunt Menu, moreover, swore that at heart she was innocent.

"Do be calm, Monsieur Narcisse. She loves you well all the same. I felt that it would not be very agreeable to you. I said to her: 'If Monsieur Narcisse learns this, he will be annoyed.' But she has scarcely lived as yet, has she? She does not know what pleases, nor what does not please. Do not weep any more, as her heart is always for you."

As neither the child nor the uncle listened to her, she turned towards Auguste, she told him how much more anxious such an adventure made her feel for her niece's future. It was so difficult to place a young girl decently! She, who had been thirty years in the employ of Messieurs Mardienne Frères, the embroiderers of the Rue Saint-Sulpice, where one could make inquiries about her, knew at the cost of what privations a work-girl made both ends meet in Paris, when she wished to remain virtuous. In spite of her good nature, though she had received Fanny from the hands of her own brother, Captain Menu, on his death-bed, she could never have been able to bring the child up with the thousand francs life annuity, which now enabled her to relinquish her needle. And she had, therefore, hoped to die in peace on seeing her with Monsieur Narcisse. But not a bit of it—Fifi goes and displeases her uncle, just for the sake of a lot of nonsense!

"Perhaps you know Villeneuve, near Lille?" said she in conclusion. "I come from there. It is a pretty large town—"

But Auguste's patience was at an end. He shook himself free of the aunt, and turned towards Bachelard whose noisy despair was calming down.

"I came to ask you for Duveyrier's new address. I suppose you know it."

"Duveyrier's address, Duveyrier's address," stammered the uncle. "You mean Clarisse's address. Wait a moment."

And he went and opened the door of Fifi's bedroom. Auguste was greatly surprised on seeing Gueulin, whom the old man had locked in, come forth. He had wished to give him time to dress himself, and also to detain him, so as to decide afterwards what he would do with him. The sight of the young man looking all upset, his hair still unbrushed, revived his anger.

"What! wretch! it's you, my nephew, who dishonours me! You soil your family, you drag my white hairs in the mire! Ah! you'll end badly, we shall see you one of these days in the dock of the assize-court!"

Gueulin listened with bowed head, feeling at once both embarrassed and furious.

"I say, uncle, you're going too far," murmured he. "There's a limit to everything. I don't think it funny either. Why did you bring me to see mademoiselle? I never asked you. You dragged me here. You drag everybody here."

But Bachelard, again overcome with tears continued:

"You've taken everything from me, I had only her left.

You'll be the cause of my death, and I won't leave you a sou, not a sou!"

Then Gueulin, quite beside himself, burst out:

"Go to the deuce! I've had enough of it! Ah! it's as I've always told you! here they come, here they come, the annoyances of the morrow! See how it succeeds with me, when for once in a way I've been fool enough to take advantage of an opportunity. Of course! the night was very pleasant; but, afterwards, go to blazes! one will be blubbering like a calf for the rest of one's life."

Fifi had dried her tears. When having nothing to do she at once felt bored, and so had taken up her needle again and was embroidering the stole, raising her large pure eyes from time to time to look at the two men, and feeling quite bewildered by their anger.

"I am in a great hurry," Auguste ventured to observe. "Please give me the address, just the name of the street and the number, I require nothing further."

"The address," said the uncle, "wait a bit, directly."

And, carried away by his feelings which were overflowing, he caught hold of Gueulin's hands.

"You ungrateful fellow, I was keeping her for you, on my word of honour! I said to myself: If he's good, I'll give her to him. Oh! in a proper manner, with a dowry of fifty thousand francs. And, you dirty beast! you can't wait, you go and take her like that, all on a sudden!"

"No, let me be!" said Gueulin, affected by the old chap's kindness of heart. "I see very well that the annoyances are going to continue."

But Bachelard dragged him before the young girl and asked her:

"Come now, Fifi, look at him: would you have loved him?"

"If it would have pleased you, uncle," answered she.

This kind reply quite broke his heart. He wiped his eyes, blew his nose, and almost choked. Well! he would see. He had always wished to make her happy. And he suddenly sent Gueulin off about his business.

"Be off. I will think about it."

Meanwhile, aunt Menu had again taken Auguste aside to explain her ideas to him. Was it not true? a workman would have beaten the child, and a clerk would have given her no end of children. With Monsieur Narcisse, on the contrary, she had the chance of having a dowry which would enable her to marry

decently.   Thank goodness, they belonged to too good a family;
the aunt would never have allowed the niece to misconduct herself, to fall from the arms of one lover into the arms of another.
No, she wished her to be in a proper sort of position.

Just as Gueulin was leaving, Bachelard called him back.

"Kiss her on the forehead, I permit it."

And then he went himself and put him outside the door,
after which he returned to Auguste, and placing his hand on
his heart, he said :

"It's no joke ; I give you my word of honour that I intended
giving her to him, later on."

"And the address ? " asked the other, losing all patience.

The uncle appeared surprised, as though he thought he had
answered him before.

"Eh ɪ what ? Clarisse's address ?   Why, I don't know it."

Auguste made an angry gesture.   Everything was going
wrong ; there seemed to be a regular plot to render him
ridiculous !   Seeing him so upset, Bachelard made a suggestion.
No doubt, Trublot knew the address, and they might find him
at his employer's, the stockbroker Desmarquay.   And the
uncle, with the obliging manner of one accustomed to knock
about, offered to accompany his young friend.   The latter
accepted.

"Listen ! " said the uncle to Fifi, after kissing her in his
turn on the forehead, " here's the sugar from the café all the
same, and three four-sou bits for your money-box.   Behave
well whilst awaiting my orders."

Tho young girl, looking very modest, continued drawing her
needle with exemplary application.   A ray of sunshine, coming
from over a neighbouring roof, enlivened the little room, gilded
this nook of innocence, into which the noise of the passing
vehicles did not even penetrate.   All the poetry of Bachelard's
nature was stirred.

"May God bless you, Monsieur Narcisse ! " said aunt Menu
to him as she saw him to the door.   " I am more easy now.
Only listen to the dictates of your heart, for it will inspire
you."

The driver had again fallen asleep, and he grumbled when the
uncle gave him Monsieur Desmarquay's address in the Rue
Saint-Lazare.   No doubt the horse was asleep also, for it required quite a hail of blows to get him to move.   At length,
the cab rolled painfully along.

"It's hard all the same," resumed the uncle after a pause.

U

"You can't imagine the effect it had on me when I saw Gueulin in his shirt. No, one must have gone through such a thing to understand it."

And he went on, entering into every detail, without noticing Auguste's increasing uneasiness. At length the latter, feeling his position becoming falser and falser, told him why he was in such a hurry to find Duveyrier.

"Berthe with that counter-jumper!" cried the uncle. "You astonish me, sir!"

And it seemed that his astonishment was especially on account of his niece's choice. However, after a little reflection, he became very indignant. His sister Eléonore had a great deal to reproach herself with. He would have nothing more to do with the family. Of course, he was not going to mix himself up with the duel; but he considered it indispensable.

"Thus, just now, when I saw Fifi with a man, my first thought was to murder every one. If the same thing should ever happen to you—"

A painful start of Auguste's caused him to interrupt himself.

"Ah! true, I was forgetting. My story does not interest you."

Another pause ensued, whilst the cab swayed in a melancholy fashion. Auguste, whose valour grew less and less at each turn of he wheel, abandoned himself to the jolts, a cadaverous look on his face, his left eye half closed with a headache. Why ever did Bachelard consider the duel indispensable? It was not the place of the culprit's uncle to urge one to shed blood. And his brother's words rang in his ear: "It's stupid, you'll get yourself spitted;" an obstinate and importunate phrase, which seemed to end by assimilating itself with the very pain of his neuralgia. He would certainly be killed; he had a presentiment he would; and this lugubrious attack of feeling completely annihilated him. He fancied himself dead, and wept over his own corpse.

"I told you Rue Saint-Lazare," called out the uncle to the driver. "It isn't at Chaillot. Turn to the left."

At length the cab stopped. Out of prudence they sent up for Trublot, who came down bareheaded to talk to them in the doorway.

"You know Clarisse's address?" asked Bachelard.

"Clarisse's address? Why, of course! Rue d'Assas."

They thanked him, and were about to re-enter their cab, when Auguste asked in his turn:

"What's the number?"

"The number? Ah! I don't know the number."

At this, the husband declared that he preferred to give up seeing Duveyrier altogether. Trublot did all he could to try and remember. He had dined there once, it was just behind the Luxembourg; but he could not recollect whether it was at the end of the street, or on the right or the left. But he knew the door well; oh! he could have said at once, "That's it." Then the uncle had another idea: he begged him to accompany them in spite of Auguste's protestations, and his talking of returning home and not wishing to disturb any one any further. Trublot, however, refused in a constrained manner. No, he would not trust himself in that hole again. And he avoided giving the real reason, a most amazing adventure, a jolly hard slap he had received from Clarisse's new cook, one evening he had gone and pinched her before her range. Could anybody understand such a thing? a slap for a polite attention, just for the sake of becoming acquainted! Such a thing had never happened to him before; he was quite bewildered by it.

"No, no," said he, seeking an excuse, "I don't intend putting my feet again inside a place where one's bored as one is there. You know Clarisse has become unbearable, something abominable, and more the lady than ladies themselves! Besides that, she has had her family with her, since her father's death—quite a tribe of hawkers, the mother, two sisters, a big scoundrel of a brother, and even an invalid aunt; you know, the sort of people who sell dolls in the streets. You've no idea how dirty and unhappy Duveyrier looks amongst them all!"

And he related that on the rainy day, when the counsellor found Clarisse waiting in a doorway, she had been the first to complain, reproaching him, with tears in her eyes, with never having respected her. Yes, she had left the Rue de la Cerisaie exasperated by the suffering which her personal dignity had undergone, and which she had for a long while repressed. Why did he always take his decoration off when he came to see her? Did he happen to think that she would soil his decoration? She was willing to be friends with him again; but first of all he would have to swear to her on his honour that he would keep his decoration on, for she required his esteem; she would not have her feelings hurt every moment in that way. And Duveyrier, discomfited by this quarrel, completely regained, confused and affected, had sworn: she was right; he considered her very noble-minded.

"He no longer takes his ribbon off," added Trublot. "I

think that she makes him sleep with it on. It flatters the girl in the presence of her family. Moreover, fat Payan, having devoured her twenty-five thousand francs' worth of furniture, she has gone in this time for thirty thousand francs' worth. Oh, it's all over ; she's got him down on the ground, under her foot, and his nose in her skirts. What a liking some people have for buttered bun !"

" Well, I'm off, as Monsieur Trublot can't come," said Auguste, whose worries were increased by all these stories.

But Trublot then declared that he would accompany them all the same ; only, he would not go up ; he would merely show them the door. And, after fetching his hat, and giving a pretext for going out, he joined them in the cab.

"Rue d'Assas," said he to the driver. "Straight down the street ; I'll tell you when to stop."

The driver swore. Rue d'Assas, by Jove ! there were people who liked going about. However, they would get there when they did get there. The big white horse steamed away without making hardly any progress, his neck dislocated in a painful bow at every step.

Bachelard was already relating his misfortune to Trublot. Such things always made him talkative. Yes, with that pig Gueulin, a most delicious little thing! He had found them both in dishabille. But at this point of his story he recollected Auguste, who, gloomy and doleful, was sitting in a heap in a corner of the cab.

"Ah ! true ; I beg your pardon !" murmured he ; "I keep forgetting."

And, addressing Trublot, he added :

"Our friend has met with a misfortune in his home also, and that is why we are trying to find Duveyrier. Yes, he found his wife last night—"

He finished with a gesture, then added simply :

"Octave, you know."

Trublot, always plain-spoken, was about to say that it did not surprise him. Only, he caught back his words, and replaced them by others, full of disdainful anger, and the explanation of which the husband did not dare to ask him for :

" What an idiot that Octave is !" said he.

At this appreciation of adultery there ensued another pause. Each of the three men was buried in his own reflections. The cab scarcely moved at all. It seemed to have been rolling for hours over a bridge, when Trublot, who was the first to emerge from his thoughts, ventured on making this judicious remark :

"This cab doesn't get along very fast."

But nothing could increase the horse's pace. It was eleven o'clock when they reached the Rue d'Assas. And there they wasted nearly another quarter of an hour, for in spite of Trublot's boasts, he could not find the door. At first, he allowed the driver to go along the street to the very end without stopping him; then he made him drive up and down three times over. And on his precise indications, Auguste kept entering every tenth house; but the doorkeepers all answered that they knew no one of the name. At length, a greengrocer pointed out the door to him. He went in with Bachelard, leaving Trublot in the cab.

It was the big rascal of a brother who admitted them. He had a cigarette stuck between his lips, and blew the smoke into their faces as he showed them into the drawing-room. When they asked for Monsieur Duveyrier, he stood looking at them in a jocular manner without answering. Then he disappeared, perhaps to fetch him. In the middle of the blue satin drawing-room, all luxuriously new, yet already stained with grease, one of the sisters, the youngest, was seated on the carpet scouring out a saucepan which she had brought from the kitchen; whilst the other, the eldest, was hammering with her clenched fists on a magnificent piano, the key of which she had just found. On seeing the gentlemen enter they had both raised their heads; neither, however, left off her occupation, but continued on the contrary hammering and scouring more energetically than ever. Five minutes passed, yet no one came. The visitors, feeling almost deafened, stood looking at each other, when some yells, issuing from a neighbouring room, completely terrified them; it was the invalid aunt being washed.

At length, an old woman, Madame Bocquet, Clarisse's mother, passed her head through a partly opened door, not daring to show any more of her person because of the filthy dress she had on.

"What do you gentlemen desire?" asked she.

"Why, Monsieur Duveyrier!" exclaimed the uncle losing patience. "We have already told the servant. Let him know that Monsieur Auguste Vabre and Monsieur Narcisse Bachelard wish to see him."

Madame Bocquet shut the door again. The eldest of the sisters was now mounted on the music stool, and was hammering away with her elbows, whilst the youngest was scraping the saucepan with an iron fork, so as to get all she could out of it.

Another five minutes passed by. Then, in the midst of the uproar, which did not seem to disturb her in the least, Clarisse appeared.

"Ah ! it's you !" said she to Bachelard, without even looking at Auguste.

The uncle was quite taken aback. He would not have known her, she had grown so fat. The big devil of a wench, once as skinny as a scarecrow and as curly as a poodle, was becoming quite the little mother, clammy, and her hair all shining with pomatum. She did not give him time to say a word, but at once roughly told him that she did not want in her home such a talebearer as him, who went and told Alphonse all sorts of horrible things ; yes, exactly so, he had accused her of sleeping with Alphonse's friends, of picking them up behind his back by the shovelful ; and he could not deny it, for Alphonse himself had told her.

"You know, my old fellow," added she, "if you've come to tipple, you may as well get out at once. The old life's done with. I now intend to be respected."

And she displayed her passion for the genteel, which had grown, and had become her fixed idea. Seized with periodical fits of rigour, she had thus driven away her lover's friends one by one, forbidding them to smoke, insisting on being addressed as Madame and on receiving morning calls. Her old superficial and borrowed funniness had all departed ; and she retained merely the exaggeration of her part of a grand lady, who at times broke out in foul words and obscene gestures. Little by little solitude was again enveloping Duveyrier : there was no longer the pleasant nook, but a ferociously middle-class abode, amidst the filth and uproar of which he met with all the annoyances of his own home. As Trublot said, one did not feel more bored at the Rue de Choiseul, and this was much less dirty.

"We haven't called on your account," replied Bachelard recovering himself, used as he was to the lively receptions of such ladies. "We must speak to Duveyrier."

Then Clarisse looked at the other gentleman. She took him for a bailiff, knowing that Alphonse was already in a mess.

"Oh ! after all, I don't care," said she. "You can take him and keep him if you like. It's not so very pleasant to have to dress his pimples !"

She no longer even took the trouble to conceal her disgust, certain, moreover, that all her cruelties only attached him to her the more.

And, opening a door, she added :

"Here ! come along, as these gentlemen persist in seeing you."

Duveyrier, who seemed to have been waiting behind the door, entered and shook their hands, trying to conjure up a smile. He no longer had the youthful air of bygone days, when he used to spend the evening at her rooms in the Rue de la Cerisaie ; he looked overcome with weariness, he was mournful and much thinner, starting at every moment, as though he were uneasy about something behind him.

Clarisse remained to listen. Bachelard, who did not intend to speak before her, invited the counsellor to lunch.

"Now, do accept, Monsieur Vabre wants you. Madame will be kind enough to excuse—"

But the latter had at length caught sight of her sister hammering on the piano, and she slapped her and turned her out of the room, taking the same opportunity to cuff and drive away the little one with her saucepan. There was a most infernal uproar. The invalid aunt in the next room again started off yelling, thinking they were coming to beat her.

"Do you hear, my darling?" murmured Duveyrier, "these gentlemen have invited me to lunch."

But she was not listening to him, she was trying the instrument with frightened tenderness. For a month past, she had been learning to play the piano. It was the secret dream of her whole life, a far away ambition the realization of which could alone stamp her a woman of society. Having satisfied herself that there was nothing broken, she was about to prevent her lover from going, simply to annoy him, when Madame Bocquet once more bobbed her head in at the door, again hiding her skirt.

"Your music-master," said she.

At this Clarisse changed her mind, and called to Duveyrier :

"That's it, be off ! I'll lunch with Théodore. We don't want you."

The music-master, Théodore, was a Belgian with a large rosy face. She at once sat down before the instrument, and rubbing her fingers to make them less stiff, she placed them on the keys. For a moment Duveyrier, who was visibly greatly annoyed, hesitated. But the gentlemen were waiting for him, so he went to put on his boots. When he returned she was splashing about amongst the scales, emitting a tempest of false notes, which were making Auguste and Bachelard quite ill.

Yet he, who went half mad when his wife played selections from
Mozart or Beethoven, stood for a minute behind his mistress,
seeming to enjoy the sounds, in spite of the nervous contrac-
tions of his face; and, turning towards his two visitors, he murmured :

"She has a most extraordinary taste for music."

After kissing her on the hair, he discreetly withdrew, leaving
her with Théodore. In the anteroom, the big rascal of a
brother asked him in his jocular way for a franc for tobacco.
Then, as they went downstairs, Bachelard expressed surprise at
his conversion to the charms of the piano, and he swore he had
never disliked it, he talked of the ideal, saying how much
Clarisse's simple scales stirred his soul, yielding to his continual mania for having a bright side to his coarse masculine
appetites.

Down below, Trublot had given the driver a cigar, and was
listening to his history with the liveliest interest. The uncle
insisted on lunching at Foyot's; it was the proper time, and
they could talk better whilst eating. Then, when the cab had
managed to start off again, he told everything to Duveyrier,
who became very grave.

Auguste's uneasiness seemed to have increased at Clarisse's,
where he had not opened his mouth; and now, worn out by this
interminable drive, his head entirely a prey to a violent aching,
he abandoned himself.

When the counsellor questioned him as to what he intended
doing, he opened his eyes, and remained a moment filled with
anguish, then he repeated his former phrase :

"Why fight, of course ! "

Only, his voice was weaker, and he added as he closed his
eyes, as though to ask to be left alone,

"Unless you have anything else to suggest."

Then the gentlemen held a grand council in the midst of
the laborious jolts of the vehicle. Duveyrier, the same as
Bachelard, considered the duel indispensable; he was deeply
affected by it, on account of the blood likely to be spilt, a long
black stream of which he pictured soiling the stairs of his property; but honour demanded it, and one cannot compound with
honour. Trublot had broader views: it was too stupid to place
one's honour in what out of decency he termed a woman's
frailty. And Auguste approved what he said by a weary blink
of his eyelids, thoroughly incensed at last by the bellicose rage
of the two others, whose duty it was on the contrary to have

been conciliatory. In spite of his fatigue, he was obliged to relate once more the scene of the night before, the blow he had
given and the blow he had received; and soon the fact of the
adultery was lost sight of, the discussion bore solely upon these
two blows: they were commented upon, and analysed, as a
satisfactory solution was sought for.

"What refinement!" Trublot ended by contemptuously saying. "If they hit each other, well! they're quits."

Duveyrier and Bachelard looked at one another, evidently
shaken in their opinions. But just then they arrived at the restaurant, and the uncle declared that they would first of all have a
good lunch. It would help to clear their ideas. He stood treat,
ordering a copious meal, with costly dishes and wines, which
kept them three hours in a private room. The duel was not
even once mentioned. From the very beginning, the conversation had necessarily turned on the question of women, Fifi and
Clarisse were during the whole time explained, turned inside out, and pulled to pieces. Bachelard now admitted himself to have been in the wrong, so as not to appear to the counsellor as having been vilely chucked over; whilst the latter,
taking his revenge for the evening when the uncle had seen him
weep in the middle of the empty rooms in the Rue de la Cerisaie,
lied about his happiness, to the point of believing in it and being affected by it himself. Seated before them, Auguste, prevented by his neuralgia both from eating and drinking, appeared
to be listening, an elbow on the table, and a confused look in
his eyes. At dessert, Trublot recollected the driver, who had
been forgotten outside; and full of sympathy he sent him the
remnants of the dishes and what was left in the bottles; for,
said he, from certain things he had let drop, he had a suspicion
the man was an ex-priest. Three o'clock struck. Duveyrier
complained of being assessor at the next sitting of the assizes;
Bachelard, who was now very drunk, spat sideways on to Trublot's trousers, without the latter noticing it; and the day
would have been finished there, amidst the liqueurs, if Auguste
had not suddenly roused himself with a start.

"Well, what's going to be done?" asked he.

"Well! young 'un," replied the uncle, speaking most familiarly, "if you like, we'll settle matters nicely for you. It's stupid
to fight."

No one appeared surprised at this conclusion. Duveyrier
signified his approval with a nod of the head. The uncle continued :

"I'll go with Monsieur Duveyrier and see the fellow, and he shall apologise, or my name isn't Bachelard. The mere sight of me will make him cave in, just because I shall have no business there. I don't care a hang for anyone!"

Auguste shook him by the hand; but he did not seem to feel relieved, the pains in his head had become so unbearable. At length, they left the private room. Down in the street, the driver was still at lunch, inside the cab; and, completely intoxicated, he had to shake the crumbs out, digging Trublot fraternally in the stomach. Only, the horse, which had had nothing at all, refused to walk, with a despairing wag of the head. They pushed him, and he ended by going down the Rue de Tournon, as though he were rolling along. Four o'clock had struck, when the animal at length stopped in the Rue de Choiseul. Auguste had had the cab seven hours. Trublot, who remained inside, engaged it for himself, and declared that he would wait there for Bachelard, whom he wished to invite to dinner.

"Well! you have been a time," said Théophile to his brother, as he hastened to meet him. "I thought you were dead."

And directly the gentlemen had entered the warehouse, he related how the day had passed. He had been watching the house ever since nine o'clock. But nothing particular had occurred. At two o'clock, Valérie had gone to the Tuileries gardens with their son Camille. Then, towards half past three, he had seen Octave go out. And that was all. Nothing moved, not even at the Josserands'. Saturnin, who had been seeking his sister under the furniture, having gone up to ask for her, Madame Josserand had shut the door in his face, doubtless to get rid of him, saying that Berthe was not there. Since then, the madman had been prowling about with clenched teeth.

"Very well," said Bachelard, "we'll wait for the gentleman. We shall see him come in from here."

Auguste, whose head was in a whirl, was making great efforts to keep on his legs. Then, Duveyrier advised him to go to bed. There was no other cure for headache.

"Go up now, we no longer require you. We will inform you of the result. My dear fellow, you know you should avoid all emotions."

And the husband went up to lie down.

At five o'clock, the two others were still waiting for Octave. The latter, without any definite object, simply desirous of having some fresh air and of forgetting the events of the night, had at first passed before "The Ladies' Paradise," where he had stopped to wish Madame Hédouin good-day, as she stood in the doorway, dressed in deep mourning; and as he informed her of his having left the Vabres', she had quietly asked him why he did not return to her. It had all been settled in a moment, without a previous thought upon the subject. When he had again wished her good-day, after promising to come on the morrow, he continued his stroll, his mind filled with a vague regret. Chance was for ever upsetting his calculations. Various projects absorbed his thoughts, and he had been wandering about in the neighbourhood for an hour or more, when, on raising his head, he found himself in the obscure turning of the Passage Saint-Roch. Opposite to him, Valérie was taking leave of a bearded gentleman, at the door of a low lodging-house in the darkest corner. She blushed and hastened away, pushing open the padded door of the church; then, seeing that the young man was following her and smiling, she preferred to await him under the porch, where they conversed together very cordially.

"You run away from me," said he. "Are you then angry with me?"

"Angry?" repeated she, "why should I be angry? Ah! they may quarrel and eat each other up if they like, it doesn't matter to me!"

She was speaking of her relations. And she at once gave vent to her old rancour against Berthe, making at first simply allusions so as to sound the young man; then, when she felt he was secretly weary of his mistress, being still exasperated with the night's proceedings, she no longer restrained herself, but poured out her heart. To think that that woman had accused her of selling herself—she, who never accepted a sou, not even a present! Yes, though, a few flowers at times, some bunches of violets. And now everybody knew which of the two was the one to sell herself. She had prophesied that one day it would be known how much she could be bought for.

"It cost you more than a bunch of violets, did it not?" asked she.

"Yes, yes," murmured he basely.

In his turn he let out some disagreeable things about Berthe, saying that she was spiteful, and even making her out to be too fat, as though seeking to avenge himself for the worry she was causing him. He had been waiting all day for her husband's seconds, and he was then returning home to see if any one had called. It was a most stupid adventure; she might very well

have prevented this duel taking place.   He ended by relating
all that had occurred at their ridiculous meeting—their quarrel,
then Auguste's arrival on the scene, before they had even exchanged a caress.

"On all I hold most sacred," said he, "I had not even
touched her."

Valérie laughed, and was getting quite excited.   She gradually yielded to the tender intimacy of this exchange of confidences, drawing nearer to Octave as though to some female
friend who knew all.   At times, a devotee coming from the
church disturbed them ; then the door gently closed to again,
and they once more found themselves alone in the drum, hung
with green baize, as though in the innermost recesses of some
discreet and religious asylum.

" I scarcely know why I live with such people," resumed she,
returning to the subject of her relations.   "Oh ! no doubt, I
am not free from reproach on my side.   But, frankly, I cannot
feel any remorse, they affect me so little.   And yet if I were to
tell you how much love bores me !"

"Come now, not so much as all that !" said Octave gaily.
" People are not always as silly as we were yesterday.   There
are blissful moments."

Then she confessed herself.   It was not entirely the hatred
she felt for her husband, the continual fever which shook his
frame, his impotence, nor yet his perpetual blubbering like a
little boy, which had caused her to misbehave herself six
months after her marriage ; no, she often did it involuntarily,
solely because her head got filled with things of which she was
unable to explain the why and the wherefore.   Everything
gave way ; she became quite ill, and could almost kill herself.
Then, as there was nothing to restrain her, she might as well
take that leap as another.

" But really now, do you never have a nice time of it ?" again
asked Octave.

" Well, never like people describe," replied she.

He looked at her full of a pitying sympathy.   All for
nothing, and without the least pleasure.   It was certainly not
worth the trouble she gave herself, in her continual fear of
being caught.   And he especially felt a certain relief to his
pride, for he had always suffered a little at heart from her old
disdain.   He recalled the circumstance to her.

" You remember, after one of your attacks ?"

" Oh ! yes, I remember.   Still, I did not dislike you ; but listen ! it is far better as it is, we should be detesting each other now."

She gave him her little gloved hand. He squeezed it, as he repeated :

" You are right, it is better as it is. Really, one only cares for the women one has had nothing to do with."

It was quite a blissful moment. They stood for a while hand in hand, deeply affected. Then, without another word, they pushed open the padded door of the church, inside which she had left her son Camille in care of the woman who let out the chairs. The child had fallen asleep. She made him kneel down, and did the same herself for a minute, burying her face in her hands, as though in the midst of a fervent prayer. And she was rising to her feet when Abbé Mauduit, who was coming from a confessional, greeted her with a paternal smile.

Octave had simply passed through the church. When he returned home every one was on the alert. Trublot alone, who was dreaming in the cab, did not see him. Tradespeople standing at their doors looked at him gravely. The stationer opposite was still surveying the front of the house, as though to search the very stones ; but the charcoal-dealer and the greengrocer had already become calmer, and the neighbourhood was relaps- . ing into its chilly dignity. In the doorway as Octave passed, Lisa, who was gossiping with Adèle, had to content herself with merely staring at him ; and both resumed their complaints of the dear price of poultry beneath the stern look of Monsieur Gourd, who bowed to the young man. As the latter was going up to his room Madame Juzeur, who had been on the watch ever since the morning, slightly opened her door, and, seizing hold of his hands, drew him into her anteroom, where she kissed him on the forehead and murmured : ·

" Poor child ! There, I won't keep you. Come back and talk to me when it's all over."

And he had scarcely reached his own apartment when Duveyrier and Bachelard called. At first, amazed at seeing the uncle, he wished to give them the names of two of his friends. But these gentlemen, without answering, spoke of their age, and preached him a sermon on his misconduct. Then, as in the course of conversation he announced his intention of leaving the house at the earliest possible moment, they both solemnly declared that that proof of his discretion was quite sufficient. There had been more than enough scandal, the time had come when respectable people had the right to expect them to make the sacrifice of their passions. Duveyrier accepted Octave's notice to quit on the spot and withdrew, whilst behind his back Bachelard invited the young man to dine with him that evening.

"Mind, I count upon you. We're on the spree, Trublot is waiting below. I don't care a button for Eléonore. But I don't wish to see her, and I'll go down first, so that no one shall meet us together."

He took his departure, and, five minutes later, Octave, delighted with the issue of affairs, joined him below. He slipped into the cab, and the melancholy horse, which had been dragging the husband about for seven hours, limped along with them to a restaurant near the Halles, where some marvellous tripe was to be obtained.

Duveyrier had gone back to Théophile in the warehouse. Valérie also had just come in, and all three were talking together when Clotilde herself returned from a concert. She had gone there, moreover, with a mind perfectly at ease, certain, said she, that some arrangement satisfactory to every one would be arrived at. Then ensued a pause, a momentary embarrassment between the two families. Théophile, seized with an abominable fit of coughing, was almost spitting his teeth out. As it was to their mutual interest to be reconciled, they ended by taking advantage of the emotion into which the new family troubles had plunged them. The two women embraced, Duveyrier swore to Théophile that the Vabre inheritance was ruining him, yet he promised to indemnify him by remitting his rent for three years.

"I must go and tranquillise poor Auguste," at length observed the counsellor.

He was ascending the stairs when some terrible cries, resembling those of an animal being butchered, issued from the bedroom. It was Saturnin who, armed with his kitchen knife, had noiselessly crept as far as the alcove ; and there, his eyes as red as flaming coals, his mouth covered with foam, he had rushed upon Auguste.

"Tell me, where have you put her ?" cried he. "Give her back to me or I'll bleed you like a pig !"

The husband, suddenly roused from his painful slumber, tried to fly. But the madman, with the strength of his fixed idea, had caught him by the tail of his shirt, and, pushing him back on the mattress, placing his neck on the edge of the bed, over a basin which happened to be there, he held him in the position of an animal at the slaughter-house.

SATURNIN IN A FIT OF MADNESS ATTEMPTING TO BLEED AUGUSTE LIKE A PIG.

p. 318.

"Ah! it's all right this time. I'm going to bleed you—I'm going to bleed you like a pig!"

Fortunately, the others arrived and were able to release the victim. But Saturnin, who was raving mad, had to be shut up; and, two hours later, the commissary of police having been sent for, he was taken for the second time to the Asile des Moulineaux, with the consent of the family. Poor Auguste lay trembling. He said to Duveyrier, who informed him of the arrangement that had been come to with Octave,

"No, I should have preferred to have fought the duel. One cannot defend oneself against a madman. Why has he such a mania for wishing to bleed me, the brigand? because his sister has made a cuckold of me? Ah! I've had enough of it, my friend, I've had enough of it, on my word of honour!"

CHAPTER XVI.

On the Wednesday morning, when Marie brought Berthe to
Madame Josserand, the latter, bursting with anger at the
thought of an adventure which she felt was a sad blow to her
pride, became quite pale and unable to utter a word.

She caught hold of her daughter's hand with the roughness
of a teacher dragging a refractory scholar to the black-hole,
and, leading her to Hortense's room, she pushed her inside,
saying at length :

"Hide yourself, never show yourself again. You will kill
your father if you do."

Hortense, who was washing, remained lost in wonder.
Red with shame, Berthe threw herself on the tumbled bed, and
burst into sobs. She had expected an immediate and violent
explanation. She had prepared a whole line of defence, determined to shout also directly her mother went too far ; and this
silent harshness, this way of treating her like a little girl who
has eaten a pot of jam, left her without strength, bringing her
back to the terrors of her childhood, to the tears she used to
shed in corners, with great promises of future obedience.

"What's up? What ever have you done?" asked her sister,
whose astonishment increased on seeing her wrapped in an old
shawl which Marie had lent her. "Has poor Auguste fallen ill
at Lyons?"

But Berthe would not answer. No, later on ; there were
things she could not speak about ; and she beseeched Hortense
to go away, to let her have the room to herself, so that she
could at least weep there in peace. The day passed thus.
Monsieur Josserand had gone off to his office, without having
the faintest idea of what had occurred ; then, when he returned
home in the evening, Berthe still remained in hiding. As she
had refused all food, she ended by ravenously devouring the
little dinner which Adèle brought to her in secret. The maid
remained watching her, and, in presence of her appetite, said:

"Don't worry yourself so much, pick up your strength. The

house is quite quiet. And as for any one being killed or wounded, there's nobody hurt at all."

"Ah!" said the young woman.

She questioned Adèle, who gave her a long account of how the day had passed, the duel which had not come off, what Monsieur Auguste had said, and what the Duveyriers and the Vabres had done. She listened to her, and seemed to live again, gobbling everything up, and asking for more bread. In all truth it was foolish of her to take the matter so much to heart when the others seemed to be already consoled!

So, on Hortense coming to join her towards ten o'clock, she greeted her gaily, and with dry eyes. And, smothering their laughter, they amused themselves when she tried on one of her sister's dressing-gowns which was too tight for her: her bosom, which marriage had developed, almost burst the material. All the same, she would be able to get it on to-morrow by altering the buttons. Both fancied themselves back again in the days of their youth, all alone in this room where they had spent years side by side. This touched them and brought them nearer to one another in an affection which they had not felt for many a long day. They had to sleep together, for Madame Josserand had got rid of the little bed which used to be Berthe's. When they were stretched side by side, with the candle blown out, and their eyes wide open in the darkness, they talked for a long while, unable to get to sleep.

"So you won't tell me?" asked Hortense again.

"But, my darling," answered Berthe, "you're not married. I really can't. It's a quarrel I've had with Auguste. He came back, you know—"

And as she interrupted herself, her sister resumed impatiently,

"Get along with you! What a fuss! Good heavens! at my age, I'm quite old enough to know!"

Then Berthe confessed herself, at first choosing her words, then letting out everything, talking of Octave and talking of Auguste. Hortense listened as she lay on her back in the dark, and merely uttered a few words to question her sister or to give an opinion: "What did he say to you then? And you, how did you feel? Well, that's funny, I shouldn't like that! Ah! really, so that's the way!" Midnight, one o'clock, then two struck; still they went on with the story, their limbs little by little irritated by the sheets, and themselves gradually becoming drowsy. In this semi-hallucination Berthe forgot her sister,

x

and began to think aloud, relieving alike her body and her mind of the most delicate confidences.

"Oh! as for me, with Verdier, it will be very simple," declared Hortense, abruptly.   "I shall do just as he wishes."

At the mention of Verdier's name Berthe made a movement of surprise. She thought the marriage was broken off, for the woman with whom he had been living for fifteen years past had just had a child, at the very moment that he intended leaving her.

"Do you then expect to marry him all the same?" asked she.

"Well! and why not? I was stupid enough to wait too long. But the child will die. It's a girl, and all scrofulous."

And, spitting out the word "mistress," with a feeling of disgust, she displayed all the hatred of a virtuous middle-class woman of a marriageable age against the creature who had been so long living with a man. It was all a manœuvre, her brat, and nothing more! Yes, a pretext she had invented, when she saw that Verdier, after buying her some chemises so as not to send her away naked, wished to habituate her to an approaching separation, by sleeping out more and more frequently. In short, one would wait and see.

"Poor woman!" Berthe was unable to help exclaiming.

"How, poor woman!" cried Hortense sourly. "It's easy to see that you also have things to reproach yourself with!"

She at once regretted her cruelty, and taking her sister in her arms, kissed her and swore that she did not mean it.   Then they were silent. But still they could not sleep, so continued the story, their eyes wide open in the darkness.

The next morning, Monsieur Josserand did not feel very well. Up till two o'clock, he had persisted in addressing wrappers, in spite of a lowness of spirits, and of a gradual loss of strength, of which he had been complaining for some time. He got up, however, and dressed himself; but, when he was on the point of starting for his office, he felt so feeble that he sent a messenger with a letter to inform the brothers Bernheim of his indisposition.

The family were about to have their breakfast. They took the meal without any tablecloth, in the dining-room, still full of the fumes of the dinner of the previous evening. The ladies would come in anyhow, still wet from recent washing of themselves, and their hair simply gathered up in a knot. On seeing her husband remain, Madame Josserand decided not to hide Berthe any longer; she was already sick of all the mystery,

and was moreover expecting every minute to see Auguste
come up and create a disturbance.

"What ! you're going to breakfast with us ! whatever is the
matter ?" asked the father in great surprise, on beholding his
daughter, her eyes heavy with sleep, her bosom half bursting
through Hortense's too tight dressing-gown.

"My husband has written to say that he is obliged to stay
at Lyons," answered she, "so I thought of spending the day
with you."

It was a story which had been arranged between the two
sisters. Madame Josserand, who maintained her stiffness of a
schoolmistress, did not give her the lie. But the father looked
at Berthe, in a confused way, and as though foreboding some
misfortune ; and the story appearing rather extraordinary to
him, he was about to ask how the shop would get on without
her, when she went and kissed him on both cheeks, in the gay
and wheedling way of other days.

"Is it really true ? You are not hiding anything from me ?"
murmured he.

"What an idea ! why should I hide anything from you ?"

Madame Josserand merely allowed herself to shrug her
shoulders. What was the use of all those precautions ? to gain
an hour, perhaps ; it was not worth while : the father would
always have to receive the blow in the end. The breakfast,
however, passed off most pleasantly. Monsieur Josserand,
delighted at finding himself between his two daughters again,
fancied they were back in the old days, when, scarcely awake,
they used to amuse him with the recital of their girlish dreams.
To him, they still retained their delightful odour of youth, as,
with their elbows on the table, they dipped their bread into
their coffee, and laughed with their mouths full. And all the
past seemed to return, when, opposite to them, he beheld the
inflexible countenance of their mother, enormous and overflowing in an old green silk dress, which she was wearing out on a
morning without stays.

But a regrettable scene spoilt the end of the breakfast. All
on a sudden, Madame Josserand addressed the servant :

"Whatever are you eating ?"

For some little while past she had been watching her.
Adèle, dragging her shoes after her, turned clumsily round the
table.

"Nothing, madame," replied she.

"How ! nothing ! You're chewing ; I'm not blind. See !

you've still got your mouth full of it. Oh ! it's no use drawing in your cheeks ; its easy to see in spite of that. And you've got some in your pocket, haven't you ? "

Adèle became confused, and tried to draw back. But Madame Josserand caught hold of her by the skirt.

" For a quarter of an hour past, I've been watching you take something out of there and thrust it under your nose, after hiding it in your hand. It must be something very good. Let me see what it is."

She dived into the pocket in her turn, and withdrew a handful of cooked prunes. The juice was still trickling from them.

" What is this ? " cried she furiously.

" Prunes, madame," said the servant, who, seeing herself caught, became insolent.

" Ah ! you eat my prunes ! So that's why they go so quickly and never again appear on the table ! I could never have believed it possible ; prunes ! in a pocket ! "

And she also accused her of drinking her vinegar. Everything disappeared ; one could not even leave a potato about without being certain of never seeing it again.

" You're a regular gulf, my girl."

" Give me sufficient to eat," retorted Adèle boldly, " and then I won't touch your potatoes."

This was too much. Madame Josserand rose from her seat, majestic and terrible.

" Hold your tongue, and don't answer me ! Oh ! I know, it's the other servants who've spoilt you. Directly a simpleton arrives in a house from the country, all the hussies in the place at once put her up to all sorts of horrors. You no longer go to mass, and now you steal ! "

Adèle, who had indeed been worked up by Lisa and Julie, did not yield.

" When I was a simpleton, as you say, you should not have taken advantage of me. It's ended now."

" Leave the room, I discharge you ! " cried Madame Josserand, pointing to the door with a tragical gesture.

She sat down quite shaken, whilst the maid, without hurrying herself, dragged her shoes after her and swallowed another prune before returning to the kitchen. She was discharged in this way regularly once a week, so that it no longer caused her the least emotion. A painful silence ensued at the table. At length Hortense observed that it was no good always discharging her if she was always kept. No doubt she stole, and was becoming insolent; but it might just as well be her as another, for she at least consented to wait upon them, whereas any one else would not have put up with them for a week, even though she were allowed to drink the vinegar and to stuff her pockets full of prunes.

The breakfast, however, finished in the most affectionate intimacy. Monsieur Josserand, deeply moved, spoke of poor Saturnin, who had had to be taken away the day before during his absence from home; and as he believed in a sudden fit of raving madness, with which his son had been seized in the middle of the shop, for such was the story that had been told him. Then, as he complained of never seeing Léon, Madame Josserand, who had become dumb again, curtly declared that she was expecting him that very day, perhaps he would come to lunch. For a week past the young man had broken off his relations with Madame Dambreville, who, to keep her promise, wished to marry him to a dry and swarthy widow; but he was determined to marry a niece of Monsieur Dambreville, a very rich and lovely creole, who had arrived at her uncle's in the month of September, after the death of her father in the West Indies. And there had been terrible scenes between the two lovers; Madame Dambreville, devoured by jealousy, refused to give her niece to Léon, not caring to find herself supplanted by that adorable flower of youth.

"How is the marriage getting on?" asked Monsieur Josserand discreetly.

At first the mother replied in well-chosen phrases, on account of Hortense. Now, she was at the feet of her son, a young fellow who was sure to succeed; and she would even throw his name in the father's face at times, saying that, thank goodness! he took after her, and would never leave his wife without a pair of shoes. She little by little warmed with her subject.

"In short, he's had enough of it! It was all very well for a while, and did him no harm. But, if the aunt doesn't give him the niece, good night! he'll cut off all supplies. I think he's quite right."

Hortense, out of decency, sipped her coffee, making a show of obliterating herself behind the cup; whilst Berthe, who for the future might hear anything, gave a slight pout of repugnance at her brother's successes. The family were about to rise from table, and Monsieur Josserand, who was more cheerful and feeling much better, was talking of going to his office all the same, when Adèle brought in a card. The person was waiting in the drawing-room.

"What, it's her! and at this hour of the morning!" exclaimed Madame Josserand. "And I who haven't got my stays on! So much the worse! it's time I gave her a piece of my mind!"

The visitor was Madame Dambreville. The father and his two daughters remained talking in the dining-room, whilst the mother directed her steps to the drawing-room. But she stopped at the door before opening it, and anxiously examined her old green silk dress, trying to button it up, picking off the threads gathered from the floors, and driving in her immense bosom with a tap.

"Excuse me, dear madame," said the visitor with a smile. "I was passing, so could not resist calling to see how you were."

She was all laced up, and had her hair done in the most correct style, while she conversed in the easy way of an amiable woman, who had just come up to wish a friend good day. Only, her smile trembled, and behind her society graces one could detect a frightful anguish, with which her whole frame quivered. She at first talked of all sorts of things, avoiding any mention of Léon's name, but at length she took from her pocket a letter which she had just received from him.

"Oh! such a letter, such a letter," murmured she, in an altered voice, half-broken with sobs. "Whatever is it he has to complain of, dear madame? He says he will never come to our house again!"

And her feverish hand held out the letter, which quite shook as she offered it to Madame Josserand. The latter read it coldly. It was a breaking off of the acquaintance in three lines of most cruel conciseness.

"Really!" said she as she returned the letter, "Léon is not perhaps altogether wrong—"

But Madame Dambreville at once began to praise up the widow—a woman scarcely thirty-five years old, most accomplished and sufficiently rich, who would make a Minister of her husband, she was so active. In short, she had kept her promises, she had found a fine match for Léon; whatever had he to be angry about? And, without waiting for a reply, making up her mind with a nervous start, she named Raymonde, her niece. Really now, was it possible? a chit of sixteen, a young savage who knew nothing of life!

"Why not?" Madame Josserand kept repeating at each interrogation, "why not, if he loves her?"

No! no! he did not love her—he could not love her!

Madame Dambreville struggled, and gradually abandoned herself.

"Come," cried she, "I only ask him for a little gratitude. It's I who have made him, it's thanks to me that he is an auditor, and he will receive a higher appointment on his wedding-day. Madame, I implore you, tell him to return to me, tell him to do me that pleasure. I appeal to his heart, to your motherly heart, yes, to all that is noble in your nature—"

She clasped her hands, her words became inarticulate. A pause ensued, during which they were standing face to face. Then suddenly she burst out into the most bitter sobs, vanquished, and no longer mistress of herself.

"Not with Raymonde," stuttered she, "oh! no, not with Raymonde!"

It was the rage of love, the cry of a woman who refuses to become old, who hangs on to the last man in the ardent crisis of the change of life. She had seized hold of Madame Josserand's hands, she bathed them with her tears, owning everything to the mother, humbling herself before her, repeating that she alone had any influence over her son, swearing to be as devoted as a servant, if she would only make him return to her. Of course, she had not come to say all this; she had promised herself, on the contrary, to let none of it be known; but her heart was breaking—it was not her fault.

"Keep quiet, my dear, you make me quite ashamed," replied Madame Josserand, angrily. "I have daughters who might hear you. I know nothing, and I don't wish to know anything. If you have affairs with my son, you must settle them together. I will never place myself in a questionable position."

Yet she loaded her with advice. At her age, one should resign oneself to the inevitable. God would be of great help to her. But she must yield up her niece, if she wished to offer her sacrifice to heaven as an expiation. Moreover, the widow did not suit Léon at all; he required a wife with a pleasant face to preside at his dinner-table. And she spoke admiringly of her son, flattered in her pride, minutely detailing him, and showing him to be worthy of the loveliest women.

"Just think, dear friend, he is not yet thirty. I should be grieved to appear unkind, but you might be his mother. Oh, he knows what he owes you, and I myself am filled with gratitude. You will remain his guardian angel. Only, when a thing is ended, it is ended. You could not possibly have hoped to have kept him always!"

And as the wretched woman refused to listen to reason, wishing simply to have him back, and at once, the mother grew quite angry.

"Do have done, madame! It is kind on my part to be so obliging. The boy will have no more of it! it is easily to be understood. Look at yourself, pray! It is I now who would call him back to his duty, if he submitted again to your exactions; for, I ask you, what good can there be in it for both of you in future? It so happens that he is coming here, and if you have counted on me—"

Of all these words, Madame Dambreville only heard the last phrase. For a week past she had been running about after Léon, without succeeding in seeing him. Her face brightened up; she uttered this cry from her heart:

"As he is coming, I shall stay!"

From that moment she made herself at home, seating herself like a heavy mass in an arm-chair, her eyes fixed on vacancy, declining any further questioning with the obstinacy of an animal which will not yield, even when beaten. Madame Josserand, bitterly regretting having said too much, exasperated with this sort of mile-stone which had become a fixture in her drawing-room, yet not daring to turn her out, ended by leaving her to herself. Moreover, some sounds coming from the dining-room made her feel uneasy. She fancied she recognised Auguste's voice.

"On my word of honour! madame, one never heard of such a thing before!" said she, violently slamming the door. "It is most indiscreet!"

It was indeed Auguste, who had come up to have the explanation with his wife's parents which he had been meditating since the day before. Monsieur Josserand, feeling jollier still, and more inclined for a little enjoyment than for office duties, was proposing a walk to his daughters, when Adèle came and announced Madame Berthe's husband. It created quite a scare. The young woman turned pale.

"What! your husband?" said the father. "But he was at Lyons! Ah! you were not speaking the truth. There is some misfortune; for two days past I have seemed to feel it."

And, as she rose from her seat, he detained her.

"Tell me, have you been quarrelling again? about money, is it not? Eh? perhaps because of the dowry, of the ten thousand francs we have not paid him?"

"Yes, yes, that's it," stammered Berthe, who released herself and fled.

Hortense also had risen. She ran after her sister, and both took refuge in her room. Their flying skirts left a breath of panic behind them, the father suddenly found himself alone at the table, in the middle of the silent dining-room. All the signs of illness returned to his countenance, a cadaverous paleness, a desperate weariness of life. The hour which he dreaded, which he had been awaiting with shame, mingled with anguish, had arrived. His son-in-law was about to speak of the assurance ; and he would have to own to the swindling expedient to which he had consented.

"Come in, come in, my dear Auguste," said he in a choking tone of voice. "Berthe has just told me of your quarrel. I'm not very well, and they've been spoiling me. I regret immensely not being able to give you that money. I did wrong in promising, I know—"

He continued painfully, with the air of a guilty man making avowals. Auguste listened to him in surprise. He had been obtaining information, and knew all about the way he had been taken in with the assurance ; but he would not have dared to demand the payment of the first ten thousand francs, for fear that the terrible Madame Josserand might first send him to old Vabre's tomb to receive the ten thousand francs due from him. However, as the matter was named to him, he started on that. It was a first grievance.

"Yes, sir, I know all. You completely took me in with your lies. I don't mind so much not having the money ; but it's the hypocrisy of the thing which exasperates me ! Why all that nonsense about an assurance which did not exist ? Why give yourself such airs of tenderness and affection, by offering to advance sums which, according to you, you would not be entitled to receive till three years later ? And you were not even blessed with a sou ! Such behaviour has only one name in every country."

Monsieur Josserand opened his mouth to exclaim : " It is not I ; it is them ! " But he was ashamed to accuse the family ; he bowed his head, thus accepting the responsibility of the disgraceful action. Auguste continued :

"Moreover, every one was against me, even that Duveyrier behaved like a rascal, with his scoundrel of a notary ; for I asked to have the assurance mentioned in the contract, as a guarantee, and I was made to shut up. Had I insisted, though, you would have been guilty of swindling. Yes, sir, swindling !"

At this accusation, the father, who was very pale, rose to his

feet, and he was about to answer, to offer his labour, to purchase his daughter's happiness with all of his existence that remained to him, when Madame Josserand, quite beside herself
through Madame Dambreville's obstinacy, no longer thinking of
her old green silk dress, now splitting, through the heaving of
her angry bosom, entered like a blast of wind.

"Eh? what?" cried she; "who talks of swindling? Is it
you, sir? You would do better, sir, to go first to Père-Lachaise
cemetery to see if it's your father's pay-day!"

Auguste had expected this, but he was all the same horribly
annoyed. She went on, with head erect, and quite crushing in
her audacity:

"We've got them, your ten thousand francs. Yes, they're
there in a drawer. But we will only give them you when
Monsieur Vabre returns to give you the others. What a
family! a gambler of a father who lets us all in, and a thief of
a brother-in-law who pops the inheritance into his own pocket!"

"Thief! thief!" stammered Auguste, unable to contain himself any longer; "the thieves are here, madame!"

They both stood with heated countenances in front of each
other. Monsieur Josserand, quite upset by all this wrangling,
separated them. He beseeched them to be calm; and, trembling all over, he was obliged to sit down again.

"Any how," resumed the son-in-law after a pause, "I won't
have any strumpet in my home. Keep your money and keep
your daughter. That is what I came up to tell you."

"You are changing the subject," quietly observed the mother.
"Very well, we will discuss the fresh one."

But the father, too weak to rise, surveyed them with a
frightened air. He no longer understood what they were
talking about. Who was the strumpet? Then when, on
listening to them, he learnt that it was his daughter, something
gave way within him—there was a gaping wound, through
which the rest of his life slowly ebbed away. Good heavens!
was his child to be the cause of his death? Was he to be
punished for all his weakness through her, whom he had not
known how to bring up? The idea that she was in debt, and
continually quarrelling with her husband, was already the bane
of his old age, and made him endure all the torments of his
own life over again. And now she had descended to adultery,
to that last degree of woman's wickedness, which roused the
worthy man's simple, honest indignation. Speechless and icy
cold, he listened to the quarrel of the other two.

"I told you she would deceive me!" cried Auguste with an air of indignant triumph.

"And I answered that you were doing everything to lead to such a result!" declared Madame Josserand victoriously. "Oh! I do not pretend that Berthe is right; what she has done is simply idiotic; and she won't lose anything by waiting. I shall let her know what I think of it. But, however, as she is not present, I can state the fact, you alone are guilty."

"What! I guilty?"

"Undoubtedly, my dear fellow. You don't know how to deal with women. Here's an instance! Do you even deign to come to my Tuesday receptions? No, you perhaps put in an appearance three times during the season, and then only stay half-an-hour. Though one may have headaches, one should be polite. Oh! of course, it's no great crime; any how it judges you, you don't know how to live."

Her voice hissed with a slowly gathered rancour; for, on marrying her daughter, she had above all counted on her son-in-law to fill her drawing-room. And he brought no one, he did not even come himself; it was the end of one of her dreams, she would never be able to struggle against the Duveyriers' choruses.

"However," added she ironically, "I force no one to come and amuse himself in my home."

"The truth is, it is not very amusing there," replied he, out of all patience.

This threw her into a towering rage.

"That's it, insult away! Learn, sir, that I might have all the high life of Paris if I wished, and that I was not looking to you to help me to keep my rank in society!"

There was no longer any question of Berthe, the adultery had disappeared before this personal quarrel. Monsieur Josserand continued to listen to them, as though he were tossing about in the midst of some nightmare. It was not possible, his daughter could not have caused him this grief; and he ended by painfully rising again from his seat and going, without saying a word, in search of Berthe. Directly she was there, she would throw herself into Auguste's arms, and then everything would be explained and forgotten. He found her in the midst of a quarrel with Hortense, who was urging her to implore her husband's forgiveness, having already had enough of her, and being unwilling to share her room any longer. The young woman resisted, yet she ended by following her father. As they returned to the dining-room, where the breakfast cups were still scattered over the table, Madame Josserand was exclaiming :

"No, on my word of honour ! I don't pity you."

On catching sight of Berthe she stopped speaking, and again retired into her stern majesty. When his wife appeared before him, Auguste made a gesture of protest, as though to remove her from his path.

"Come," said Monsieur Josserand in his gentle and trembling voice, "what is the matter with you all ? I can't make it out ; you will drive me mad with all your quarrelling. Your husband is mistaken, is he not, my child ? You will explain things to him. You must have a little consideration for your old parents. Embrace each other, now come, do it for my sake."

Berthe, who would all the same have kissed Auguste, stood there awkwardly, and half-choked by her dressing-gown, on seeing him draw back with an air of tragical repugnance.

"What ! you refuse to, my darling ?" continued the father. "You should take the first step. And you, my dear boy, encourage her, be indulgent."

The husband at length gave free vent to his anger.

"Encourage her, not if I know it ! I found her in her chemise, sir ! and with that man ! Do you take me for a fool, that you wish me to kiss her ! In her chemise, sir !"

Monsieur Josserand stood lost, in amazement. Then he caught hold of Berthe's arm.

"You say nothing ; can it be true ? On your knees, then !"

But Auguste had reached the door. He was hastening away.

"Your comedies are useless ! they don't take me in ! Don't try to shove her on my shoulders again, I've had her once too often. You hear me, never again ! I would sooner go to law about it. Pass her on to some one else, if she's in your way. And, besides, you're no better than she is !"

He waited till he was in the anteroom, and then further relieved himself by shouting out these last words :

"Yes, when one makes a strumpet of one's daughter, one should not push her into a respectable man's arms !"

The outer door banged, and a profound silence ensued. Berthe had mechanically gone back to her seat at the table, lowering her eyes, and looking at the coffee dregs in the bottom of her cup ; whilst her mother sharply walked about, carried away by the tempest of her violent emotions. The father, utterly worn out, and with a face as white as that of a corpse, had sat down all by himself at the other end of the room, against the wall. An odour of rancid butter, butter of inferior quality purposely bought at the Halles, quite infected the apartment.

"Now that that vulgar person has gone," said Madame Josserand, "one may be able to hear oneself speak. Ah! sir, these are the results of your incapacity. Do you at length acknowledge your errors? think you that such quarrels would be picked with either of the brothers Bernheim, with one of the owners of the Saint-Joseph glass works? No, you cannot think so. If you had listened to me, if you had simply pocketed your employers, that vulgar person would have been at our feet, for he evidently only wants money. Have money and people will respect you, sir. It is better to create envy than pity. Whenever I have had twenty sous, I have always said that I had forty. But you, sir, you don't care if I go out barefooted, you have disgracefully deceived your wife and your daughters in dragging them through this beggar's existence. Oh! do not deny it, it is the cause of all our misfortunes!"

Monsieur Josserand, with a lifeless look in his eyes, had not even stirred. She had stopped before him, with an enraged desire for a row; then, seeing he did not move, she continued to pace the room.

"Yes, yes, be disdainful. You know it will not affect me much. And we will see if you will again dare to speak ill of my relations after all that yours have done. Uncle Bachelard is quite a star! my sister is most polite! Listen, do you wish to know my opinion? well! it is that if my father had not died, you would have killed him. As for your father—"

Monsieur Josserand's face became whiter than ever as he remarked:

"I beseech you, Eléonore. I abandon my father to you, and also all my relations. Only, I beseech you, let me be. I do not feel well."

Berthe, taking pity on him, raised her head.

"Do leave him alone, mamma," said she.

So, turning towards her daughter, Madame Josserand resumed more violently than ever:

"I've been keeping you for the last, you won't lose by waiting! Yes, ever since yesterday I've been bottling it up. But, I warn you, I can no longer keep it in—I can no longer keep it in. With that counter-jumper, I can scarcely believe it! Have you, then, lost all pride? I thought that you were making use of him, that you were just sufficiently amiable to cause him to interest himself in the business downstairs ; and I assisted you, . I encouraged him. In short, tell me what advantage you saw in it all ? ”

“ None whatever,” stammered the young woman.

“ Then why did you take up with him ? It was even more stupid than wicked.”

“ How absurd you are, mamma : one can never explain such things.”

Madame Josserand was again walking about.

“ Ah ! you can't explain ! Well ! but you ought to be able to ! There is not the slightest shadow of sense in misbehaving oneself like that, and it is this which exasperates me ! Did I ever tell you to deceive your husband ? did I ever deceive your father ? He is here, ask him. Let him say if he ever caught me with any other man.”

Her pace slackened and became quite majestic ; and she slapped herself on her green bodice, driving her breasts back under her arms.

“ Nothing, not a fault, not the least forgetfulness, even in thought. My life has been a chaste one. Yet God knows what I have had to put up with from your father ! I have had every excuse ; many women would have avenged themselves. But I had some sense, and that saved me. Therefore, as you see, he has not a word to say against me. He remains there on his chair without being able to make a single complaint. I have right on my side, I am virtuous. Ah ! you big ninny, you have no idea how stupid you have been ! ”

And she doctorally gave a lecture on morality in its bearings to adultery. · Was not Auguste now in a position to act the master to her ? She had supplied him with a terrible weapon. Even if they lived together again, she could never have the least argument with him, without being shut up at once. Eh ? a pretty position ! how pleasant it would be, always having to bend her back ! It was all over, she must now bid good-bye to all the little benefits she might have secured from an obedient husband, from whom she might have exacted every kindness and consideration. No, it were far better to live virtuous, than to no longer have the upper hand in one's own home !

“ Before heaven !” said she, “I swear I would have restrained myself, even if the Emperor had pestered me ! One loses too much.”

She took a few steps in silence, apparently reflecting, and then added,

“ Moreover, it is the greatest possible shame.”

Monsieur Josserand looked at her, looked at his daughter, and his lips moved, though no sound came from them; and his whole suffering being conjured them to put an end to this cruel explanation. But Berthe, who bent before violence, was wounded by her mother's lesson. She at length rebelled, for she was quite unconscious of her fault, thanks to the old education which she had received when a girl in search of a husband.

"Well!" said she, boldly planting her elbows on the table, "you should not have made me marry a man I did not love. Now I hate him, and I have taken another."

And so she went on. All the story of her marriage was again gone over in her short phrases, which she let out little by little: the three winters spent in angling for men, the fellows of every colour into whose arms she was thrown, and the ill-success attending this offer of her body in the authorised thoroughfares of middle-class drawing-rooms; then, all that which mothers teach dowerless girls, a regular course of decent and permitted prostitution, the contact of the flesh when dancing, hands abandoned behind doors, the immodesty of innocence speculating on the appetites of simpletons; then, the husband hooked one fine evening, just like a street-walker landing her man, the husband caught behind a curtain, excited and falling into the trap, in the fever of his desire.

"In short, he bores me and I bore him," declared she. "It's not my fault, we don't understand one another. As early as the morrow of our wedding-day, he looked as though he thought we had taken him in; yes, he was cold and put out, just like when he has a bad day's sale. For my part, I did not amuse myself particularly with him. Really! I don't think much of marriage if it offers no more pleasure than that! And that's how it all began. So much the worse! it was bound to come; I'm not the most guilty."

She left off speaking, but shortly added with an air of profound conviction:

"Ah! mamma, how well I understand you now! You remember, when you told us you had had more than enough of it."

Madame Josserand, standing up before her, had been listening for a minute with indignant amazement.

"Eh? I said that!" cried she.

But Berthe, warming with her subject, would not stop.

"You have said so twenty times. And, besides, I should have liked to have seen you in my place. Auguste is not kind like papa. You would have been fighting together about money matters before a week had passed. He would precious soon have made you say that men are only good to be taken in ! "

" Eh ? I said that ! " repeated the mother quite beside herself.

She advanced so menacingly towards her daughter, that the father held out his hands in a suppliant gesture imploring mercy. The sounds of the two women's voices struck him to the heart unceasingly ; and, at each shock, he felt the wound extend. Tears gushed from his eyes as he stammered :

" Do leave off, spare me."

" No, it is dreadful ! " resumed Madame Josserand in louder tones than ever. " This wretched creature now pretends I am the cause of her shamelessness ! You will see she will soon make out that it is I who have deceived her husband. So, it's my fault ! for that is what you seem to mean. It's my fault ! "

Berthe remained with her elbows on the table, very pale, but resolute.

"It's very certain that if you had brought me up differently—"

She did not finish. Her mother gave her a clout with all her might, and such a hard one that it banged Berthe's head down on to the table-cover. Her hand had been itching to give it, ever since the day before ; it had been making her fingers tingle, the same as in those far-off days when the child used to over-sleep herself.

"There !" cried she, "that's for your education ! Your husband ought to have beaten you to a jelly."

The young woman did not rise, but sat there sobbing, her cheek pressed against her arm. She forgot her twenty-four years, this clout brought her back to the slaps of other times, to a whole past of timorous hypocrisy. All her resolution of an emancipated grown-up person melted away in the great sorrow of a little girl.

But, on hearing her weep so bitterly, the father was seized with a terrible emotion. He at length got up, quite distracted, and he pushed the mother away, saying :

" You wish then to kill me between you ? Tell me, must I go on my knees to you ? "

Madame Josserand, having relieved her feelings, and having nothing to add, was withdrawing in a royal silence, when she found Hortense listening behind the door as she suddenly opened it. This caused a fresh outburst.

" Ah ! so you were listening to all this filth ? The one does the most horrible things, and the other takes a delight in hearing about them; the two make the pair. But, good heavens ! who ever was it that brought you up ? "

Hortense, without being in the least moved, entered the room.

" It was not necessary to listen, one can even hear you in the kitchen. The servant is wriggling with laughter. Besides, I'm old enough to be married ; there is no harm in my knowing."

" Verdier, eh ? " resumed the mother bitterly. " That's all the satisfaction you give me. Now, you are waiting for the death of a brat. You may wait, she's big and plump, so I've been told. It serves you right."

A rush of bile gave a yellow hue to the young girl's skinny countenance And, with clenched teeth, she replied :

" Though she's big and plump, Verdier can leave her. And I will make him leave her sooner than you think, just to spite you all Yes, yes, I will get married without any one else's assistance. They're far too solid, the marriages you put together ! "

Then, as her mother was advancing towards her, she added :

" Ah ! you know, I don't intend to be slapped ! Take care."

They looked each other straight in the eyes, and Madame Josserand was the first to yield, hiding her retreat beneath an air of scornful domination. But the father thought the battle was going to begin again. Then, when, surrounded by these three women, he beheld this mother and these daughters, all those he had loved, end by devouring one another, he felt a whole world give way beneath him and went off to seek refuge in the bedroom, as though wounded to death and desirous of dying there in peace. In the midst of his sobs, he kept repeating :

" I can bear it no longer—I can bear it no longer— "

The dining-room became once more wrapped in silence. Berthe, her cheek on her arm, and still heaving long nervous sighs, was growing calmer. Hortense had quietly seated herself at the other end of the table, and was buttering the remainder of a roll, so as to pull herself together again. Then, she made her sister positively desperate by a host of sad remarks : their home was becoming quite unbearable; in her place, she would sooner receive cuffs from her husband than from her mother, for it was more natural ; when she married Verdier, she would send her mother to the right about, so as to have no such scenes in her home. At this moment Adèle came to clear the table ; but Hortense continued, saying that they would receive notice to quit, if that sort of thing went on ;

and the servant was of the same opinion : she had been obliged
to shut the kitchen window, for Lisa and Julie were already
poking their noses in that direction.　She nevertheless thought
it all awfully funny too, she was still laughing at it ; Madame
Berthe had come in for it sadly, she was the most hurt of the
lot.　Then, rolling her big body about, she uttered a profoundly
philosophical remark : after all, the house did not care, the
thing was to live well, every one would have forgotten all
about madame and her two gentlemen in a week.　Hortense,
who nodded her approval of what she said, interrupted her to
complain of the butter, which was quite uneatable.　Well !
butter at twenty-two sous could only be poison.　And, as it
left a stinking deposit at the bottom of the saucepans, Adèle
was explaining that it was not even economical, when a dull
thud, a distant shake of the floor, suddenly caused them to
listen intently.

Berthe, all anxiety, at length raised her head.

" What's that ? " asked she.

" It's perhaps madame and the other lady, in the drawing-
room," said Adéle.

Madame Josserand had started with surprise, as she crossed
the drawing-room.　A woman was there, all alone.

" What ? you again ? " cried she, when she had recognised
Madame Dambreville, whom she had forgotten.

The latter did not stir.　The family quarrels, the noisy
voices, the slamming of doors, seemed to have passed over her
without her having felt the least breath of them.　She remained
immovable, looking into vacancy, buried in a heap in her lovesick mania.　But there was something at work within her, the
advice of Léon's mother had upset her, and was deciding her to
dearly purchase a few remnants of happiness.

" Come," resumed Madame Josserand roughly, " you can't,
you know, sleep here.　I have had a note from my son, he is
not coming."

Then Madame Dambreville spoke, her mouth all clammy
from her long silence, and as though she were just waking up.

" I am going, pray excuse me.　And tell him from me that
I have reflected.　I consent.　Yes, I will reflect still further,
and perhaps I may help him to marry that girl, as he insists
upon it.　But it is I who give her to him, and I wish him to
ask me for her, me alone, you understand !　Oh ! he must
come back, he must come back ! "

Her ardent voice became quite beseeching.　She added in a

lower tone, in the obstinate way of a woman who, after sacrificing everything, clings to a last satisfaction,

"He shall marry her, but he must live with us. Otherwise nothing will be done. I would sooner lose him."

And she went off. Madame Josserand was most charming again. In the anteroom, she said all sorts of consoling things, she promised to send her son submissive and tender, that very evening, affirming that he would be delighted to live at his aunt-in-law's. Then, when she had shut the door behind Madame Dambreville's back, filled with a pitying tenderness she thought :

"Poor boy ! what a price she will make him pay for it !"

But, at this moment, she also heard the dull thud, which caused the boards to tremble. Well ? what was it ? was the servant smashing all the crockery, now ? She hastened to the dining-room, and questioned her daughters.

"What is it ? Is the sugar-basin broken ?"

"No, mamma. We don't know."

She turned round, looking for Adèle, when she beheld her listening at the door of the bedroom.

"Whatever are you doing ?" cried she. "Everything is being smashed in your kitchen, and your're there spying on your master. Yes, yes, one begins with prunes, and one ends with something else. For some time past, you have had a way about you which greatly displeases me; you smell of men, my girl—"

The servant stood looking at her with wide open eyes. At length she interrupted her.

"That's not what's the matter. I think master has fallen down in there."

"Good heavens ! she's right," said Berthe turning pale, "it was just like some one falling."

They entered the room. Monsieur Josserand, seized with a fainting fit, was lying on the floor before the bed ; his head had come in contact with a chair, and a little stream of blood was issuing from the right ear. The mother, the two daughters and the servant surrounded and examined him. Berthe, alone, wept, again seized with the bitter sobs which the blow had called forth. And, when the four of them raised him to place him on the bed, they heard him murmur :

"It's all over. They've killed me."

CHAPTER XVII.

MONTHS passed by, and spring had come again. At the house in the Rue de Choiseul, every one was talking of the approaching marriage of Octave and Madame Hédouin.

Matters, however, were not so far advanced. Octave was again in his old place at " The Ladies' Paradise," the business of which developed daily. Since her husband's death, Madame Hédouin was unable to attend properly to the incessantly growing concern by herself. Her uncle, old Deleuze, nailed to his easy-chair by rheumatism, troubled himself about nothing ; and, naturally, the young man, who was very active and a constant prey to the mania for doing business on a large scale, had in a little while reached a position of decisive importance in the house. Moreover, still irritated by his silly amours with Berthe, he no longer dreamed of utilizing women, but even dreaded them. He thought the best thing for him to do was to become Madame Hédouin's partner, and then to commence the dance of millions. Recollecting therefore the ridiculous repulse he had met with at her hands, he treated her as though she were a man, which was the way she wished to be treated.

From this moment their relations became most intimate. They would shut themselves for hours together in the small room right at the back. In former days, when he had sworn to himself to seduce her, he had pursued certain tactics there, trying to take advantage of her commercial emotions, whispering figures close to her neck, watching for the days of heavy takings to profit by her enthusiasm. Now, he was simply good-natured, having no other aim but to push the business. He no longer even desired her, though he retained the recollection of her gentle quiver when waltzing with him on Berthe's wedding-night. Perhaps she had loved. In any case it was best to remain as they were ; for, as she justly said, the business demanded a great amount of order, and it would be impolitic to wish for things which would disturb them from morning till night.

Seated together at the narrow desk, they would often forget themselves, after going through the books and settling the orders. He would then return to his dreams of enlargement. He had sounded the owner of the next house, and had found him willing to sell. They would give notice to the second-hand dealer and to the umbrella man, and then establish a special department for silk. She, very grave, would listen, not daring to venture yet. But she felt an increasing sympathy for Octave's commercial faculties, recognising her own will in his, her taste for business, the serious and practical side of her character, beneath his gallant exterior of an amiable trader. And he displayed besides a warmth, an audacity, which were wanting in her, and which filled her with emotion. It was introducing fancy into trade, the only fancy that had ever troubled her. He was becoming her master.

At length, as they sat side by side one evening examining some invoices beneath the scorching flame of a gas-jet, she said slowly :

"I have spoken to my uncle, Monsieur Octave. He consents, so we will buy the house. Only—"

He interrupted her joyfully to exclaim :

"Then the Vabres are done for !"

She smiled, and murmured reproachfully :

"Do you detest them, then? It is not proper on your part ; you are the last who should wish them ill."

She had never spoken to him of his relations with Berthe. This sudden allusion embarrassed him immensely, without his exactly knowing why. He blushed and tried to stammer out some explanation.

"No, no, it does not concern me," resumed she, still smiling and very calm. "Excuse me, it quite escaped me ; I never intended to speak to you on the subject. You are young. So much the worse for those who are willing, is it not so? It is the place of the husbands to guard their wives, when the latter are unable to guard themselves."

He experienced a sensation of relief, on understanding that she was not angry. He had often dreaded a coldness on her part if she came to know of his former connection.

"You interrupted me, Monsieur Octave," resumed she, gravely. "I was about to add that if I purchase the next house, and thus double the importance of my business, it will be impossible for me to remain single. I shall be obliged to marry again."

Octave sat lost in astonishment.   What ! she already had a husband in view, and he was in ignorance of it !   He at once felt that his position there was compromised.

"My uncle," continued she, "told me so himself.   Oh, there is no hurry just yet.   I have only been eight months in mourning ; I shall wait till the autumn.   Only, in trade one must put one's heart on one side, and consider the necessities of the situation.   A man is absolutely necessary here."

She discussed all this calmly, like a matter of business, and he gazed on her regular and healthy beauty, on her pure complexion beneath her neatly arranged black hair.   Then he regretted not having, since her widowhood, renewed the effort to become her lover.

"It is always a very serious matter," stammered he ; "it requires reflection."

No doubt, she was quite of that opinion.   And she spoke of her age.

"I am already old ; I am five years older than you, Monsieur Octave—"

Deeply agitated, yet thinking he understood, he interrupted her, and seizing hold of her hands, he repeated :

"Oh, madame ! oh, madame ! "

But she rose from her seat and released herself.   Then she turned down the gas.

"No, that's enough for to-day.   You have some very good ideas, and it is natural I should think of you to put them into execution.   Only there will be a deal of worry ; we must thoroughly study the project.   I know that at heart you are very serious.   Think the matter over on your side, and I will think it over on mine.   That is why I have named it to you. We can talk about it again later on."

And things remained thus for weeks.   The establishment continued just the same as usual.   As Madame Hédouin always maintained her smiling serenity when in Octave's company, without an allusion to the slightest tender feeling, he affected on his side a similar peace of mind, and he ended by becoming like her, healthfully happy, placing his confidence in the logic of things.   She often repeated that sensible things always happened of themselves.   Therefore she was never in a hurry. The gossip which commenced to circulate respecting her intimacy with the young man did not in the least affect her.   They waited.

In the Rue de Choiseul, therefore, the entire house vowed that the marriage was as good as accomplished.   Octave had given up his room to lodge in the Rue Neuve-Saint-Augustin near "The Ladies' Paradise." He no longer visited any one, neither the Campardons, nor the Duveyriers, who were quite shocked at the scandal of his amours. Monsieur Gourd himself, whenever he saw him, pretended not to recognise him so as to avoid having to bow. Only Marie and Madame Juzeur, on the mornings when they met him in the neighbourhood, went and stood a moment in some doorway to have a chat with him. Madame Juzeur, who passionately questioned him respecting Madame Hédouin, tried to persuade him to call upon her, so as to be able to talk the matter over nicely; and Marie, who was greatly distressed, complaining of again being in the family way, and who told him of Jules's amazement and of her parents' terrible anger. Then, when the rumour of his marriage became more persistent, Octave was surprised to receive a low bow from Monsieur Gourd. Campardon, without exactly making friends again, gave him a cordial nod across the street; whilst Duveyrier, calling one evening to buy some gloves, showed himself most amiable. The entire house was beginning to pardon him.

Moreover, the house had resumed its course of middle-class respectability. Behind the mahogany doors fresh abysses of virtue were forming. The gentleman on the third floor came to work one night a week; the other Madame Campardon passed by with her rigid principles; the maid-servants displayed dazzlingly white aprons; and, in the lukewarm silence of the staircase, the pianos alone, on every floor, gave vent to the same waltzes, a distant, and, so to say, religious music.

However, the uneasiness caused by the adulterous act was still there, imperceptible to uneducated people, but most disagreeable to those of refined morals. Auguste obstinately persisted in not taking his wife back, and so long as Berthe lived with her parents, the scandal would not be effaced, there would ever linger a material vestige of it. None of the tenants, moreover, publicly related the true version of the story, which would have been awkward for everybody. Of a common accord, without even agreeing together, it had been decided to say that the quarrel between Auguste and Berthe was on account of the ten thousand francs, a mere question of money. This was far more decent. This being understood, there was no harm in talking of the matter before young ladies. Would the parents pay, or would they not? And the drama became quite simple, for not an inhabitant of the neighbourhood was surprised or indignant at the idea that money matters could be the cause of blows in a family. It is true that in reality this pleasant arrangement did not prevent things being as they were; and, in spite of its calm in the presence of misfortune, the house cruelly suffered in its dignity.

It was Duveyrier especially who, as landlord, carried the burden of this persistent and unmerited misfortune. For some time past Clarisse had been torturing him to such a pitch, that he would at times come home to his wife to weep. But the scandal of the adultery had struck him to the heart; he saw, said he, the passers-by look at his house from top to bottom, that house which his father-in-law and he had striven to decorate with every domestic virtue; and as this sort of thing could not be allowed to last, he talked of purifying the building for his personal honour. Therefore, he urged Auguste, in the name of public decency, to become reconciled with his wife. Unfortunately Auguste resisted, backed up in his rage by Théophile and Valérie, who had definitely installed themselves at the pay-desk, and who were delighted with the existing discord. Then as matters were going badly at Lyons, and the silk warehouse was in jeopardy for want of capital, Duveyrier conceived a practical idea. The Josserands were probably longing to get rid of their daughter: the thing to do was to offer to take her back, but only on condition that they paid the dowry of fifty thousand francs. Perhaps uncle Bachelard would yield to their entreaties and give the money. At first, Auguste violently refused to be a party to any such arrangement; even were the sum a hundred thousand francs, he would not think it sufficient. Then, becoming very anxious as his April payments drew near, he had given in to the counsellor's arguments, as the latter pleaded the cause of morality and spoke merely of a good action to be done.

When they were agreed, Clotilde selected the Abbé Mauduit for negotiator. It was a delicate matter, only a priest could interfere in it without compromising himself. It so happened, that the reverend man was deeply grieved by the deplorable catastrophes which had befallen one of the most interesting households of his parish; and he had already offered his advice, his experience, and his authority, to put an end to a scandal at which the enemies of religion might take delight. However, when Clotilde spoke to him of the dowry, asking him 'to be the bearer of Auguste's conditions to the Josserands, he bowed his head, and maintained a painful silence.

"It is money due that my brother asks for," repeated she. "It is no bargain, understand. Moreover, my brother insists upon it."

"It is necessary and I will go," said the priest at length.

The Josserands had been expecting the proposal for days. Valérie must have spoken of it, all the tenants were discussing the affair : were they so hard up as to be forced to keep their daughter? would they be able to obtain the fifty thousand francs to get rid of her? Since the question had reached this point, Madame Josserand had been in a constant rage. What! after having had such trouble to marry Berthe at first, she now had to marry her a second time ! Everything was upset, the dowry was again demanded, all the money worries were going to commence afresh ! Never before had a mother had such a task to go through twice over. And all owing to the fault of that silly fool, whose stupidity went so far as to make her forget her duty.

The house was becoming a hell upon earth; Berthe suffered a continual torture, for even her sister Hortense, furious at no longer sleeping alone, never uttered a sentence without introducing some insulting allusion into it. She was even reproached with the food she ate. When one had a husband somewhere, it was all the same very funny that one should go and share one's parents' meals, which were already too sparing. Then, the young woman, in despair, would sob in corners, accusing herself of being a coward, but unable to pick up sufficient courage to go downstairs and throw herself at Auguste's feet, and say :

"Here ! beat me, I cannot be more unhappy than I am."

Monsieur Josserand alone showed some affection for his child. But that child's faults and tears were killing him ; he was dying through the cruelties of the family, with an unlimited holiday from business, spent mostly in bed. Doctor Juillerat who attended him, talked of a decomposition of the blood : it was a dissolution of the entire system, during which each organ was attacked, one after the other.

"When you have made your father die of grief, perhaps you will be satisfied ! " cried the mother.

And Berthe scarcely dared enter the invalid's room. Directly the father and daughter met, they wept together, and did each other a great deal of harm.

At length, Madame Josserand came to a grand decision : she invited uncle Bachelard, resolved to humiliate herself once

more. She would have given the fifty thousand francs out of
her own pocket, if she had possessed them, so as not to have to
keep that big married girl, whose presence dishonoured her
Tuesday receptions. But she had learnt some shocking things
about the uncle, and if he did not do as she wished, she intended,
once for all, to give him a bit of her mind.

During dinner, Bachelard behaved in a most abominable
manner. He had arrived in an advanced stage of intoxication ;
for, since he had lost Fifi, he had fallen into the lowest depths
of vice. Fortunately, Madame Josserand had not invited any
one else, for fear of losing their esteem. He fell asleep at
dessert whilst relating some of his drivelling old rake's very
mixed stories, and they were obliged to wake him up to take
him into Monsieur Josserand's room. Everything had been
prepared there with a view of acting on the old drunkard's
feelings : before the father's bed were two arm-chairs, one for
the mother, the other for the uncle. Berthe and Hortense
would stand up. One would see whether the uncle would
again dare to deny his promises in the face of a dying man, in
such a sad room, dimly lighted by a smoky lamp.

" Narcisse," said Madame Josserand, "the situation is a grave
one—"

And, slowly and solemnly, she explained this situation, her
daughter's regrettable misfortune, the husband's revolting
venality, the painful resolution she had been obliged to come to
of giving the fifty thousand francs, so as to put a stop to the
scandal which covered the family with shame. Then she
severely continued :

" Remember what you promised, Narcisse. On the evening of
the signing of the marriage contract, you again slapped your
chest and swore that Berthe might rely on her uncle's
affection. Well ! where is this affection ? the moment has
arrived to display it. Monsieur Josserand, join me in showing
him his duty, if your weak state of health will allow you to
do so."

In spite of his great repugnance, the father murmured, out
of love for his daughter :

" It is true; you promised, Bachelard. Come, before I leave
you for ever, do me the pleasure of behaving as you should."

But Berthe and Hortense, in the hope of working upon the
uncle's feelings, had filled his glass once too often. He was in
such a fuddled condition, that one could not even take advantage of him.

"Eh? what?" stuttered he, without having the least necessity for exaggerating his intoxication. "Never promise— Don't understand—Tell me again, Eléonore."

The latter recommenced her story, made weeping Berthe embrace him, beseeched him for the sake of her husband's health, and proved to him that in giving the fifty thousand francs, he would be fulfilling a sacred duty. Then, as he began to doze off again, without appearing to be in the least affected by the sight of the invalid or of the chamber of sickness, she abruptly broke out into the most violent language.

"Listen! Narcisse, this sort of thing has been lasting too long—you're a scoundrel! I know of all your beastly goings-on. You've just married your mistress to Gueulin, and you've given them fifty thousand francs, the very amount you promised us. Ah! it's decent; little Gueulin plays a pretty part in it all! And you, you're worse still, you take the bread from our mouth, you prostitute your fortune, yes! you prostitute it, by robbing us of money which was ours for the sake of that harlot!"

Never before had she relieved her feelings to such an extent. Hortense busied herself with her father's medicine, so as not to show her embarrassment. Monsieur Josserand, who was made far worse by this scene, tossed about on his pillow, and murmured in a trembling voice:

"I beseech you, Eléonore, do be quiet; he will give nothing. If you wish to say such things to him, take him away that I may not hear you."

Berthe, on her side, sobbed louder than ever and joined her father in his entreaties.

"Enough, mamma, do as papa asks. Good heavens! how miserable I am to be the cause of all these quarrels! I would sooner leave you all, and go and die somewhere."

Then, Madame Josserand deliberately put the question to the uncle.

"Will you, yes or no, give the fifty thousand francs, so that your niece may hold her head up?"

Regularly scared, he tried to go into explanations.

"Listen a moment. I found Gueulin and Fifi together. What could I do? I was obliged to marry them. It wasn't my fault."

"Will you, yes or no, give the dowry you promised?" repeated she furiously.

He wavered, his intoxication increased to such a pitch that he could scarcely find words to utter,

"Can't, word of honour!—Completely ruined. Otherwise, at once—Candidly you know—"

She interrupted him with a terrible gesture, and declared :

"Good, then I shall call a family council and have you declared incapable of managing your affairs. When uncles become drivelling, it's time to send them to an asylum."

At this, the uncle was seized with intense emotion. He glanced about him, and found the room had a sinister aspect with its feeble light ; he looked at the dying man who, held up by his daughters, was swallowing a spoonful of some black liquid ; and his heart overflowed, he sobbed as he accused his sister of never having understood him. Yet, he had already been made unhappy enough by Gueulin's treachery. They knew he was very sensitive, and they did wrong to invite him to dinner, to make him sad afterwards. In short, in place of the fifty thousand francs, he offered all the blood in his veins.

Madame Josserand, who was quite worn out, had decided to leave him to himself, when the servant announced Doctor Juillerat and the Abbé Mauduit. They had met on the landing, and entered together. The doctor found Monsieur Josserand much worse, he was still suffering from the shock occasioned by the scene in which he had been forced to play a part. When, on his side, the priest wished to take Madame Josserand into the drawing-room, having, he said, a communication to make to her, the latter guessed on what subject he had called, and answered majestically that she was with her family and prepared to hear everything there ; the doctor himself would not be in the way, for a physician was also a confessor.

"Madame," then said the priest with slightly embarrassed gentleness, "you behold in the step I am taking an ardent desire to reconcile two families—"

He spoke of God's pardon, and of the great joy it would be to him to be able to reassure all honest hearts, by putting an end to an intolerable state of things. He called Berthe a miserable child, which again caused her tears to flow ; and all this in such a paternal manner, in such choice expressions, that there was no need for Hortense to retire. However, he was obliged to come to the fifty thousand francs : there seemed to be nothing more but for the husband and wife to embrace each other, when he stated the formal condition of the payment of the dowry.

"My dear Abbé Mauduit, allow me to interrupt you," said Madame Josserand. "We are deeply moved by your efforts.

But never, you understand me ! never will we traffic in our daughter's honour.   People who have already become reconciled over this child's back !   Oh ! I know all, they were at daggers drawn, and now they are inseparable, reviling us from morning till night.   No, such a bargain would be a disgrace—"

"It seems to me though, madame—" ventured the priest.

But she drowned his voice, as she superbly continued :

"See ! my brother is here.   You can question him.   He was again saying to me only a little while ago : 'Here are the fifty thousand francs, Éléonore, settle this miserable matter !'   Well! ask him what reply I made.   Get up, Narcisse.   Tell the truth."

The uncle had already again fallen asleep in an arm-chair, at the end of the room.   He moved, and uttered a few discon- . nected words.   Then, as his sister insisted, he placed his hand on his heart, and stammered :

"When duty speaks, one must obey.   The family comes before everything."

"You hear him ?" cried Madame Josserand, with a triumphant air.   "No money, it's disgraceful !   Tell those people from us that we don't die, to avoid having to pay.   The dowry is here, we would have given it ; but, now that it's exacted as the price of our daughter, the matter becomes too disgusting. Let Auguste take Berthe back first, and then we will see later on."

She had raised her voice, and the doctor, who was examining his patient, was obliged to make her leave off.

"Speak lower, madame !" said he.   " Your husband suffers."

Then the Abbé Mauduit, whose embarrassment had increased, went up to the bedside, and found some kind words to say. And he afterwards withdrew, without again referring to the matter, hiding the confusion of having failed beneath his amiable smile, with a curl of grief and disgust on his lips.   As the doctor went off in his turn, he roughly informed Madame Josserand that there was no hope for the invalid : the greatest precautions must be taken, for the least emotion might carry him off.   She was thunderstruck, and returned to the dining-room, where her two daughters and their uncle had already withdrawn, to let Monsieur Josserand rest, as he seemed disposed to go to sleep.

"Berthe," murmured she, "you have killed your father The doctor has just said so."

And they all three, seated round the table, gave way to their grief, whilst uncle Bachelard, also in tears, mixed himself a glass of grog.

When Auguste learnt the Josserands' answer, his rage against his wife knew no bounds, and he swore he would kick her away, the day she came to ask for forgiveness. Yet in reality, he wanted her; there was a voidness in his life, he seemed to be out of his element, amidst the new worries of his abandonment, quite as grave as those of his married life. Rachel, whom he had kept on simply to annoy Berthe, robbed him and quarrelled with him now, with the cool impudence of a spouse; and he ended by regretting all the little advantages of a joint existence, the evenings spent in boring each other, and then the costly reconciliations between the warm sheets. But he had especially had enough of Théophile and Valérie, who were quite at home downstairs now, filling the warehouse with their importance. He even suspected them at times of pocketing some of the money, without the least compunction. Valérie was not like Berthe, she was delighted to throne herself at the pay-desk; only Auguste fancied that he noticed she attracted men, even in face of her fool of a husband, whose persistent cough veiled his eyes with continuous tears. Therefore he might just as well have had Berthe there. She at least did not have the whole street passing along the counters.

Besides all this, another more serious anxiety bothered him: " The Ladies' Paradise " was prospering, and already menaced his business, which decreased daily. He certainly did not regret that miserable Octave, yet he was just, and recognised that the fellow possessed very great abilities. How swimmingly everything would have gone, had they only got on better together! He was seized with the most tender regrets; there were hours when, sick of his loneliness, feeling life giving way beneath him, he felt inclined to go up to the Josserands and ask them to give Berthe back to him for nothing.

Duveyrier too, moreover, did not yield, and, more and more cut up by the moral disfavour into which such an affair threw his building, he was for ever urging his brother-in-law to a reconciliation. He even pretended to put faith in Madame Josserand's words, as reported by the priest: if Auguste took back his wife unconditionally, they would certainly pay him the dowry on the morrow. Then, as the latter again flew into a frightful rage at the repetition of this statement, the counsellor appealed more especially to his heart. He would take him along the quays, on his way to the Palais de Justice; he preached to him of the forgiveness of injuries in a voice choked with emotion, and fed him with a cowardly and lamentable philosophy, according to which the only possible felicity was to put up with woman, as one could not do without her.

Duveyrier was visibly declining, and made the entire Rue de Choiseul anxious on account of the sadness of his gait and the paleness of his countenance, on which the red blotches gathered and spread. An unavowable misfortune seemed to have overtaken him. It was Clarisse who still fattened, and overflowed, and who tortured him. As fast as she developed a middle-class obesity, he found her all the more unbearable with her fine education, and her rigorous gentility. Now, he was not allowed to address her familiarly in the presence of her family; yet, in his presence, she would put her arms round her music master's neck, and do all manner of things which intensely grieved him. Having on two occasions caught her with Théodore, he had flown into a rage, and then had begged her pardon on his knees, consenting to share with everyone. Moreover, to keep him humble and submissive, she was continually alluding in terms of repugnance to his pimples; she had even had the idea of passing him on to one of her cooks, a strapping wench accustomed to dirty work; but the cook would have nothing to do with the gentleman.

Each day, life became more and more cruel for Duveyrier at this mistress's where he encountered all the worries of his own home again, but this time in the midst of a regular hell. The whole tribe of hawkers, the mother, the big blackguard of a brother, the two little sisters, even the invalid aunt, impudently robbed him, lived on him openly, to the point of emptying his pockets during the nights he slept there. His position was also becoming a serious one in another respect: he had got to the end of his money, he trembled at the thought of being compromised on his judicial bench; he could certainly not be removed; only, the young barristers were beginning to look at him in a saucy kind of way, which made it awkward for him to administer justice. And, when driven away by the filth and the uproar, seized with disgust of himself, he flew from the Rue d'Assas and sought refuge in the Rue de Choiseul, his wife's malignant coldness completed the crushing of him. Then, he would lose his head, he would look at the Seine on his way to the court, with thoughts of jumping in some evening when a final suffering should impart to him the requisite courage.

Clotilde had noticed her husband's emotion, and felt anxious and irritated with that mistress of his who did not even make a man happy in his misconduct. But, for her part, she was greatly annoyed by a most deplorable adventure, the consequences of which quite revolutionized the house. On going upstairs one morning for a handkerchief, Clémence had caught Hippolyte with that abortion Louise, and, since then, she had taken to slapping him in the kitchen for the least thing, which of course greatly interfered with the attendance. The worst was that madame could no longer close her eyes to the illicit connection existing between her maid and her footman; the other servants laughed, the scandal was reported amongst the tradespeople, it was absolutely necessary to oblige them to get married if she wished to retain them; and, as she continued to be very well satisfied with Clémence, she thought of nothing but this marriage.

To negotiate between lovers who were for ever fighting with each other seemed such a delicate affair, that she decided on employing the Abbé Mauduit, whose moralizing character seemed specially suited to the occasion. Her servants, moreover, had been causing her a great deal of trouble for some time past. When down in the country, she had noticed the intimacy of her big hobbledehoy Gustave with Julie; she had at one moment thought of sending the latter about her business though regretfully, for she liked her cooking; then, after sound reflection, she had decided to keep her, prefering that the youngster should have a mistress at home, a clean girl who would never be any trouble. There is no knowing what a youth may get hold of outside, when he begins too young. She was watching them therefore, without saying a word; and, now, the other two must needs worry her with their affair.

It so happened that one morning, as Madame Duveyrier was preparing to call on the priest, Clémence came and announced that the Abbé Mauduit was taking the extreme unction up to Monsieur Josserand. After meeting him on the staircase, the maid had returned to the kitchen, exclaiming:

"I said that he would come again this year!"

And, alluding to the castastrophes which had befallen the house, she added:

"It has brought ill-luck to everyone."

This time, the priest did not arrive too late, and that was an excellent sign for the future. Madame Duveyrier hastened to Saint-Roch, where she awaited the Abbé Mauduit's return. He listened to her, and for a while maintained a sad silence, then

he was unable to refuse to enlighten the maid and the footman
on the immorality of their position. Moreover, the other matter would have obliged him to return shortly to the Rue de
Choiseul, for poor Monsieur Josserand would certainly not last
through the night; and he mentioned that he saw in this circumstance a cruel, but happy opportunity for reconciling Auguste and Berthe. He would try and arrange the two affairs
simultaneously. It was high time that heaven consented to
bless their efforts.

"I have prayed, madame," said the priest. "The Almighty
will triumph."

And indeed, that evening at seven o'clock, Monsieur Josser-
and's death agony began. The entire family was there, except-
ing uncle Bachelard who had been sought for in vain in all the
cafés, and Saturnin who was still confined at the Asile des Moulineaux. Léon, whose marriage was most unfortunately post-
poned through his father's illness, displayed a dignified grief.
Madame Josserand and Hortense showed some courage. Berthe
alone sobbed so loudly, that, so as not to affect the invalid, she
had gone and stowed herself away in the kitchen, where Adèle,
taking advantage of the general confusion, was drinking some
mulled wine. Monsieur Josserand expired in the quietest fashion; it was his honesty which finished him. He had passed a useless life, and he went off like a worthy man tired of the wicked
things of the world, heart-broken by the quiet indifference of
the only beings he had ever loved. At eight o'clock, he stammered out Saturnin's name, turned his face to the wall, and expired. No one thought him dead, for all had dreaded a terrible
agony. They sat patiently for some time, letting him, as they
thought, sleep. When they found he was already becoming
cold, Madame Josserand, in the midst of the general wailing,
flew into a passion with Hortense, whom she had instructed to
fetch Auguste, counting on restoring Berthe to the latter's arms
amidst the great grief of her husband's last moments.

"You think of nothing!" said she, wiping her eyes.

"But, mamma," replied the girl in tears; "no one thought
papa would go off so suddenly! You told me not to go for
Auguste till nine o'clock, so as to be sure of keeping him till
the end."

The sorely afflicted family found some distraction in this
quarrel. It was another matter gone wrong; they never
succeeded in anything. Fortunately, there was still the funeral
to take advantage of to bring the husband and wife together.

The funeral was a pretty decent one, though it was not so grand as Monsieur Vabre's. Moreover, it did not give rise to nearly the same excitement in the house and the neighbourhood, for the deceased was not a landlord; he was merely a quiet-going body whose demise did not even disturb Madame Juzeur's slumbers. Marie, who had been hourly expecting her confinement since the day before, was the only one who expressed regret at having been unable to assist the ladies in laying the poor gentleman out. Downstairs, Madame Gourd contented herself with rising, as the coffin passed, and bowing inside her room, without coming as far as the door. The entire house, however, went to the cemetery: Duveyrier, Campardon, the Vabres, and Monsieur Gourd. They talked of the spring and of the early crops, which would be greatly interfered with by the heavy rains they were having. Campardon was surprised to see Duveyrier looking so unwell; and, as the counsellor turned pale when the coffin was brought downstairs, and seemed about to faint, the architect murmured:

"He has smelt the earthy odour. God grant that the house may not sustain any further losses!"

Madame Josserand and her daughters had to be supported to their coach. Léon, assisted by uncle Bachelard, was most attentive, whilst Auguste followed behind in an embarrassed way. He got into another coach with Duveyrier and Théophile. Clotilde detained the Abbé Mauduit, who had not officiated, but who had gone to the cemetery, wishing to give the family a proof of his sympathy. The horses started on the homeward journey more gaily; and she at once asked the priest to return to the house with them, for she felt that the time was favourable. He consented.

The three mourning coaches silently drew up in the Rue de Choiseul with the relations. Théophile at once rejoined Valérie, who had remained behind to superintend a general cleaning, the warehouse being closed.

"You may pack up," cried he, furiously. "They're all at him. I bet he'll end by begging her pardon!"

They all, indeed, felt a pressing necessity for putting an end to the unpleasantness. Misfortune should at least be good for something. Auguste, in the midst of them, understood very well what they wanted; and he was alone, without strength to resist, and filled with shame. The relations slowly walked in under the porch hung with black. No one spoke. On the stairs, the silence continued, a silence full of deep thought;

whilst the crape skirts, soft and sad, ascended higher and higher. Auguste, seized with a final feeling of revolt, had taken the lead, with the intention of quickly shutting himself up in his own apartments; but, as he opened the door, Clotilde and the priest, who had followed close behind, stopped him. Directly after them, Berthe, dressed in deep mourning, appeared on the landing, accompanied by her mother and her sister. They all three had red eyes; Madame Josserand especially was quite painful to behold.

"Come, my friend," simply said the priest, overcome by tears.

And that was sufficient. Auguste gave in at once, seeing that it was better to make his peace at that honourable opportunity. His wife wept, and he wept also, as he stammered:

"Come in. We will try not to do it again."

Then the relations kissed all round. Clotilde congratulated her brother; she had had full confidence in his heart. Madame Josserand showed a broken-hearted satisfaction, like a widow who is no longer the least affected by the most unhoped-for happiness. She associated her poor husband with the general joy.

"You are doing your duty, my dear son-in-law. He who is now in heaven thanks you."

"Come in," repeated Auguste, quite upset.

But Rachel, attracted by the noise, now appeared in the anteroom; and Berthe hesitated a moment in presence of the speechless exasperation which caused the maid to turn ghastly pale. Then she sternly entered, and disappeared with her black mourning in the shadow of the apartment. Auguste followed her, and the door closed behind them.

A deep sigh of relief ascended the staircase, and filled the house with joy. The ladies pressed the hands of the priest whose prayers had been granted. Just as Clotilde was taking him off to settle the other matter, Duveyrier, who had lagged behind with Léon and Bachelard, arrived walking painfully. The happy result had all to be explained to him; but he, who had been desiring it for months past, scarcely seemed to understand, a strange expression overspreading his face, and his mind a prey to a fixed idea, the torture of which quite absorbed him. Whilst the Josserands regained their apartments, he returned to his own, behind his wife and the priest. And they had just reached the anteroom, when some stifled cries caused them to start.

"Do not be uneasy, madame. It is the little lady upstairs in labour," Hippolyte complaisantly explained. "I saw Dr. Juillerat run up just now."

Then, when he was alone, he added philosophically:

"One goes, another comes."

Clotilde made the Abbé Mauduit comfortable in the drawing-room, saying that she would first of all send him Clémence; and, to help him to while away the time, she gave him the "Revue des Deux Mondes," which contained some really charming verses. She wished to prepare her maid for the interview. But on entering her dressing-room, she found her husband seated on a chair.

Ever since the morning, Duveyrier had been in a state of agony. For the third time he had caught Clarisse with Théodore; and, as he complained, the whole family of hawkers, the mother, the brother, the little sisters, had fallen upon him, and driven him downstairs with kicks and blows; whilst Clarisse had called him a poverty-stricken wretch, and furiously threatened him with the police if he ever dared to show himself there again. It was all over; down below the doorkeeper had told him that for a week past a very rich old fellow had been anxious to provide for madame. Then, driven away, and no longer having a warm nook to nestle in, Duveyrier, after wandering about the streets, had entered an out-of-the-way shop and purchased a pocket revolver. Life was becoming too sad; he could at least put an end to it, as soon as he had found a suitable place for doing so. This selection of a quiet corner was occupying his mind, as he mechanically returned to the Rue de Choiseul to assist at Monsieur Josserand's funeral. Then, when following the corpse, he had had a sudden idea of killing himself at the cemetery: he would go to the furthest end and hide behind a tombstone. This flattered his taste for the romantic, the necessity for a tender ideal, which was wrecking his life, beneath his rigid middle-class attitude. But, as the coffin was being lowered into the grave, he began to tremble, seized with an earthy chill. The spot would decidedly not do; he would have to seek elsewhere. And, having returned in a worse state than ever, entirely a prey to this one idea, he sat thinking on a chair in the dressing-room, trying to decide which was the most suitable place in the house: perhaps the bedroom, beside the bed, or simply just where he was, without moving.

"Will you have the kindness to leave me to myself?" said Clotilde to him.

He already had his hand on the revolver in his pocket.

" Why ? " asked he, with an effort.

" Because I wish to be alone."

He thought that she wanted to change her dress, and that she would not even let him see her bare arms, so repugnant he felt was he to her. For an instant he looked at her with his dim eyes, and beheld her so tall, so beautiful, with a complexion clear as marble, her hair gathered up in deep golden tresses. Ah ! if she had only consented, how everything might have been arranged ! He rose stumblingly from his chair, and, opening his arms, tried to take hold of her.

" What now ? " murmured she, greatly surprised. " What's the matter with you ? Not here, surely. Have you the other one no longer then ? It is going to begin again, that abomination ? "

And she exhibited such utter disgust, that he drew back. Without a word, he left her, stopping in the anteroom as he hesitated for a moment ; then, as there was a door facing him, the door of the closet, he pushed it open ; and, without the slightest hurry, he sat down. It was a quiet spot, no one would come and disturb him there. He placed the barrel of the little revolver in his mouth, and pulled the trigger.

Meanwhile, Clotilde, who had been struck since the morning by his strange manner, had listened to ascertain if he were obliging her by returning to Clarisse. On learning where he had gone, by a creak peculiar to that door, she no longer bothered herself about him, and was at length in the act of ringing for Clémence, when the dull report of a fire-arm filled her with surprise. Whatever was it ? it was just like the noise a saloon rifle would make. She hastened to the anteroom, not daring at first to question him ; then, as a strange sound issued from where he was, she called him, and on receiving no answer opened the door. The bolt had not even been fastened. Duveyrier, stunned by fright more than by the injury he had received, remained squatting, in a most lugubrious posture, his eyes wide open, and his face streaming with blood. He had missed his object. After grazing his jaw, the bullet had passed out again through the left cheek. And he no longer had the courage to fire a second time.

" What ! that is what you come to do here ? " cried Clotilde quite beside herself. " Just go and kill yourself outside ! "

She was most indignant. Instead of softening her, this

spectacle threw her into a supreme exasperation. She bullied
him, and raised him up without the least precaution, wishing
to carry him away so that no one should see him in such a
place. In that closet! and to miss killing himself too! It was
too much.

Then, whilst she supported him to lead him to the bedroom,
Duveyrier, who had his throat filled with blood, and whose teeth
were dropping out, stuttered between two rattles:

"You never loved me!"

And he burst into sobs, he bewailed the death of poetry, that
little blue flower which it had been denied him to pluck. When
Clotilde had put him to bed, she at length became softened,
seized with a nervous emotion in the midst of her anger. The
worst of it was that Clémence and Hippolyte were coming in
answer to the bell. She at first talked to them of an accident:
their master had fallen on his chin; then she was obliged to
abandon this fable, for on going to wipe up the blood, the footman had found the revolver. The wounded man was still losing a great deal of blood, when the maid remembered that
Dr. Juillerat was upstairs attending to Madame Pichon, and
she hastened to him, meeting him on the staircase, on his way
home after a most successful delivery. The doctor immediately
reassured Clotilde; perhaps the jaw would be slightly out of its
place, but her husband's life was not in the least danger. He
was proceeding to dress the wound, in the midst of basins of
water and red stained rags, when the Abbé Mauduit, uneasy at
all this commotion, ventured to enter the room.

"Whatever has happened?" asked he.

This question completed upsetting Madame Duveyrier. She
burst into tears, at the first words of explanation. The priest,
fully aware of the hidden miseries of his flock, had moreover quite
understood matters. Already whilst waiting in the drawing-
room he had been taken with a feeling of uneasiness, and almost
regretted the success which had attended his efforts, that
wretched young woman whom he had once more united to her
husband without her showing the slightest remorse. He was
filled with a terrible doubt, perhaps God was not with him.
And his anguish still further increased as he beheld the
counsellor's fractured jaw. He went up to him, bent upon
energetically condemning suicide. But the doctor, who was
very busy, thrust him aside.

"After me, my dear Abbé Mauduit. By-and-by. You can
see very well that he has fainted."

CLOTILDE LEADING AWAY HER HUSBAND AFTER HIS ATTEMPTED
SUICIDE.

p. 358.

And indeed, directly the doctor touched him, Duveyrier had lost consciousness. Then Clotilde, to get rid of the servants who were no longer needed, and whose staring eyes embarrassed her very much, murmured, as she wiped her eyes :

"Go into the drawing-room. Abbé Mauduit has something to say to you."

The priest was obliged to take them there. It was another unpleasant piece of business. Hippolyte and Clémence followed him in profound surprise. When they were alone together, he began preaching them a rather confused sermon : heaven rewarded good behaviour whereas a single sin led one to hell ; moreover, it was time to put a stop to scandal and to think of one's salvation. Whilst he spoke thus, their surprise turned to bewilderment ; with their hands hanging down beside them, she with her slender limbs and tiny mouth, he with his flat face and his big bones like a gendarme, they exchanged anxious glances ! Had madame found some of her napkins upstairs in a trunk? or was it because of the bottle of wine they took up with them every evening ?

"My children," the priest ended by saying, "you set a bad example. The greatest of crimes is to pervert one's neighbour, and to bring the house where one lives into disrepute. Yes, you live in a disorderly way which unfortunately is no longer a secret to anyone, for you have been fighting together for a week past."

He blushed ; a modest hesitation caused him to choose his words. Meanwhile the two servants had sighed with relief. They smiled now and strutted about in quite a happy manner. It was only that ! really there was no occasion to be so frightened !

"But it's all over, sir," declared Clémence, glancing at Hippolyte in the fondest manner. "We have made it up. Yes, he explained everything to me."

The priest, in his turn, exhibited an astonishment full of sadness.

"You do not understand me, my children. You cannot continue to live together, you sin against God and man. You must get married."

At this, their amazement returned. Get married ! whatever for ?

"I don't want to," said Clémence. "I've quite another idea."

Then the Abbé Mauduit tried to convince Hippolyte.

"Come, my fine fellow, you who are a man, use your influence with her; talk to her of her honour. It will change
nothing in your mode of living. Be married."

The footman grinned in a jocular and embarrassed manner.
At length he declared, as he looked down at the toes of his
boots :

"I daresay, I don't say the contrary; but I'm already
married."

This answer put a stop to all the priest's moral preaching.
Without adding a word, he folded up his arguments, and put
religion, now become useless, back into his pocket, deeply regretting ever having risked it in such a disgraceful matter.
Clotilde, who rejoined him at this moment, had heard everything; and she gave vent to her indignation in a furious gesture. At her order, the footman and the maid left the room,
one behind the other, looking very serious, but in reality feeling
highly amused. After a short pause, Abbé Mauduit complained
bitterly : why expose him in that manner? why stir up things
it was far better to let rest? The condition of affairs had now
become most disgraceful. But Clotilde repeated her gesture :
so much the worse! she had far greater worries. Moreover,
she would certainly not send the servants away, for fear the
whole neighbourhood learnt the story of the attempted suicide
that very evening. She would decide what to do later on.

"You will not forget, will you? the most complete repose,"
urged the doctor, coming from the bedroom. "He will get
over it perfectly, but all fatigue must be avoided. Take
courage, madame."

And, turning towards the priest he added :

"You can preach him a sermon later on, my dear friend. I
do not give him up to you yet. If you are returning to Saint-
Roch, I will accompany you; we can walk together."

They both went downstairs, and the house once more resumed
its great peacefulness. Madame Juzeur had lingered in the
cemetery, trying to ensnare Trublot whilst reading the inscriptions on the tombstones with him, and, in spite of his little
liking for fruitless flirtations, he had been obliged to bring her
back to the Rue de Choiseul in a cab. The sad mishap which
had befallen Louise had filled the poor lady with melancholy.
When they reached their destination, she was still speaking of
the wretched creature whom she had sent back the day before
to the foundling hospital : a cruel experience, a final illusion
destroyed, which, at the same time, carried away her hope of

ever finding a virtuous maid-servant. Then, when in the doorway, she ended by inviting Trublot to come and have a chat with her sometimes. But he excused himself on account of his work.

At this moment, the other Madame Campardon passed them. They bowed to her. Monsieur Gourd informed them of Madame Pichon's happy deliverance. Then they were all of Monsieur and Madame Vuillaume's opinion : three children for a mere clerk was rank madness; and the doorkeeper even gave a hint that if another came the landlord would give them notice to quit, for too many children degraded a building. But they ceased talking as a veiled lady, leaving behind her an odour of verbena, lightly glided into the vestibule, without saying a word to Monsieur Gourd, who pretended not to see her. That morning he had prepared everything in the distinguished gentleman's apartment on the third flcor for a night of work.

Moreover, he had only just time to cry out to the other two :
" Take care ! they would run over us like dogs."

It was the carriage of the second floor people who were going out. The horses pawed the ground beneath the porch, the father and the mother, reclining on the back seat, smiled at their children, two lovely fair children, whose little hands were contending for a bunch of roses.

" What people ! " murmured the indignant doorkeeper. " They did not even go to the funeral, for fear of being as polite as others. They splash one, yet if one only chose to speak ! "

" What now ? " asked Madame Juzeur deeply interested.

Then Monsieur Gourd related that some one had come from the police, yes, from the police ! The man on the second floor had written such a disgusting novel, that he was going to be sent to Mazas prison.

" The most horrible things ! " continued he, in a tone of disgust. " It's full of filthiness about the most respectable people. It is even said that the landlord is mentioned in it; exactly, Monsieur Duveyrier himself ! What cheek ! Ah ! they do well to hide themselves and never to associate with any of the other tenants ! We know now what they manufacture, with their air of keeping themselves to themselves. And yet, you see, they have their carriage, and they sell their filth for its weight in gold ! "

It was this thought especially which exasperated Monsieur

Gourd. Madame Juzeur only read poetry, Trublot declared that he knew nothing of literature. Yet, they were both blaming the gentleman for defiling the house which sheltered his family in his writings, when some ferocious yells, and some most abominable expressions, came from the farthest end of the courtyard.

"You big cow! you were only too glad to have me, to let your men out! You hear me, you damned camel! there's no need to send some one to tell you!"

It was Rachel, whom Berthe had sent about her business, and who was relieving her feelings on the servants' staircase. This quiet and respectful girl, whom even the other servants could never get to talk, had suddenly given way to a fit of passion, similar to the bursting of a main sewer. Already beside herself because of madame's return to her husband, whom she had been robbing at her ease during their separation, she had become simply furious when told to fetch a porter to take away her trunk. Standing up in the kitchen, Berthe listened in a bewildered sort of way; whilst Auguste, who was at the door for the purpose of turning her out, received the vile expressions and the atrocious accusations full in the face.

"Yes, yes," continued the enraged servant, "you didn't turn me out, on the night when your lover was obliged to dress himself in the midst of my saucepans, whilst I kept your cuckold waiting at the door, to give you time to get cool again! Ah! you strumpet!"

Filled with shame, Berthe went and hid herself in the bedroom. But Auguste could not retire: he turned pale and trembled all over at these filthy revelations, shouted out on a staircase; and the only words he could find to say, to express his anguish at thus learning all the coarse details of the intrigue just at the very moment he had forgiven it, were, "Wretched woman! wretched woman!" The other servants had all come out on to the landings of their kitchens. They leant over the balusters, and did not miss a word; but even they were astonished at Rachel's violence. Little by little, a feeling of consternation drove them away. It ended by passing all limits. Lisa summed up the general opinion by saying:

"Ah! no, one may gossip, but it's not right to treat one's employers thus."

Every one went off, leaving the girl to relieve her feelings all by herself, for it was becoming awkward listening to things which were unpleasant for everybody; more especially, as she took to abusing the whole house. Monsieur Gourd was the first to return to his room, observing that one could do nothing with a woman in a passion. Madame Juzeur, whose delicacy was deeply wounded by this cruel disclosure of love, seemed so upset, that Trublot, much against his wish, was obliged to see her to her apartment for fear she might faint. Was it not unfortunate? everything had been settled, there no longer remained the least subject for scandal, the house was already resuming its peaceful respectability, and now this horrid creature must needs go and again stir up things which had been buried in oblivion, and which no one cared anything more about!

"I'm only a servant, but I'm respectable!" yelled she, throwing all her strength into the cry. "And there's not one of you lady strumpets in the whole of your wretched house who can say the same! Never fear, I'm going, you all disgust me too much!"

The Abbé Mauduit and Doctor Juillerat were slowly descending the stairs. They too had heard. A great peacefulness now reigned over all: the courtyard was empty, the staircase deserted; the doors seemed walled up, not a curtain at the windows moved; and all that issued from the closed apartments was a silence full of dignity.

The priest halted beneath the porch, as though worn out with fatigue.

"What miseries!" murmured he sadly.

The doctor nodded his head as he replied:

"Such is life."

They would make these avowals to one another when leaving in company the chamber of death or the bedside of a mother and her new-born babe. In spite of their opposite beliefs, they agreed at times on the question of human infirmities. They were both in the same secrets: if the priest listened to the ladies' confessions, the doctor, on the other hand, had for thirty years past attended the mothers in their confinements and prescribed for the daughters.

"Heaven is abandoning them," remarked the priest.

"No," said the doctor, "do not mix heaven up in the matter. They are either ill or badly brought up, that is all."

And, without pausing, he spoilt this conclusion by violently accusing the Empire: under a republican government, things would certainly go much better. But, in the midst of these flights of a mediocre man, came the just observations of an old practitioner, thoroughly acquainted with the wrong side of his neighbourhood. He spoke his mind about the women, those whom a doll-like education corrupted or stultified, others whose sentiments and whose passions were perverted by a hereditary neurosis; he did not show himself, however, more tender towards the men, fellows who finished ruining their constitutions, beneath their hypocritical good behaviour; and, in the midst of his jacobinical outburst, there sounded the stubborn knell of a caste, the decomposition and collapse of the middle-classes, whose rotten supports were cracking of themselves. Then, he again floundered, he talked of the barbarians, and announced universal happiness.

"I am more religious than you are," concluded he.

The priest seemed to have been silently listening. But he did not hear, he was entirely taken up by his sad reverie. After a pause, he murmured:

"If they are unconscious, may heaven have mercy upon them!"

Then, they left the house, and slowly followed the Rue Neuve-Saint-Augustin. A fear of having said too much kept them silent, for they both had need to be careful in their positions. As they raised their heads, on arriving at the end of the street, they beheld Madame Hédouin smiling at them, at the door of "The Ladies' Paradise." Standing behind her was Octave, also laughing. That very morning they had settled on their marriage, after a serious conversation. They would wait till the autumn. And they were both full of joy at having at length arranged the matter.

"Good day, my dear Abbé Mauduit!" said Madame Hédouin gaily. "And you, doctor, always paying visits?"

And, as the latter congratulated her on her good looks, she added:

"Oh! if there were only me, you might give up business at once."

They stood conversing a moment. The doctor having mentioned Marie's confinement, Octave seemed delighted to hear of his former neighbour's happy delivery. But, when he learnt that it was a third daughter, he exclaimed:

"Can't her husband manage a boy, then? She thought she might still get Monsieur and Madame Vuillaume to put up with a boy; but they'll never stomach another girl."

"I should think not," said the doctor. "They have both taken to their bed, the news of their daughter's pregnancy

upset them so much. And they sent for a notary, so that
their son-in-law should not even inherit their furniture."

There was a little chaff. The priest alone remained silent,
with his eyes cast on the ground. Madame Hédouin asked
him if he was unwell. Yes, he felt very tired, he was going to
take a little rest. And, after a cordial exchange of good wishes,
he went down the Rue Saint-Roch, still accompanied by the
doctor. On arriving before the church, the latter abruptly
said :

" A bad customer, eh ? "

" Who is ? " asked the priest in surprise.

" That lady who sells linen. She does not care a pin for
either of us. No need for religion, nor for medicine. All the
same, when one is always so well, it is no longer interesting."

And he went on his way, whilst the priest entered the
church.

A bright light penetrated through the broad windows, with
their white panes edged with yellow and pale blue. Not a
sound, not a movement, troubled the deserted nave, wherein
the marble facings, the crystal chandeliers, and the gilded
pulpit, slumbered in the peaceful brightness. It was the quiet,
the substantial comfort of a middle-class drawing-room, with
the coverings taken off the furniture for the grand evening reception. All by herself, a woman, in front of the chapel of Our
Lady of the Seven Dolours, was watching the tapers burn as
they emitted an odour of melting wax.

Abbé Mauduit intended to go up to his room. But a great
agitation, a violent necessity, had forced him to enter the
church and kept him there. It seemed to him that God was
calling him, with a confused and far-off voice, the orders proceeding from which he was unable to catch. He slowly crossed
the church, and was trying to read within himself, to quiet his
alarms, when, suddenly, as he passed behind the choir, a super-
human spectacle shook his entire frame.

It was beyond the marble chapel of the Virgin, as white as
a lily, beyond the gold and silver plate of the chapel of the
Adoration, with its seven golden lamps, its golden candelabra,
and its golden altar shining in the tawny shadow of the aureate
stained windows; it was in the depths of this mysterious night,
past this tabernacle background, a tragical apparition, a simple
yet harrowing drama : Christ nailed to the cross, between the
Virgin Mary and Mary Magdalen, weeping at his feet; and the
white statues, which an invisible light coming from above

caused to stand out from against the bare wall, seemed to advance and increase in size, making the bleeding humanity of this death, and these tears, the divine symbol of eternal woe.

The priest, thoroughly distracted, fell on his knees. He had whitened that plaster, arranged that mode of lighting, prepared that phenomenon; and, now that the hoarding was removed, the architect and the workmen gone, he was the first to be thunderstruck at the sight. From the terrible severity of the Calvary came a breath which overpowered him. He fancied he felt the Almighty passing over him; he bent beneath this breath, filled with misgivings, tortured by the thought that he was perhaps a bad priest.

Oh, Lord! had the hour struck for no longer covering the ills of this decomposed world with the mantle of religion? Was he no longer to assist in the hypocrisy of his flock, no longer to be always there, like a master of the ceremonies, to direct the order of its follies and its vices? Was he then to let all collapse, even though the Church herself might be carried away by the fall? Yes, such was the order no doubt, for the strength to go farther forward in human misery was abandoning him, he was agonizing through powerlessness and disgust. All the abominations he had mingled with since the morning, were stifling him. And, with his hands ardently clasped before him, he prayed for pardon, pardon for his lies, pardon for the weak complaisances, and the base promiscuousness. The fear of God came over him, he beheld God disowning him, forbidding him any longer to abuse His name, a God of anger resolved at last to exterminate the guilty. All the worldly man's tolerances disappeared before the unbridled scruples of his conscience, and there only remained the faith of the believer, terrified and struggling in the uncertainty of salvation. Oh, Lord! which was the straight road, what should be done in the midst of that expiring society which even contaminated its priests?

Then, the Abbé Mauduit, his eyes fixed on the Calvary, sobbed aloud. He wept like the Virgin Mary and Mary Magdalen, he mourned for truth dead, for heaven empty. And right beyond the marble ornaments and the jewelled plate, the great plaster Christ was without a drop of blood.

CHAPTER XVIII

In December, the eighth month of her mourning, Madame Josserand for the first time accepted an invitation to dine out. It was merely at the Duveyriers', almost a family gathering, with which Clotilde opened her Saturday receptions of the new winter. The day before, Adèle had been told that she would have to help Julie with the washing-up. The ladies were in the habit of thus lending their servants to each other on the days when they gave parties.

"And above all, try and put a little more go into yourself," said Madame Josserand to her maid-of-all-work. "I don't know what you've got in your body now, you're as limp as rags. Yet you're fat and plump."

Adèle was simply nine months gone in the family way. For a long time she had thought she was merely growing stouter, which greatly surprised her however; and she would get into a perfect rage, with her ever hungry empty stomach, on the days when madame triumphantly showed her to her guests: ah, well! those who accused her of weighing her servant's bread might come and look at that great glutton, it was not likely she got so fat by merely licking the walls! When, in her stupidity, Adèle at length became aware of her misfortune, she restrained herself twenty times from telling the truth to her mistress, who was really taking advantage of her condition to make the neighbourhood think that she was at length feeding her.

But, from this moment, terror stultified her entirely. Her village ideas once more took possession of her obtuse skull. She thought herself damned, she fancied that the gendarmes would come and take her, if she admitted her pregnancy. Then, all her low cunning was made use of to hide it. She concealed the feelings of sickness, the intolerable headaches, the terrible constipation from which she suffered ; twice she thought she would drop down dead before her kitchen fire, whilst stirring some sauces. The pain that she had endured for the

two last months with the obstinacy of a heroic silence was indeed frightful.

Adèle went up to bed that night about eleven o'clock. The
thought of to-morrow evening terrified her : more drudgery,
more bullying by Julie! and she could scarcely move about.
Yet, to her, her confinement was still an uncertain and far-off
affair, she preferred not to think of it, vaguely hoping that it
would no longer trouble her. She had, therefore, made no pre-
parations, and was without an idea, without a plan. She was only
comfortable when in her bed, stretched out on her back. As it
had been freezing since the day before, she kept her stockings
on, blew out her candle, and pulling the clothes tightly about
her waited to get warm.

During the night she was seized with labour pains, and a
desire came over her to move about, so as to walk them off.
She therefore lighted the candle and began to wander round the
room, her tongue dried up, tormented with a burning thirst,
and her cheeks on fire. Hours passed in this cruel wandering,
without her daring to put on her shoes, for fear of making a
noise, whilst she was only protected against the cold by an old
shawl thrown across her shoulders. Two o'clock struck, then
three o'clock.

Not a soul stirred in the adjoining rooms, every one was
snoring ; she could hear Julie's sonorous hum, whilst Lisa made
a kind of hissing noise like the shrill notes of a fife. Four
o'clock had just struck, when seized with a violent pain, she
felt that the end was approaching, and could not restrain
uttering a loud cry.

At this the occupants of the other rooms began to rouse up.
Voices thick with sleep were heard saying : "Well! what?
who's being murdered?—Some one's being taken by force !—
Don't dream out loud like that!" Dreadfully frightened, she drew
the bed-clothes over the new-born child, which was uttering
plaintive cries like a little kitten. But she soon heard Julie
snoring again, after turning over ; whilst Lisa, once more asleep,
no longer uttered a sound. Then she experienced an immense
relief, an infinite comfort of calm and repose, and lay as one
dead.

She must have dozed thus for the best part of an hour.
When six o'clock struck, the consciousness of her position
awoke her again. Time was flying, she rose up painfully, and
did whatever things came into her head, without deciding on
them beforehand. A frosty moon shone full into the room.

After dressing herself, she wrapped the infant up in some old
rags, and then folded a couple of newspapers around it. It
uttered no cry now, yet its little heart was beating.

Not one of the servants was about as yet, and after getting
slumbering Monsieur Gourd to unfasten the door from his room,
she was able to go out and lay her bundle in the Passage
Choiseul, the gates of which had just been opened, and then
quietly return upstairs. She met no one. For once in her
lifetime, luck was on her side !

She immediately set about tidying her room, after which,
utterly worn-out, and as white as wax, she again lay down.
It was thus that Madame Josserand found her, when she had
made up her mind to go upstairs towards nine o'clock, greatly
surprised at not seeing Adèle come down. The servant having
complained of a violent attack of diarrhœa which had kept her
awake all night, madame exclaimed :

"Of course ! you must have eaten too much again ! You
think of nothing else but stuffing yourself."

The girl's paleness, however, made her uneasy, and she
talked of sending for the doctor ; but she was glad to save the
three francs, when Adèle vowed that she merely needed rest.
Since her husband's death, Madame Josserand had been living
with her daughter Hortense on an allowance made her by the
brothers Bernheim, but which did not prevent her from bitterly
alluding to them as persons who lived on the brains of others ;
and she spent less than ever on food, so as not to descend to a
lower level of society by quitting her apartments and giving up
her Tuesday receptions.

"That's right ; sleep," said she. "There is some cold beef
left which will do for this morning, and to-night we dine out.
If you cannot come down to help Julie, she will have to do
without you."

The dinner that evening at the Duveyriers' was a very cordial
one. All the family was there : the two Vabres and their wives,
Madame Josserand, Hortense, Léon, and even uncle Bachelard,
who behaved well. Moreover, they had invited Trublot to fill
a vacant place, and Madame Dambreville, so as not to separate
her from Léon. The latter, after his marriage with the niece,
had once again fallen into the arms of the aunt, who was still
necessary to him. They were seen to arrive together in all the
drawing-rooms, and they would apologise for the young wife,
whom a cold or a feeling of idleness, said they, kept at home.
That evening the whole table complained of scarce knowing

her : they loved her so much, she was so beautiful! Then,
they talked of the chorus which Clotilde was to give at the end
of the evening ; it was the "Blessing of the Daggers" again,
but this time with five tenors, something complete and magisterial. For two months past, Duveyrier himself, who had become quite charming, had been looking up the friends of the
house, and saying to every one he met: "You are quite a
stranger, come and see us ; my wife is going to give her choruses
again." Therefore, half through the dinner, they talked of
nothing but music. The happiest good nature and the most
free-hearted gaiety prevailed throughout.

Then, after the coffee, and whilst the ladies sat round the
drawing-room fire, the gentlemen formed a group in the parlour
and began to exchange some grave ideas. The other guests
were now arriving. And among the earliest were Campardon,
Abbé Mauduit, and Doctor Juillerat, without including the
diners, with the exception of Trublot, who had disappeared on
leaving the table. They almost immediately commenced talking politics. The debates in the Chamber deeply interested the
gentlemen, and they had not yet given over discussing the success of the opposition candidates for Paris, all of whom had been
returned at the May elections. This triumph of the dissatisfied
portion of the middle-classes made them feel anxious at heart,
in spite of their apparent delight.

"Dear me!" declared Léon, "Monsieur Thiers is certainly a
most talented man. But he puts such acrimony into his
speeches on the Mexican expedition that he quite spoils their
effect."

He had just been named to a higher appointment, through
Madame Dambreville's influence, and had at once joined the
government party. The only thing that remained in him of
the famished demagogue was an unbearable intolerance of all
doctrines.

"Not long ago you were accusing the government of every
sin," said the doctor smiling. "I hope that you at least voted
for Monsieur Thiers."

The young man avoided answering. Théophile, whose
stomach was no longer able to digest his food, and who was
worried with fresh doubts as to his wife's constancy, exclaimed :

"I voted for him. When men refuse to live as brothers, so
much the worse for them!"

"And so much the worse for you, as well, eh?" remarked

Duveyrier, who, speaking but little, uttered some very profound observations.

Théophile, greatly scared, looked at him. Auguste no longer dared admit that he had also voted for Monsieur Thiers. Then, every one was very much surprised to hear uncle Bachelard utter a legitimist profession of faith : he thought it the most genteel. Campardon seconded him warmly ; he had abstained from voting himself, because the official candidate, Monsieur Dewinck, did not offer sufficient guarantees as regards religion ; and he furiously declaimed against Renan's " Life of Jesus," which had recently made its appearance.

" It is not the book that should be burnt, it is the author ! " repeated he.

" You are, perhaps, too radical, my friend," interrupted the priest in a conciliatory tone. " But, indeed, the symptoms are becoming terrible. There is some talk of driving away the pope, the revolution has invaded parliament. We are walking on the edge of a precipice."

" So much the better ! " said Doctor Juillerat simply.

Then, the others all protested. He renewed his attacks against the middle classes, prophesying that there would be a clean sweep, the day when the masses wished to enjoy power in their turn ; and the others loudly interrupted him, exclaiming that the middle classes represented the virtue, the industry, and the thrift of the nation. Duveyrier was at length able to make himself heard. He owned it before all: he had voted for Monsieur Dewinck, not that Monsieur Dewinck exactly represented his opinions, but because he was the symbol of order. Yes, the saturnalia of the Reign of Terror might one day return. Monsieur Rouher, that remarkable statesman who had just succeeded Monsieur Billault, had formally prophesied it in the Chamber. He concluded with these striking words :

" The triumph of the opposition, is the preliminary subsidence of the structure. Take care that it does not crush you in falling ! "

The other gentlemen held their peace, with the unavowed fear of having allowed themselves to be carried away even to compromising their personal safety. They beheld workmen begrimed with powder and blood, entering their homes, violating their maid-servants and drinking their wine. No doubt, the Emperor deserved a lesson ; only, they were beginning to regret having given him so severe a one.

" Be easy ! " concluded the doctor scoffingly. " We will manage to save you from the bullets."

But he was going too far, they set him down as an original.
It was, moreover, thanks to this reputation for originality, that
he did not lose his connection.   He continued, by resuming with
Abbé Mauduit their eternal quarrel respecting the approaching
downfall of the Church.   Léon now sided with the priest : he
talked of Providence and, on Sundays, accompanied Madame
Dambreville to nine o'clock mass.

Meanwhile, the guests continued to arrive, the drawing-room
was becoming quite filled with ladies.   Valérie and Berthe were
exchanging little secrets like two good friends.   The other
Madame Campardon, whom the architect had brought no doubt
in place of poor Rose, who was already in bed upstairs and
reading Dickens, was giving Madame Josserand an economical
recipe for washing clothes without soap ; whilst Hortense,
seated all by herself and expecting Verdier, did not take her
eyes off the door.   But suddenly Clotilde, while conversing
with Madame Dambreville, rose up and held out her hands.
Her friend Madame Octave Mouret, had just entered the room.
The marriage had taken place early in November, at the end of
her mourning.

"And your husband?" asked the hostess.   "He is not going
to disappoint me, I hope ?"

"No, no," answered Caroline with a smile.   "He will
be here directly ; something detained him at the last
moment."

There was some whispering, glances full of curiosity were
directed towards her, so calm and so lovely, ever the same, with
the pleasant assurance of a woman who succeeds in everything
she undertakes.   Madame Josserand pressed her hand, as
though she were delighted to see her again.   Berthe and Valérie
left off talking and examined her at their ease, studying her
costume, a straw colour dress covered with lace.   But, in the
midst of this quiet forgetfulness of the past, Auguste, whom the
political discussion had left quite cool, was giving signs of indignant amazement as he stood near the parlour door.   What! his
sister was going to receive the family of his wife's former lover !
And, in his marital rancour, there was a touch of the jealous
anger of the tradesman ruined by a triumphant competition ;
for "The Ladies' Paradise," by extending its business and creating a special department for silk, had so drained his resources,
that he had been obliged to take a partner.   He drew near, and
whilst every one was making much of Madame Mouret, he
whispered to Clotilde :

"You know, I will never put up with it."

"Put up with what?" asked she, greatly surprised.

"I do not mind the wife so much, she has not done me any harm. But if the husband comes, I shall take hold of Berthe by the arm, and leave the room in the presence of everybody."

She looked at him, and then shrugged her shoulders. Caroline was her oldest friend, she was certainly not going to give up seeing her, just to satisfy his caprices. As though anyone even recollected the matter. He would do far better not to rake up things forgotten by everybody but himself. And as, deeply affected, he looked to Berthe for support, expecting that she would get up and follow him at once, she calmed him with a frown; was he mad? did he wish to make himself more ridiculous than he had ever been before?

"But it is in order that I may not appear ridiculous!" retorted he in despair.

Then Madame Josserand inclined towards him, and said in a severe tone of voice:

"It is becoming quite indecent; everyone is looking at you. Do behave yourself for once in a way."

He held his tongue, but without submitting. From this moment a certain uneasiness existed amongst the ladies. The only one who preserved her smiling tranquillity was Madame Mouret, now sitting beside Clotilde and opposite Berthe. They watched Auguste, who had retired to the window recess where his marriage had been decided, not so very long before. His anger was bringing on a headache, and he now and again pressed his forehead against the icy cold panes.

Octave did not arrive till very late. As he reached the landing, he met Madame Juzeur, who had just come down, wrapped in a shawl. She complained of her chest, and had got up on purpose not to disappoint the Duveyriers. Her languid state did not prevent her falling into the young man's arms, as she congratulated him on his marriage.

"How delighted I am with such a splendid result, my friend! Really! I was quite in despair about you, I never thought you would have succeeded. Tell me, you rascal, how did you manage to get over her?"

Octave smiled and kissed her fingers. But some one who was bounding upstairs with the agility of a goat, disturbed them; and, greatly surprised, they fancied they recognised Saturnin. It was indeed Saturnin, who a week before had left the Asile des Moulineaux, where for a second time Doctor Chassagne declined to detain him any longer, still considering him not sufficiently mad. No doubt he was going to spend the evening with Marie Pichon, just as in former days, when his parents had company. And those bygone times were suddenly evoked. Octave could hear an expiring voice coming from above, singing the ballad with which Marie whiled away her vacant hours ; he beheld her once more eternally alone, beside the crib in which Lilitte slumbered, and awaiting Jules's return with all the complacency of a gentle and useless woman.

"I wish you every happiness with your wife," repeated Madame Juzeur, tenderly squeezing Octave's hands.

In order not to enter the drawing-room with her, he was purposely occupying some time in removing his overcoat, when Trublot, in his dress clothes, bareheaded, and looking quite upset, came from the passage leading to the kitchen.

"You know she's not at all well !" murmured he, whilst Hippolyte announced Madame Juzeur.

"Who isn't ?" asked Octave.

"Why Adèle, the servant upstairs."

Hearing there was something the matter with her, he had gone up quite paternally, on leaving the dinner-table. It must have been a very severe attack of cholerine ; a good glass of mulled wine was what she ought to have, and she had not even a lump of sugar. Then, as he noticed that his friend smiled in an indifferent sort of way, he added :

"Hallo ! I forgot, you're married, you joker ! This sort of thing no longer interests you. I never thought of that when I found you with Madame Anything you like except that !"

They entered together. The ladies were just then speaking of their servants, and were taking such interest in the conversation, that they did not notice them at first. All were complacently approving Madame Duveyrier, who was trying to explain, in an embarrassed way, why she continued to keep Clémence and Hippolyte : he was rough, but she dressed her so well, that one could not help shutting one's eyes to other matters. Neither Valérie nor Berthe could succeed in securing a decent girl ; they had given it up in despair, after trying every registry office, the good-for-nothing servants from which had done no more than pass through their kitchens. Madame Josserand violently abused Adèle, of whom she related some fresh abominable and stupid doings of an extraordinary character ; and yet she did not send her about her business. As for the other Madame Campardon, she was quite enthusiastic in her praises of Lisa : a pearl, not a thing to reproach her with, in short one of those deserving domestics to whom one gives prizes.

"She is quite one of the family now," said she. "Our little Angèle is attending some lectures at the Hôtel de Ville, and Lisa accompanies her. Oh ! they might remain out together for days, we should not be in the least anxious."

It was at this moment that the ladies caught sight of Octave. He was advancing to wish Clotilde good-evening. Berthe looked at him ; then, without the least affectation, she resumed her conversation with Valérie, who had exchanged with him the affectionate glance of disinterested friendship. The others, Madame Josserand, Madame Dambreville, without throwing themselves at him, surveyed him with sympathetic interest.

"So here you are at last !" said Clotilde, who was most amiable. "I was beginning to tremble for the chorus."

And, as Madame Mouret gently scolded her husband for being so late, he made some excuses.

"But, my dear, I was unable to come sooner. I am most sorry, madame. However, I am now entirely at your disposal."

Meanwhile, the ladies were anxiously watching the window recess into which Auguste had retired. They received a momentary fright when they beheld him turn round at the sound of Octave's voice. His headache was no doubt worse, he had a restless look about the eyes, which seemed full of the darkness of the street. He at length appeared to make up his mind, and returning to his former position beside his sister's chair, he said :

"Send them away, or else we will leave."

Clotilde again shrugged her shoulders. Then, Auguste seemed disposed to give her time to consider : he would wait a few minutes longer, more especially as Trublot had taken Octave into the parlour. The other ladies were still uneasy, for they had heard the husband whisper in his wife's ear :

"If he comes back here, you must get up and follow me. Otherwise, you may return to your mother's."

In the parlour, the gentlemen greeted Octave quite as cordially. If Léon made a point of showing a little coolness, uncle Bachelard and even Théophile seemed to declare, as they held out their hands to Octave, that the family forgot everything. He congratulated Campardon, who, decorated two days previously, now wore a broad red ribbon ; and the beaming architect scolded him for never calling now and then to pass an hour with his wife : though one got married, it was scarcely nice to forget friends of fifteen years' standing. But the young man felt quite surprised and anxious as he stood before Duveyrier. He had not seen him since his recovery. He looked uneasily at his jaw all out of place, dropping too much on the left side, and which now gave a horrid squinting expression to his countenance. Then, when the counsellor spoke, he had another surprise : his voice had lowered two tones, it had become quite sepulchral.

"Don't you think him much better thus ?" said Trublot to Octave, as they returned to the drawing-room door. "It positively gives him a certain majestic air. I saw him presiding at the assizes, the day before yesterday—Listen ! they are talking of it."

And indeed the gentlemen had abandoned politics to take up morality. They were listening to Duveyrier as he gave some details of an affair in which his attitude had been particularly noticed. He was even about to be named a president and an officer of the Legion of Honour. It was respecting an infanticide already a year old. The unnatural mother, a regular savage, as he said, happened to be the boot-stitcher, his former tenant, that tall pale and friendless girl, whose pregnant condition had roused Monsieur Gourd's indignation so much. And besides that, she was altogether stupid ! for, without reflecting that her appearance would betray her, she had gone and cut her child in two and kept it at the bottom of a bonnet-box. She had naturally told the jury quite a ridiculous romance : a seducer who had deserted her, misery, hunger, and then a fit of mad despair on seeing herself unable to supply the little one's wants : in a word, the same story they all told. But it was necessary to make an example. Duveyrier congratulated himself on having summed up with that lucidity, which often decided a jury's verdict.

"And what was your sentence ?" asked the doctor.

"Five years," replied the counsellor in his new voice, which seemed both hoarse and sepulchral. "It is time to oppose a dyke to the debauchery which threatens to submerge Paris."

Trublot nudged Octave's elbow ; they were both acquainted with the facts of the attempt at suicide.

"Eh ? you hear him ?" murmured he. "Without joking, it improves his voice : it stirs one more, does it not ? it goes straight to the heart, now. Ah ! if you had only seen him, standing up, draped in his long red robes, with his mug all

askew ! On my word ! he quite frightened me, he was extraordinary, oh ! you know ! a style in his majesty enough to make
your flesh creep ! "

But he left off speaking, and listened to the ladies in the
drawing-room, who were again on the subject of servants. That
very morning, Madame Duveyrier had given Julie a week's
notice : she had nothing certainly to say against the girl's
cooking ; only, good behaviour came before everything in her
eyes. The truth was that, warned by Doctor Juillerat, and
anxious for the health of her son whose little goings-on she
tolerated at home, so as to keep them under control, she had
had an explanation with Julie, who had been unwell for some
time past : and the latter, like a genteel cook, whose style was
not to quarrel with her employers, had accepted her week's
notice. Madame Josserand at once shared Clotilde's indignation : yes, one should be very strict on the question of morality ;
for instance, if she kept that slut Adèle in spite of her dirty
ways, and her stupidity, it was because the girl was virtuous.
Oh ! on that point, she had nothing whatever to reproach her
with !

"Poor Adèle ! when one only thinks !" murmured Trublot,
again affected at the thought of the wretched creature, half
frozen upstairs beneath her thin blanket.

Then, bending towards Octave's ear, he added with a
chuckle :

"I say, Duveyrier might at least take her up a bottle of claret!"

" Yes, gentlemen," the counsellor was continuing, " statistics
will bear me out, the crime of infanticide is increasing in the
mos frightful proportions. Sentiment prevails to too great an
extent in the present day, and far too much consideration is
shown to science, to your pretended physiology, all of which
will end by there soon being neither good nor evil. One cannot cure debauchery ; the thing is to destroy it at its root."

This refutation was addressed above all to Doctor Juillerat,
who had wished to give a medical explanation of the boot-
stitcher's case.

The other gentlemen also exhibited great severity and disgust : Campardon could not understand vice, uncle Bachelard
defended infancy, Théophile demanded an inquiry, Léon discussed the question of prostitution in its relations with the
state ; whilst Trublot, in answer to an inquiry of Octave's,
talked of Duveyrier's new mistress, who was a decent sort of
woman this time, rather mature, but romantic, with a soul ex-

panded by that ideal which the counsellor required to purify
love; in short, a worthy person who gave him a peaceful home,
imposing upon him as much as she liked and sleeping with his
friends, without making any unnecessary fuss. And the Abbé
Mauduit alone remained silent, his eyes fixed on the ground,
his mind sorely troubled, and full of an infinite sadness.

They were now about to sing the "Blessing of the Daggers."
The drawing-room had filled up, a flood of rich dresses was crushing in the brilliant light from the chandelier and the lamps,
whilst gay bursts of laughter ran along the rows of chairs; and,
in the midst of the buzz, Clotilde in a low voice roughly
chided Auguste, who, on seeing Octave enter with the other
gentlemen of the chorus, had caught hold of Berthe's arm to
make her leave her seat. But he was already beginning to
yield, feeling more and more embarrassed in the presence of the
ladies' dumb disapproval, whilst his head had become entirely
the prey of triumphant neuralgia. Madame Dambreville's
stern looks quite drove him to despair, and even the other
Madame Campardon was against him. It was reserved to
Madame Josserand to finish him off. She abruptly interfered,
threatening to take back her daughter and never to pay him
the fifty thousand francs dowry; for she was always promising
this dowry with the greatest coolness imaginable. Then, turning towards uncle Bachelard, seated behind her, and next to
Madame Juzeur, she made him renew his promises. The uncle
placed his hand on his heart: he knew his duty, the family before everything ! Auguste repulsed on all sides, beat a retreat,
and again sought refuge in the window recess, where he
once more pressed his burning forehead against the icy cold
panes.

Then, Octave experienced a singular sensation as though his
Paris life was beginning over again. It was as though the two
years he had lived in the Rue de Choiseul had been a blank.
His wife was there, smiling at him, and yet nothing seemed to
have passed in his existence : to-day was the same as yesterday,
there was neither pause nor ending. Trublot showed him the
new partner standing beside Berthe, a little fair fellow very neat
in his ways, who gave her, it was said, no end of presents.
Uncle Bachelard, who was now going in for poetry, was revealing himself in a sentimental light to Madame Juzeur, whom he
quite affected with some intimate details respecting Fifi and
Gueulin. Théophile, devoured by doubts, doubled up by violent
fits of coughing, was imploring Doctor Juillerat in an out-of-the-

way corner to give his wife something to quiet her. Campardon, his eyes fixed on cousin Gasparine, was talking of the diocese of Evreux, and jumping from that to the great works of the new Rue du Dix Décembre, defending God and art, sending the world about its business, for at heart he did not care a hang for it, he was an artist! And behind a flower-stand there could even be seen the back of a gentleman whom all the marriageable girls contemplated with an air of profound curiosity : it was Verdier, who was talking with Hortense, the pair of them having an acrimonious explanation, again putting off their marriage till the spring, so as not to turn the woman and her child into the street in the depth of winter.

Then, the chorus was sung afresh. The architect, with his mouth wide open, gave out the first line. Clotilde struck a chord, and uttered her cry. And the other voices burst forth, the uproar increased little by little, and spread with a violence which scared the candles and caused the ladies to turn pale. Trublot, having been found wanting among the basses, was being tried a second time as a barytone. The five tenors were much noticed, Octave especially, to whom Clotilde regretted being unable to give a solo. When the voices fell, and she had applied the soft pedal, imitating the cadenced and distant footsteps of a departing patrol, the applause was deafening, and she, together with the gentlemen, had every praise showered upon them. And at the farthest end of the adjoining room, right behind a triple row of men in evening dress, one beheld Duveyrier clenching his teeth so as not to cry aloud with anguish, with his mouth all on one side, and his festering eruptions almost bleeding.

The tea coming next, unrolled the same procession, distributed the same cups and the same sandwiches. For a moment, the Abbé Mauduit found himself once more in the middle of the deserted drawing-room. He looked, through the wide open door, on the crush of guests ; and vanquished, he smiled, he again cast the mantle of religion over this corrupt middle-class society, like a master of the ceremonies draping the canker, to stave off the final decomposition. He must save the Church, as heaven had not answered his cry of misery and despair.

At length, the same as on every Saturday, when midnight struck, the guests began to withdraw. Campardon was among the first to leave, with the other Madame Campardon. Léon and Madame Dambreville were not long in maritally following them.   Verdier's back had long ago disappeared, when Madame Josserand went off with Hortense, bullying her for what she called her romantic obstinacy.   Uncle Bachelard, very drunk from the punch he had taken, detained Madame Juzeur a moment at the door, finding her advice full of experience quite refreshing.   Trublot, who had stolen some sugar for Adèle, was making for the passage leading to the kitchen, when the presence of Berthe and Auguste in the anteroom embarrassed him, and he pretended to be looking for his hat.

But, just at this minute, Octave and his wife, escorted by Clotilde, also came out and asked for their wraps.   There ensued a few seconds of embarrassment.   The anteroom was not large, Berthe and Madame Mouret were pressed against each other, whilst Hippolyte was searching for their things. They both smiled.   Then, when the door was opened, the two men, Octave and Auguste, brought face to face, did the polite, each stepping aside.   At length, Berthe consented to pass out first, after an exchange of bows.   And Valérie, who was leaving in her turn with Théophile, again looked at Octave in the affectionate way of a disinterested friend.   He and she alone might have told each other everything.

"Good-bye," repeated Clotilde graciously to the two families, before returning to the drawing-room.

Octave stopped short.   He had just caught sight on the next floor of the partner, the neat little fair fellow, taking his departure like the rest, and whose hands Saturnin, who had just left Marie, was pressing in an outburst of savage tenderness, stuttering the while: "Friend—friend—friend—" A singular feeling of jealousy at first darted through him.   Then, he smiled.   It was the past ; and he again recalled his amours, all his campaign of Paris, the complaisances of that good little Pichon, the repulse he received from Valérie of whom he preserved a pleasant recollection, his stupid connection with Berthe which he regretted as pure waste of time.   Now, he had transacted his business, Paris was conquered ; and he gallantly followed her whom in his heart he still styled Madame Hédouin, every now and then stooping to see that the train of her dress did not catch in the stair-rods.

The house had once more resumed its grand air of middleclass dignity.   He fancied he could hear Marie's distant and expiring ballad.   Beneath the porch he met Jules coming in : Madame Vuillaume was at death's door and refused to see her daughter. Then, that was all, the doctor and the priest retired last and still arguing; Trublot had slyly gone up to Adèle to attend to her; and the deserted staircase slumbered in a heavy warmth with its chaste doors enclosing respectable alcoves. One o'clock was striking, when Monsieur Gourd, whom Madame Gourd was snugly awaiting in bed, turned out the gas. Then, the whole house lapsed into silent darkness, as though annihilated by the decency of its sleep. Nothing remained, life resumed its level of indifference and stupidity.

On the following morning, Adèle dragged herself down to her kitchen, so as to allay suspicion. A thaw had set in during the night, and she opened the window, feeling stifled, when Hippolyte's voice rose furiously from the depths of the narrow courtyard.

"You dirty hussies! Who has been emptying her slops out of the window again? Madame's dress is quite spoilt!"

He had hung out one of Madame Duveyrier's dresses given him to brush, and he found it all spattered with sour broth. Then, from the top to the bottom, the servants appeared at their windows and violently exculpated themselves. The sluice was open and a rush of the most abominable words flowed from the foul spot. In times of thaw, the walls were steeped with humidity, and quite a pestilence ascended from the obscure little courtyard, all the hidden corruptions of the different floors seeming to melt and ooze out by this common sewer of the house.

"It wasn't me," said Adèle leaning out. "I've only just come."

Lisa abruptly raised her head.

"Hallo! so you're on your legs again. Well what was the matter? Is it true you almost croaked?"

"Oh! yes, I had such colics, and not at all funny, I can tell you!"

This put a stop to the quarrel. Valérie and Berthe's new servants, a big camel and a little jade, as they were termed, looked curiously at Adèle's pale face. Victoire and Julie also wished to see her, and stretched their necks, and leant their heads back. They all had an idea there was something wrong, for it was unnatural to have such gripes and yell out as she did.

" Perhaps you've had something which didn't agree with you," said Lisa.

The others burst out laughing, another rush of foul language overflowed, whilst the wretched creature, awfully frightened, stammered :

"Hold your tongues, with your nasty words ! I'm quite ill enough as it is. You don't want to finish me off, do you ? "

No, of course not. She was as stupid as stupid could be, and dirty enough to disgust a whole neighbourhood ; but they all held too closely together to wish to bring her into any trouble. And they naturally turned to abusing their masters and mistresses ; they criticised the party of the previous evening with looks of profound repugnance.

"So they've all made it up again now ? " asked Victoire as she sipped her glass of syrup and brandy.

Hippolyte, who was wiping madame's dress, replied :

"They've no more heart than my shoes. When they've spat in one another's faces, they wash themselves with it, to make one believe they're clean."

"They must manage to agree somehow or other," said Lisa. "Otherwise, it wouldn't take long before our turn came."

But there was a moment of panic. A door opened, and the servants were already diving back into their kitchens, when Lisa announced that it was only little Angèle : there was nothing to fear with her, she understood. And, from the foul spout, there again arose all the rancour of the domestics in the midst of the poisonous stench caused by the thaw. There was a grand spreading out of all the dirty linen of the last two years. It was quite consoling not to be ladies and gentlemen, when one beheld the masters and mistresses living in the midst of it all, and apparently enjoying it, as they were preparing to go through it all again.

"Eh ! I say, you, up there ! " suddenly shouted Victoire, "was it with Mug-askew that you had what didn't agree with you ? "

At this, a ferocious yell of delight quite shook the stinking cesspool. Hippolyte actually tore madame's dress ; but he did not care, it was far too good for her as it was ! The big camel and the little jade were bent over the hand-rails of their windows, wriggling in a mad burst of laughter. Adèle, however, who was quite scared, and who was half asleep through weakness, started, and she retorted in the midst of the jeers :

"You're all of you heartless things. When you're dying, I'll come and dance at your bedsides."

"Ah ! mademoiselle," resumed Lisa, leaning out to speak to Julie, "how happy you must feel at leaving such a wretched house in a week ! On my word, one becomes wicked here in spite of oneself. I wish you a better home in your next place."

Julie, her arms bare, and dripping with the blood from a turbot she had been just cleaning for that evening's dinner, returned to the window beside the footman. She shrugged her shoulders and concluded with this philosophical reply :

"Dear me ! mademoiselle, here or there, they're all alike. In the present day, whoever has been in the one has been in the other. It's all Filth and Company."

THE END.

42, CATHERINE STREET, STRAND,
MARCH, 1887.

VIZETELLY & CO.'S NEW BOOKS, AND NEW EDITIONS.

THEOPHILE GAUTIER'S FAMOUS ROMANCE OF LOVE AND PASSION.

Handsomely printed on vellum-texture paper, with Chapter headings and tailpieces in various tints, and with 17 high-class Etchings from designs by Toudouze.
Price 10s. 6d., elegantly bound.

MADEMOISELLE DE MAUPIN.

By THEOPHILE GAUTIER.

"Gautier is an inimitable model. His manner is so light and true, so really creative, his fancy so alert, his taste so happy, his humour so genial, that he makes illusion almost as contagious as laughter."—MR. HENRY JAMES.

In crown 8vo, illustrated with page Engravings, price 3s. 6d., attractively bound.

PAPA, MAMMA, AND BABY.

By GUSTAVE DROZ.

TRANSLATED WITHOUT ABRIDGMENT FROM THE 130TH FRENCH EDITION.

"Monsieur Gustave Droz is the painter of a slightly factitious state of society which toys with pleasant vices like the eighteenth century played at pastorals. One must read his master-piece—'Monsieur, Madame et Bébé'—to understand all the painted grace of that circle. No doubt the tone is a trifle exaggerated, but the artist's great merit lies in his having depicted characters which will certainly live as excellent studies of the society of the period."—EMILE ZOLA.

"The story of the courtship of the pair is exquisitely realistic and charmingly attractive, and like praise must also be given to the various pictures of their married life. Of course the book is highly sensuous, yet this general tone is relieved by so many passages of a neutral affection, and by a style at once so light, graceful, and humorous, that even a prude might hesitate to condemn it. The *intimité galante* of life, the lover who is a husband, and the wife who is in love with the man she has married, have never before been so attractively portrayed."—*Pictorial World.*

NEW BOOK BY THE AUTHOR OF "A MUMMER'S WIFE."

To be Ready during April,

In crown 8vo, price 3s. 6d.

A MERE ACCIDENT: A Realistic Story.

By GEORGE MOORE.

NEW WORK BY THE AUTHOR OF "THE IRONMASTER."

In crown 8vo, 3s. 6d.

CLOUD AND SUNSHINE. (Noir et Rose.)

By GEORGES OHNET.

Translated with the Author's sanction from the 60th French Edition by
MRS. HELEN STOTT.

NEW NOVEL BY THE AUTHOR OF "THE IRONMASTER."

To be Ready during June.

In Crown 8vo, price 7s. 6d.

WILL. (Volonté.)

By GEORGES OHNET.

In Picture Cover, 1s. With Humorous Illustrations by LANCELOT SPEED.

KING SOLOMON'S WIVES : Or the Mysterious Mines.

By HYDER RAGGED,

AUTHOR OF "HE, SHE, OR IT!" "GUESS!" &c.

In crown 8vo, 2s. 6d.

A CITY GIRL. A Realistic Story.

By JOHN LAW.

NEW REALISTIC NOVELS.

M. EMILE ZOLA'S NEW NOVEL.

To be Ready during June.

In Crown 8vo, with Page Illustrations, Price 6s.

THE SOIL. (La Terre.)

By EMILE ZOLA.

FLAUBERT'S MASTERPIECE.

In crown 8vo, beautifully printed on vellum-texture paper, and Illustrated with Six Etchings, by French Artists, price 6s., elegantly bound.

MADAME BOVARY: Provincial Manners.

By GUSTAVE FLAUBERT.

TRANSLATED BY ELEANOR MARX-AVELING. With an Introduction and Notes of the proceedings against the author before the "Tribunal Correctionnel" of Paris.

M. EMILE ZOLA ON "MADAME BOVARY."

"The first characteristic of the naturalistic novel, of which 'Madame Bovary' is the type, is the exact reproduction of life, the absence of every romantic element. The scenes themselves are every day ones; but the author has carefully sorted and balanced them in such a way as to make his work a monument of art and science. It is a true picture of life presented to us in an admirably selected frame. All extraordinary invention is therefore banished from it. One no longer encounters in its pages children marked at their birth, then lost, to be found again in the last chapter; nor secret drawers containing documents which come to light at the right moment for the purpose of saving persecuted innocence.

"The whole of 'Madame Bovary,' even in its slightest incidents, possesses a heartrending interest—a new interest, unknown prior to the appearance of this book—the interest of reality, of the drama of daily life. It grips your very vitals with an invincible power, like some scene you have witnessed, some event which is actually happening before your eyes. The personages of the story are among your acquaintances, you have assisted at their proceedings twenty times over. You are in your own sphere in this work, and all that transpires is even dependent upon your surroundings. It is this which causes such profound emotion."

BLACKWOOD'S MAGAZINE ON "MADAME BOVARY."

"Flaubert wrote his great masterpiece 'Madame Bovary' deliberately in his maturity: and the notoriety which carried him with it into the law-courts, made him a martyr in a society that was by no means fastidious. Seldom before has an author concentrated such care and thought on a single work. Each separate chapter is wrought out with an exactness of elaboration to which the painting of the Dutch school is sketchy and superficial."

NEW REALISTIC NOVELS—*continued.*

In crown 8vo, with Ornamental Initials and Vignettes, and a Portrait of the Author, Etched by BOCOURT *from a drawing by* FLAUBERT's *niece. Price 6s.*

SALAMBO.

By GUSTAVE FLAUBERT.

TRANSLATED FROM THE FRENCH "ÉDITION DÉFINITIVE" BY J. S. CHARTRES, AND PREFACED BY AN ESSAY ON FLAUBERT's WORKS.

Press Opinions on Mr. J. S. Chartres's Translation of "Salambo."

" Some little while ago there was published an extraordinary bad translation of Flaubert's 'Salambo' [by M. French Sheldon]. By some means (there are so many of these means) it was puffed as even in our time few if any books so bad have been puffed. Names of all sorts and conditions of men ('the highest authorities in the land,' said the advertisement) were pressed into its service. And hand in hand with the puffing went some dark warnings against other possible translations, which would inevitably be spurious, infamous, and I know not what else. The reason of this warning is now clear. Another translation has appeared, done by Mr. J. S. Chartres, and published by Vizetelly, which is much superior to its predecessor."—*The World.*

" We are able to declare that this second translation, the work of Mr. Chartres, and published by Messrs. Vizetelly, is very much the better of the two."—*Saturday Review.*

In crown 8vo, with Etchings by MULLER, *from designs by* JEANNIOT. *Price 6s.*

GERMINIE LACERTEUX.

By EDMOND AND JULES DE GONCOURT.   [*In April.*

" 'GERMINIE LACERTEUX' fixes a date in our contemporary literature. For the first time the lower classes are studied by writers who are masters of observation and style. And I repeat it is not a question of a more or less interesting story, but of a complete lesson of moral and physical anatomy. The novelist throws a woman on to the slab of the amphitheatre, the first woman that comes to his hand, the servant girl crossing the street with her apron on; he patiently dissects her, shows each muscle, gives full play to the nerves, seeks for causes and relates results; and this suffices to uncover a whole bleeding corner of humanity. The reader feels the sobs rising in his throat, and it happens that this dissection becomes a heartrending spectacle, full of the highest morality.'—EMILE ZOLA.

TWELFTH THOUSAND.

With 32 highly finished page Engravings, cloth gilt, price 3s. 6d.

SAPPHO: Parisian Manners.

By ALPHONSE DAUDET.

UNABRIDGED TRANSLATION FROM THE 100TH FRENCH EDITION.

"The book may, without exaggeration, be described as a glowing picture of Parisian life, with all its diversity of characters, with its Bohemian and half-world circles that are to be found nowhere else; with all its special immorality, in short, but also with the touch of poetry that saves it from utter corruption, and with the keen artistic sense that preserves its votaries from absolute degradation."—*Daily Telegraph.*

*** VIZETELLY & CO.'S Edition of " SAPPHO" is the only complete one. It contains every line of the original work and fifty pages more matter than any other.*

Shortly. In crown 8vo. Price 3s. 6d.	*Uniform with " A CRUEL ENIGMA."*
# A CRUEL ENIGMA.	# A LOVE CRIME.
## By PAUL BOURGET.	## By PAUL BOURGET.
Translated without abridgment from the 18th French Edition.	*Translated with abridgment from the 17th French Edition.*

Specimen of the Engravings in DAUDET'S "SAPPHO."

"Alone in the little garden of the restaurant they were kissing each other and eating their fish. All at once, from a rustic arbour built among the branches of the plane-tree at whose foot their table was set out, a loud and bantering voice was heard : 'I say, there, when you've done billing and cooing——,' and the leonine face and ruddy beard of Caoudal the sculptor appeared through an opening in the woodwork of the hut."

NEW ONE-VOLUME NOVELS.

A NOVEL OF JEWISH LIFE.
In crown 8vo, price 7s. 6d.

DR. PHILLIPS: A Maida Vale Idyll.
BY FRANK DANBY.

In crown 8vo, price 7s. 6d.

THE MEADOWSWEET COMEDY.
BY T. A. PINKERTON.   [*Ready in April.*

In crown 8vo, price 3s. 6d.

MY BROTHER YVES.
BY PIERRE LOTI.
Translated from the 17th French Edition.   [*Ready in April.*

Third Edition, in crown 8vo, price 3s. 6d.

DISENCHANTMENT.
BY F. MABEL ROBINSON.
AUTHOR OF "MR. BUTLER'S WARD."

"'DISENCHANTMENT' is a novel of considerable power. There is not one of the characters which does not become more and more an actual man or woman as one turns the pages. . . . The book is full of humour and the liveliest and healthiest appreciation of the tender and emotional side of life, and the accuracy—the almost relentless accuracy—with which the depths of life are sounded, is startling in the work of an almost unknown writer."—*Pall Mall Gazette.*

"Some of the scenes are given with remarkably impressive power. . . . The book is altogether of exceptional interest as an original study of many sides of actual human nature."—*The Graphic.*

Fifth Edition, in crown 8vo, with Frontispiece, price 6s.

A DRAMA IN MUSLIN.
BY GEORGE MOORE.
AUTHOR OF "A MUMMER'S WIFE," "A MODERN LOVER," &c.

"Mr. George Moore's work stands on a very much higher plane than the facile fiction of the circulating libraries. The hideous comedy of the marriage-market has been a stock topic with novelists from Thackeray downwards; but Mr. Moore goes deep into the yet more hideous tragedy which forms its afterpiece, the tragedy of enforced stagnant celibacy, with its double catastrophe of disease and vice."—*Pall Mall Gazette.*

In crown 8vo, price 5s.

ICARUS.
BY THE AUTHOR OF "A JAUNT IN A JUNK."

"A clever book with an original and ingenious idea. . . . Well fitted to amuse the leisure of men and women of the world."—*Morning Post.*

"The tale is admirably told."—*St. Stephen's Review.*

In crown 8vo, price 5s.

IN THE CHANGE OF YEARS.
BY FÉLISE LOVELACE.

"The author is but too true to human nature, as Thackeray and other great artists have been before her."—*Academy.*

THE NOVELS OF FEDOR DOSTOIEFFSKY.

TRANSLATED FROM THE ORIGINAL RUSSIAN.

Third Edition.   In crown 8vo, 450 pages, price 6s.

CRIME AND PUNISHMENT.

A RUSSIAN REALISTIC NOVEL.

By FEDOR DOSTOIEFFSKY.

OPINIONS OF THE PRESS.

The Athenæum.

"Outside Russia the name of Fedor Dostoieffsky was till lately almost unknown. Yet Dostoieffsky is one of the most remarkable of modern writers, and his book, 'CRIME AND PUNISHMENT,' is one of the most moving of modern novels. It is the story of a murder and of the punishment which dogs the murderer; and its effect is unique in fiction. It is realism, but such realism as M. Zola and his followers do not dream of. The reader knows the personages—strange, grotesque, terrible personages they are—more intimately than if he had been years with them in the flesh. He is constrained to live their lives, to suffer their tortures, to scheme and resist with them, exult with them, weep and laugh and despair with them; he breathes the very breath of their nostrils, and with the madness that comes upon them he is afflicted even as they. This sounds extravagant praise, no doubt; but only to those who have not read the volume. To those who have, we are sure that it will appear rather under the mark than otherwise."

Pall Mall Gazette.

"The figures in the grand, gloomy picture are a handful of men and women taken haphazard from the crowd of the Russian capital. They are nearly all poor. The central figure in the novel is one of those impecunious 'students,' the outcomes of whose turbulent brains have often been a curse where they were intended to be a blessing to their country. Sonia is a figure of tragic pathos. . . . . A strange fascination attracts Raskolnikoff to seek her out in her own lodgings, a bare little room in an obscure street of St. Petersburg; and there, in the haunt of impurity and sin, the harlot and the assassin meet together to read the story of Lazarus and Dives. In that same den Rodia confesses his crime, and, in anguish almost too deep for words, the outcast girl implores the criminal, for God's sake, to make atonement."

The Spectator.

"In our opinion Dostoieffsky's finest work is 'CRIME AND PUNISHMENT.' Though never Zolaesque, Dostoieffsky is intensely realistic, calls a spade a spade with the most uncompromising frankness. He describes sin in its most hideous shapes; yet he is full of tenderness and loving-kindness for its victims, and shows us that even the most abandoned are not entirely bad, and that for all there is hope—hope of redemption and regeneration. Dostoieffsky sounded the lowest depths of human nature, and wrote with the power of a master. None but a Russian and a genius could draw such a character as Rodia Raskolnikoff, who has been aptly named the 'Hamlet of the Madhouse.'"

The World.

"The publisher has done good work in publishing 'CRIME AND PUNISHMENT,' a translation of Dostoieffsky's much-praised novel—a little over-praised, perhaps, but a strong thing, beyond all question."

Westminster Review.

"'CRIME AND PUNISHMENT' is powerful, and not without a certain weird fascination."

Second Edition, in crown 8vo, with Portrait and Memoir, price 5s.

INJURY AND INSULT.   By FEDOR DOSTOIEFFSKY.

TRANSLATED FROM THE ORIGINAL RUSSIAN BY F. WHISHAW.

"That 'Injury and Insult' is a powerful novel few will deny. Vania is a marvellous character. Once read, the book can never be forgotten."—*St. Stephen's Review.*

"A masterpiece of fiction. The author has treated with consummate tact the difficult character of Natasha 'the incarnation and the slave of passion.' She lives and breathes in these vivid pages, and the reader is drawn into the vortex of her anguish, and rejoices when she breaks free from her chain."—*Morning Post.*

In crown 8vo, price 5s.

THE FRIEND OF THE FAMILY, & THE GAMBLER.

TRANSLATED FROM THE ORIGINAL RUSSIAN BY F. WHISHAW.

"There are three Russian novelists who, though, with one exception, little known out of their own country, stand head and shoulders above most of their contemporaries. In the opinion of some not indifferent critics, they are superior to all other novelists of this generation. Two of them, Dostoieffsky and Turgenieff, died not long ago, the third, Lyof Tolstoi, still lives. The one with the most marked individuality of character, probably the most highly gifted, was unquestionably Dostoieffsky."—*Spectator.*

To be followed by

THE IDIOT.   THE BROTHERS KARAMASOFF.
UNCLE'S DREAM, & THE PERMANENT HUSBAND.

THE NOVELS OF COUNT LYOF TOLSTOI.

COUNT TOLSTOI'S MASTERPIECE.

Second Edition. In One Volume, 8vo, 780 pages, 7s. 6d.

ANNA KARENINA: A Russian Realistic Novel. By
COUNT LYOF TOLSTOI.

"To say that the book is fascinating would be but poor praise. It is a drama of life, of which every page is palpitating with intense and real life, and its grand lesson, 'Vengeance is Mine, I will repay,' is ever present."—*Pall Mall Gazette.*

"It has not only the very hue of life, but its movement, its advances, its strange pauses, its seeming reversions to former conditions, and its perpetual change, its apparent solations, its essential solidarity. It is a world, and you live in it while you read, and long afterwards."—*Harper's Monthly.*

COUNT TOLSTOI'S GREAT REALISTIC NOVEL.

Second Edition. In Three Vols., 5s. each.

WAR AND PEACE.   By COUNT LYOF TOLSTOI.

1. BEFORE TILSIT.   2. THE INVASION.   3. THE FRENCH AT MOSCOW.

"Incomparably Count Tolstoi's greatest work is 'War and Peace.'"—*Saturday Review.*

"Count Tolstoi's magnificent novel."—*Athenæum.*

"Count Tolstoi's admirable work may be warmly recommended to novel readers. His pictures of Imperial society—the people who move round the Czar—are as interesting and as vivid as his battle scenes."—*St. James's Gazette.*

"The interest of the book is not concentrated in a hero and a heroine. The other personages are studied with equal minute elaboration . . . and pass before us in scenes upon which the author has lavished pains and knowledge. He describes society as it appears to a calm, severe critic. He understands and respects goodness, and sets before us all that is lovable in Russian domestic life."—*Pall Mall Gazette.*

With Frontispiece. In One Volume, 3s. 6d.

A HERO OF OUR TIME.   By M. U. LERMONTOFF.

"Lermontoff's genius was as wild and erratic as his stormy life and tragic end. But it had the true ring, and his name is enrolled among the literary immortals of his country. 'A Hero of Our Time' is utterly unconventional, possesses a weird interest all its own, and is in every way a remarkable romance."—*Spectator.*

During May, in crown 8vo, with a Portrait and Memoir of Count Tolstoi, price 5s.

CHILDHOOD, BOYHOOD, AND YOUTH.

THE MERMAID SERIES.

" I lie and dream of your full MERMAID wine."
Master Francis Beaumont to Ben Jonson.

Now Publishing,
In Half-Crown monthly vols., post 8vo.   Each volume
containing from 400 to 500 pages, bound in cloth with cut or uncut edges.

An Unexpurgated Edition of

THE BEST PLAYS

of

THE OLD DRAMATISTS,

Under the General Editorship of HAVELOCK ELLIS.

LTHOUGH a strong and increasing interest is felt to-day in the great Elizabethan dramatists who are grouped around Shakespeare, no satisfactory attempt has hitherto been made to bring their works before the public in a really popular manner.   With the exception of such monumental and for most readers inaccessible editions as those of Dyce and Bullen, they have either been neglected or brought out in a mutilated and inadequate form.   Some of the most delightful of them, such as Middleton and Thomas Heywood, and even Beaumont and Fletcher are closed to all, save the few, and none of them are obtainable in satisfactory editions at moderate prices.

In the MERMAID SERIES it is proposed to issue the best plays of the Elizabethan and later Dramatists, those plays which, with Shakespeare's, constitute the chief contribution of the English spirit to the literature of the world.   The Editors who have given their assistance to the undertaking include men of literary eminence, who have already distinguished themselves in this field, as well as younger writers of ability.   The first volume will contain a general introduction by Mr. J. A. Symonds, dealing with the Elizabethan Drama generally, as the chief expression of English national life at one of its points of greatest power and expansion.

Each volume will contain on an average five complete Plays, prefaced by an Introductory Notice of the Author. Great care will be taken to ensure, by consultation among the Editors, that the Plays selected are in every case the *best* and most representative—and not the most conventional, or those which have lived on a merely accidental and traditional reputation. A feature will be made of plays by little known writers, which although often so admirable are now almost inaccessible. The names of the Editors will be sufficient guarantee for the quality of the selection. In every instance the utmost pains will be taken to secure the best text, the spelling will be modernised, and brief but adequate notes will be supplied.

In no case will the Plays undergo any process of expurgation. It is believed that, although they may sometimes run counter to what is called modern taste, the free and splendid energy of Elizabethan art, with its extreme realism and its extreme idealism—embodying, as it does, the best traditions of the English Drama—will not suffer from the frankest representation.

Carefully etched Portraits of those Dramatists of whom authentic portraits exist will be given as frontispieces to the various volumes, and every pains will be taken to ensure typographical accuracy and excellence, and to produce the series in a satisfactory manner in every respect.

Now ready—

MARLOWE. Edited by HAVELOCK ELLIS. With a General Introduction by J. A. SYMONDS.

To be followed by

MASSINGER. Edited by ARTHUR SYMONS.

MIDDLETON. With an Introduction by A. C. SWINBURNE.

BEAUMONT AND FLETCHER (2 vols.). Edited by J. St. LOE STRACHEY.

DEKKER. Edited by ERNEST RHYS.

WEBSTER AND CYRIL TOURNEUR. Edited by J. A. SYMONDS.

SHIRLEY. Edited by EDMUND GOSSE.

ARDEN OF FEVERSHAM and other Plays attributed to Shakespeare. Edited by ARTHUR SYMONS.

OTWAY. Edited by the Hon. RODEN NOEL.

FORD. Edited by HAVELOCK ELLIS.

THOMAS HEYWOOD. Edited by J. A. SYMONDS.

Also by CONGREVE, BEN JONSON (2 vols.), CHAPMAN, MARSTON, WILLIAM ROWLEY AND FIELD, DRYDEN, WYCHERLEY, LEE, &c.

NEW STORY BY THE AUTHOR OF "THE CHEVELEY NOVELS."

In Crown 8vo, attractively bound, price 3s. 6d.

HIS CHILD FRIEND.

BY THE AUTHOR OF "A MODERN MINISTER," "SAUL WEIR," &c.

"Is told tenderly and with graphic skill. All the characters are well and truthfully drawn."—*Academy.*

A STORY OF THE STAGE.

In Crown 8vo, with eight tinted page engravings, price 2s. 6d.

SAVED BY A SMILE.

BY JAMES SIREE.

Second Edition. In crown 8vo, with page engravings, price 2s. 6d.

MY FIRST CRIME.

BY G. MACÉ, FORMER "CHEF DE LA SÛRETÉ" OF THE PARIS POLICE.

"An account by a real Lecoq of a real crime is a novelty among the mass of criminal novels with which the world has been favoured since the death of the great originator Gaboriau. It is to M. Macé, who has had to deal with real *juges d'instruction*, real *agents de la sûreté*, and real murderers, that we are indebted for this really interesting addition to a species of literature which has of late begun to pall."—*Saturday Review.*

A BOOK FOR THE PRESENT CRISIS.

Second Edition. In crown 8vo, paper cover, price 1s., or cloth, 1s. 6d.

IRISH HISTORY FOR ENGLISH READERS.

BY WILLIAM STEPHENSON GREGG.

"The history is one that every Englishman *ought* to read. As an outline to be filled up by wider reading it is an admirable little book."—*Literary World.*

Shortly will be published in Shilling Volumes, with picture covers,

CAPITAL STORIES.

THE EARLIER VOLUMES WILL INCLUDE:

THE CHAPLAIN'S SECRET. BY LÉON DE TINSEAU.

AVATAR. BY THÉOPHILE GAUTIER.

(*The above work evidently suggested "Doctor Jekyll and Mr. Hyde."*)

COLONEL QUAGG'S CONVERSION; and Other Stories.
BY GEORGE AUGUSTUS SALA.

THE MONKEYS' REVENGE. BY LÉON GOZLAN.

THE MARCHIONESS'S TEAM. BY LÉON DE TINSEAU.

MR. E. C. GRENVILLE-MURRAY'S WORKS.

Third and Cheaper Edition, in post 8vo, 434 pp., with numerous Page and other Engravings, handsomely bound, price 5s.

IMPRISONED IN A SPANISH CONVENT:

AN ENGLISH GIRL'S EXPERIENCES.

"Intensely fascinating. The *exposé* is a remarkable one, and as readable as remarkable."—*Society.*

"Excellent specimens of their author in his best and brightest mood."—*Athenæum.*

"Highly dramatic."—*Scotsman.*   "Strikingly interesting."—*Literary World.*

"Instead of the meek cooing dove with naked feet and a dusty face who had talked of dying for me, I had now a bright-eyed rosy-cheeked companion who had cambric pocket-handkerchiefs with violet scent on them and smoked cigarettes on the sly."—*Page 75.*

New and Cheaper Edition, Two Vols. large post 8vo, attractively bound, price 15s.

UNDER THE LENS: SOCIAL PHOTOGRAPHS.

ILLUSTRATED WITH ABOUT 300 ENGRAVINGS BY WELL-KNOWN ARTISTS.

CONTENTS:— JILTS — ADVENTURERS AND ADVENTURESSES — HONOURABLE GENTLEMEN (M.P.s)—PUBLIC SCHOOLBOYS AND UNDERGRADUATES—SPENDTHRIFTS —SOME WOMEN I HAVE KNOWN—ROUGHS OF HIGH AND LOW DEGREE.

"Brilliant, highly-coloured sketches. . . . containing beyond doubt some of the best writing that has come from Mr. Grenville-Murray's pen."—*St. James's Gazette.*

"Limned audaciously, unsparingly, and with much ability."—*World.*

"Distinguished by their pitiless fidelity to nature."—*Society.*

At the Eton and Harrow Cricket Match: *from "UNDER THE LENS."*

MR. E. C. GRENVILLE-MURRAY'S WORKS—*continued.*

Seventh Edition, in post 8vo, handsomely bound, price 7s. 6d.

SIDE-LIGHTS ON ENGLISH SOCIETY:

Sketches from Life, Social and Satirical.

ILLUSTRATED WITH NEARLY 300 CHARACTERISTIC ENGRAVINGS.

CONTENTS:—FLIRTS. — ON HER BRITANNIC MAJESTY'S SERVICE. — SEMI-DETACHED WIVES.—NOBLE LORDS.—YOUNG WIDOWS.—OUR SILVERED YOUTH, OR NOBLE OLD BOYS.

"This is a startling book. The volume is expensively and elaborately got up; the writing is bitter, unsparing, and extremely clever."—*Vanity Fair.*

"Mr. Grenville-Murray sparkles very steadily throughout the present volume, and puts to excellent use his incomparable knowledge of life and manners, of men and cities, of appearances and facts. Of his several descants upon English types, I shall only remark that they are brilliantly and dashingly written, curious as to their matter, and admirably readable."—*Truth.*

"No one can question the brilliancy of the sketches, nor affirm that 'Side-Lights' is aught but a fascinating book. . . . . . . The book is destined to make a great noise in the world."—*Whitehall Review.*

Third Edition, with Frontispiece and Vignette, price 2s. 6d.

HIGH LIFE IN FRANCE UNDER THE REPUBLIC:

SOCIAL AND SATIRICAL SKETCHES IN PARIS AND THE PROVINCES.

"Take this book as it stands, with the limitations imposed upon its author by circumstances, and it will be found very enjoyable. . . . . The volume is studded with shrewd observations on French life at the present day."—*Spectator.*

"A very clever and entertaining series of social and satirical sketches, almost French in their point and vivacity."—*Contemporary Review.*

"A most amusing book, and no less instructive if read with allowances and understanding."—*World.*

"Full of the caustic humour and graphic character-painting so characteristic of Mr. Grenville-Murray's work, and dealing trenchantly yet lightly with almost every conceivable phase of social, political, official, journalistic and theatrical life."—*Society.*

MR. E. C. GRENVILLE-MURRAY'S WORKS—*continued.*

Second Edition, in large 8vo, tastefully bound, with gilt edges, price 10s. 6d.

FORMING A HANDSOME VOLUME FOR A PRESENT.

PEOPLE I HAVE MET.

Illustrated with 54 tinted Page Engravings, from Designs by FRED. BARNARD.

THE RICH WIDOW (reduced from the original engraving).

"Mr. Grenville-Murray's pages sparkle with cleverness and with a shrewd wit, caustic or cynical at times, but by no means excluding a due appreciation of the softer virtues of women and the sterner excellences of men.   The talent of the artist (Mr. Barnard) is akin to that of the author, and the result of the combination is a book that, once taken up, can hardly be laid down until the last page is perused."—*Spectator.*

"All of Mr. Grenville-Murray's portraits are clever and life-like, and some of them are not unworthy of a model who was more before the author's eyes than Addison—namely, Thackeray." —*Truth.*

"Mr. Grenville-Murray's sketches are genuine studies, and are the best things of the kind that have been published since 'Sketches by Boz,' to which they are superior in the sense in which artistically executed character portraits are superior to caricatures."—*St. James's Gazette.*

"No book of its class can be pointed out so admirably calculated to show another generation the foibles and peculiarities of the men and women of our times."—*Morning Post.*

An Edition of "PEOPLE I HAVE MET" is published in small 8vo, with Frontispiece and other page Engravings, price 2s. 6d.

In post 8vo, 150 engravings, cloth gilt, price 5s.

JILTS AND OTHER SOCIAL PHOTOGRAPHS.

Uniform with the above.

SPENDTHRIFTS AND OTHER SOCIAL PHOTOGRAPHS.

MR. GEORGE AUGUSTUS SALA'S WORKS.

"It was like your imperence to come smonchin' round here, looking after de white folks' washin."

In One Volume, demy 8vo, 560 pages, price 12s., the FIFTH EDITION of

AMERICA REVISITED,

FROM THE BAY OF NEW YORK TO THE GULF OF MEXICO, & FROM LAKE MICHIGAN TO THE PACIFIC, INCLUDING A SOJOURN AMONG THE MORMONS IN SALT LAKE CITY.

ILLUSTRATED WITH NEARLY 400 ENGRAVINGS.

"In 'America Revisited' Mr. Sala is seen at his very best; better even than in his Paris book, more evenly genial and gay, and with a fresher subject to handle."—*World.*

"Mr. Sala's good stories lie thick as plums in a pudding throughout this handsome work."—*Pall Mall Gazette.*

MR. G. A. SALA'S WORKS—*continued.*

In demy 8vo, handsomely printed on hand-made paper, with the Illustrations on India paper mounted (only 250 copies printed), price 10s. 6d.

UNDER THE SUN:
ESSAYS MAINLY WRITTEN IN HOT COUNTRIES.

A New Edition, containing several Additional Essays, with an Etched Portrait of the Author by BOCOURT, and 12 full-page Engravings.

"There are nearly four hundred pages between the covers of this volume, which means that they contain plenty of excellent reading."—*St. James's Gazette.*

Uniform with the above, with Frontispiece and other Page Engravings.

DUTCH PICTURES, and PICTURES DONE WITH A QUILL.

The Graphic remarks: "We have received a sumptuous new edition of Mr. G. A. Sala's well-known 'Dutch Pictures.' It is printed on rough paper, and is enriched with many admirable illustrations."

"Mr. Sala's best work has in it something of Montaigne, a great deal of Charles Lamb—made deeper and broader—and not a little of Lamb's model, the accomplished and quaint Sir Thomas Brown. These 'Dutch Pictures' and 'Pictures Done with a Quill' should be placed alongside Oliver Wendell Holmes's inimitable budgets of friendly gossip and Thackeray's 'Roundabout Papers.' They display to perfection the quick eye, good taste, and ready hand of the born essayist—they are never tiresome."—*Daily Telegraph.*

UNDER THE SUN, and DUTCH PICTURES AND PICTURES DONE WITH A QUILL *are also published in crown 8vo, price 2s. 6d. each.*

Third and Cheaper Edition, in demy 8vo, cloth gilt, price 6s.

A JOURNEY DUE SOUTH;
TRAVELS IN SEARCH OF SUNSHINE,

INCLUDING

MARSEILLES, NICE, BASTIA, AJACCIO, GENOA, PISA, BOLOGNA, VENICE, ROME, NAPLES, POMPEII, &c.

ILLUSTRATED WITH 16 FULL-PAGE ENGRAVINGS BY VARIOUS ARTISTS.

"In 'A Journey due South' Mr. Sala is in his brightest and cheeriest mood, ready with quip and jest and anecdote, brimful of allusion ever happy and pat."—*Saturday Review.*

Eighth Edition, in crown 8vo, 558 pages, attractively bound, price 2s. 6d., or gilt at the side and with gilt edges, 3s.

PARIS HERSELF AGAIN.
BY GEORGE AUGUSTUS SALA.

WITH 350 CHARACTERISTIC ILLUSTRATIONS BY FRENCH ARTISTS.

'On subjects like those in his present work, Mr. Sala is at his best."—*The Times.*

"This book is one of the most readable that has appeared for many a day. Few Englishmen know so much of old and modern Paris as Mr. Sala."—*Truth.*

"'Paris Herself Again' is infinitely more amusing than most novels. There is no style so chatty and so unwearying as that of which Mr. Sala is a master."—*The World.*

A BUCK OF THE REGENCY: *from "DUTCH PICTURES."*

"Mr. Sala's best work has in it something of Montaigne, a great deal of Charles Lamb—made deeper and broader—and not a little of Lamb's model, the accomplished and quaint Sir Thomas Brown. These 'Dutch Pictures' and 'Pictures Done With a Quill' should be placed alongside Oliver Wendell Holmes's inimitable budgets of friendly gossip and Thackeray's 'Roundabout Papers.' They display to perfection the quick eye, good taste, and ready hand of the born essayist—they are never tiresome." —*Daily Telegraph.*

VIZETELLY'S ONE-VOLUME NOVELS.

CHEAPER ISSUE.

"The idea of publishing cheap one-volume novels is a good one, and we wish the series every success."—*Saturday Review.*

2s. 6d. each.

FIFTH EDITION.

THE IRONMASTER; OR, LOVE AND PRIDE.

By GEORGES OHNET.

TRANSLATED WITHOUT ABRIDGMENT FROM THE 146TH FRENCH EDITION.

"This work, the greatest literary success in any language of recent times, has already yielded its author upwards of £12,000."

THIRD EDITION.

NUMA ROUMESTAN; OR, JOY ABROAD AND GRIEF AT HOME.

By ALPHONSE DAUDET.

TRANSLATED BY Mrs. J. G. LAYARD.

"'Numa Roumestan' is a masterpiece; it is really a perfect work; it has no fault, no weakness. It is a compact and harmonious whole."—MR. HENRY JAMES.

SECOND EDITION.

THE CORSARS; OR, LOVE AND LUCRE.

By JOHN HILL, AUTHOR OF "THE WATERS OF MARAH," "SALLY," &c.

"It is indubitable that Mr. Hill has produced a strong and lively novel, full of story, character, situations, murder, gold-mines, excursions, and alarms. The book is so rich in promise that we hope to receive some day from Mr. Hill a romance which will win every vote."—*Saturday Review.*

The Book that made M. Ohnet's reputation, and was crowned by the French Academy.

SECOND EDITION.

PRINCE SERGE PANINE.

By GEORGES OHNET. AUTHOR OF "THE IRONMASTER."

TRANSLATED, WITHOUT ABRIDGMENT, FROM THE 110TH FRENCH EDITION.

"This excellent version is sure to meet with large success on our side of the Channel."—*London Figaro.*

BETWEEN MIDNIGHT AND DAWN.

By INA L. CASSILIS, AUTHOR OF "SOCIETY'S QUEEN," &c.

"An ingenious plot, cleverly handled."—*Athenæum.*

"The interest begins with the first page, and is ably sustained to the conclusion."—*Edinburgh Courant.*

ROLAND; OR THE EXPIATION OF A SIN.

By ARY ECILAW.

"A novel entitled 'Roland' is creating an immense sensation in Paris. The first, second, and third editions were swept away in as many days. The work is charmingly written."—*The World.*

VIZETELLY'S ONE-VOLUME NOVELS—*continued.*
3s. 6d. each.

NINTH EDITION, CAREFULLY REVISED, AND WITH A SPECIAL PREFACE.

A MUMMER'S WIFE. A Realistic Novel.

By GEORGE MOORE, Author of "A Modern Lover."

"A striking book, different in tone from current English fiction. The woman's character is a very powerful study."—*Athenæum.*

"A Mummer's Wife, in virtue of its vividness of presentation and real literary skill, may be regarded as a representative example of the work of a literary school that has of late years attracted to itself a good deal of notoriety."—*Spectator.*

"'A Mummer's Wife' holds at present a unique position among English novels. It is a conspicuous success of its kind."—*Graphic.*

THIRD EDITION.

COUNTESS SARAH.

By GEORGES OHNET, Author of "The Ironmaster."

TRANSLATED, WITHOUT ABRIDGMENT, FROM THE 118th FRENCH EDITION.

"The book contains some very powerful situations and first-rate character studies."—*Whitehall Review.*

"To an interesting plot is added a number of strongly-marked and cleverly drawn characters."—*Society.*

THIRD EDITION.

MR. BUTLER'S WARD.

By MABEL ROBINSON.

"A charming book, poetically conceived, and worked out with tenderness and insight."—*Athenæum.*

"The heroine is a very happy conception, a beautiful creation whose affecting history is treated with much delicacy, sympathy, and command of all that is touching."—*Illustrated News.*

"All the characters are new to fiction, and the author is to be congratulated on having made so full and original a haul out of the supposed to be exhausted waters of modern society. . . . ."—*Graphic.*

THE THREATENING EYE.

By E. F. KNIGHT, Author of "A Cruise in the Falcon."

"There is a good deal of power about this romance."—*Graphic.*

"Full of extraordinary power and originality. The story is one of quite exceptional force and impressiveness."—*Manchester Examiner.*

THE FORKED TONGUE.

By R. LANGSTAFF DE HAVILLAND, M.A., Author of "Enslaved," &c.

"In many respects the story is a remarkable one. Its men and women are drawn with power and without pity; their follies and their vices are painted in unmistakable colours, and with a skill that fascinates."—*Society.*

THIRD EDITION.

A MODERN LOVER.

By GEORGE MOORE, Author of "A Mummer's Wife."

"Mr. Moore has a real power of drawing character, and some of his descriptive scenes are capital."—*St. James's Gazette.*

"It would be difficult to praise too highly the strength, truth, delicacy, and pathos of the incident of Gwynnie Lloyd, and the admirable treatment of the great sacrifice she makes. The incident is depicted with skill and beauty."—*Spectator.*

"Kiss me, dear," said Athenaïs.

In large crown 8vo, beautifully printed on toned paper, price 5s., or handsomely bound with gilt edges, suitable in every way for a present, 6s.

An Illustrated Edition of M. Ohnet's Celebrated Novel.

THE IRONMASTER; OR, LOVE AND PRIDE.

CONTAINING 42 FULL-PAGE ENGRAVINGS BY FRENCH ARTISTS, PRINTED SEPARATE FROM THE TEXT.

VIZETELLY'S ONE VOLUME NOVELS—*continued.* 3s. 6d. each.

PRINCE ZILAH.

By JULES CLARETIE.

Translated from the 57th French edition.

"M. Jules Claretie has of late taken a conspicuous place as a novelist in France."—*Times.*

THE TRIALS OF JETTA MALAUBRET.

(NOIRS ET ROUGES.)

By VICTOR CHERBULIEZ, OF THE FRENCH ACADEMY.

TRANSLATED BY THE COUNTESS G. DE LA ROCHEFOUCAULD

"'Jetta Malaubret' deals with the experiences of a young girl who is taken from a convent and deliberately plunged into a sort of society calculated to teach her the utmost possible amount of worldly wisdom—to say nothing of worse things—in the shortest possible time. The characterization and dialogue are full of piquancy and cleverness."—*Society.*

In post 8vo, with numerous Page and other Engravings, cloth gilt, price 3s. 6d.,

NO ROSE WITHOUT A THORN;

AND OTHER TALES.

By F. C. BURNAND, H. SAVILE CLARKE, R. E. FRANCILLON, &c.

"By the aid of the chimney with the register up Mrs. Lapscombe's curiosity was, to certain extent, gratified."—*Page* 19.

In post 8vo, with numerous Page and other Engravings, cloth gilt, price 3s. 6d.

THE DOVE'S NEST,

AND OTHER TALES.

By JOSEPH HATTON, RICHARD JEFFERIES, H. SAVILE CLARKE, &c.

ZOLA'S POWERFUL REALISTIC NOVELS.

TRANSLATED WITHOUT ABRIDGMENT.

ILLUSTRATED WITH PAGE ENGRAVINGS BY FRENCH ARTISTS.

In crown 8vo, price 6s. each.

Mr. HENRY JAMES on ZOLA'S NOVELS.

"A novelist with a system, a passionate conviction, a great plan—incontestable attributes of M. Zola—is not now to be easily found in England or the United States, where the story-teller's art is almost exclusively feminine, is mainly in the hands of timid (even when very accomplished) women, whose acquaintance with life is severely restricted, and who are not conspicuous for general views. The novel, moreover, among ourselves, is almost always addressed to young unmarried ladies, or at least always assumes them to be a large part of the novelist's public.

"This fact, to a French story-teller, appears, of course, a damnable restriction, and M. Zola would probably decline to take *au sérieux* any work produced under such unnatural conditions. Half of life is a sealed book to young unmarried ladies, and how can a novel be worth anything that deals only with half of life? These objections are perfectly valid, and it may be said that our English system is a good thing for virgins and boys, and a bad thing for the novel itself, when the novel is regarded as something more than a simple *jeu d'esprit*, and considered as a composition that treats of life at large and helps us to *know.*"

NANA.

From the 127th French Edition.

THE "ASSOMMOIR."   (The Prelude to "NANA.")

From the 97th French Edition.

PIPING HOT!   (POT-BOUILLE.)

From the 63rd French Edition.

GERMINAL; OR, MASTER AND MAN.

From the 47th French Edition.

THE RUSH FOR THE SPOIL.   (LA CURÉE.)

From the 34th French Edition.

THE LADIES' PARADISE.   (The Sequel to "PIPING HOT!")

From the 50th French Edition.

ABBÉ MOURET'S TRANSGRESSION.

From the 31st French Edition.

THÉRÈSE RAQUIN.

The above Works are published without Illustrations, price 5s. each.

HIS MASTERPIECE?   (L'ŒUVRE.)

With a Portrait of M. EMILE ZOLA, Etched by BOCOURT.

ZOLA'S REALISTIC NOVELS—*continued.*

THE FORTUNE OF THE ROUGONS.
From the 24th French Edition.

HOW JOLLY LIFE IS!
From the 44th French Edition.

THE CONQUEST OF PLASSANS.
From the 23rd French Edition.

A LOVE EPISODE.
From the 52nd French Edition.

HIS EXCELLENCY EUGÈNE ROUGON.
From the 22nd French Edition. [*Shortly.*

FAT AND THIN. (LE VENTRE DE PARIS.)
From the 24th French Edition. [*In May.*

The following are published, in large octavo, price 7s. 6d. per Vol.

Each Volume contains about 100 Engravings, half of which are page-size.

1. NANA. 2. THE ASSOMMOIR. 3. PIPING HOT.

DESIGNS BY BELLENGER, BERTALL, CLAIRIN, GILL, VIERGE, &c.

THE BOULEVARD NOVELS.
Pictures of French Morals and Manners.

In small 8vo, attractively bound, price 2s. 6d. each.

NANA'S DAUGHTER.
BY ALFRED SIRVEN and HENRI LEVERDIER.
From the 35th French Edition.

THE YOUNG GUARD.
BY VAST-RICOUARD.
From the 15th French Edition.

THE WOMAN OF FIRE.
BY ADOLPHE BELOT.
From the 30th French Edition.

ODETTE'S MARRIAGE.
BY ALBERT DELPIT.
From the 22nd French Edition.

THE VIRGIN WIDOW.
BY A. MATTHEY.

A LADIES' MAN.
BY GUY DE MAUPASSANT.
From the 50th French Edition.

SEALED LIPS.
BY F. DU BOISGOBEY.

VIZETELLY'S HALF-CROWN SERIES.

PARIS HERSELF AGAIN. By George Augustus Sala. Ninth Edition. 558 pages and 350 Engravings.

"On subjects like those in his present work, Mr. Sala is at his best."—*The Times.*

"This book is one of the most readable that has appeared for many a day. Few Englishmen know so much of old and modern Paris as Mr. Sala."—*Truth.*

UNDER THE SUN. Essays Mainly Written in Hot Countries. By George Augustus Sala. A New Edition. Illustrated with 12 page Engravings and an etched Portrait of the Author.

"There are nearly four hundred pages between the covers of this volume, which means that they contain plenty of excellent reading."—*St. James's Gazette.*

DUTCH PICTURES and PICTURES DONE WITH A QUILL. By George Augustus Sala. A New Edition. Illustrated with 8 page Engravings.

"Mr. Sala's best work has in it something of Montaigne, a great deal of Charles Lamb—made deeper and broader—and not a little of Lamb's model, the accomplished and quaint Sir Thomas Brown. These 'Dutch Pictures' and 'Pictures Done with a Quill,' display to perfection the quick eye, good taste, and ready hand of the born essayist—they are never tiresome."—*Daily Telegraph.*

HIGH LIFE IN FRANCE UNDER THE REPUBLIC. Social and Satirical Sketches in Paris and the Provinces. By E. C. Grenville-Murray. Third Edition, with a Frontispiece.

"A very clever and entertaining series of social and satirical sketches, almost French in their point and vivacity." —*Contemporary Review.*

"A most amusing book, and no less instructive if read with allowances and understanding."—*World.*

PEOPLE I HAVE MET. By E. C. Grenville-Murray. A New Edition. With 8 page Engravings from Designs by F. Barnard.

"Mr. Grenville-Murray's pages sparkle with cleverness and with a shrewd wit, caustic or cynical at times, but by no means excluding a due appreciation of the softer virtues of women and the sterner excellencies of men."—*Spectator.*

"All of Mr. Grenville-Murray's portraits are clever and life-like, and some of them are not unworthy of a model who was more before the author's eye than Addison—namely, Thackeray."—*Truth.*

A BOOK OF COURT SCANDAL.

CAROLINE BAUER AND THE COBURGS. From the German, with two carefully engraved Portraits.

"Caroline Bauer's name became in a mysterious and almost tragic manner connected with those of two men highly esteemed and well remembered in England—Prince Leopold of Coburg, and his nephew, Prince Albert's trusty friend and adviser, Baron Stockmar."—*The Times.*

THE STORY OF THE DIAMOND NECKLACE, Told in Detail for the First Time. A New Edition. By Henry Vizetelly. Illustrated with an authentic representation of the Diamond Necklace, and a Portrait of the Countess de la Motte, engraved on steel, and other Engravings.

"Had the most daring of our sensational novelists put forth the present plain unvarnished statement of facts as a work of fiction, it would have been denounced as so violating all probabilities as to be a positive insult to the common sense of the reader. Yet strange, startling, incomprehensible as is the narrative which the author has here evolved, every word of it is true."—*Notes and Queries.*

GUZMAN OF ALFARAQUE. A Spanish Novel, translated by E. Lowdell. Illustrated with highly finished steel Engravings from Designs by Stahl.

"The wit, vivacity and variety of this masterpiece cannot be over-estimated."—*Morning Post.*

In large 8vo, 160 pages and 130 Engravings, price 1s.

GORDON AND THE MAHDI.
An Illustrated Narrative of the Soudan War.

"This wonderfully good shilling's worth should command a wide sale."—*Illustrated News.*

In paper covers, 1s. each ; or cloth gilt, 2s. 6d.

PATTER POEMS.
HUMOROUS AND SERIOUS, FOR READINGS AND RECITATIONS.
BY WALTER PARKE.
WITH ILLUSTRATIONS BY J. LEITCH.

"'Patter Poems' include many sparkling and merry lays, well adapted for recitation. and sure of the approval of the audience." —*Saturday Review.*

THE
COMIC GOLDEN LEGEND.
BY WALTER PARKE.
WITH ILLUSTRATIONS BY J. LEITCH.

"The stories are told in bright and luminous verses in which are dexterously wrought parodies of a good many present and some past poets."—*Scotsman.*

SONGS OF SINGULARITY.
BY WALTER PARKE.
ILLUSTRATED WITH 60 ENGRAVINGS.

In paper covers, 1s. ; or in parchment binding, gilt on side, 2s. 6d.

ADMIRABLY SUITED FOR PRIVATE REPRESENTATION.

THE PASSER-BY.
A COMEDY IN ONE ACT.
BY FRANÇOIS COPPÉE, of the French Academy.
TRANSLATED BY LUIGI, AUTHOR OF "THE RED CROSS," &c.

"A translation exceedingly well done."—*Whitehall Review.*

NEW SATIRICAL POEM, BY A WELL-KNOWN POET.

In crown 8vo, price 1s.

LUCIFER IN LONDON,
AND HIS REFLECTIONS ON LIFE, MANNERS, AND THE PROSPECTS OF SOCIETY.

"Decidedly witty and original."—*Sunday Times.*

In crown 8vo, price 2s. 6d.

IN STRANGE COMPANY.
BY JAMES GREENWOOD (the "Amateur Casual").
ILLUSTRATED WITH A PORTRAIT OF THE AUTHOR, ENGRAVED ON STEEL.

VIZETELLY'S SIXPENNY SERIES OF AMUSING AND ENTERTAINING BOOKS.

CECILE'S FORTUNE. By F. DU BOISGOBEY.

THE THREE-CORNERED HAT. By P. A. DE ALARCON.

THE BLACK CROSS MYSTERY. By H. CORKRAN.

THE STEEL-NECKLACE. By F. DU BOISGOBEY.

THE GREAT HOGGARTY DIAMOND. By W. M. THACKERAY.

CAPTAIN SPITFIRE, AND THE UNLUCKY TREASURE. By P. A. DE ALARCON.

MATRIMONY BY ADVERTISEMENT; And Other Adventures of a Journalist. By C. G. PAYNE. *Engravings.*

VOTE FOR POTTLEBECK! The Story of a Politician in Love. By C. G. PAYNE. *Engravings.*

YOUNG WIDOWS. By E. C. GRENVILLE-MURRAY. 50 *Engravings.*

THE DETECTIVE'S EYE. By F. DU BOISGOBEY.

THE STRANGE PHANTASY OF DR. TRINTZIUS. By AUGUSTE VITU.

A SHABBY GENTEEL STORY. By W. M. THACKERAY.

THE RED LOTTERY TICKET. By F. DU BOISGOBEY.

Will be ready shortly—

THE FIDDLER AMONG THE BANDITS. By ALEXANDRE DUMAS.

TARTARIN OF TARASCON. By ALPHONSE DAUDET.

THE PRIMA DONNA'S HUSBAND. By F. DU BOISGOBEY.

THE ABBÉ CONSTANTIN. By LUDOVIC HALÉVY.

THE RESULTS OF A DUEL. By F. DU BOISGOBEY.

Other Volumes are in Preparation.

In One Volume, large imperial 8vo, price 3s., or single numbers price 6d. each,

THE SOCIAL ZOO;

Satirical, Social, and Humorous Sketches by the Best Writers.

Copiously Illustrated in many Styles by well-known Artists.

OUR GILDED YOUTH. By E. C. GRENVILLE-MURRAY.

NICE GIRLS. By R. MOUNTENEY JEPHSON.

NOBLE LORDS. By E. C. GRENVILLE-MURRAY.

FLIRTS. By E. C. GRENVILLE-MURRAY.

OUR SILVERED YOUTH. By E. C. GRENVILLE-MURRAY.

MILITARY MEN AS THEY WERE. By E. DYNE FENTON.

In demy 4to, handsomely printed and bound, with gilt edges, price 12s.

A HISTORY OF CHAMPAGNE;

WITH NOTES ON THE OTHER SPARKLING WINES OF FRANCE.

By HENRY VIZETELLY.

CHEVALIER OF THE ORDER OF FRANZ-JOSEF,
WINE JUROR FOR GREAT BRITAIN AT THE VIENNA AND PARIS EXHIBITIONS OF 1873 AND 1878.

Illustrated with 350 Engravings,

FROM ORIGINAL SKETCHES AND PHOTOGRAPHS, ANCIENT MSS., EARLY PRINTED
BOOKS, RARE PRINTS, CARICATURES, ETC.

"A very agreeable medley of history, anecdote, geographical description, and such like matter, distinguished by an accuracy not often found in such medleys, and illustrated in the most abundant and pleasingly miscellaneous fashion."—*Daily News.*

"Mr. Henry Vizetelly's handsome book about Champagne and other sparkling wines of France is full of curious information and amusement. It should be widely read and appreciated."—*Saturday Review.*

"Mr. Henry Vizetelly has written a quarto volume on the 'History of Champagne,' in which he has collected a large number of facts, many of them very curious and interesting. Many of the woodcuts are excellent."—*Athenæum.*

"It is probable that this large volume contains such an amount of information touching the subject which it treats as cannot be found elsewhere. How competent the author was for the task he undertook is to be inferred from the functions he has discharged, and from the exceptional opportunities he enjoyed."—*Illustrated London News.*

"A veritable *édition de luxe*, dealing with the history of Champagne from the time of the Romans to the present date. . . . An interesting book, the incidents and details of which are very graphically told with a good deal of wit and humour. The engravings are exceedingly well executed."—*The Wine and Spirit News.*

MR. HENRY VIZETELLY'S POPULAR BOOKS ON WINE.

"Mr. Vizetelly discourses brightly and discriminatingly on crus and bouquets and the different European vineyards, most of which he has evidently visited."—*The Times.*

"Mr. Henry Vizetelly's books about different wines have an importance and a value far greater than will be assigned them by those who look merely at the price at which they are published."—*Sunday Times.*

Price 1s. 6d. ornamental cover; or 2s. 6d. in elegant cloth binding.

FACTS ABOUT PORT AND MADEIRA,

GLEANED DURING A TOUR IN THE AUTUMN OF 1877.

By HENRY VIZETELLY,

WINE JUROR FOR GREAT BRITAIN AT THE VIENNA AND PARIS EXHIBITIONS OF 1873 AND 1878.

With 100 Illustrations from Original Sketches and Photographs.

BY THE SAME AUTHOR.

Price 1s. 6d. ornamental cover; or 2s. 6d. in elegant cloth binding.

FACTS ABOUT CHAMPAGNE,

AND OTHER SPARKLING WINES.

COLLECTED DURING NUMEROUS VISITS TO THE CHAMPAGNE AND OTHER VITICULTURAL DISTRICTS OF FRANCE AND THE PRINCIPAL REMAINING WINE-PRODUCING COUNTRIES OF EUROPE.

Illustrated with 112 Engravings from Sketches and Photographs.

Price 1s. ornamental cover; or 1s. 6d. cloth gilt.

FACTS ABOUT SHERRY,

GLEANED IN THE VINEYARDS AND BODEGAS OF THE JEREZ, & OTHER DISTRICTS.

Illustrated with numerous Engravings from Original Sketches.

Price 1s. in ornamental cover; or 1s. 6d. cloth gilt.

THE WINES OF THE WORLD,

CHARACTERIZED AND CLASSED.

In small post 8vo, ornamental scarlet covers, 1s. each.

THE GABORIAU AND DU BOISGOBEY SENSATIONAL NOVELS.

> " Ah, friend, how many and many a while
> They've made the slow time fleetly flow,
> And solaced pain and charmed exile,
> BOISGOBEY and GABORIAU!"
>
> *Ballade of Railway Novels in " Longman's Magazine."*

IN PERIL [OF HIS LIFE.

" A story of thrilling interest, and admirably translated."—*Sunday Times.*

THE LEROUGE CASE.

" M. Gaboriau is a skilful and brilliant writer, capable of so diverting the attention and interest of his readers that not one word or line in his book will be skipped or read carelessly."—*Hampshire Advertiser.*

OTHER PEOPLE'S MONEY.

" The interest is kept up throughout, and the story is told graphically and with a good deal of art."—*London Figaro.*

LECOQ THE DETECTIVE. Two Vols.

" In the art of forging a tangled chain of complicated incidents involved and inexplicable until the last link is reached and the whole made clear, Mr. Wilkie Collins is equalled, if not excelled, by M. Gaboriau."—*Brighton Herald.*

THE GILDED CLIQUE.

" Full of incident, and instinct with life and action. Altogether this is a most fascinating book."—*Hampshire Advertiser.*

THE MYSTERY OF ORCIVAL.

" The Author keeps the interest of the reader at fever heat, and by a succession of unexpected turns and incidents, the drama is ultimately worked out to a very pleasant result. The ability displayed is unquestionable."—*Sheffield Independent.*

DOSSIER NO. 113.

" The plot is worked out with great skill, and from first to last the reader's interest is never allowed to flag."—*Dumbarton Herald.*

THE LITTLE OLD MAN OF BATIGNOLLES.

THE SLAVES OF PARIS. Two Vols.

" Sensational, full of interest, cleverly conceived, and wrought out with consummate skill."—*Oxford and Cambridge Journal.*

THE CATASTROPHE. Two Vols.

" 'The Catastrophe' does ample credit to M. Gaboriau's reputation as a novelist of vast resource in incident and of wonderful ingenuity in constructing and unravelling thrilling mysteries."—*Aberdeen Journal.*

THE COUNT'S MILLIONS. Two Vols.

" To those who love the mysterious and the sensational, Gaboriau's stories are irresistibly fascinating. His marvellously clever pages hold the mirror up to nature with absolute fidelity; and the interest with which he contrives to invest his characters proves that exaggeration is unnecessary to a master."—*Society.*

INTRIGUES OF A POISONER.

"The wonderful Sensational Novels of Emile Gaboriau."—*Globe.*

THE OLD AGE OF LECOQ, THE DETECTIVE. Two Vols.

"The romances of Gaboriau and Du Boisgobey picture the marvellous Lecoq and other wonders of shrewdness, who piece together the elaborate details of the most complicated crimes, as Professor Owen with the smallest bone as a foundation could reconstruct the most extraordinary animals."—*Standard.*

IN THE SERPENTS' COILS.

"This is a most picturesque, dramatic, and powerful sensational novel. Its interest never flags. Its terrific excitement continues to the end. The reader is kept spellbound."—*Oldham Chronicle.*

THE DAY OF RECKONING. Two Vols.

"M. du Boisgobey gives us no tiresome descriptions or laboured analyses of character; under his facile pen plots full of incident are quickly opened and unwound. He does not stop to moralise; all his art consists in creating intricacies which shall keep the reader's curiosity on the stretch, and offer a full scope to his own really wonderful ingenuity for unravelling."—*Times.*

THE SEVERED HAND.

"The plot is a marvel of intricacy and cleverly managed surprises."—*Literary World.*

"Readers who like a thoroughly entangled and thrilling plot will welcome this novel with avidity."—*Bristol Mercury.*

BERTHA'S SECRET.

"'Bertha's Secret' is a most effective romance. We need not say how the story ends, for this would spoil the reader's pleasure in a novel which depends for all its interest on the skilful weaving and unweaving of mysteries."—*Times.*

WHO DIED LAST? OR THE RIGHTFUL HEIR.

"Travellers at this season of the year will find the time occupied by a long journey pass away as rapidly as they can desire with one of Du Boisgobey's absorbing volumes in their hand."—*London Figaro.*

THE CRIME OF THE OPERA HOUSE. Two Vols.

"We are led breathless from the first page to the last, and close the book with a thorough admiration for the vigorous romancist who has the courage to fulfil the true function of the story-teller, by making reflection subordinate to action."—*Aberdeen Journal.*

Lately published Volumes.

THE RED BAND. Two Vols.—THE GOLDEN TRESS.

FERNANDE'S CHOICE—THE NAMELESS MAN.

THE PHANTOM LEG.—THE ANGEL OF THE CHIMES.

THIEVING FINGERS.—THE CONVICT COLONEL.

HIS GREAT REVENGE. 2 Vols.—A RAILWAY TRAGEDY.

THE MATAPAN AFFAIR. — A FIGHT FOR A FORTUNE.

THE GOLDEN PIG; OR, THE IDOL OF MODERN PARIS. 2 Vols.

PRETTY BABIOLE.—THE CORAL PIN. Two Vols.

THE THUMB STROKE.—THE JAILER'S PRETTY WIFE.

In double volumes, bound in scarlet cloth, price 2s. 6d. each.

NEW EDITIONS OF THE
GABORIAU AND DU BOISGOBEY
SENSATIONAL NOVELS.

1.—THE MYSTERY OF ORCIVAL, AND THE GILDED CLIQUE.
2.—THE LEROUGE CASE, AND OTHER PEOPLE'S MONEY.
3. LECOQ, THE DETECTIVE.   4.—THE SLAVES OF PARIS.
5.—IN PERIL OF HIS LIFE, AND INTRIGUES OF A POISONER.
6.—DOSSIER NO. 113, AND THE LITTLE OLD MAN OF BA-
TIGNOLLES.   7.—THE COUNT'S MILLIONS.
8.—THE OLD AGE OF LECOQ, THE DETECTIVE.
9.—THE CATASTROPHE.   10.—THE DAY OF RECKONING.
11.—THE SEVERED HAND, AND IN THE SERPENTS' COILS.
12.—BERTHA'S SECRET, AND WHO DIED LAST?
13.—THE CRIME OF THE OPERA HOUSE. 17.—THE CORAL PIN.
14.—THE MATAPAN AFFAIR, AND A FIGHT FOR A FORTUNE.
15.—THE GOLDEN PIG.   18.—HIS GREAT REVENGE.
16.—THE THUMB STROKE, AND PRETTY BABIOLE.
19.—JAILER'S PRETTY WIFE, AND ANGEL OF THE CHIMES.
20.—A RAILWAY TRAGEDY, AND THE CONVICT COLONEL.
21.—THE PHANTOM LEG, AND THIEVING FINGERS.

In small post 8vo, ornamental covers, 1s. each ; in cloth, 1s. 6d.

VIZETELLY'S POPULAR FRENCH NOVELS.

TRANSLATIONS OF THE BEST EXAMPLES OF RECENT FRENCH
FICTION OF AN UNOBJECTIONABLE CHARACTER.

"They are books that may be safely left lying about where the ladies of the family can pick them up and read them. The interest they create is happily not of the vicious sort at all."
SHEFFIELD INDEPENDENT.

FROMONT THE YOUNGER & RISLER THE ELDER. By A. DAUDET.

"The series starts well with M. Alphonse Daudet's masterpiece."—*Athenæum.*
"A terrible story, powerful after a sledge-hammer fashion in some parts, and won-derfully tender, touching, and pathetic in others, the extraordinary popularity whereof may be inferred from the fact that this English version is said to be ' translated from the fiftieth French edition.' "—*Illustrated London News.*

SAMUEL BROHL AND PARTNER. By V. CHERBULIEZ.

"Those who have read this singular story in the original need not be reminded of that supremely dramatic study of the man who lived two lives at once, even within himself. The reader's discovery of his double nature is one of the most cleverly managed of sur-prises, and Samuel Brohl's final dissolution of partnership with himself is a remarkable stroke of almost pathetic comedy."—*The Graphic.*

THE DRAMA OF THE RUE DE LA PAIX. By A. BELOT.

"A highly ingenious plot is developed in 'The Drama of the Rue de la Paix,' in which a decidedly interesting and thrilling narrative is told with great force and passion, relieved by sprightliness and tenderness."—*Illustrated London News.*

MAUGARS JUNIOR. By A. THEURIET.

One of the most charming novelettes we have read for a long time."—*Literary World.*

WAYWARD DOSIA, & THE GENEROUS DIPLOMATIST.
By Henry Gréville.

"As epigrammatic as anything Lord Beaconsfield has ever written."—*Hampshire Telegraph.*

A NEW LEASE OF LIFE, & SAVING A DAUGHTER'S DOWRY. By E. About.

"'A New Lease of Life' is an absorbing story, the interest of which is kept up to the very end."—*Dublin Evening Mail.*

"The story, as a flight of brilliant and eccentric imagination, is unequalled in its peculiar way."—*The Graphic.*

COLOMBA, & CARMEN. By P. Mérimée.

"The freshness and raciness of 'Colomba' is quite cheering after the stereotyped three-volume novels with which our circulating libraries are crammed."—*Halifax Times.*

"'Carmen' will be welcomed by the lovers of the sprightly and tuneful opera the heroine of which Minnie Hauk made so popular. It is a bright and vivacious story."—*Life.*

A WOMAN'S DIARY, & THE LITTLE COUNTESS. By O. Feuillet.

"Is wrought out with masterly skill and affords reading, which although of a slightly sensational kind, cannot be said to be hurtful either mentally or morally."—*Dumbarton Herald.*

BLUE-EYED META HOLDENIS, & A STROKE OF DIPLO-MACY. By V. Cherbuliez.

"'Blue-eyed Meta Holdenis' is a delightful tale."—*Civil Service Gazette.*

"'A Stroke of Diplomacy' is a bright vivacious story pleasantly told."—*Hampshire Advertiser.*

THE GODSON OF A MARQUIS. By A. Theuriet.

"The rustic personages, the rural scenery and life in the forest country of Argonne, are painted with the hand of a master. From the beginning to the close the interest of the story never flags."—*Life.*

THE TOWER OF PERCEMONT & MARIANNE. By George Sand.

"George Sand has a great name, and the 'Tower of Percemont' is not unworthy of it."—*Illustrated London News.*

THE LOW-BORN LOVER'S REVENGE. By V. Cherbuliez.

"'The Low-born Lover's Revenge' is one of M. Cherbuliez's many exquisitely written productions. The studies of human nature under various influences, especially in the cases of the unhappy heroine and her low-born lover, are wonderfully effective."—*Illustrated London News.*

THE NOTARY'S NOSE, AND OTHER AMUSING STORIES. By E. About.

"Crisp and bright, full of movement and interest."—*Brighton Herald.*

DOCTOR CLAUDE; OR, LOVE RENDERED DESPERATE. By H. Malot. Two vols.

"We have to appeal to our very first flight of novelists to find anything so artistic in English romance as these books."—*Dublin Evening Mail.*

THE THREE RED KNIGHTS; OR, THE BROTHERS' VENGEANCE. By P. Féval.

"The one thing that strikes us in these stories is the marvellous dramatic skill of the writers."—*Sheffield Independent.*

Bradbury, Agnew, & Co.,   [Printers, Whitefriars.